THE ASSASSINATION
OF
SHERLOCK HOLMES

Books by

CRAIG JANACEK

THE FURTHER ADVENTURES OF SHERLOCK HOMES
LIGHT IN THE DARKNESS°
TREASURE TROVE INDEED!^*
THE ASSASSINATION OF SHERLOCK HOLMES

THE DR. WATSON TRILOGY
THE ISLE OF DEVILS
THE GATE OF GOLD
THE RUINS OF SUMMER*

OTHER NOVELS
THE ANGER OF ACHILLES PETERSON
THE OXFORD DECEPTION

§

°Portions previous published in:
The MX Book of New Sherlock Holmes Stories Part I: 1881 to 1889;
David Marcum, Editor; MX Publishing

^Portions previously published in:
The MX Book of New Sherlock Holmes Stories Part IV: 2016 Annual;
David Marcum, Editor; MX Publishing
The MX Book of New Sherlock Holmes Stories Part VI: 2017 Annual;
David Marcum, Editor; MX Publishing
and
Holmes Away from Home: Tales of the Great Hiatus;
David Marcum, Editor; Belanger Books

*Coming soon

THE ASSASSINATION OF SHERLOCK HOLMES

THE FURTHER ADVENTURES OF SHERLOCK HOLMES

CRAIG JANACEK

This book is a work of fiction. Names, characters, places, and incidents either are the product of the author's imagination or are used fictitiously and are not to be construed as real. Any resemblance to actual events, locales, or persons, living or dead, is entirely coincidental.

Cover illustration by Frederic Dorr Steele (1873-1944) from 1903

(in public domain)

TO OWEN & DANICA

"It is not the critic who counts;
not the man who points out how the strong man stumbles,
or where the doer of deeds could have done them better.
The credit belongs to the man who is actually in the arena,
whose face is marred by dust and sweat and blood;
who strives valiantly;
who errs,
who comes short again and again,
because there is no effort without error and shortcoming;
but who does actually strive to do the deeds;
who knows great enthusiasms,
the great devotions;
who spends himself in a worthy cause;
who at the best knows in the end the triumph of high achievement,
and who at the worst, if he fails,
at least fails while daring greatly,
so that his place shall never be with
those cold and timid souls who neither know victory nor defeat....
There is little use for the being whose tepid soul
knows nothing of great and generous emotion,
of the high pride, the stern belief, the lofty enthusiasm,
of the men who quell the storm and ride the thunder."

The Man in the Arena
Theodore Roosevelt (1858-1919)

CONTENTS

ACKNOWLEDGMENTS

First and foremost, I must give a grateful acknowledgment to Sir Arthur Conan Doyle (1859-1930) for the use of the Sherlock Holmes characters. Without his words, these cases could not have been written.

For reference, I consider Leslie S. Klinger's *The New Annotated Sherlock Holmes* (2005 & 2006) to be the definitive edition. I frequently consulted Jack Tracy's *The Encyclopedia Sherlockiana, or A Universal Dictionary of the State of Knowledge of Sherlock Holmes and His Biographer John H. Watson, M.D.* (1977), Matthew E. Bunson's *Encyclopedia Sherlockiana, an A-to-Z Guide to the World of the Great Detective* (1994), and Bruce Wexler's *The Mysterious World of Sherlock Holmes* (2008).

Four works in particular were inspirational for some of the settings found herein, including Sir Arthur Conan Doyle's gothic horror story *The Ring of Thoth* (1890), Mark Twain's novelette *A Murder, a Mystery, and a Marriage* (written 1876, published 2001), Peter Ackroyd's *London: The Biography* (2001), and Paul Talling's *London's Lost Rivers* (2011).

Finally, this trilogy of stories also owes a massive debt to David Marcum, author and editor of several wonderful compilations of Sherlockian tales, whose praise and encouragement prompted me to continue unearthing these lost cases of Mr. Sherlock Holmes, written long ago by his biographer Dr. John H. Watson.

LITERARY AGENT'S FOREWORD

For someone whose life has touched the hearts of so many people throughout the last one hundred plus years, Sherlock Holmes' career ended not with a bang, but a whimper.[1]

For a brief time, the reading public was convinced that Holmes did meet his glorious, albeit tragic, end in 1891, when he was thought to have nobly sacrificed himself at Reichenbach Falls in order to ensure the destruction of the malevolent Professor Moriarty. However, upon his sensational return from the Great Hiatus in 1894, Holmes threw himself back into a series of cases, some of which – such as *The Adventure of the Six Napoleons* – showcased the heights of his power, while others – such as *The Adventure of the Veiled Lodger* – were much more commonplace.

These uneven investigations continued until 1903, when Holmes suddenly retired to an estate on the South Downs. After that date, only two more cases – neither written by Dr. Watson – appeared in the official records, one of which (*The Adventure of the Lion's Mane*) detailed a trivial matter that occurred in 1907 near his villa, while the other (*His Last Bow*) took place on the eve of The Great War in 1914.

We know from Dr. Watson's own pen that the mystery of the simian-like Professor Presbury, chronicled as *The Adventure of the Creeping Man*, was 'one of the very last cases handled by Holmes before his retirement from practice.' But the Canon is curiously silent about the true closing case of Holmes' official career as the world's first consulting detective. Did some undisclosed horrible tragedy drive him into premature retirement, or did he deem that some great unrecorded feat of

---

[1] A paraphrase of the final lines of the great poem 'The Hollow Man' by T.S. Eliot (1888-1965), which allude to the failed gunpowder plot of Guy Fawkes.

detection was finally sufficient to serve as the capstone to an unprecedented, and to this day unrivaled, career?

It was to reconcile this puzzling debate that I went searching for an account of that lost case which made Holmes resolve that it was time to finally hang up his perhaps apocryphal deerstalker's cap. Unfortunately, what I discovered was not that tale. But perhaps these papers contain something equally singular and important in the closure of a career, and even of a life?

I will not bore you with a prolonged narrative of my search. Suffice it to say that it was long and dusty. However, it began with an inspiration that I like to think was worthy of Holmes himself. Much effort has been made by many fine scholars to locate the actual site of Holmes' retirement villa. The sprinkling of clues in the Canon have been followed with scrupulous care, and strong suspects, such as Birling Manor Farm, between the Seven Sisters and Eastbourne and near Went Hill, have been identified. While this hunt is a worthwhile pursuit on its own merits, it is unlikely to reveal any manuscripts of note. Holmes very rarely bothered to record any literary account of his own cases, and the few instances that have been preserved (*The Adventures of The Lion's Mane* and the *Blanched Soldier*) lack Dr. Watson's characteristic vigor. And certainly Watson would not have been likely to send any completed texts to Holmes, not after enduring years of disparagement from his friend about Watson's overly romantic style of writing.

Therefore, if I wished to locate some other entombed tin box, for the one kept at Cox & Co. surely appears to have been heavily damaged by a bomb that fell during the Blitz,[2] I must instead turn my eyes to other locales that might hide potential treasure troves. To that end, the question was not 'Where was the site of Sherlock Holmes' retirement?' but rather, 'Where was the final domicile of his great biographer, Dr. John H. Watson?'

That was the problem that I ultimately solved in order to present these tales to you now. I do not, at the moment, wish to disclose the exact location, in hopes that from some unexplored corner further manuscripts may one day appear. What I unearthed was quite damaged by over a hundred years of damp and rot. Painstaking restoration work was required to bring the pages into a readable condition. In the translation to printable or digital form, a conscious decision was made to adopt American spellings of such words as 'colour' and 'theatre.' If this seems contrary to the spirit of its original author, the fault is entirely mine. Annotations were added in order to assist Sherlockian scholars studying these newly-

---

[2] Sources vary as to whether this was due to a V-1 or V-2 rocket, or from a Luftwaffe-dropped bomb.

discovered cases.

Furthermore, while the papers appear to tell a unified narrative, for reasons known only to Dr. Watson, he decided to separate them into three tales, the individual bundles tied up with decaying red tape. While each tale is enjoyable on its own, they are perhaps enhanced when read as part of the complete narrative of Holmes' temporary return from the Happy Isles of Retirement.

Herein, you will learn how Holmes' peace was shattered by a message that threatened all that he and Dr. Watson accomplished over the years, and perhaps even his very life. But fear not, friends of Mr. Sherlock Holmes, for 'beyond this place of wrath and tears... and yet the menace of the years, finds and shall find [Holmes] unafraid.'[3]

So 'come, my friends, it is not too late to seek a newer world. Push off... for my purpose holds, to sail beyond the sunset, and the baths of all the western stars...'[4] And read the story of the way a career ended, not with a whimper, but a bang.

§

---

[3] A paraphrase of several lines from 'Invictus' by William Ernest Henley (1849-1903): 'Beyond this place of wrath and tears / Looms but the Horror of the shade, / And yet the menace of the years / Finds and shall find me unafraid. / It matters not how strait the gate, / How charged with punishments the scroll, / I am the master of my fate, / I am the captain of my soul.'

[4] An excerpt from that great meditative poem on the conflicting emotions of retirement and advancing old age, 'Ulysses' by Alfred, Lord Tennyson (1809-1892): 'Come, my friends, / 'T is not too late to seek a newer world. / Push off, and sitting well in order smite / The sounding furrows; for my purpose holds / To sail beyond the sunset, and the baths / Of all the western stars, until I die. / It may be that the gulfs will wash us down: / It may be we shall touch the Happy Isles, / And see the great Achilles, whom we knew. / Tho' much is taken, much abides; and tho' / We are not now that strength which in old days / Moved earth and heaven, that which we are, we are; / One equal temper of heroic hearts, / Made weak by time and fate, but strong in will / To strive, to seek, to find, and not to yield.'

THE ADVENTURE OF THE PHARAOH'S CURSE

On referring to my notes, I see that it was a mild morning on the last day of October in 1909 when Inspector Lestrade appeared upon my doorstep. The boisterous equinoctial gales of fall had past, leaving the trees in the yard behind my home stripped bare and puddles in the fallow garden. After many years where I imagined that my wounds had fully healed, with the advance of time and the change in the weather, I felt again their once familiar ache.[5] At the time, I was busy in my study with the writing up an adventure from my extensive archive of cases investigated by Sherlock Holmes over the years of our mutual association. Little did I know at the time that the facts of that particular undertaking paled in comparison to the most remarkable and dramatic events that were about to unfold.

I was experimenting with a new technique, which I had adopted after reading about the practice by Mr. Jefferson of Virginia. I was using one of his polygraph machines to simultaneously create a duplicate of the adventure I was documenting.[6] I had sadly learned over the years that banks such as Cox & Co. can be robbed, that residences can catch on fire, and that hounds can on occasion feast upon pages of foolscap. Some manuscripts had already passed out of my possession into the hands of private individuals, but I had firmly determined that those future cases

---

[5] Watson is believed to have been born in 1852, which would make him 58 years old at the time of this adventure.

[6] The polygraph machine used by President Thomas Jefferson was not a lie-detector, as the term has now come to be used, but rather an ingenious 1803 device to copy a piece of writing. Examples are preserved at both Monticello and the Smithsonian Museum of American History.

which were not yet ready for publication would be best preserved in duplicate form.

Needless to say, I was quite surprised to look up from this work and find his face peering at me from the other side of my desk. He was dapperly dressed, but the years had not been kind to Lestrade, whose sallow-faced, furtive features in the best of times can only have been described as either bulldoggish or ferret-like, and now appeared most similar to a wrinkled leather sack. Still, while he was not without faults, he was a good man in his own way, and reminded me of some of the fine old days. My wife must have seen him in and bade him wait for a natural pause to my activity, so as to not interrupt the train of my thoughts.

My mustached lips curled upwards at the once-familiar sight of the Scotland Yarder. "Well, well, Inspector, it is a pleasure to see you again. It has been, what, eight years?"

"Indeed, Doctor," he nodded sadly, his eyes dark. I noted that he wore a light brown dustcoat and leather leggings rather than his official uniform, which I deduced represented his travelling outfit. "I don't get down to Southsea much, I am afraid."[7]

"Yes, well I find that it suits me. While the bustle of London's five millions may be intoxicating to a man of eight and twenty, the charms of the largest city on earth can begin to wear thin when the years start to mount. And as long as I have a Bradshaw's close to hand, I can always rely upon the remarkable British train system to have me at Waterloo Station in but a shade over two hours, should the London season promise a new exhibition of Expressionists at a Bond Street Gallery, or a singer of great repute at Covent Garden."

As I spoke Lestrade looked about my study, examining the rows of books upon my shelves. "You've done quite well for yourself, Doctor."

"Yes, well..."

"Don't get me wrong, Doctor. I daresay you deserve it. You have been instrumental over the years in helping Mr. Holmes bring to justice some right dangerous individuals, who would be a general menace to the peaceful British public if left free to roam the streets."

"My role has always been a minor one."

"Perhaps, but who took a bullet for him off the Edgeware Road? Who subdued Colonel Moran when he was about to strange Holmes? Who carried Holmes away from the poisonous clouds of the Cornish Horror? And who dragged him from the burning wreck of the *Friesland*, eh?[8] In

---

[7] From this we can deduce that sometime between 1904 and 1909, Watson sold his home and practice in Queen Anne Street (as noted in *The Adventure of the Illustrious Client*) and also retired to the south coast of England.

[8] This unrecorded case was mentioned in *The Adventure of the Norwood*

any case, I don't even mention the folks whose suffering you've alleviated and whose lives you've saved in the course of your original vocation."

"So what can I do for you, Inspector? Is someone ill?"

"No, Doctor. I am fortunately not here in your professional capacity. But I do need your help. There have been some strange occurrences at the..."

I laughed. "My help? I think not. It is Holmes that you require."

He signed heavily. "As you might know, Doctor, Mr. Holmes has refused several most princely offers from some of the greatest names in Europe to take up cases again, and on every occasion he has refused. Needless to say, any attempts from the C.I.D. have been rapidly rebuffed. He has made it clear that his retirement is definite and permanent."

"And you believe that I may be able to induce him to alter his stance?" I laughed. "Holmes has never heeded my opinion before. Why should he change now?"

"He will listen to this story, Doctor, for it is both fantastic and tragic. And I daresay that the tragedy part hits close to home this time."

I frowned. "I do not know to what you refer, Inspector. However, if your case is such a strong one, then I cannot fathom why you would need my presence?"

"I've learned a thing or two from watching Mr. Holmes over the years, Doctor. You are the only one to whom he ever listened," he said with tenacious persistence.

"I am afraid that I cannot..."

"It is but three hours to Eastbourne," he interrupted, his tone pleading. "From there we can hire a coach to finish the last few miles to Fulworth."[9]

The look upon his face was so defeated that I could not but feel for the man. His condescending attitude over the years had rankled at times, but we had once coursed the moors of Devon together. My heart was not as hard as that of Holmes. "Very well, Inspector. I will do what I can."

And so it happened that I found myself, after six years of quietude, once more flying along in the corner of a first-class carriage, *en route* to see Holmes, and ultimately to witness the onset of another adventure, one perhaps more thrilling than any we had experienced before.

§

Of course, I first rushed downstairs to explain the matter to my

---

Builder, but here we learn more about Watson's role in the adventure.

[9] The general whereabouts of Holmes' retirement abode was described in the Preface to *His Last Bow.* However, no such village of Fulworth has ever been located, suggesting that Watson changed the name to protect his friend's privacy.

understanding wife. I then rapidly perused my overnight bag, ensuring that it was adequately stocked with all of the necessary accoutrements. My recollection of the journey is a pleasant one, for the weather was fine, the train swift, and my companion a reminder of exciting days past. During the ride, I repeatedly attempted to elucidate from Lestrade some details of the case that was so difficult and important that it required drawing Holmes away from his soothing retreat. However, the Inspector only shook his head and replied that it was too sad a tale to have to tell twice, and that he preferred to wait until we were in the presence of Holmes. I shrugged at this unusual reticence from the normally-loquacious Lestrade, but was well used to such treatment at the hands of Holmes, who often withheld facts until they could be presented for the most dramatic effect. Unable to hardly draw another word from Lestrade, I therefore settled myself down in the corner of the carriage, drew my hat down over my eyes, and sank into the deepest of thoughts.

As I have previously documented, Holmes retired to the South Downs in 1904, shortly after the grotesque case of Professor Presbury and his wolf-hound Roy. Although he was but five and fifty years of age, attacks of rheumatism, likely brought on by years of complete and utter disregard for his health, had taken their toll. Furthermore, to his nimble mind, the criminal world had grown commonplace and sterile, lacking all traces of audacity and romance. There was little doubt that he was able to retire comfortably. While it was true that he never varied his fees, save when he chose to remit them entirely, that is not to say that he never raised the base level as the years passed and one century slipped into another. As Holmes' fame spread, his paying clients increasingly came from the cream of London's society and the great royal houses of Europe. I therefore have it on good confidence that Holmes comfortably draws an income of over nine hundred pounds a year, with his primary expenditure the maintenance of his bee-keeping apparatus.[10]

Although he had considered both the valleys of Surrey[11] and the moors of the Cornish peninsula, Holmes eventually settled upon the Downs for reasons he has so-far neglected to share. I thought that perhaps it was because the tranquil beauty of the place was a perfect counterpart to his

[10] Compare this to the income of Ms. Mary Sutherland, who in 1889 drew £100 a year (*A Case of Identity*), Mr. Grant Munro, who in 1888 drew £700-800 a year (*The Yellow Face*), and finally the salary of his brother Mycroft, who in 1895 was paid only £450 a year to occasionally run the British Government (*The Adventure of the Bruce-Partington Plans*)!

[11] The most famous of which is called by the evocative name of 'Holmesdale.' Sadly, the name of the vale derives not from the Great Detective, but from the Holm Oak, an evergreen oak which was once common in the area.

intrinsic grim humor. His estate was magnificently situated so as to command a view of the Channel, and what was once a small farm had principally been allowed to turn fallow. Only one small clearing near his villa was maintained in order to serve as the lair of his arthropod companions. Excepting myself, I was unaware that Holmes had any particular friends who might call upon him. Here amid his books, he lived what I thought must be a lonely life, but it seemed to suit Holmes' simple wants and eccentric needs.

Much to our surprise, Holmes was not at home when Lestrade and I arrived. We were met by his old housekeeper Martha, who looked exceptionally flustered at the appearance of unexpected guests.[12] My explanation of pressing matters which precluded the sending of a telegraph announcement fell upon deaf ears.

"I am sorry, sirs, but he is out walking," said the housekeeper tersely. "Do you wish to wait?" She motioned diffidently to the sofa in the sitting room. "Mr. Holmes doesn't much encourage visitors."

While I myself had stopped in many times before, I still could hardly reconcile the tidy status of Holmes' current accommodations with his Bohemian habits from the days that we shared a flat in Baker Street. Every item was neatly in its place, with nary a reeking chemical experiment or bullet hole in sight. I recognized some scientific charts which, along with some books, appeared to be the only objects that had travelled with him from 221B. Although Holmes would have denied it, I always suspected that Holmes had a considerable artistic side to his nature, and this tendency had finally manifested itself with a line of well-chosen modern water-colors and some very choice etchings that were hung neatly on the walls.

Fortunately, Lestrade and I had not a long delay to our mission, for I soon heard rustling on the soft gravel walk which could only come from the distinctive loping gait belonging to my friend. Before he could even come into view, the high, somewhat strident tones of his precise voice called out, "I was wondering who you would bring for support, Lestrade. My first hypothesis was the Home Secretary, and I half suspected you might try to enlist the Premier himself."

"How did you know it was me, Mr. Holmes?" Lestrade asked.

Holmes' eager, clear-cut face appeared from around the corner, but the paleness to which I had grown accustomed over our long acquaintance in the fogs of Baker Street had vanished under a healthy glow of the countryside. He threw his loose-limbed figure into the chair opposite us

---

[12] While some commentators have seen fit to identify Martha with Mrs. Hudson, the fact that Watson does not address her as such seems to disprove such assertions.

and let out a dry chuckle that was as near a thing to a laugh as ever passed his lips. "When I spot in my pathway a boot-print with the left foot twisted inwards, and suddenly smell the distinctive 4711 *Eau de Cologne*, surely it can only mean that the celebrated Inspector Lestrade has honored me with another visit, however futile his errand. I must admit, however, that this dragooning of Watson is a novel tactic of which I much approve. It has been far too long since his previous week-end visit." He turned to me. "My dear Watson, I am delighted to find you on my step."

"It is good to see you too, Holmes," said I, shaking him warmly by the hand.

"And, Lestrade, by my calculations, it has been three months, one week, and five days since you last attempted to coax me back to London with some seemingly 'impossible' case. You might think that after a span of six years that you would have learned that my answer has not varied. Fortunately, you always seem to manage to solve them in the end, even if it takes you far longer than it really should. For example, you handled the Porter Murder with less than your usual, that's to say, you handled it fairly well. I suppose congratulations are in order."

"It was Tooley."

"Of course it was Tooley, Holmes said acerbically.[13] "That much was plain from a simple reading of the agony columns of the *Daily Telegraph*."

"And where have you been, Holmes?" I asked, hoping to spare the poor Inspector any further brunt of Holmes' ill-concealed scorn.

"If you must know, Watson, I was engaged on my daily excursion. It is a delightful day, so I strolled out to enjoy the superb air. The sea air, the sunshine, what else does a man require? We walked along the cliff path which, as you know leads, via a steep descent, down to the beach. But as the tide was in, we did not descend, and simply skirted the cliffs."

"'We?'" I inquired, hopefully. "Were you accompanying someone on this walk?"

Holmes snorted. "Merely a figure of speech, Watson. But look around you," he gestured to the windows which opened out onto the view of the fields and the brilliant blue sky. "Why should I ever leave the salubrious airs and soothing life of my little Sussex home for the choking fumes and deep gloom of London?" He shook his head. "No, I have no desire to immerse myself back into the bustle of these feverish days."

"But, Mr. Holmes, only you can bring light to this darkness!" Lestrade interjected.

Holmes sighed. "Really, Lestrade. I think you have been reading too much of Watson's embellished tales. For the most part, the London

---

[13] Who exactly Tooley killed in the 'Porter Murder,' and why, are questions lost to time, as this case never made its way into the papers of the day.

criminal has been a dull fellow ever since the death of the unlamented Professor Moriarty. Yes, after my return from abroad we handled several cases not without interest, but for the most part, there was nothing that had not been done before. However, I suppose you will not leave until I have at least heard you out and pointed you in the right direction to solve your trivial matter, eh?"

"This is a most serious one, Mr. Holmes. I would not have come otherwise."

"Well, at least I can offer you a cigar and some afternoon tea first." With a ring of the bell to signal Martha, three steaming cups soon appeared. From a small pot, which appeared to be made of gold, with a great set of rubies set around the circumference, Holmes added a dash of honey to our cups. "This is from my own hives, of course," he explained for the benefit of Lestrade as we sipped it cautiously. "It is mixed with a small amount of royal jelly, which provides it with some remarkable properties. It has done wonders for my knees, for example, which are now largely without pain, excepting only during the rain. Which is, of course, an unfortunately all too common occurrence."

The splendor of the pot was in such contrast to his homely ways and simple life that I could not help commenting upon it.

"Oh, yes, a small token from the Sultan. I am not proud that I once consulted for a cruel despot, but sometimes international politics take precedent over niceties."[14] He reached for his cherry wood pipe, which he kept on top of a busby whose moldering bearskin had seen better days, and proceeded to slowly light it. When complete, he leaned languidly back in his chair in that familial attitude. "Now, Lestrade, let us hear about this little mystery of yours. If you must relate it, pray let me have all of the facts. The smallest point may be the most essential."

"I will start at the beginning, Mr. Holmes, if you promise to hear me out till the end."

Holmes shrugged. "If you insist. I suppose that my routine for the day has already been disrupted. What are a few more minutes?"

"The grotesque mystery in question is taking place at the British Museum," explained Lestrade. I noted that Holmes smiled in acknowledgement of a place where he spent many a day at the onset of his career. "It began with the disappearance of several items of intrinsic value."

Holmes pulled out his pocket watch and studied it. "Items vanish from museums across the globe every day. I fail to see how this is an event that

---

[14] In *The Adventure of the Blanched Soldier,* Holmes reported that he took a case for Sultan of Turkey, who at that time was Abdul Hamid II the Damned, a brutal and paranoid dictator who was eventually overthrown.

concerns me."

"First of all, Mr. Holmes, the honor of our nation is at stake!" cried Lestrade. "The Louvre and the Kaiser Friedrich Museum will be laughing at us if word of this gets out. Not to mention that every thief in the country will catch word that the Museum is easy pickings. It will be a free-for-all."

Holmes shook his head. "I have done my bit for Queen and Country, Lestrade. Their honor now rests in younger hands. I am afraid that I cannot help you. I believe that there is a train from Eastbourne at half-past three that you might catch if you finish your tea."

"You promised to hear me out, Mr. Holmes!" he cried in despair.

Holmes sighed and waved his hand. "Very well. Proceed."

"Just last night..." stammered Lestrade, anxiously.

"You are as bad as Watson, Lestrade,'" interrupted Holmes, tetchily. "Don't tell it from the wrong-end! Pray give us the essential facts from the commencement."

"Yes, well, the events in question began approximately a month ago," stammered Lestrade.

"Give me a date, Lestrade. Approximations are of little use."

Lestrade consulted his notebook. "Yes, well, it was on the 30th of September that the first item was noticed to have gone missing. This was a gold cup from the Backworth Hoard."

"You say that the theft was noted on the 30th, interrupted Holmes. "Do they not check every item every day?"

"A cursory inspection is made, of course, Mr. Holmes. But the thief did not leave a bare spot on the velvet. Rather, they left something in its place that was a rough approximation of the cup's shape and size."

"Ah, so you suspect a forger?" I interjected.

Lestrade shook his head. "No, Doctor. The item left behind could never have been mistaken for the cup upon anything but the most general looking-over. In fact, it was a visitor to the museum who pointed it out to one of the curators, as they were confused why it was situated in the Ancient Britain gallery."

Holmes' eyes narrowed with seeming interest. "What was it?"

"It was a scarab."

"What?" I exclaimed. "A beetle?"

"Yes, Doctor, or at least a plaster amulet of one."

A single bushy eyebrow twitched, signifying that Holmes' interest had certainly been peaked, even if he endeavored to conceal it. "Peculiar. And these scarabs have now been left multiple times?"

"Yes, Mr. Holmes. The list of missing objects is growing by the day. Almost every morning it is noted that a new item has vanished. A Celtic torc from the Wolverton Hoard, a jewel encrusted ring from the Rhayader

Treasure, a silver shield from the Cheshire Barrow, a horned helmet from the Backwater Bequest. I could go on. And in every instance, a scarab is left in its place."

"Most curious."

"That's but the least of it, Mr. Holmes. The presence of these substituted objects immediately suggested to the inspector on the case that these thefts were somehow linked to the Museum's Egyptian Collection."

Holmes nodded. "It is a reasonable hypothesis, I suppose. But was there another detective on the case before you, Lestrade?"

"Yes, Patterson got it. Over the years, he has become the unofficial go-to man whenever the Yard comes across a crime that has something to do with art."

Holmes sniffed. "Ah, well, perhaps it is just as well that they called you in, Lestrade. In our sole expedition together Patterson managed to bag only the small game, while allowing the prize to roam free, despite me leaving him all the necessary details in Pigeonhole M. So please recapitulate for me what Patterson has thus far discovered?"

"He found that the Museum's night guards are divided into regular patrols. The building is so large that it requires multiple guards to cover its entire expanse. The Egyptian and Assyrian rooms have two men that regularly work it. One man, Mr. Dominic Bedford, has worked at the Museum for over twenty years. He has the reputation of being an honest man and his service record has been exemplary. He is due for retirement with full pension in less than a year."

"Perhaps his pension is insufficient to cover his expenses and he has decided to supplement his income?" I offered.

Holmes considered this for a moment and then shook his head. "It is too early to form hypotheses, Watson. We are not yet in possession of all of the facts." He looked back at Lestrade. "And the other guard?"

"The other guard, Mr. Andrew Morrison, has only been employed at the Museum for two months."

"Well, there is your answer, Inspector," I decided. "He is your most likely suspect. He sought employment solely for the purpose of gaining unimpeded entrance to the Museum."

"Yes, that was Patterson's conclusion as well, Doctor. He focused his efforts on investigating the background of Mr. Morrison and found some irregularities. But Morrison cannot be the culprit."

"What leads you to assume that, Lestrade?" asked Holmes, who was, despite himself, beginning to look somewhat interested.

"The simple matter that Mr. Morrison has vanished."

Holmes snorted in amusement. "And why do you not think that Mr. Morrison is even now spending his ill-gotten wealth somewhere upon the

Riviera?"

"Because the thefts have continued, Mr. Holmes."

"Most peculiar. The problem does present some features of interest. I will admit that the sequence does not appear logical. If Morrison was the thief, he would hardly draw notice to himself by vanishing in the midst of the investigation. And how would he continue to perform his burglaries? I presume that Patterson thus re-focused his efforts upon Mr. Bedford?"

"Yes, but Bedford cannot be the thief either. You see, six nights ago Mr. Bedford refused to report for work. He has not been back since. And yet, the thefts are still taking place. Why, just last night, while the streets surrounding the Museum were constantly patrolled by constables, half of the Lewis Chessman vanished."

If Holmes was disturbed by this appalling news, he hid it well. "And what reason did Mr. Bedford provide to explain his absence from work?"

"He claimed that he saw one of the Egyptian statues moving on its own. He said that the Museum was cursed! He did not wish to vanish like Mr. Morrison."

Holmes chuckled and shook his head. "Perhaps we should exhaust all natural explanations before we begin to invoke those from beyond the veil, Lestrade."

Lestrade looked miserable. "Yes, Patterson thought the same."

"So what was his next course of action?"

"Patterson decided that he would spend the night in the Museum. He wished to witness the statue for himself and determine if it was somehow linked to the thefts."

Holmes nodded. "It would be a bizarre coincidence if it was not. So what did Patterson discover?"

Lestrade shook his head. 'That's just it, Mr. Holmes. In the morning, Patterson was dead."

Holmes sat up abruptly as if he had been galvanized, his pipe half-way to his lips. "What!?" he exclaimed.

"Yes, he was horribly strangled. And that is why we need you, Mr. Holmes. You are the one man in all of England, nay, in all of Europe, who could get to the bottom of this terrible matter. We are utterly powerless, and I fear that this is just the beginning. Would you let another man die because you failed to act? Would you fail to avenge poor Patterson?"

If Holmes had a weakness it was that he was accessible to flattery, and also, to be fair, to the invocation of justice. The two forces made him lay down his pipe with a sigh of resignation and push back his chair. "I know little of such matters." He leaned back and with one of his long, thin arms, took down the great index volume which was labeled 'C.' Holmes laid it upon the table before him and his eyes moved slowly over the chronicle of old cases, a veritable mine of accumulated data from a lifetime of adventure.

"Let me see. Conk-Singleton forgery case," he read. "Copper Beeches. That huge brute was a nasty customer. I have some memory that you made a chronicle of it, Watson, though I was unable to applaud you upon the result. Crispin, the cracksman. Crocodile, in the Westbourne. Noteworthy incident, that! Crooked Man, one of your more superficial tales, Watson. Crossbow Murders. Do you recall that tricky case, Watson?[15] Crosby, the banker. What a terrible death, that. Cultists, in Wapping. Cuneiform, and its relation to Ogham inscriptions.[16] Here we are! Good old index. You can't beat it. Listen to this, Watson. Curses in Caribbean Voodooism, with a reference to Eckermann. And more relevant to today, Curses in Egyptian Mythology." He turned over the pages with reluctance, and after a short perusal he set the great tome aside with a sneer of disdain.

"Bollocks, Lestrade, bollocks! What have we to do with mummies that cause stormy seas, or who magically strike down those who desecrate their final resting places? It's it too fantastic. We detour into the realm of fairy tales and fiction. I have travelled from one side of the globe to the other, from Chicago to Khartoum, from Nassau to Lhassa, and I have seen many a strange sight, but I have never seen anything to make me believe in the existence of the supernatural."[17]

"But surely," I said, "the curse might not necessarily be a mystical force? Perhaps there is a scientific explanation? I have read, for example, that some deadly mold could grow in the long-enclosed tomb only to be released when it was opened to the air. The ancient priests may have even deliberately placed the mold therein to punish future grave robbers."

"Excellent, Watson! As you say, the idea of an actual curse cannot be seriously entertained. I think we have been down this road once before, have we not? Where your friend Mr. Ferguson saw vampires, we saw an all too human motive. I think the same principal will apply here. We need not invoke a realm beyond the senses."

"So you will investigate this matter, Mr. Holmes?" asked Lestrade, his

---

[15] Unfortunately, it appears that Watson neglected to ever record the cases of Crispin, the Westbourne Crocodile, or the Crossbow Murders.

[16] Cuneiform is the earliest known writing of the Sumerians. Ogham is a Medieval Irish alphabet which survived only on several hundred stone monuments throughout Ireland and Wales. There is no known link between the two.

[17] Holmes is known to have spent time in Chicago in the time preceding the Great War (*His Last Bow*), but no Canonical source mentions him visiting prior to 1909, the setting for this tale.

tone hopeful.

"Yes, I suppose I must, if only to prove a point. If we start at once, we should be in London shortly after the Museum closes for the night."

"I would join you, if you will have me," I added.

"Are you sure that you wish to go, Watson? One man is missing and another is dead, so the task is certain to be a dangerous one."

"Of course, Holmes. It's been almost eight years since I was last shot."

He gazed at me with a curious expression. "I must continuously guard myself from these little outbursts of your pawky humor, Watson. They are as unpredictable as the weather, I fear."

"Shall we depart, then? Once more unto the breach."[18] I said smiling.

Holmes sighed. "Well, at least I can pay a visit to the Nevill's on Northumberland Avenue to ease the rheumatism in my knees. The South Downs have many qualities, but medicinal baths are not one of them."

§

Thus it was that on a bright fall afternoon Holmes and I found ourselves in the company of Inspector Lestrade seated a first-class carriage traveling nor-westward at fifty miles per hour while bound for Victoria Station. It was an ideal fall day, with a light blue sky dotted with gauzy white clouds. There was an invigorating nip in the air, which shook off years of accumulated rust from my limbs. It was not until we were well-started upon our journey, rushing along the reddening countryside, past several pretty little towns, that Holmes appeared to relax. His long, gaunt form was wrapped in a long, grey travelling cloak, and his head covered by a close-fitting ear-flapped cloth cap. The rack above us was stocked with our small travelling valises, in the event that the problem at the Museum precluded a return to our homes that same evening.

We had the carriage to ourselves, so Holmes finally set aside his walking stick, and proceeded to light his old, oily black clay pipe. "Well, Lestrade," said he, when finished with this task. "We have a clear run here of two hours with which you can fill in the remaining details of your investigation."

"What would you like to know, Mr. Holmes?"

"First of all, how many items in total have been stolen?"

Lestrade consulted his official notebook. "Since the thirtieth of September, there have been twenty-nine items that have been noted as

---

[18] A reference to Shakespeare's famous line: "Once more unto the breach, dear friends" (*Henry V*, Act III, Scene 1). This may also be an allusion to Holmes' famous line 'The game is afoot,' which itself derives from Shakespeare's *Henry IV*, Part I, Act III, Scene 1.

missing. The collection is enormous, so it is possible that other small objects have been overlooked."

"Still, we have roughly twenty-nine items in thirty-two days. That is suggestive, don't you think, Lestrade?"

"Is it, Mr. Holmes? I hadn't remarked that it was particularly noticeable."

"Oh, yes. I would be much obliged if you would provide me with a list of the objects and the days that they were reported missing."

"I thought you might need that, Mr. Holmes, and had a duplicate account drawn up." Lestrade extracted a piece of paper and handed it over to Holmes.

My friend merely tucked it into his breast pocket and then continued his questioning. "First of all, there are other players in this case that have yet to be mentioned, are there not? What of the guards in the Ancient Britain Galleries, under whose very noses the treasures have vanished? In my experience, most night guards are elderly, uneducated, and given to excess consumption of spirits."

Lestrade nodded as if he anticipated this question. "There are two guards assigned to the Britain Galleries, as well as the adjoining rooms along the eastern side of the second floor. They are required to make rounds of this section of the museum several times during the night. But during the other hours they can often be found resting in small cubicles."

"'Sleeping' would perhaps be a more accurate term, would it not?"

"As you say, Mr. Holmes, though they deny it, of course. Neither man has been at the Museum for as long as Mr. Bedford. The first man, whose name is Edward Rucastle, has been at his post for eight years, coming there soon after finishing his schooling."

"Rucastle?" I asked. I glanced at Holmes. "Do you think it could be the same lad?"

Holmes' grey eyes gleamed. "The boy's name was Edward, if I recall correctly. He is about six and twenty-years of age, Lestrade?"

Lestrade nodded. "That sounds about right. Do you know him? He is a sour man, none too bright, and not very popular with his fellows. But for all the minor complaints, the Museum's Director has had no serious reason to doubt his loyalty."

Holmes shook his head. "It may simply be a coincidence. We must converse with him at some point, Lestrade. Pray continue."

"The other man was only hired a few months ago. His name is Quincy Seraphim and he is a retired sergeant of the Army. Coldstream Guards, I believe. He is nearing fifty, with a quiet, unassuming manner."

"Surely he must be a prime suspect," I exclaimed. "He had access, and if he started working there just before thefts began..."

"Indeed, Watson. But he is perhaps too obvious a suspect. Would not a clever man wait some time before beginning his crime spree? Otherwise, he simply calls all of the attention to himself."

"Not if he is using the scarabs as a distraction," I argued.

Holmes nodded thoughtfully. "A valid point, Watson. Using them as a blind would be a clever tactic. But why murder poor Patterson in the Egyptian Gallery, which is a floor away and on the opposite side of the Great Court? No, no, we will undoubtedly need to question Mr. Seraphim, but I would not rush to condemn him."

"And there is another objection to your scenario, Doctor," said Lestrade. "The Museum is well aware that the night guards it employs do not generally hail from the cream of society. They must have good references, of course, but it is a lonely and thankless job. The pay is not miserly, but it is hardly extravagant either. So the Museum has in place measures to ensure that no guard walks home with a pound of gold in his pocket. First, there are two guards for each section so that they watch each other. For a guard to be involved, they would likely need to be in collusion. And then in the morning, the entire lot of them must line up by the Montague Place entrance, where they are searched before being let out the door."

"One of them could offer the searcher some metallic arguments to overlook things," I offered.

"I think not, Doctor," said Lestrade severely. "This is not left in private hands. An officer from the Yard does this duty, and even they are rotated regularly."

I was still unsatisfied. "Surely they could conceal the stolen objects somewhere in the museum and a confederate could then recover it during the day?"

Holmes laughed aloud. "Excellent, Watson! It is a great aid to put yourself in the other fellow's place and think of what you would do if you were so criminally inclined."

However, Lestrade was shaking his head. "We had the same thought, Doctor. But it seems that the Museum had taken steps to prevent that over thirty years ago. The Principal Librarian, Sir Edward Bond, long ago received an anonymous note.[19] In it, some enterprising rouge carefully detailed forty-two different ways that the Museum was vulnerable to thieves. With the advice of the Yard, they acted upon this note and secured all of these former chinks in their armor. One such gap mentioned in the note was just as you suggest, Doctor, so all potential

---

[19] Sir Edward Bond was an actual Librarian at the British Museum from 1873-1888. Perhaps Holmes favored him because he wrote an influential book on English Charters, a topic in which Holmes was also very interested?

hiding spots have long since been sealed off."

"Odd that such a famous paleographer as Sir Edward would never be able to identify the anonymous writer of such a note," said Holmes dryly.[20] "But there is one other guard whose part in this drama has not yet come into focus. What has befallen the missing Mr. Andrew Morrison?"

"Ah, that is a good question, Mr. Holmes," replied Lestrade. "We don't rightly know."

"You must be more precise, Lestrade. You said the man has gone missing, but failed to provide any of the necessary details to elucidate whether he is conspirator or victim."

"Yes, well, we are uncertain of that. As I noted, Mr. Holmes, on the twenty-fourth of October Mr. Morrison was on duty in the Egyptian and Assyrian Galleries. Mr. Bedford was still working on that night and the two of them passed each other regularly. Bedford claims that Morrison was acting entirely normally. He was last seen at nine o'clock in the morning. But when it was time for the guard line-up, Morrison never appeared. The Director immediately called in the Yard, and Patterson had a squad of constables hurriedly sweep the place, but they found no sign of him. Finally they had to open the doors to the public. But to this day, no one has ever seen Mr. Morrison alive again."

"Hmmm," Holmes pondered this information. "And his particulars? You said there were irregularities?"

"Well, Mr. Holmes, Patterson sent a man round to Morrison's residence. This proved to be a boarding-house on Godalming Road. He had been residing there since late August, just a few days before he obtained the job at the Museum, and he lived quietly and paid his bills regularly. He never returned for his items, which were admittedly few in number and of little value. But the odd part was that on the ledger, he noted his previous address as being a place on Rotherhithe Street. But when Patterson's man called there, they had no recollection of him."

"So it was a fake address?" I asked.

Lestrade shook his head. "Not exactly, Doctor. His name was in their book as well, but even though it has been a span of only two months, no one could recall the man. It is as if he had slipped entirely from their memory."

"A handy trick, that, if you are up to no good," observed Holmes.

"The landlady at Godalming Road noted that Morrison's identity papers said that he had been born in Richmond. So Patterson sent a man

---

[20] One wonders if this was Holmes' subtle way of admitting that he wrote the anonymous letter. In the days before he and Watson took on the flat at 221B Baker Street, Holmes had rooms on Montague Street, directly across from the Museum.

round there too."

Holmes nodded approvingly. "I must say that Patterson's methods are to be commended. He was most thorough in this case."

"Ah, I see it now," I exclaimed. "Let me guess, Inspector. He found that Morrison had never been born in Richmond?"

"On the contrary, Doctor," Lestrade replied. "The records were quite clear. Morrison had been born on 18 December 1854. He also died there on 6 January 1905."

Holmes chuckled dryly. "So, your Mr. Morrison assumed the identity of a dead man. Very clever, indeed. While it is possible that this was done for some benign reason, I think we must accept the strong likelihood that this was done explicitly for the purpose of infiltrating the Museum."

"But Mr. Holmes," Lestrade protested. "Morrison vanished six days before the murder of Inspector Patterson, and the thefts have continued up through last night."

"Yes, that does present a difficulty. As of now, I am not yet in possession of all of the facts with which to further an explanation of Mr. Morrison's precise role. However, there is another question that we must ask ourselves. Surely the British Museum has gold from Greece, Persia, and many other distant lands. Why are only the treasures of Ancient Britain vanishing? It would be impossible to sell such unique objects on the open market, and no fence wants stuff of the sort that you can neither melt nor sell. The gold objects are one thing, but the Lewis Chessman? Worthless! Except perhaps to a few exceptionally rich collectors of limited scruples."

"Well, the rumors going round the Museum is that it is revenge," said Lestrade cautiously.

"Revenge upon whom?"

"Revenge upon the nation of Britain."

"For what action?"

"For committing the ransacking of the Pharaoh's tomb."

Holmes laughed heartily. "Let them believe that, Lestrade. But it does raise another interesting question. There is no earthly reason why those scarabs were substituted for the treasures. You said that they were plaster, did you not?"

"Yes, what of it?"

"Not stone or faience?"

"No, I don't believe so."

"So why does the ghost of a four thousand year old mummy need to leave behind a modern copy?"

With that cryptic pronouncement, Holmes refused to say another word about the matter until he was on the scene of the action. He briefly glanced at the list of missing objects and then buried himself in a selection of the evening papers. Lestrade and I were left hoping that the gleam in Holmes' eyes suggested that his hand was already upon some clue.

§

We arrived at Victoria Station just as it was the light was fading to dusk. A thick fog had descended and caused the lines of London's dark, shapeless buildings to take on a dull neutral tint. On the streets the men were out in force with their long poles lighting the lamps, which gave off their soft, parchment-colored light. At the curb, Lestrade hailed a hansom cab and ordered the driver to take us to the Museum.

"Belay that, my good man," countermanded Holmes. "The Alpha Inn."

As the cab set off for this destination, Lestrade's eyebrows rose in surprise. "Do you fancy a pint, Mr. Holmes?"

"I fancy a word with Mr. Dominic Bedford."

"And you expect to find him at the Alpha Inn?"

"I cannot say with absolute certainty, of course, however, I think the likelihood is very high."

"Why so, Holmes?" I asked.

"As we strode through the passenger foyer at the station, I noted that it was shortly after half past five o'clock. Unless the hours of the Museum have been altered since I retired to the Downs, I know that this is very near the time when the night watchmen congregate at the Inn to share a small beer before starting their duties."

"But Mr. Bedford has refused to report for work," I protested.

"True, Watson, but the habits of many years do not change overnight. He is well used to the company of his fellows, and may still seek them out, even if he does not join them afterwards on their trek to the Museum's doors."

A few minutes later we found ourselves in Bloomsbury, at that small public house on the corner of Oxford Street and Coptic Street. Although a score of years had passed since we first crossed that threshold looking for the origin of a singular goose, the same white-aproned landlord, his face even ruddier and more weathered, continued to stand guard behind the bar.

"Good evening, Mr. Windigate," Holmes called. "I trust you are well? Is Mr. Bedford a guest of the house this evening?"

"Ah, yes, Mr. Holmes," said that man, clearly recognizing my famous friend. "He is indeed. You see the stout and swarthy fellow in the corner, nursing a beer? The one with the grizzled hair and whiskers?"

"Indeed!" replied Holmes with a triumphant glance in Lestrade's direction. "Well, prosperity to your house, sir," he said, sliding a pair of shillings across the bar.

When we approached the indicated table, the older man looked up at us with unfriendly brown eyes. However, when he recognized Lestrade, his manner changed to one of servility. "What can I do for you, Inspector?"

"This here is Mr. Sherlock Holmes and his companion, Dr. Watson. They have some questions for you."

"I've answered plenty of questions. I've got no more information for you."

Holmes slid into the seat opposite Bedford and turned the full force of his gaze upon the man. "Come now, Mr. Bedford. You are a man of the world, are you not? You have seen some near sixty years in your day, and you have fiddled at many a music hall in Shadwell."

I was sufficiently familiar with my friend's methods to be able to follow his reasoning. I observed that the peculiar blue clay on his boots might signify to Holmes that the man trod in some particular district of town, and noted that the red inflammation on the left side of Bedford's neck provided the data for Holmes' deduction of the man's free-time habits.[21] However, the man's eyes grew larger and larger as Holmes' narration went on. "You are a wizard, Mr. Holmes," he whispered in amazement. "How could you know all that?"

"It is my business to know things, Mr. Bedford. That is my trade, or at least was. Just as I know that your tale of a cursed statue is ridiculous. Don't tell me you honestly believe such nonsense."

The man only shook his head. "I am very sorry, Mr. Holmes. But I saw what I saw, and you can't tell me otherwise. There is a black statue in the gallery, about yea high," he held out his hands about three feet apart. "It sits in a glass case, where no one can touch it, and no breeze could make it stir. But it moves, I tell you. It is some form of dark magic, I am sure of that. I will swear to it in a court of law, or before the King himself, if need be." His voice vibrated with terror.

"That won't be necessary," said Holmes mildly.

But the man's excitement could not be contained. "And then there was the murdered inspector, the thin red band encircling his throat, and his purple-colored face screwed up into a horrible contorted mask. I will never forget it. It's devilish, Mr. Holmes, devilish!" cried Bedford, his voice rising with a mad, unreasoning terror. "It is not of this world.

---

[21] We are unable to verify that the clay of Shadwell, part of London's notorious East End, is marked by a particular shade of blue, but the affliction of Mr. Bedford is known in medical slang as a 'Fiddler's Neck.'

Something has come into that museum which is beyond the ken of reason."

Holmes shook his head. "I am not prepared to admit the possibility of diabolical intrusions into the affairs of men."

"Denying the power of the Father of Evil does not lessen Him, Mr. Holmes. No one in their right mind would go near that crypt at night, and only the foolhardy would approach it by day. No, it's more than a man's nerves can stand." He reached for his glass and rapidly drained it.

Lestrade vainly attempted to get some additional words out of Mr. Bedford, but the man mutely shook his head. Holmes could tell that Bedford would say no more that night and motioned Lestrade and I towards the door. He glanced at me and his lips curled up in a crooked grin. "It will not be the first time we have ventured into a haunted crypt, eh, Watson? And this one has been nicely set up for us in the heart of London. We don't have to first trudge three miles through the Berkshire grass-lands. Shall we see what awaits us at the British Museum?"

§

We regained our cab, which swept us along Great Russell Street before turning on Great Orme Street, a narrow thoroughfare lined with high, thin, yellow-brick edifices. There was hardly a corner of London that did not remind me of some adventure that Holmes and I had coursed together. Holmes gestured to one house in particular. "Recall, Watson, the house of Mrs. Warren, and over there, the high red house with stone facings, where the unlamented Gorgiano met his grisly fate."

I smiled at the sight of the locale of one of his great deductions, but it was rapidly passed by our speeding cab. We soon approached the front steps of the Museum, whose sight still filled me with respectful admiration for this mighty center of learning. The original design, imitating that of a Greek temple was handsome, but in the half-century since it was completed, the soot-riddled air of London had unfortunately turned it a deep, distressing greyish-black.[22] I hoped the new Government might see fit to have it thoroughly scrubbed back to its former glory.

My eyebrows rose when we passed by the front entrance, but Lestrade explained that the building was shut tight for the night, and only the rear doors were still accessible. The cab turned at Montague Street, and I thought to glance over at Holmes. His heavily-lidded eyes appeared deep in thought at the sight of his old rooms. Finally turning again along the

---

[22] The building that houses the collection of the British Museum has never really been completed. Expansions and improvements continue up to the modern day. Watson is probably referring to the opening of the forecourt in 1852.

northeast side of the Museum, we reached our goal.

At the sight of Lestrade descending from the cab, a uniformed guard held open the door. When we entered the back foyer, a man of about fifty years of age threw aside a journal and sprang up to meet us. He was stout and approaching corpulence, with a face filled with drooping rolls of skin. Wispy tufts of hair swept over his pate, while narrowed eyes squinted from behind thick spectacles. His suit was rumpled and his cravat loosely knotted. He held out a hand, which possessed a somewhat limp grasp, but his manner was affable.

With a raise of his bushy eyebrows I detected that this man recognized my still-famous friend. "Ah, Mr. Holmes, it is a great pleasure," said he, excitably. "Inspector Lestrade had given us hope that you might soon be making an appearance upon the scene, but I hardly dared believe it would be tonight."

"Mr. Holmes, allow me to introduce Mr. Walter Brundage, the Keeper of Egyptian and Assyrian Antiquities at the Museum, said Lestrade."[23] As he led us to his office, Brundage smiled broadly. "I am also a great admirer of yours, Mr. Holmes. And this must be Dr. Watson. We are indebted to you, sir. I have read every story you have written. You know, I am myself a detective of sorts."

I raised my eyebrows in surprise. "Oh, yes?"

"Indeed, early in my career I was assigned to investigate why papyrus scrolls from our excavation sites, and supposedly guarded by our local agents, kept appearing in the collections of antiquity dealers across Europe. We were being forced to buy our own scrolls at inflated rates! It was quite a scandal."

"And did you find the source of the leaks?" I inquired politely.

"It was the local guards, of course. They are always loyal to those who pay them the most, which was not us, I am afraid. That is why I think you should more closely study the guards here. It is one of them. I am certain of it."

Holmes had listened to this unsolicited advice with uncharacteristic patience. "And you have other talents, as well, Mr. Brundage, do you not? I have heard tales of looters rewarded, customs officials bribed, and antiquities smuggled in diplomatic pouches."

Brundage laughed merrily. "Guilty as charged, Mr. Holmes. Of course, amassing the finest collection of Egyptian antiquities in the world is not a simple task. We are constantly racing the French, the Germans, even the

---

[23] There was no Walter Brundage at the Museum in 1909, but Watson commonly changed names of people that appeared in his tales. We can safely assume that this is in fact Ernest Alfred Thompson Wallis Budge (1857-1934), who was Keeper from 1894-1924.

Americans, for each new piece that is pulled from the ground. Every tactic needs to be employed, no matter what the legality. Of course, it's not like the locals miss it. Every item is far better off in our nice museum than lying neglected, or worse, purposefully defaced, in some sandy defile."

"And what method did you use to acquire the effigy so feared by Mr. Bedford?" Holmes asked mildly.

"Nothing nefarious there, I am afraid. That was excavated, legal and above board, by our archeologist Griffith, from the Deir el-Bahri site near Luxor.[24] It is part of a full tomb that he discovered, which belonged to a Pharaoh from the Eleventh Dynasty named Mentuhotep.[25] Griffith sent the entire contents back to us: mummy, inner painted coffin, stone sarcophagus, and all of the varied trappings required to ensure the transition of Mentuhotep's *Ka*, or life-force, from his earthly remains to the *Duat*, their version of the afterlife. Our exhibit of this magnificent find opened at the beginning of September."

"And was the statue cursed?" I interjected.

"Of course," Brundage smiled again. Many of the Egyptian royal coffins are carved with curses, you know. Mentuhotep's says something to the effect of 'Cursed be those who disturb the rest of a Pharaoh, the chosen of Amun-Ra. They that shall break the seal of this tomb will be judged by Anubis. I shall cast the fear of myself into him. Death shall come on swift wings. I shall seize his neck like a bird. An end will be made for him.'"

"Holmes!" I exclaimed. "The curse has come true! Inspector Patterson was strangled. *His neck was seized...*"

Holmes stared intently at Brundage. "You are certain of the translation?"

The man snorted in derision. "I should say so. I need not remind you that the Rosetta Stone lies a few rooms from here. You can decipher it for yourself."

"And yet, Bedford's story of a moving statue is absurd."

"Not all at, Mr. Holmes. I have seen it with my own eyes."

"What?" I exclaimed.

"Oh, yes," replied Brundage. "I will admit that I was a bit taken aback myself at first. It was perhaps six weeks past, when I noticed one morning

---

[24] Presumably Francis Llewellyn Griffith (1862-1934) an eminent British Egyptologist. Watson probably neglected to disguise his name as he only appears in the form of mentions.

[25] There were at least four Pharaohs of that name in the Eleventh Dynasty (c.2134-1991 BCE). In fact, an intact Old Kingdom tomb has never been found, so Watson either misremembered Brundage's words or one of them is exaggerating.

that the statue had turned around in the night. I thought this was rather strange, because it is protected in a glass case and I am the only one who has a key. I put it back in order, but the next day I found that it had moved again. My first guess was that someone was playing an elaborate hoax or practical joke upon me – this was before any other thefts were first noted, mind you. My great success has fostered jealousy in the eyes of some of my rivals, though I refuse to cast aspersions. I thought that perhaps one of them had managed to filch my key ring for a time and produce a replicate."

"But you have ruled out that possibility?" asked Holmes.

"Indeed. I decided to investigate, so I set up Mr. Bedford to watch over this statue in particular. He was excused from his regular rounds, and sat in front of it all night. Can you imagine who he observed that was responsible for moving it?"

"Pray tell," said Holmes.

"Absolutely nobody. No one approached the case. And when he watched, the statue was as still as a stone. But when he took his eyes off it for a moment and then looked back, he noticed that its position had actually shifted slightly. By the end of the night, it had completed a one hundred and eighty degree rotation."

Lestrade sniffed in obvious disbelief. Brundage smiled at the inspector. "That was my opinion as well, gentlemen, let me assure you. I thought that Mr. Bedford had managed to stash a flask somewhere, despite our strict injunctions to the contrary, and had overindulged. So I finally decided that I must perform the task myself. It was hardly an easy matter, but armed with a good supply of coffee, I saw it through."

"And what did you witness?"

"That Mr. Bedford was absolutely correct. There is no doubt that the statue moves on its own. It is almost impossible to see directly, like waiting for a pot to boil. But when you let your attention wander, and then look again, the progressive motion is clear."[26]

"Have you generated a hypothesis, Mr. Brundage?"

The keeper shrugged. "At first, I thought this particular effigy was nothing more than a rather large and fine example of an *ushabti*, one of the minions of the deceased. They are to be found scattered throughout every tomb in Egypt. But upon further inspection I am now convinced that

---

[26] This tale is very similar to something that happened at the Manchester Museum in 2013. The recurring event was caught on video. The ten-inch tall statue of Neb-Sanu, which dates back nearly 4,000 years and was found in a mummy's tomb, had been at the Museum for eighty years. However, it that case, a time-lapse video showed it turning during the day, apparently of its own volition. During the night, however, it remained still.

it is in fact a small *Ka* statue. It is a receptacle, and permanent home, for the released soul of the Pharaoh after he departed from this earth. It can serve as an alternative vessel if the mummy is violated."

"Are you suggesting that your museum is haunted?" asked Holmes, skeptically.

"I have requested for several of my associates from the Ghost Club to verify this occurrence, and it is completely reproducible. Therefore, having eliminated an external cause, I can only conclude that in fact we are witnessing a verifiable manifestation of the hidden spirit world that constantly surrounds us, but is just beyond the sight of insensitive eyes. It is not a difficult thing to believe if you have spent sufficient time in the Orient and have experienced other similar uncanny incidents.[27] I invite you to see for yourself, Mr. Holmes."

"I intend to," Holmes replied, coming to his feet. "Lestrade, I would ask that you summon the guards from the Britain galleries, Mr. Rucastle and Mr. Seraphim. While you perform that task, Watson and I will now take a stroll round the premises. I do not recall any other question which I desire to ask of you at the moment, Mr. Brundage, but some may arise. May I ask you to remain on site for the next few hours?"

"Of course, Mr. Holmes. Do you wish for me to accompany you?"

"No, no, I like to form my own impressions."

"Very well. Here, Mr. Holmes. You may need this." He held out a fire-proof lantern of the type carried by the guards at night. "And one more thing, I should tell you that Sir Evan Lloyd Williams, the Director and Principal Librarian of the Museum, is on his way here. The guard was instructed to notify him if you made an appearance." Brundage paused for a moment, as if to consider his words. "He is, ah, most concerned that we get to the bottom of the matter as swiftly as possible, before the confidence of the public is lost."

"Yes, I may have a question or two for him, as well," said Holmes dryly.

§

Holmes' unerring sense of direction led us directly to the series of rooms that contained the Museum's famous exhibits, despite it being many years since his last visit. Notwithstanding his initial silence I could tell that Holmes was in a jocund mood. The glamour and mystery of the place, with its sinister atmosphere of forgotten nations, appealed to the imagination of my friend. As we made our way through a series of

---

[27] Strangely enough, Holmes' time in the Orient during the Great Hiatus failed to engender a similar belief.

galleries, each filled with traces of some vanished race which had passed from this earth, Holmes finally laughed aloud. "Well, Watson, what do you make of all that nonsense?"

"I hardly know what to think, Holmes. You have demonstrated time and time again that what man fancies as supernatural in origin is, in fact, something all too prosaic. There are no vampires in Sussex, no spectral hound in Dartmoor, no miracles on Vere Street, no...."

"Yes, Watson, I appreciate your point," Holmes interrupted.

"And yet, surely there are things that science has yet to explain? What about the madness of Isadora Persano? Here we have Mr. Brundage, an educated man of science, who clearly believes that the spirit of the Pharaoh haunts this edifice."

Holmes shook his head. "Any given man is clearly capable of holding two contradictory thoughts simultaneously, Watson. Simply because Mr. Brundage has been trained in the scientific method does not preclude him from also believing in the imaginary. No, I am afraid that no ghosts are needed at this particular juncture. We shall not listen to such fancies."

"Do you have an alternate hypothesis?"

"I have told you repeatedly, Watson, that it is a mistake to hypothesize in advance of the facts. Nevertheless, at the moment, I have devised seven separate explanations. For example, Walter Brundage is an admitted thief. The public applauds him because he steals from the natives of Egypt and Persia, however, this can be a slippery slope for any man. Perhaps he favors the turf, and his debts have grown too large for his modest income? Might he be forced to supplement it from the treasures of the museum? He would not steal from his own gallery, of course, but it would not be very difficult for him to obtain a set of keys from his counterpart in charge of the Britain Galleries."

"In that case, why leave the scarabs?" I protested. "Why draw attention to the Egyptian galleries?"

Holmes shrugged. "It might be a smokescreen. He creates the legend of a cursed statue to distract us from his true intentions of plundering the British treasures."

"Surely it would have been more prudent to send the cloud of suspicion to one of the other galleries? The one containing the sculptures of Greece, for instance?"

"Yes, Watson, but his access was more limited. That would require him stealing two sets of keys."

"And the murder of Inspector Patterson? Why would Brundage commit such a foul deed?"

Holmes shook his head. "I doubt it was his intention. Perhaps Patterson began to suspect him? The cruel mind of a murderer can be difficult to fathom, but Brundage might have felt that it was his only alternative."

Any further thoughts, however, fled as we crossed the threshold into the Egyptian Gallery. While both of us had visited during the day, when it was brightly lit and thronged with the general public, the room took on an entirely different character in the pale gloom of the night. It had also been fully remodeled to accommodate the new collection amassed by Mr. Brundage. The moon was shining fitfully though the high windows, and illuminated a giant marble sphinx towering above us. I had never seen it before, but it recalled to my mind the colossal human-headed winged lions that guarded the entrance to the nearby Assyrian Chambers.[28]

Holmes paused and sniffed cautiously at the air, though I noted nothing unusual. My eyes ran along the lines of mummies and the endless array of polished cases, some of wood and some of stone. The walls and ceilings were thickly covered with a thousand strange relics from throughout the Land of the Pharaohs. In the entire chamber there was scarce an article, from the shriveled ear of wheat to the pigment-box of the painter, which had not held its own against four thousand years. Here were the flotsam and jetsam washed up by the great ocean of time from that far-off empire. From stately Thebes, from lordly Luxor, from the great temples of Heliopolis, from a hundred rifled tombs, these relics had been brought.

I glanced round at the long-silent figures that flickered vaguely up through the shadow. Tall, angular figures bearing weapons stalked in an uncouth frieze round the gallery. Above were a myriad of animal-headed statues, with viper-crowned, almond-eyed monarchs, and strange beetle-like deities cut out the blue lapis lazuli. Horus and Isis and Osiris peered down from every niche and shelf, while across the ceiling a true son of the old Nile, a great, hanging-jawed mummified crocodile was slung in a double noose.

I am not a nervous man, but the complete silence was oppressive. Neither outside nor within the walls was there a creak or murmur. It was as if the busy streets of London had faded into the mists of time. I felt that the museum was trapped under some shadow, something sinister and unnatural.

Holmes lifted his lantern, which shot a tiny tunnel of vivid yellow light upon the mournful scene. Its rays were reflected back from a construction of rough-hewn stone that rose at a slope up towards the roof, which itself was lost in the shadows above our heads. This strange monument surely

---

[28] One of the highlights of the BM, the pair of colossal lions were excavated from the entrance to the royal palace of King Ashurnasirpal II (883-859 BCE) at Nimrud by Austen Henry Layard from 1845-1851.

enclosed the disturbed remains of the Pharaoh himself, restless at being separated from the land to which he belonged. This gate of Death left a feeling of absolute horror in my mind.

"It is a pyramid of fear!" I whispered.

Holmes sighed. "Cut out the drama, Watson," he said severely. "I note that it is a pyramid."

I gathered my wits and studied the structure. "But surely the dating is wrong?"

"What do you mean, Watson?"

"The construction of pyramid tombs fell out of favor after the Fifth Dynasty. They required too many resources to build, and were judged to be excessively vulnerable to tomb robbers."

Holmes looked at me curiously. "I never grasp your full abilities, Watson."

"I read it in a book once, Holmes," I said, shrugging modestly.

"Still, I believe that you are entirely correct. While I would like to credit the artifacts themselves as being authentic, though perhaps that should not be a given when dealing with the slippery Mr. Brundage, it is abundantly clear that the Keeper has freely indulged his imagination at this juncture. The stones that make up this pyramid are not Egyptian."

"How can you be certain, Holmes?"

He stepped forward and placed his hand upon the wall of the structure. "Because no Egyptian pyramid was ever constructed from Cotswold limestone."

I looked more closely at the stones, and even I, who lack Holmes' familiarity with the dirt and stone of England, realized the truth in his words. "Yes, well, it is certainly a vivid effect."

The two of us entered the archway into the pyramid proper, which was lonely and eerie in the dim light. In the center of this singular chamber was a vertical mummy case with its horrible occupant, who stood, grim and stark, his black, shriveled face pointed towards the entry. The form was, of course, lifeless and inert, but it seemed as I gazed at it that there still lingered a small spark of vitality, some faint consciousness in its gaze. Four thousand years old, the horrid, black, withered thing seemed to reach out with its bony forearm and claw-like hand, ready to seize upon any who intruded upon its slumber. The facial features, though horribly discolored towards a deep indigo, were perfect, and the two little nut-like eyes still lurked in the depths of the black, hollow sockets like something unnatural and inhuman. The blotched skin was drawn tightly from bone to bone, and a tangled wrap of a black, coarse hair fell over the ears. Two thin teeth, like those of a rat, overlaid the shriveled lower lip. The gaunt ribs, with their parchment-like covering, were exposed, as was the sunken, leaden-hued abdomen, with the long slit where the embalmer had left his mark. Only the lower limbs were still wrapped round with coarse, yellow cerecloth and linen bandages. I think that, having experienced what I have in my life, I am as strong-nerved as any man could possibly be, but I admit that I was a bit shaken by this half-lit scene.

Near the Pharaoh stood a giant statue of Osiris, ruler of the dead, divine judge, his body swathed in depictions of mummy wrappings, his arms crossed over his chest, his hands holding the twin scepters of his rule. The stone of his tall white crown and snowy alabaster shoulders shone pale in contrast to the flat black face and hands. Before him lay a horizontal case, which contained an intricately inscribed, yellow, curled roll of paper. The museum label explained that this deceptively plain papyrus scroll has come to be known as the 'Book of the Dead,' for the secret spells within promise to unlock an occult knowledge beyond that bestowed upon ordinary mortals.

Holmes surveyed this grim tableau and then chuckled. "Well, if our friend Mr. Brundage was concerned about animating the spirit of his mummy, perhaps situating the incantations of revivification nearby was a poor choice, eh, Watson? If I ever permit you to chronicle any more of my little problems, Watson, which is admittedly unlikely, I foresee that you will enliven your pages with this account of the singular adventure of the Bloomsbury Lodger."

I recognized that Holmes was making light of the situation to defuse the tension in the air and smiled gratefully. "So where is our spinning statue?"

Holmes glanced around the other cases, which contained a magnificent collection of earthenware canopic jars, rings, precious stones, and dozens of similar objects. However, one circular case stood apart. It held only a three-foot high jet black statue of a cobra-crowned pharaoh. Although but half the size of true life and carved from the darkest basalt, its eyes shown with two polished moonstones that seemed to watch us in the darkness. The statue was not facing the mummy directly, but was instead oddly turned approximately fifteen degrees counter-clockwise.

My friend closely studied the lock for a moment and then grunted. "Well, no signs of tampering, that is for certain. The hole is unscratched. Whoever is moving this statue must be in possession of a key."

But I was hardly listening to him. "Holmes," I whispered. "The statue has moved!"

"What?" exclaimed Holmes, clearly annoyed. "Not you too, Watson." He glanced back at the statue and then paused. "That is strange, it *has* moved slightly."

I was about to respond, however, when I heard a faint sound, and felt a whiff of air and a light brushing past my elbow. It was so slight that I could scarcely be certain of it. Had something passed me in the darkness? I felt as if vague shapes swirled and swam in the unnerving gloom, each a warning of something beyond the learning of man, some unutterable dweller upon the shadowy entryway to that undiscovered country from which none have ever returned. A freezing horror threatened to take utter possession of me.

§

However, I was not able to dwell upon these fears for long, since Holmes' sardonic voice suddenly muttered that we were about to be joined by a pair of men. As usual, his strikingly acute senses heard their approach long before it became obvious to me, though I doubted him not. And eventually, I was able make out Mr. Brundage following behind an imperious white-haired gentleman, both holding lanterns that matched the one in Holmes' hand.

Brundage's voice quavered slightly as he made the introductions. "Mr. Holmes, Dr. Watson, please allow me to introduce Sir Evan Lloyd Williams, distinguished Director and Principal Librarian of the British Museum.[29]

Sir Williams was a severe looking man of about five and forty, his balding pate shining in the lantern light. He was dressed in a formal black dinner jacket over a bone white shirt. His fierce blue eyes gazed upon Holmes with what appeared to be considerable contempt. "Your name is familiar to me, sir," he said, his bushy mustache quivering as he spoke. "I have read your analysis of the Chaldean roots traced in the Cornish branch of the Celtic language. It is a masterpiece," he proclaimed, and I saw Holmes' chest puff out slightly. "A masterpiece of rank amateurism. It is so riddled with errors that they overwhelm the few areas of accuracy. I am afraid that philology is an exacting science that requires years of training. It cannot be learned over a weekend from glancing at a few minor tomes, like some cheap parlor trick."

Holmes' grey eyes narrowed at this venomous attack, but when he spoke his voice was strangely mild. "Yes, well, I am sure you have your own interpretation of the data. Pray tell, Sir Williams, as Dr. Watson and I made our way over to this gallery, we passed through a small room containing some fine objects that I have seen before in the chambers of a

---

[29] Although Watson uses a different name, the position of 'Director and Principal Librarian of the British Museum' was occupied from 1909-1931 by Sir Frederic George Kenyon (1863-1952), a flawed scholar whose lack of scientific rigor fortunately did no permanent harm to the integrity of the museum.

Mr. Nathan Garrideb. A set of fine Syracusan coins, for example. And a cabinet of Neolithic flint tools arranged chronologically with the skulls of their one-time owners. Did his estate perhaps leave them to the Museum?"

"Yes, there were a few items worthy of display, though nothing that compared to the scope of his imagination. Garrideb thought he was another Hans Sloane,"[30] sniffed Sir Williams, his lip curled in a sneer. "But in actuality, the old imbecile was a minor dilettante. These sorts of things are best left to the professionals."

Holmes bared his teeth in what some might mistake for a pained smile, and I knew to be a grimace of distaste. It was one of my friend's most evident faults that he was impatient with less astute intellects than his own, and I feared he judged the Director to be squarely in this camp. Holmes promptly did away with his weak attempt at pleasantries. It was never a great skill of his, and the Director plainly had no interest in talking with Holmes. He sniffed at the air. "I have a few questions for your, Sir Williams."

"Yes, so Brundage tells me," said the Director, while the man beside him shrank further into the shadows. "But I am afraid that is impossible. The matter is very delicate, Mr. Holmes," he intoned. "Consider the reputation of the museum. I can hardly justify speaking before..."

"Have no fear, Sir Williams. I can assure you that Dr. Watson is the very soul of discretion."

The Director faced round to study me. "Is he? Would your other clients agree, Mr. Holmes? The ones whose private lives have been laid bare in his tawdry tales? I think not."

Holmes' spine stiffened and he turned the full force of his gaze upon the man. "You can answer my questions now, Sir Williams, or you can answer them later. Perhaps we will call upon your home a bit later this evening? I am certain that your lovely wife will be happy to receive us. Or did you have plans to be out?"

It was difficult to tell for certain by the dim lantern-light, but I thought I detected that all color had drained from the man's face. Walter Brundage, for his part, was following this exchange with trepidation, but also great interest. "What do you wish to know?" Sir Williams finally croaked.

Holmes smiled like a cat that had just caught his mouse. "First of all, you have had quite a turn-over in your guards as of late. Both Mr. Morrison of this gallery, and Mr. Seraphim of the Ancient Britain rooms, are rather new, are they not?"

Sir Williams recovered his composure and managed a nonchalant

---

[30] Sir Hans Sloane (1660-1753) was a British collector, whose curiosities formed the foundation of the British Museum.

shrug. "They are a rough lot, Mr. Holmes. Turn-over happens on a regular basis."

"And in these particular cases?" Holmes inquired. "What became of their predecessors?"

The man shrugged. "I believe that the man before Seraphim was beaten by thugs down in Limehouse and crippled for life. He got some small pension from us, but was unfit for further work. And the man before Morrison died of some disease. Tetanus, I believe."

"Very good," nodded Holmes. "We have heard much about the guards. But there is one other group that has access to the Museum after hours, I think: the cleaners. When do the floors get swept?"

"Daily, of course."

"Come now, Sir Williams. Confabulations do not become a knight of the realm. You see, I know that you are not having the Museum scrubbed daily, even if your ledgers suggest otherwise. I have already inspected the floors of this room. It has not rained in London for three days, and yet, the distinctive prints of several pairs of muddy Wellingtons are plain.[31] What gentleman wears such boots when there is no chance of a shower?"

Sir Williams appeared distressed by this accusation, though Holmes expressed it more delicately than was his usual wont. "Yes, well, it is as you say, sir. The cleaners come every four days."

Holmes smiled at this confession. "Excellent. You have been most helpful, Sir Williams. I have no further questions for you at the moment, but please be ready to return to the Museum should I need to summon you. That way I will not be forced to pay a social visit to your home."

The man scurried away in a most undignified manner, Brundage trailing along behind him.

Holmes laughed as we watched them leave. "What do you make of that, Watson?"

I shook my head. "I admit that I am mystified by the whole matter. I hesitate to cast doubts upon a man of such rank, but his hostility was plain. Could Sir Williams be stealing from his own museum?"

"Yes, he does make an attractive candidate, Watson. Unfortunately, I think his hostility derives from pure snobbery. He is a feckless fool, and a shining example of someone being promoted because of his connections and not due to his ability. Sadly, his predecessor was no better, as the old fraud had little knowledge of graphology, but an unerring sense of self-promotion.[32] For his own part, Sir Evan Lloyd Williams' scholarship is

---

[31] Wellingtons were a term for rain-boots during Victorian times, named after the Iron Duke, who was the first to wear them.

[32] The predecessor was Sir Edward Maunde Thompson (1840-1929), a paleographer noted for his 'study' of William Shakespeare's supposed

burdened with critical errors, where he twists facts to fits his theories and not the other way round."

"I don't understand how you got him to answer you, when he plainly had no such desire?"

"It was evident that Sir Williams is engaged in activities with a lady, or perhaps ladies, belonging to the world's oldest profession. He had a trace of a cheap rouge stain on his collar, and he reeked of a perfume that can be had for less than a shilling."

"It could have come from his wife?"

"Tut, tut, Watson! The wife of a knight does not freshen herself with a one-shilling scent."

"Perhaps he is not married?"

Holmes sighed. "He was wearing a wedding ring, Watson."

"Well, other men have engaged in such activities and not been overly concerned. Why did he fear exposure so much?"

Holmes chuckled. "Because Sir Williams is known as one of the leading scholars of the so-called Biblical Authenticity movement.[33] To be caught *in flagrante delicto*[34] would expose him as an enormous hypocrite. Of course I do not care a farthing what the man does in his private time. I am no Milverton. The connection was a simple matter and not one of which I am overly proud. But as they say, 'desperate times....'[35] Ah, I think I spot the approach of Lestrade."

Lestrade and one other man soon appeared out of the darkness. As he stepped into the circle of yellow light thrown by our lantern, I saw that the inspector was leading a short and prodigiously stout man, no more than two inches above five feet. His head was enormous, with an unsmiling face, and a great heavy chin which rolled down in fold upon fold over his throat, and which made him appear much older than his six and twenty years. The man's protuberant eyes bulged at the sight of Holmes.

"You are Mr. Edward Rucastle, are you not?" Holmes asked.

"I am," the man answered sullenly, a shadow passing over his face.

"And your father was named Jephro?"

---

handwriting in the manuscript of the play Sir Thomas More.

[33] Supposed 'scholars' who start with the belief that the events described in the Bible are historical fact, and then twist the archeologic facts to fit their theories.

[34] Latin for 'in blazing offense.'

[35] The exact origin of this phrase is unknown. It may be a variant of a Latin proverb: *'extremis malis extrema remedia'* (extreme remedies for extreme ills). There are hints of it in *Hamlet*, Act III, Scene 2 ('Diseases desperate grown, by desperate alliances are relieved, Or not at all'), and Guy Fawkes is alleged to have said to King James I on 6 November 1605 (after his capture): 'Desperate diseases require desperate measures.'

Lestrade spluttered in indignation. "How could you possibly know that, Mr. Holmes?"

"I know it because I was once acquainted with Mr. Rucastle's father." He turned to the guard. "Do you deny it?"

"I deny nothing!" said the man, angrily. "Do you deny mangling him, Mr. Sherlock Holmes? Do you deny turning him into a broken invalid?" His cheeks were red, his brow was all crinkled, and the veins stood out at his temples with a great passion.

Holmes' eyebrows rose. "As I recall, it was your father's hound that was responsible for his injuries, Mr. Rucastle, not I."

"Oh, yes," he spluttered. "I've read the account of your lackey. It's quite the fiction. But I had the truth from my father's lips."

"If by 'lackey,' you are referring to Dr. Watson, then you should be thanking him, not insulting him. It was only due to his careful attention that your father survived that terrible wound."

"So he says. From what I hear, he almost finished the job that you began. Only the arrival of the country surgeon saved my father's life."

"Yes, well, what is true for you is true for you, and what is true for me is true for me. [36] But what matters to me, Mr. Rucastle, is not what you believe, but what sort of man you have become?"

"I don't need to answer to you. I have been an honest employee of the Museum for eight years. No man can say otherwise. Unless I am under arrest, I wish to return to my job."

"Hold, Mr. Rucastle," interjected Lestrade. "Mr. Holmes may not have an official role here, but I do. You better answer to me, or you will find yourself sleeping in a warm bunk at Bow Street."

"What do you want to know?" he replied sullenly.

Lestrade looked to Holmes for guidance, who nodded. "I only wish to know if you have anything new to add to your prior statements to Inspector Patterson," said Holmes, as placidity as he was capable. "Sometimes upon further reflection, fresh thoughts come to light."

"I don't know anything about it. I walk my rounds, just like I always have. Nobody, excepting only Seraphim and I, enters our galleries at night. I can't explain where those things vanish to, nor how those little beetles appear. I would tell you if I did."

Holmes studied him. "I believe you, Mr. Rucastle. I have no further questions for you. But where is your counterpart?"

---

[36] Holmes here is quoting from Protagoras (c.490–420 BCE), a pre-Socratic Greek philosopher and a prominent sophist. Protagoras created a major controversy during ancient times through his statement that, 'Man is the measure of all things,' meaning that there is no absolute truth, only that which individuals deem to be the truth.

"It happens to be Mr. Seraphim's night off, Mr. Holmes," interjected Lestrade.

"Oh, indeed?" Holmes said mildly. He turned to Rucastle. "And how often do the guards get the night off?"

"Every nine nights," he answered sullenly.

Holmes smiled, as if at some internal joke. "Yes, I thought as much."

Rucastle frowned, as if Holmes was treating him like a fool, but he turned and silently went back in the direction that he came. When the man was out of earshot, Lestrade looked at Holmes, who had turned and was again studying the slowly spinning statue. Lestrade glanced over at me, wondering if he should break my friend's concentration. After several minutes of uncomfortable silence, he finally cleared his throat.

"Have you come to a conclusion, Mr. Holmes?"

Holmes tore his gaze from the statue and looked over at the inspector with a peculiar smile upon his face. "I have some notions, Lestrade, but nothing definitive as of yet."

"Can you explain the statue? I fear that this may be beyond the realm of man."

"Of a sort, Lestrade. Of a sort. I do think that the answer to this piece of the puzzle hails from another place and time."

"Ancient Egypt?" I said.

"The curse?" said Lestrade, simultaneously.

"Perhaps," he replied cryptically.

"So what is our next course of action, Holmes?" I asked.

He pulled his watch from his pocket and consulted it. "The hour is getting late. I think a light supper at the Café Royal followed by some rest. How do you feel about the Northumberland Hotel, Watson?"

"But what about the thefts, Mr. Holmes?" cried Lestrade.

Holmes shrugged. "Rome was not built in a day, Lestrade. If you have some patience, I fancy that we will get to the bottom of this soon enough."

"And if more things vanish tonight while you sleep?"

"It is entirely possible, Lestrade, though your little list," Holmes patted his pocket, "tells me some nights are free of mischief. As for tonight, I put the odds at approximately two to one. Of course, even if something does occur, I have high hopes of eventually recovering most of the items intact. Good night, Lestrade. I will wire the Yard when I am ready to proceed."

With that, the two of us departed from the Museum. As we climbed aboard a hansom headed for Northumberland Avenue, Holmes laughed. "I do say, Watson, that as much as I initially resisted Lestrade's entreaties, I am glad to be back in the game, albeit for a brief while. I scarcely admitted to myself how much I missed the thrill of the chase, and this has proven to be a unique problem."

"Surely you must suspect Edward Rucastle? His presence in the Museum would otherwise be too monstrous a coincidence."

"Indeed, Watson. I must acknowledge that I did not anticipate the presence of this figure from our past. The plot does thicken."[37]

"He clearly hates you, Holmes, for in his twisted mind, he blames you for the downfall of his villainous father. Perhaps this is an elaborate scheme to lure you to your doom?"

Holmes chuckled. "Yes, well I have been coursed by more skilled hunters than the half-witted son of a petty swindler. If Colonel Sebastian Moran could not bring me down, I will not lose much sleep worrying about poor Edward Rucastle."

§

And yet, when I woke at half-past seven the following morning, the first glimmer of daylight appearing, it was clear that Holmes had gone all night without rest. I knew this was his wont when his mind was stimulated by a challenge, though it often pushed his constitution to its breaking point. The only sign of him in our adjoining rooms was a thick haze of pipe smoke in the air and a hurriedly scribbled note that contained one of Holmes' laconic messages: 'Come at once to the Museum, if convenient.'

I dressed and immediately set off to meet Holmes, forsaking my breakfast in my eagerness to hear what ratiocinations his great brain had solved during the small hours of the night. I emerged into a foggy morning light, which, by the time I arrived at my destination, was giving way to a thin watery sunshine. Despite the early hour, for the Museum had yet to open to the public, the door guard must have been alerted to allow me to pass unobstructed. I made my way back to the main Egyptian Gallery, as I was certain this was where I would find my friend.

Sure enough, Sherlock Holmes was standing under the facsimile pyramid, with a small crowd gathered about him. The room appeared much more prosaic in the clear light of day. The group included Inspector Lestrade, his face looking hopeful, Sir Evan Lloyd Williams, his expression a storm of thunderclouds, and Mr. Walter Brundage, whose appearance suggested that he had been roused long in advance of his usual waking time.

"Ah, Watson," said Holmes, "excellent, you have arrived just in time. I fear I could not have delayed these impatient gentlemen for very much longer."

"You have solved the case, Holmes?"

---

[37] A quotation of a phrase by George Villers, the Second Duke of Buckingham (1628-1687), from his play, 'The Rehearsal.'

"Yes, I hope to show you how it was done," said Holmes, smiling. "My train of reasoning began with this statue." He indicated the now-motionless black effigy across from the Pharaoh's mummy.

"Damn the statue, man!" erupted Sir Williams. "If you know who is stealing from my Museum, out with it now!"

Holmes turned to the man and said with a display of restrained civility, "I have my methods, sir. They have served me well over the years, as Inspector Lestrade will confirm, should you doubt me. I do not intend to vary them now. If you do not wish to remain, you may depart at any time."

The Director appeared furious at being denied in his own realm, but he remained rooted to the floor.

"As I was saying, the solution to the mysterious spinning statue is a rather superficial one. I first discarded the possibility of a supernatural explanation, which is the default of a weak intellect and an overactive imagination. Furthermore, while at least one key to this case exists in the possession of Mr. Brundage, we know that it is not a human hand that is turning the statue. You see, Lestrade, both Dr. Watson and I were able to confirm the testimony of Mr. Bedford, the protesting night-guard. The statue does indeed move on its own. Therefore, having eliminated the impossible, whatever explanation remained must be the truth. The statue is being turned by external forces of an entirely natural kind."

"But the statue is in a glass case!" cried Mr. Brundage, perhaps upset at Holmes' characterization of the limits of his intelligence. "What sort of forces could penetrate that?"

"The kind that only a set of hyper-acute senses might be able to detect," said Holmes smiling. "Vibrations."

The Director snorted with derision. "You are mad, Mr. Holmes. If this statue moved because of nearby vibrations, it would happen during the day, when the throngs of people are passing through this gallery, not in the dead of night."

"I did not say that the vibrations were nearby. In fact, during the day the closer vibrations of the public's footfalls serve as a sort of interference wave, and prevent the status from turning. It is their very absence after hours that allows the distant vibrations to produce the nocturnal movements. I have examined the statue myself and...."

"That's impossible," interjected Brundage. "Only I have the key."

Holmes shook his head. "It is a rather simple lock, Mr. Brundage. It took me but a few seconds to open it. As I was saying, I examined the statue this morning and found that it has a convex base. There is a subtle lump at the bottom which makes it more susceptible to vibrations than the others in the gallery whose bases are perfectly flat. The differential friction of the serpentine stone of the statue and the glass shelf upon which it sits creates the movements which some have attributed to the presence of a ghostly life-force."

"But where are the vibrations coming from, Holmes?" I asked.

"I told you last night, Watson, that the answer hails from another place and time. The other 'place' was strictly literal, while another 'time' was perhaps metaphorical. For the vibrations are caused by rumblings of trains passing through the modern tube station beneath our feet."[38]

"You must be joking, Mr. Holmes," scoffed the Director.

"I never jest, Sir Williams. As Mr. Bedford clearly described, the statue does not continuously rotate. I timed the intervals between the movements and compared them to the timing of the trains entering and exiting the station. They match perfectly."

"That is a fine piece of deduction, Mr. Holmes," said Lestrade anxiously. "But I don't see how that tells us who is robbing the Museum and killed Patterson?"

"I was getting to that, Lestrade," said Holmes, piqued by the interruption. "While I was visiting the British Museum Station, I had a pleasant conversation with the Station Master. Mr. Jack Bullinger was a wealth of information about the goings-on of his small domain. Did you know that the station is reputed to the haunted by the ghost of a daughter of an Egyptian Pharaoh?"

Lestrade stared at Holmes as if he required a trip to Bedlam. "But Mr. Holmes, you've always said that you don't believe in the Pharaoh's curse?" said he, weakly.

As if he hadn't heard Lestrade, Holmes continued. "According to Mr. Bullinger, the ghost first appeared when her mummy was accidentally destroyed during an unwrapping process by the Museum's Egyptologists."

Brundage grunted and shrugged his shoulders. "It happens sometimes. The wrappings on a mummy can be quite pasted together. There are always more where those came from."

"Yes, well, late on certain nights, the Princess's ghost appears, dressed in an impressive loincloth and headdress, and she wails and screams so loudly that the noise carries down the tunnels to the adjoining stations." He turned to me. "What do you make of that, Watson?"

Having studied my friend's methods over the span of so many years, I was sufficiently conversant so as to attempt to replicate them. I considered

---

[38] British Museum was a station on the London Underground served by the Central line and which opened 1900. In 1933, with the expansion of Holborn station, less than 100 yards away, the British Museum station was permanently closed. It was subsequently utilized as a military office and command post, but in 1989 the surface building was demolished and the remainder of the station is wholly disused.

how this information would have furthered Holmes's deductions. "Perhaps the cries are not from a ghost, but rather made by some natural process?" I ventured.

Holmes wore an amused smile at this brilliant deduction of mine. "Capital, Watson! You are scintillating this morning. And you haven't even had your coffee yet, I see. That is exactly the first solution which occurred to me. A sudden change in air pressure could create such an effect. I then turned my attention back to this gallery. Was the connection between the mummies herein and the Underground station purely a coincidence? I took another stroll around this room and noted an anomaly. If you will follow me, gentlemen?"

Holmes led us out from under the pyramid and along the eastern wall, which was lined by a series of upright, lidded stone sarcophagi, each intricately carved with hieroglyphics. "We have here a fine set of mummy cases, most of which are remarkably intact despite their great age and the vast distance that they travelled to their new home. But this one is different, wouldn't you say?" He stopped in front of one such funeral receptacle, its weathered brown granite marred by the presence of several steel rods, rivets and claps. "This one has been modified, enhanced by this clever set of levers which allow the lid to be easily opened. Is this your handiwork, Mr. Brundage?"

The man shrugged modestly. "Yes, well, before we built the pyramid, we needed something to amuse our patrons. They enjoy seeing the lid slowly raised, imagining the emergence of the horrid form within..."

"Indeed," said Holmes drily. "But I see that you use it no longer? This side is clasped by a firm lock."

Brundage hesitated for a moment. "That is correct, Mr. Holmes. Despite the best efforts of the modern engineers who made the levers, the lid was never intended by its ancient makers to be opened once it was closed. Small cracks eventually began to appear in the marble, so we desisted. I put that lock on there to deter errant school boys from trying to open it when no one was looking."

"And the key?"

"I don't carry it with me. It must be around here somewhere. Likely in the desk drawer in my office."

"No matter, for I do not require it. Like someone before me, it will be a simple matter to crack. Do you see the scratches, Lestrade?" he said, angling out the lock for inspection.

"Yes, I do," replied Lestrade. "But I still cannot follow you, Mr. Holmes. Do you suspect that the thief is stashing their loot inside?"

"The thief is certainly utilizing it for something, Lestrade," Holmes replied, as he took a set of picks from his pocket. "Look down, gentlemen.

Do you see that fine layer of marble dust that has been so kindly left by the Museum's infrequent cleaners? This morning I found a few similar grains upstairs near the case of the Chessmen."

"But there is dust everywhere, Mr. Holmes!" protested Lestrade. "How could you have known to look for some speaks that are different?"

"I knew because I was expecting to find it." Holmes stopped and turned to look at us, the opened lock now held freely in his hand. Done with it, he held it out for me to take. In spite of his aptitude for concealing his sentiments, I could easily see that Holmes was in a state of suppressed exhilaration, while I was giddy with that half-sporting, half-intellectual gratification which I unfailingly experienced when I accompanied Holmes during one of his successful investigations. "We know that none of guards could be responsible," he continued. "The precautions that prevent them from removing any objects are too fastidious. Instead, I decided that the thief must be entering the Museum from outside each night. But how?"

"A tunnel!" I exclaimed. "A secret tunnel to the Underground Station! And when the lid is opened, a difference in air pressure creates the screams that are attributed to the Princess' ghost!"

"Exactly, Watson!" He turned, and with his still-fearsome strength, threw open the stone lid upon its series of levers. "Gentlemen, I give you the entrance to the tunnel!"

But when the four of us peered eagerly inside, all we found was a thick layer of dust.

§

When Sir Williams had completed his strident exit in a fit of seemingly-justified indignation, Mr. Brundage trailing meekly behind him, Lestrade and I turned to Holmes with questioning looks. After his premature announcement, Holmes had carefully searched the inside of the sarcophagus, still hoping to find some hidden latch that might trigger the bottom portion to open into his conjectured tunnel. But after several futile minutes, Holmes was forced to admit defeat. He proceeded to slump against the side of the massive plinth that held the room's guardian sphinx. Holmes sat for some time in silence with his head sunk forward, and his eyes bent upon the silent and empty sarcophagus. I imagined his thoughts bordered upon the morbid.

It had, of course, come as a great surprise to me to see that Holmes was wrong, for only a handful of times had I known him to fail. So accustomed was I to his invariable triumphs that the very possibility of his failing had ceased to enter my head. I worried that I must reject this case from my published records, for I always preferred to dwell upon his successes. I was greatly pained at the mistake, for I knew how keenly Holmes would feel any such slip. It was his specialty to be as precise as possible, but it was obvious that the years of inactivity during his retirement had slightly dulled his once razor-sharp mind. He was obviously embarrassed, while Lestrade simply raised his eyebrows in surprise at Holmes' unexpected failure. Lestrade's opinion had shifted over the almost three decades of his acquaintance with Holmes, from one of contemptuous skepticism to that of respectful awe. But I once again saw the pale light of doubt in the inspector's eyes. I desperately hoped that this setback would not send Holmes into one of the fits of blackest depression to which he was often prey.

Holmes finally sighed and slowly stood. "I have miscalculated badly, Lestrade. I must reconsider my position," he said at last. He strode from the room in uncontrollable agitation, with a flush upon his sallow cheeks, and a nervous clasping and unclasping of his long, thin hands.

No more was said until we were ensconced in a hansom rattling our way back to the hotel. I hoped that some rest might help restore his powers. "I am afraid that this blunder denotes the true zero-point of my lifetime, Watson. You have seen me miss my mark before, but never before has my instinct played me so false. It seemed a foregone conclusion when it first flashed across my mind in the Underground station, but the one disadvantage of a dynamic brain is that one can always imagine alternative reasons which might make the scent a false one. Perhaps our day has passed? Soon these streets will be filled with motor-cars," he gestured out the window. "These hansom cabs will vanish like relics of a forgotten era. An era, unfortunately, to which you and I belong."

I endeavored to think of something reassuring to tell him, but the growing aches in my shoulder and leg told of the same truth of which he bespoke. Holmes was right. We were getting old.

Finally he was roused from his melancholy ruminations by the sight out the window. "Cabby, where are we going?" he called up to the driver. I look out and noted that we were not, as I would have expected, travelling down St. Martin's Lane.

"Sorry, sir, Trafalgar Square is blocked on accounts of the suffrage protests. We needed to go down Kingsway and Aldwych instead and then here along the Embankment."

"Ah, very good," replied Holmes, sinking back morosely into his seat. But then he sprang forward. "Stop the horse, cabby!" he commanded.

"What is it, Holmes?"

However, I received no answer. Instead, Holmes had already jumped out of the cab and was striding down the Embankment back the way we had come. The driver was futilely calling after him. I paid the man and hurried to catch my friend. Fortunately, he had not gone far. Instead he stopped at a curious spot.

"Strange, Watson, how many times have we passed this way over the years, but never really registered it into our consciousness."

"Indeed, Holmes," I exclaimed. I stared up at the great red granite obelisk that pierced the sky. It was over twenty meters high, engraved on all sides with hieroglyphs. It was flanked on two sides by giant bronze sphinxes, their inscription-dimpled patinas darkened to a midnight black.[39]

"If I recall correctly, this monument is known as Cleopatra's Needle, though it actually has little to do with that great queen, whose age cannot wither her infinite variety."[40] Tell me, Watson, what do you see that is wrong with this tableau?"

I studied it for a minute. "The sphinxes appear to be looking backwards. They should be guarding the Needle, not gazing upon it."

Holmes laughed softly to himself. "You are a conductor of light, Watson."

"Have you had some inspiration, Holmes?"

"Oh, yes. Look over there, Watson," he commanded, pointing towards Waterloo Bridge. "Do you recall that this is the locale of one of the greatest failures of my early years? For it was here that Mr. John Openshaw was decoyed and murdered by Captain James Calhoun and his two mates, minutes after I sent him away to his death. But, with age comes great wisdom. We shall not be defeated again, I think."

"Back to the Museum then?"

"Not quite yet, Watson. There is still one piece of the puzzle that remains to be tracked down."

"Where to then, Holmes?"

"No, my dear fellow. This is one task I must undertake on my own. There is no prospect of danger or I should not dream of stirring without

---

[39] The obelisk is twenty-one meters (almost seventy feet) high and weighs about two and a quarter tons. It was originally erected in the Egyptian city of Heliopolis on the orders of Thutmose III, c.1450 BCE. The inscriptions were added about two hundred years later by Ramesses II to commemorate his military victories. The obelisk was then moved to Alexandria and set up in the Caesareum, a temple built by Cleopatra in honor of Julius Caesar, by the Romans in 12 BCE. It was presented to the UK in 1819 by the ruler of Egypt, Muhammad Ali, in commemoration of the victories of Lord Nelson at the Battle of the Nile and Sir Ralph Abercromby at the Battle of Alexandria, but not installed until 1878. Cleopatra's Needle is flanked by two faux-Egyptian sphinxes cast from bronze that bear hieroglyphic inscriptions. The Sphinxes appear to be looking at the Needle rather than guarding it due to an improper installation.
[40] A paraphrase of William Shakespeare (from *Antony and Cleopatra*, Act II, Scene 2): 'I trust that age doth not wither nor custom stale my infinite variety.'

you at my side." He would say no more. By this point in our friendship I simply accepted his curiously secretive streak, which invariably led to the production of one those dramatic effects that he so clearly craved. I could attempt to guess at his exact plans, but often found that even I was often left in the dark. "I will be at the Museum by five o'clock," he continued. "I will send a note to Lestrade and all of the other players to meet me there at that hour. I trust that by that time I will have cleared up the mess that I have made of this so far. Adieu."

I watched as he hailed a passing cab and leapt aboard. The streets were crowded on the way back to the hotel, but in the event that Holmes concluded his investigations early, I did not wish to miss any potential messages sent to me there. Therefore, I spent the remainder of the morning and early afternoon at a desk jotting down notes while they were still fresh in my mind, in the hopes that they might someday be worthy of publication. This quickly passed the time and before I knew it, I looked at the clock and realized that I must proceed with haste back to the Museum, skipping my tea in the process. I sprang into a hansom and drove to the Bloomsbury, half-afraid that I might be too late to hear the dénouement of this singular mystery.

When I arrived minutes before the appointed hour, the main doors were due to remain open for a short time longer, and the galleries were still filled with crowds of assorted people. Fashionable ladies, chattering mindlessly behind gloved hands, inadvertently mingled with plodding laborers and stylishly, if modestly, attired clerks. Even a poorly-herded gaggle of children scampered amidst the ancient rubble. After some effort, I finally located Sherlock Holmes standing alone under the pyramid by the silent effigy of the long-deceased Pharaoh.

Unfortunately, Holmes' afternoon errand did not appear to have been a successful one. The expression on this face was haggard, his shoulders rounded, and he seemed to me as if he had aged ten years in a day. He leaned heavily upon his walking stick. I worried that the immense strains of this investigation and the miasmas of London were worsening his rheumatism and breaking down his once-iron vigor.

"Ah, Watson, splendid," said he with some animation, upon spying my approach. "I am glad that you are a shade early for our appointment. You have often accused me of withholding from you key facts so as to produce an astonishing effect. To rectify this balance I would like to inform you of my activities of this afternoon and allow you to draw your own conclusions before the other members of this drama appear."

"Thank you, Holmes. I would greatly appreciate that."

"My first destination was to Stepney, where amidst the reeking outcasts of Europe I visited the work yard of Gelder and Co."

"The source of the Napoleonic busts?" I exclaimed. "Is that where you suspect the scarabs were sculpted?"

He smiled and nodded. "Very good, Watson. I then proceeded directly back to the Museum."

I frowned. "But you have already thoroughly searched this gallery, and those containing the treasures of Ancient Britain. Did you overlook something?"

"No, no. My powers are not failing to such an extent. However, I was earlier guilty of leaping to a conclusion, when I had yet to perform an adequate reconnaissance of the area. The answer, or the inspiration, I should more properly say, actually lies in the nearby galleries of Ancient Greece. Finally, a few minutes' glance through the acquisition manifests of the Museum confirmed my suspicions."

"Greece!" I protested. "Nothing about this case points to anything to do with Greece!"

Holmes smiled at my outburst, but any further explanations would have to wait, as we were joined by Inspector Lestrade, Sir Evan Lloyd Williams, Mr. Walter Brundage, and three men dressed as guards: Edward Rucastle, the erstwhile Dominic Bedford, and a new man who could only be Quincy Seraphim. The latter was some fifty years in age, about five foot, nine inches in height, and once sturdily built, but now trending to portliness. The fellows' complexion was sallow, but with thick black hair and bushy side-whiskers and moustache. He wore thick glasses which accentuated his dull grey eyes. His manner was nervous and shy, that of a man more accustomed to spending long hours with the relics of the past than with the living of today.

Holmes glanced at Lestrade, who returned a significant look. I deduced from this that Lestrade had, at Holmes' suggestion, drawn a cordon of constables about the Museum. "Ah, gentlemen, thank you for coming," said Holmes.

"Inspector Lestrade, I must protest," exclaimed Sir Williams. "I do not know why we must continue to march to the whimsical commands of a failing mind. I for one have little faith..."

"And what of the faith of the British public?" interjected Holmes. "Can you explain why you delayed three weeks before calling in the assistance of Scotland Yard?" he asked acerbically.

The Director spluttered in rage, but had no ready answer to this charge of incompetence.

Holmes turned to the guard we had met at the Alpha Inn. "Mr. Bedford, I wish to personally thank you for agreeing to return. I can assure you that after tonight there will be no more talk of curses in the museum."

"Are you going to perform an exorcism, Mr. Holmes?" asked the man solemnly.

"Of a sort," said Holmes nodding. He faced round to look at Mr. Seraphim in his questioning way. "Good evening, Mr. Seraphim. I trust that you enjoyed your night off?"

"Yes, sir," replied the man, his voice proving to be very deep and husky.

"I understand that you are relatively new to the job, are you not? Do you enjoy it?"

"Indeed, sir. It is quiet and retiring. It allows me time to think. For thought is the key to all treasures, and thus I have soared above this world."[41]

Holmes' eyes kindled and a spring flush sprang into his thin cheeks. For an instant the curtain had lifted upon his intense, passionate nature, but for an instant only. When I glanced again his face had resumed that Pharaonic serenity which had made so many regard him as a machine rather than a man. He turned and again addressed the entire assembly. "To understand how these items are vanishing from the Museum, one must reconsider the sequence of events. From studying your manifests, Mr. Brundage, I see that your mummy, and its grave goods, arrived from Cairo at the end of August. From the messages sent by the Museum's representative, Mr. Griffith, you had already conceived the notion for the new design of the gallery and had already ordered a set of properly-shaped blocks of Cotswold stones to form your nouveau pyramid."

Brundage appeared tense. "Yes, what of it? I've never asserted that the pyramid was authentic. It sets the ambiance for the rest of the items, which I do guarantee to be genuine."

"So you say, Mr. Brundage, however, if your Pharaoh's mummy has been in place since early September, why did it wait until the end of the month to begin its revenge upon the people of Britain by making their ancient treasures vanish?"

"I, I cannot say," he stammered.

"And why does the Pharaoh take nights off?"

"What do you mean?" exclaimed Brundage.

"An inspection of the list of missing items provided by Inspector Lestrade makes it plain that items do not vanish every night. If the supernatural is in effect then I would not expect such laziness."

"What are you driving at, Mr. Holmes?" asked Lestrade.

"I wondered if there was some pattern to the days when no items were taken. And I soon spotted it, for it was deceptively simple. A nine day

[41] A paraphrase of Honoré de Balzac (from *The Magic Skin*, 1831): 'Thought is a key to all treasures; the miser's gains are ours without his cares. Thus I have soared above this world, where my enjoyments have been intellectual joys.'

pattern, neatly coinciding with the dates that a guard might have a night off." Holmes began to stroll in the direction of the Egyptian Gallery. I followed him with excited interest, for I was becoming convinced that every one of his words and actions were directed towards a definite end. "I postulate to you, gentlemen, that the imitation of these thefts has nothing to do with the arrival of your mummy. Instead everything was predicated upon someone else making an appearance in the museum. It is quite evident from the start that there are two men – more, perhaps, but at least two – who are involved in the plot." He turned to addressed Sir Williams. "They must have been aided by a confederate inside the Museum. As there were two guards who have only recently come into your service, Mr. Morrison and Mr. Seraphim, they are the obvious suspects."

"But, Mr. Holmes," protested Lestrade, "we've already established that the guards cannot possibly remove any objects from the Museum."

"I concur, Lestrade. The objects cannot be removed by the guards, nor does it seem possible that anyone is entering and leaving the Museum at night. I spent some time in the other galleries today and can confirm that there is no evidence of external intrusions."

"Are you suggesting another secret tunnel, Mr. Holmes?" sneered Sir Williams.

Holmes paused at the entrance to the gallery. He turned to the man and smiled ruthlessly. "Tell me, Sir Williams, how tenuous is the position of a Director who not only allows his Museum to be plundered, but who proudly displays fraudulent imitations?"

"How dare you, sir!" exclaimed the Director. "Do you wish for me to file a charge of libel? Every item has been carefully authenticated by one of our specialists. There are no fakes in this museum!"

"And if there were, would they have any value?" asked Holmes, mildly. Though his tone and manner suggested extreme nonchalance, I knew Holmes far too well. He was feigning this attitude, and was about to perform another of his famous conjuring tricks.

"Of course not!"

"I was hoping you would say that, Sir Williams." In a paroxysm of sudden energy, Holmes pivoted and raised his cane far above his head. With a demonical force that he had carefully masked behind a feeble manner, he swiftly brought the stick down upon the neck of the guardian sphinx. A loud thud made it evident that his cane was weighted with lead, turning it into a formidable weapon. As Sir Williams and Mr. Brundage made horrified cries, with frenzied eagerness Holmes struck the statue several more times. A series of cracks appeared in the marble, and the head splintered off from the body and fell heavily. I watched, astonished, as it scattered into fragmented shards upon the floor. The most amazing thing of all, however, was not Holmes' act of wanton destruction, but the fact that the sphinx was plainly hollow. And from the collar of the shattered neck poked the wizened head of a dust-covered man.

§

At the sound, Mr. Seraphim gave a violent start and dropped his guard's lantern, while the rest of the spectators raised their voices in confusion and protest. Once the general outcry had died down, Lestrade and a hastily-summoned uniformed constable hauled the thief from a cunningly hidden hatch set into the top of the statue. He was between thirty and forty years of age, with dark brown hair and whiskers, though he currently appeared like a cookie that had been sprinkled with confectioner's sugar. His eyes gleamed with a deep malevolence and his huge powerful hands clenched spasmodically from within the pair of steel handcuffs in which they were enclosed. A supply of water, wrapped sandwiches, a dark lantern, and a squeeze bag filled with some sort of sealant were also retrieved from within the hollow cavity.

I have always had a quick eye for faces. "Why, it's Parker!" I exclaimed.

Holmes laughed. "Yes, Watson," said he, as he faced the astonished company. "When I heard that Inspector Patterson had been strangled, I immediately considered the possibility that a garrotter was involved.[42] I am sorry that I once considered you to be harmless, Parker. I am afraid that your career is about to end on the gallows."

"But how on earth did you realize that he was in the sphinx?"

"As I mentioned to you and Lestrade at the beginning, Watson, I found the idea of a curse to be absurd. And yet, I will admit that the observation of the spinning effigy with my own eyes gave me pause for a moment. However, once I determined scientifically how it was being moved, I then took as my starting hypothesis that there was nothing supernatural transpiring in the museum. While I have combatted some evils over the years, both small and great, there are none that can reach out from four millennia ago. If you recall my old axiom, Watson, you may deduce that, if there was no way out of the museum at night, then logically the thief must have still been within. But all of the possible hiding spots

---

[42] Watson never tells us how he recognizes Parker, as he is only alluded to by Holmes in *The Adventure of the Empty House*. Presumably Lestrade picked him up on the advice of Holmes, and Watson then saw him at the trial of Colonel Sebastian Moran. Here we find an example of Holmes being too blasé, for clearly a professional garrotter cannot be too harmless, and Inspector Patterson paid the ultimate price of Parker being free.

had long ago been sealed. So he therefore must have created his own. A chance encounter on the Embankment, plus a stroll through the Greek Galleries,[43] prompted me to recall my Homer."[44]

"Beware of Greeks bearing gifts."[45]

"Exactly, Watson!"

"I was not aware that you had read it."

"During my retirement, I have attempted to rectify certain of my limitations, perhaps at the expense of some room in my little brain attic. One such deficiency was the set of classics that I ignored during my university days. However, as this case proves, you never know what item of knowledge may come in handy someday. Like Ulysses before him, it was a bold stratagem," Holmes continued. "Having obtained the item for the evening, Parker would climb into the Trojan Sphinx, and wait for the last morning rounds of the guards before the Museum opened for the day. He would then exit, apply a sealing paste to close his hatch, and blend in with the gathering crowds. After a suitable period of time, he would simply stroll out the front door with the object in his pocket."

"But how did you know it was this statue in particular, Mr. Holmes?" asked Lestrade.

"I have, as my friend Watson may have remarked once or twice, an abnormally acute set of senses. In this case, a faint but specific scent was apparent which seemed to center upon this statue. It may have been a small mistake on the part of Parker to utilize that particular substance as the base of his sealing paste, for I have spent much of the last three years surrounded by it as the fruit of my leisured ease."

"What was it?" asked Lestrade.

"Beeswax, likely mixed with marble dust. An ingenious device, if not

---

[43] The faux sphinx has long ago been removed from Museum. It may be theorized that the conspirators were inspired by a colossal marble lion tomb monument from Knidos in the Greek part of Asia-Minor (modern day Turkey). This lion was carved c.350-200 BCE and weighs some six tons. Made from one piece of marble, it was mounted on a base crowning a funerary monument. The monument itself was square with a circular interior chamber and a stepped-pyramid roof. The monument was originally set on a headland terminating in a sheer cliff that falls some 200 feet into the sea. The hollow eyes of the lion were probably originally inset with colored glass, and the reflection of light may have been an aid to sailors navigating the notoriously difficult coast. The lion was found in 1859 by the architect Richard Pullan, who was a member of an expedition sent to acquire pieces of Greek sculpture and architecture for the British Museum.

[44] The Trojan Horse never appears directly in either the *Iliad* or the *Odyssey*, though Homer alludes to it in the latter volume. The story is primarily found in the 'Posthomerica' of Quintus of Smyrna.

[45] A well-known quote from Virgil's *Aeneid.*

for the distinctive aroma. A survey of the Museum ledgers confirmed my suspicion. You see, Lestrade, this particular item," he patted the side of the broken sphinx, "was added after the rest of the exhibit on the twenty-second of September. Shortly after its installation, the thefts began."

"But why did the Museum accept a forgery?" I asked.

"According to the manifest, the sphinx was donated to the Museum by a wealthy Greek aristocrat. The name is listed as Baron Adonis Schwartz, but I suspect that to be a pseudonym.[46] The certificate of authenticity purporting to be from Griffiths is an obvious forgery, though that fact is likely not apparent to anyone who is not an expert on graphology. I believe, Watson, that I see a hint of the hand of our old friend Archie Stamford in the distinctive slant of the ash grapheme.[47] Mr. Brundage, who was never one to look a gift horse in the mouth, took the sphinx at face value and installed it in the entryway to the gallery."[48]

By the flush of his cheeks, it appeared Brundage at least had the good graces to feel some shame at his actions which inadvertently led to both the plunder of his museum and the death of an inspector.

"But you said that there were two men involved?" I noted.

"Indeed, Watson. The entire business took a cool hand, but it was still too risky for Parker to move about the Museum at night. He would enter the building every night before closing, and conceal himself in the Sphinx during the period of time between closing and the first rounding of the guards. He would then be passed the stolen treasures by his accomplice. This job was made much easier when Mr. Morrison vanished and Mr. Bedford was too terrorized to return to work. That was the reason for the introduced scarabs, to accentuate the possibility that the Museum was haunted by the curse of a long-dead Pharaoh. Unfortunately for Inspector Patterson, the thieves did not account for the possibility that the gallery would be occupied two evenings ago. While his accomplice was forced to hurriedly pick the lock and hide within Mr. Brundage's 'improved' sarcophagus, Parker must have climbed from the Sphinx, slipped up

---

[46] Holmes never describes who he suspects as playing the role of Baron Schwartz. The most likely suspect is Baron Gruner (since Schwartz means 'black' and Gruner means 'green'), who was one of the most dangerous men in Europe and who clearly survived his encounter with Holmes in *The Adventure of the Illustrious Client.*

[47] The 'ash' (or 'aesc') grapheme is the now-archaic ligature of the letters 'a' and 'e,' as in Ægypt.

[48] Strangely enough, this phrase does not appear to derive from the Trojan Horse! It seems to come from the fact that horses' gums recede as they age, which makes the teeth appear to grow long. Thus, checking the teeth of a horse is a way of checking for old age.

behind Patterson, and did him in."

"So who was his accomplice, Mr. Holmes?" asked Lestrade breathlessly.

"A cold-blooded scoundrel who has greatly deserved punishment, but has slipped from the touch of the law many times in the past, as he rose from crime to crime. Still, I think he must have spent at least one stint in Newgate, where he became acquainted with the other players in this drama. But this time he will join Parker in the dock upon a capital charge. That would be Mr. Quincy Seraphim, also known to us as Mr. James Windibank."

§

The supposed guard made a break for it, but was swiftly corralled by a pair of Lestrade's stalwart constables. The man's brow was drenched with moisture, and his lips had turned stark white, making his face take on a ghastly appearance. Windibank, as I will now call him, looked numbed and dazed, as if he was about to collapse if not held up by the men gripping his upper arms. His head was sunk upon his breast, like one who was utterly defeated. Never, certainly, have I seen a plainer confession of guilt upon a human countenance.

While the Director and Mr. Brundage had slunk off in silent shame at the shared incompetence that allowed such nefarious events to occur in their Museum, the reinstated Mr. Bedford smiled broadly at this exciting beginning to the night's shift. I remained behind with Lestrade and his trio of large, able-bodied policemen in order to interrogate both Holmes and his pair of prisoners.

"How did you know it was Seraphim, Holmes?" I asked. "I thought for certain it would be Edward Rucastle."

Holmes sniffed. "Really, Watson, it was quite elementary. I suspected it as soon as Lestrade described Mr. Seraphim as 'retiring and shy' in the same breath that it was noted that Seraphim was a former sergeant of the Army. As an old campaigner, Watson, how many sergeants do you know that can be described as 'shy'?"

"None, Holmes."

"Exactly. And once I finally laid eyes upon him I became certain. Mr. Windibank here has always been fond of a disguise. In this case, he used one very similar to the one that he once employed for his transformation into Mr. Hosmer Angel. There was a new wig, different glasses, some lifts in his shoes, and a different tone to his voice, all of which would have been sufficient to fool most people. Fortunately, I am not most people. His choice of sobriquet was also rather unoriginal.[49] His fatal mistake, however, was when he quoted from Balzac. Then I knew my man."

By the end of this speech, Windibank appeared to have regained some measure of bitter composure. He turned to Holmes with a chilly sneer. "You've got nothing on me, Mr. Holmes. You are correct that I spent a short time in Newgate, and that has forced me to find jobs under an assumed name, for no one wants to hire a known criminal. But I have been an honest employee since I started here at the Museum."

Holmes laughed. "I doubt that there is an honest bone in your body, Mr. Windibank. And many a man has been hanged on far slighter evidence than we have on you. If Parker here refuses to squeal, there is always our old friend Beppo. I believe that he will be happy to identify you as the man with whom he contracted."

"Beppo, the sculptor!" I exclaimed.

"None other, Watson. Who else in London do you think would be capable of carving such a magnificent statue, while simultaneously keeping quiet about it? Not some respectable artist, to be certain! That is who I tracked down at the masonry yard in Stepney. I spent a few hours this afternoon upon Saffron Hill and at Goldini's Restaurant before someone was willing to admit that they knew of Beppo's whereabouts. I learned that he had been generously taken back by his former manager. Unfortunately, Beppo is not long for this world. I doubt that he shall live another month. He has contracted chalicosis."

"Stonecutter's Disease!"

"Indeed, Watson, the long years of inhaling stone dust have ravaged his lungs. His face was an ashen white, while his lips and the corners of his nostrils were tinged with a shade of blue. So he has little to fear as far as retribution should he talk to us." He turned back to the villain. "I think that was the full chain of events, Mr. Windibank, or would you care to try to contradict me again?"

Windibank suddenly dropped the defiant attitude which had characterized him, and the ferocity of a dangerous wild beast gleamed in his dark eyes, distorting his once handsome features. "You will regret this, Holmes," he snarled.

"That may prove to be a difficult task, Mr. Windibank, for your neck is forfeited," said Holmes. "There is a four-wheeler waiting to convey you to Bow Street. You will not be walking the streets of London again, I think."

As the constables led the furious pair away, Lestrade shook his head in wonderment. "I've always said, Mr. Holmes, that we at the Yard are damned proud of you. But this one may be your crowning achievement. We cannot thank you enough for catching a pair of police-killers."

---

[49] Since a 'seraphim' is the highest rank in the hierarchy of angels.

Holmes waved away the compliment, though his smile showed that it had pleased him. "Say no more of it, Lestrade. To you, and to you only, belongs the credit of the remarkable arrest which you have effected. And now, Watson, I think that something nutritious would not be out of place. I can recall a place in Westminster where the port is rather above mediocrity."

§

Holmes and I were soon seated in Simpson's, at a small table in the front window where we could look down at the rushing stream of life through the Strand and wonder at how greatly the kaleidoscope had changed in appearance since we first began our association so many years prior.

"I fear, Watson," said Holmes, "that you will not improve any reputation that I may still retain by adding the Case of the Sphinx's Riddle to your annals, should your collection remain open. I have been lethargic in mind and wanting in that mixture of imagination and reality which formed the basis of my art."

"Not at all, Holmes," I replied slowly, still processing all that had transpired earlier. "It was but a temporary eclipse of your powers. So it was nothing more than an astonishing coincidence that Edward Rucastle happened to be working at the Museum?"

"My dear fellow, as I believe I once said, 'life is infinitely more extraordinary than anything which the mind of man could conceive. The strange happenstances, the delightful chain of events leading to the most outrageous results can make all fiction, with its traditionalisms and foreseen finishes most stale, flat, and unprofitable.'[50] Or, as one of your crude fellow scribblers might have said: 'Truth is stranger than fiction'"[51]

"So Windibank hired the thugs who maimed his predecessor?"

"I believe that we can take that as a forgone conclusion."

"And what of Mr. Morrison?" I asked.

Holmes shook his head. "An unraveled thread, I am afraid, Watson. Life, unlike fiction, is often messy. Not everything has an answer. Mr. Windibank and Parker have little incentive to disclose this answer to us, for whatever their defense, I am afraid that they are destined for a date with the hangman. Either Morrison was an innocent bystander, and he was

---

[50] Holmes is paraphrasing himself (from *A Case of Identity*), which is itself a paraphrase of *Hamlet*, Act I, Scene 2.
[51] Mark Twain: 'Truth is stranger than fiction, but it is because Fiction is obliged to stick to possibilities; Truth isn't' (from *Following the Equator*, 1897). It was also attributed to Lord Byron in his *Don Juan*.

done away with in some incredibly clever fashion, or he was a third accomplice. If the latter, we may never learn his identity, for there is a curious honor among thieves."

We ordered a bottle of the famous Warre's vintage of which Holmes had spoken, and once our glasses were poured, I offered a toast to the successful conclusion of a challenging case.

Holmes, however, failed to match my cheer. He appeared distracted, his nervous fingers twirling the meerschaum pipe from which many unsavory odors had emanated over the years. I watched as his bushy eyebrows twitched ever so slightly, which always signified some internal disappointment and irritation.

"What is it, Holmes? You should be happy to have had one last chance to exercise your gifts. You have brought a pair of desperate men to justice."

He shook his head. "I cannot exactly say, Watson. There is no data to support this, but every instinct that I possess cries out that this case was far too simple."

"Simple!" I cried. "Surely you jest, Holmes! A man concealing himself in a hollow Sphinx, thereby eluding Scotland Yard for weeks?"

"It is hardly difficult to fool Lestrade and company, Watson. I fear they have learned little of my techniques."

"But surely it was a unique case in the annals of crime?"

Holmes shrugged. "Perhaps. However, it brings to mind the devious artifice of Jonas Oldcastle, does it not?"

"The Norwood Builder? I suppose there are some elements that are similar," I conceded. "But what does that prove?"

"Perhaps nothing...." However, anything further Holmes might have planned to say was interrupted when the *maître d'hôtel* appeared at our table. He bowed slightly and handed a slip of paper to my friend. "A telegram for you, Mr. Holmes."

Holmes took it from the man and carelessly glanced at the paper. He then straightened in his seat and crumpled it in his fist. He frowned and looked up at me. "Did you tell anyone that we were dining here, Watson?"

"No."

"Are you certain? No one? Lestrade? Your wife?"

I shook my head. "No one."

Holmes broke eye contact with me and proceeded to stare intently at the other occupants of the restaurant. I tried to follow his gaze, but saw nothing out of the ordinary. After a few minutes, he abandoned this pursuit and looked down at the telegram again.

"What do you fear, Holmes?" I asked breathlessly.

"I do not know for certain, Watson. But look for yourself." He smoothed the paper out upon the table and pushed it over to me. I stared down at the curious inscription, which ran thus:

> N1 § P1 C1 Pa8 W13 § P1 C2 Pa2 W65 § P1 C1 Pa1
> W72 § P1 C1 Pa18 W1 § P2 C1 Pa9 W63 § P1 C1 Pa1
> W56 § P2 C4 Pa29 W72 § – MORTLOCK

"Who, then, is Mortlock?" I asked.

"Mortlock, Watson, is a *nom-de-plume*, of course. You must recall our ally of sorts, that shifty and evasive personality who attempted to aid us in the affair at Birlstone?"

"Porlock?"

"Yes, of course. Do you not see, Watson? That particular name was obviously chosen for two reasons. First, because of its final rhyme with that latter half my own given name. And second, because the initial syllable would convey the message that that individual so-called could be induced to provide information if properly recompensed."

"I admit that I am not following you, Holmes. Do you believe that Porlock has resurfaced after all these years?"

Holmes shook his head violently. "No, no, Watson. I think that the name used herein is a message beyond what is encoded in this cryptic combination of letters, numbers, and symbols. Recall your days at Winchester, Watson. What does the Latin root 'mort' denote?"

I finally understood what he was trying to tell me, and the thought chilled me to the bones. "It means 'death' of course."

"Exactly, Watson. Exactly. But whose death?"

"Surely we can determine that by deciphering the message itself?"

"Yes, Watson, but how?"

"Is this not the same book cipher that Porlock once employed?"

"Not at all. Look at it, Watson. Porlock's code did not use so many letters, nor these funny symbols. We must apply all of our reason to the problem of what method is herein being employed."

I studied it for a moment. "Well, it seems to be to be quite simple."

Holmes' right eyebrow rose in surprise. "Oh? You have broken it?"

"Almost, Holmes, almost. Surely the symbol is nothing more than a break, and the 'W' stands for 'word.'"

"I will accept that as a point of departure."

"Then the 'Pa' must be 'page.'"

Holmes shook his head. "There are difficulties, Watson. The printing of various editions of the same story can be quite numerous, and the paginations differ between them. Even if we were able to guess the name of the book, how are we to determine which edition to utilize?"

"Paragraph!" I cried.

"Good, Watson, good! No matter what font and spacing a printer uses, unless they deviate from the author's master plan, the separation between paragraphs should remain intact."

"Then the next sign, 'C1' stands for 'chapter the first,' no doubt."

"Excellent, Watson. Your deduction of twenty years ago has finally proven correct, unless I am much deceived. But now we encounter further difficulties. If we know the chapter number, then what do we make of the 'P' symbol?"

"That is obvious, Holmes," I said triumphantly.

"Is it?" he asked archly.

"Of course, Holmes. It stands for 'part.'"

"Part! That is brilliant, Watson. Surely that allows us to narrow our search down to books which are divided into multiple parts, within which the chapter numbers are repeated. You can see that the first three words come from Chapter 1 of Part 1, while the fifth word can only be found in Chapter 1 of Part 2. Only a few authors would employ such an eccentric numbering strategy."

"But what about the 'N1?'"

"Unless I am very much mistaken, that is not a word, but rather the symbol that identifies for us the book itself."

"But there must be thousands of books that begin with the letter 'N,'" I protested.

"True enough, but you will note, Watson, that there is no second letter. So this is a book with only one word in the title. That should help considerably."

A long silence followed, during which we sat pondering this mystery. I finally spoke. "I am sorry, Holmes, but I cannot think of any novels with one word titles that start with 'N.' The closest I can come up with would be Dickens' '*Nicholas Nickelby*.'"

Holmes slumped back in his seat. "No, no, Watson, that will not do. You have one 'N' too many. We are undone, I fear. I was hoping that a man of letters such as yourself...." He stopped at stared at me, a wild look in his eyes. "Could it be...?" he cried.

"What is it, Holmes?"

When he opened his mouth, a laugh tinged with a hint of madness echoed forth. "I fear we were off target with our last conclusion, Watson. Mortlock is not trying to make this too difficult for us. His goal is to deliver a message, is it not? He would not have picked a book that was too obscure. He has it, and he imagined that we would have it too. In short, Watson, it is a very popular book."

"So you know it? I have not known you to read much popular fiction, save only the most sensational literature."

"Yes, I fear that I do. I once remarked that it was a work of superficial romanticism. Follow me, Watson."

He rose from his seat and shrugged on his great overcoat. With a wave of his hand, Holmes directed that the bill be sent to him. I hurried to keep up with him as he set off eastwards along the Strand, dodging cabs and omnibuses. At the first junction with Lancaster Place, I watched as Holmes stopped before a cheap newsstand. The front shelves were filled with the scent of freshly printed pages while, in the rear, moldered a forlorn assortment of dusty novels. Next to the structure, a boy was bawling out headlines of the latest edition of the evening paper.

"Why, Mr. Holmes, I'll be," said the news-vendor. "It's been a long time. What'll it be tonight? *The Evening Standard* has a nice story about a bold robbery at St. Paul's Cathedral. That's right up your alley, I reckon."

"Not tonight, Carter," Holmes said. "It's a novel that I require. The first chronicle of a novice biographer, who applied to it a somewhat fantastic sobriquet."

The man shrugged. "Doubt I have something with so many fancy words, but it's yours if I got it, Mr. Holmes."

He turned to me, an inscrutable look in his grey eyes. "You see the significance of the 'N1' now, do you not, Watson?"

"Ah, yes. It is clear. The first novel by that writer."

"Can you still not deduce the name?"

"I am afraid not, Holmes. There are new writers appearing every day, it seems. I cannot possibly keep up with them all."

"Well, Watson, this tale might not have seen the light of day if we had not thwarted the Red Leech." He sighed and shook his head before turning back to the newsman. "Carter, give me a copy of '*A Study in Scarlet.*'"

"What?" I cried. "Holmes, you cannot think that I had anything to do with this?"

"Not at all, Watson. But it was sent by a man who knows far too much about me. He has studied my methods, as so carefully laid out by you in your tales."

"My dear Holmes, I certainly never intended...."

He forestalled my protest. "It is no matter, Watson. It is, as they say, water under the bridge."

Holmes took the slim volume from the newsman Carter and tucked it under his arm. He then strode down towards the Thames and out onto Waterloo Bridge. He did not pause until he came to the streetlamp in very middle. He set the volume upon the top of the balustrade and flipped to the first chapter. "Now let us see what Chapter 1 has in store for us. Jot down the words, Watson." He counted silently. "Paragraph eight, word thirteen, is 'what.' That is an auspicious beginning. Now let us try the next one. Paragraph ten, word fifteen, is 'walks.' – 'What walks.'" Holmes' eyes were gleaming with nervous anticipation and his fingers danced upon the page as he moved along. "The next word is 'on.' I think we are on the right track, Watson." He continued until the phrase was complete. "What – walks – on – no – legs – at – midnight?"

"You must be mistaken, Holmes. Certainly it is a different book. That phrase is gibberish."

"Is it, Watson?" he stared at me intently. "Do you not recall the lessons of your Greek master? What was the riddle of the Sphinx?"

I considered this for a moment. "'What is the creature that walks on four legs in the morning, two legs at noon and three in the evening?' And the answer is 'Man,' of course."

"Do you see, Watson?" his voice was deadly serious. "Mortlock's question is a progression of the Sphinx's riddle. Morning, noon, evening. And now: 'What walks on no legs at midnight?' Midnight being the very end of the metaphorical day."

"What?"

"A corpse." He shook his head grimly. "These are much deeper waters that I had originally thought. I fear that once more the game is afoot."

I attempted to buoy his spirits. "You have always answered that call, Holmes. Why is it now cause for alarm?"

"Because, Watson, this time I do not even know what game we are playing."

The two of us sat in silence for some minutes, the rough water rushing against the stones beneath us. We gazed out at the fog-shrouded sky over the vast murky River, a spiritual counterpart to one in a far-away dusty land, and our eyes strained to glimpse what mystery lay beyond the curtain.

§

THE PROBLEM OF THREADNEEDLE STREET

I t was with some measure of hesitation that I took up my pen in order to chronicle the incident of the Sphinx's Riddle, for never before in the long and storied career of Mr. Sherlock Holmes had I witnessed such a mysterious conclusion to a case. At first glance, it appeared that Holmes had very neatly tied up all of the loose threads, sending both Parker and Windibank on well-deserved trips to Newgate and possibly even the gallows after that. However, the arrival of the encoded telegram, with its Sphinx-like riddle ascribed to one Mortlock, whomever he may be, suggested that we swam in far deeper waters than I had originally suspected.

I nonetheless did my best to set down the facts as I knew them at the time. Over the nearly three decades of our association, I have learned several artifices from my good friend Mr. Sherlock Holmes. One is to conceal the links between a series of deductions, so as to suddenly present the conclusion and thereby produce a startling effect. He has performed this act innumerable times for the benefit of his clients, the inspectors of Scotland Yard, and even me. However, in this particular case, I felt that some cruel trick was being played upon Holmes himself, for he had been presented with a disquieting close to an apparently simple case. Could he shake off the mental rust that must have accumulated over the last six years of his retirement and reason back from this message, and the crimes that preceded it, to the prime mover of the drama? Who was Mortlock?

It was with these thoughts turning over in my brain that I lay down for a restless sleep. When I finally awoke the following morning, I found the lanky form of Holmes pacing back and forth in the sitting room of the hotel's suite, his chin sunk upon his breast, and his hands thrust into his trouser pockets. His aquiline face was drawn and his grey eyes shone with grim determination. I could deduce from the fact that the room was literally ankle-deep in newspapers that Holmes had experienced little repose the prior night.

"Ah, good morning, Watson," said he, amiably. "I see that you too had a late night."

I was heartened to see that he was in a good humor, despite the threat which loomed over us. "Let me guess, Holmes. You deduced this from the dark circles under my eyes and the hasty way by which I have shaved my cheeks."

He laughed merrily. "You are making progress, Watson, my dear fellow, but you forgot the most important clue of all, from which the final inference could be made."

I glanced over at the mirror hanging upon the wall. Even after all this time, I was still somewhat surprised to not find the once thin-as-a-lath fellow of nine and twenty years, but rather a stout, thick-necked, middle-sized man of fifty-seven. Only the moustache over my square jaw remained unchanged, even as it fell from the passing tides of fashion. Some things simply fit a man's face and cannot be altered. But I could not spot Holmes' final clue. "And what is that, Holmes?"

"I believe that I have stressed to you before, Watson, the critical importance of observing any peculiarities upon a man's hands. In this case, your right hand has both a heightened redness upon the callus of the second finger and numerous stains of a blue iron gall ink. From this, one may safely conclude that you have been engaged upon the task of setting down the events of the last two days into one of your little sketches. Since I am well aware that once you start upon such a task, you like to see it through, it is simple enough to hypothesize that you remained up late through the night working upon it."

"Indeed, Holmes, and I must say that I am disquieted by the message from the so-called Mortlock."

He nodded in agreement. "As you know, Watson, when I was in active practice, it was my method to never miss any advertisements in the agony columns. They are a wealth of information and a hunting-ground for the student of the unusual. During my retirement, I have entirely given up such habits. But if I am to deduce the identity of our Mr. Mortlock, I need to revert to my previous ways. As you can see, I have therefore arranged for the local news agent to send up not only fresh editions of every paper, but as many older copies that he could get his hands upon. I have just been looking though all of them in order to master the particulars of what is transpiring in this vast city teeming with over five millions of people."

I glanced at the jumble of newspapers on the floor, from the *Times* to the *Morning Post* to the *Daily Chronicle*, *Daily Telegraph*, and many others. "Would it not be simpler to just question Parker or Windibank? If they were put up to the job by someone, surely they must know the identity of the mastermind?"

Holmes shook his head. "It is rare to find an informer, for their lifespan is short and filled with fear."

"And did you discover anything of note in the papers?"

"Nothing conclusive. But there are some interesting items worthy of following up. Perhaps one of them will prove to be the thread that I require."

"So you plan to remain in London for some time?"

"Indeed. I cannot conduct this inquiry from Sussex, that much is certain," said he, chuckling. "If I may ask for your co-operation, my dear Watson, you would confer a great favor upon me by staying on as well."

"On the contrary," I answered, "I should wish nothing better."

Holmes raised one of his bushy eyebrows. "We may have several hard and dangerous days' and nights' work in front of us. Are you certain?"

"Of course, Holmes."

"Very good," said he, smiling. "I have often said that there is no man who is better worth having at my side when I am in a tight place, and I think we may find ourselves betwixt the devil and the deep sea before the matter is clear.[52] Ha! This is like the old days, then! Well, if we are to continue this, we shall need a London base. The Northumberland Hotel may be fine for a night or two, but it is hardly an adequate headquarters for conducting an investigation. And our sanctum at Baker Street is no more. It is a great pity that Mrs. Hudson has sold the flat to an insurance company and retired to Brighton."

"Unfortunately, I sold my house on Queen Anne Street as well."

Holmes snorted with amusement. "I think not, Watson. Even if you had not set up your shingle in Southsea, I fear that your good wife would little stand my particular habits for very long."

"You do her a discredit, Holmes."

"Ah, I did not mean to offend you, Watson. Of course, I do not mean to disparage your lovely wife, of whom I wholeheartedly approve. But my ways would be difficult for any woman to become accustomed. Not to mention that there may be an element of danger, to which I would fain expose her."

"A hotel then? The Langham, for instance."

Holmes laughed. "Your tastes have become refined over the years, Watson. When I first met you, you were bunking in some nameless hotel on the Strand. Now you wish to lay your head in a room next to royalty.

---

[52] The first recorded citation of 'the Devil and the deep sea' is from Robert Monro's 'His expedition with the worthy Scots regiment called Mac-keyes' (1637).

61

Have your scribblings sold so well that you can afford such luxury?"

I blushed. "I suppose that I have become accustomed to a certain degree of comfort over the years."

"Yes, well, a hotel poses certain other problems. You can only keep the maids out for so long."

"Why would you bar the maids? Do you suspect that they may disrupt your unique, and shall we say, somewhat untidy, methods of organization?"

"No, I suspect them of being spies."

"Truly?"

"One can never be too certain, Watson. No, there are only three men that I trust implicitly in London, and two of them are standing in this room."

"And the third?"

Holmes glanced at his pocket watch. "I think, at the present moment, we will find the answer to that question at number 22 Pall Mall, across from a certain club of little renown."

§

Before we departed the hotel, I dashed off a telegram to my wife informing her that I would be detained for several more days. Having read every one of the manuscripts, published and private, describing my past adventures in the company of Sherlock Holmes, I doubted that this news would come as a great surprise to her.

We engaged a hansom to take us and our bags the short distance beyond Trafalgar Square to the address where resided none-other than Mycroft Holmes, Sherlock's elder brother. As we drove, we passed my former club,[53] the shipping office of the Adelaide-Southampton Line, and finally the headquarters of a real estate firm, to which Holmes motioned. "I may have need of you, Watson, in the next few days to investigate on your own some thread of this tangled skein. I shall hope that you will endeavor to improve upon your performance from the time when you vainly attempted to learn the identity of the occupants of Charlington Hall."

"But Williamson was the key to the whole scheme of Jack Woodley!" I cried, with some heat. "If we had just learned that he was a defrocked priest, all would have been made plain."

"Perhaps, Watson, perhaps," said Holmes, reluctantly. "But here we

---

[53] This must be a reference to the United Service Club, a gentleman's club founded for the use of senior army and navy officers. It sat at 116 Pall Mall until it was disbanded in 1978.

are."

We stopped at a fine neo-classical columned building, across from the bow-windows of the Diogenes Club. It was a strategic location, for his rooms were at the epicenter of that group of buildings from which the vast holdings of the British Empire were directed, both night and day. Mycroft's chambers were on the first floor, and I briefly wondered if Mr. Melas still occupied the floor above some twenty years later. After we climbed the steps and rang the bell, the door was opened by Mycroft's ancient butler.

We were promptly shown into the library, where our host awaited us in the comfort of a large basket chair. Mycroft's appearance had changed little in the twenty years since I had first met him. He was still that strange mixture of similarity – in his light grey eyes and sharp expression – and difference – in his massively corpulent frame – to his younger brother. Like Sherlock, he cared little for the vagaries of fashion, and wore a suit that may have dated from the early days of Victoria's reign. This rumpled and somewhat slovenly appearance contrasted greatly with the regal austerity of his surroundings.

A place more unlike 221B Baker Street could not be found. Every small object was tidily in its place. While Mycroft also possessed shelves of books, these were fine, leather-bound and gilt-edged, rather than thumbed-through and bursting with clippings. The table was free of acid stains and steaming chemical beakers, holding instead a gold snuff box, ivory pipe-rack, and crocodile-skin tobacco pouch. The walls were not besprinkled with a tangled skein of diagrams tracing some convoluted criminal endeavor, but rather a series of precisely colored maps detailing every corner of the Empire upon which the sun never sets. These were interspersed by a beautiful carved-wood and glass barometer, as well as a portrait of a man which I strongly suspected to be a Rembrandt self-portrait. There was ne'er a bullet-hole in sight.

"Ah, Sherlock," said Mycroft, setting down a cup of tea. "I expected you a half-hour ago."

If Holmes was surprised, he hid it well. "Your agents informed you that I was back in London?"

"Precisely. It is rather past when you normally dine. I suppose Dr. Watson overslept?"

"Precisely," Holmes smiled.

"By the way, Doctor, it is a great pleasure to see you looking so hearty." He glanced back at his brother. "But why are you still here, Sherlock? I read the official report on the British Museum. You should have noted the irregularity of the Sphinx a tad sooner, don't you think, my dear boy?"

"How so?" asked Holmes with some asperity.

"By the age of the marble, Sherlock! Can you honesty tell me that a newly carved statue has the same appearance as one that has been sitting in the sands of Egypt for the last three thousand years?"

"The sculptor washed it in a solution of acid. This method produced a weathered effect."

"Ah, that was a clever idea," said Mycroft appreciatively. "I admit that I had not considered it. So why are you still in town, Sherlock? Do you think Lestrade incapable of tracking down the stolen items? Or has another one of your petty puzzles of the police-court arisen? I always said that you would be bored on the Downs and would be looking for some excuse to creep back to London."

"I assure you, Mycroft, that I intend to return to my apiary as soon as this matter is settled. But there are complications."

"Very well then, I shall ask Stanley to make up the guest rooms."

And that is how I became temporary flat-mates with not one, but two, Holmes brothers.

§

Eventually our host departed for his offices on Whitehall, while Holmes busied himself writing a series of telegrams. I was sitting with my feet outstretched to the cheerful blaze of the fire in an attempt to ward off some of the cold damp of the bleak November day, when Stanley announced a pair of visitors for Sherlock. He promptly showed in the familiar face of Inspector Gregson and another man with whom I was unacquainted. Despite his advancing years, Gregson still managed to look robust, energetic, and gallant in his official uniform. The second man was nearer sixty than fifty, somewhat portly and dignified. Both his hair and beard were a snowy white, and horn-billed glasses accentuated his deep brown eyes. His dark suit was somber, but finely cut. And yet the distraught expression upon his face was that of a man who has seen his worst fears come to pass.

"Ah, Gregson," drawled Holmes, "I am back in London for but a few days, and already the lonely inspectors of Scotland Yard come a calling. Have the criminal classes really been so enlivened in my absence?"

Although it must have been several years since they had last seen each other, Gregson wasted no time on pleasantries. "There has been a robbery at the Bank of England, Mr. Holmes! I have brought Mr. Randolph Ellis Winthrop, the Bank Governor, straight away to see you."

Holmes yawned. "Another Worthington Gang? A simple heist at the Old Lady of Threadneedle Street contains little of interest, Gregson. I am rather occupied just now, and I desire no distractions. Pray tell, how exactly did you find me?"

"You left no forwarding address at the Northumberland, but the man at the door recalled which cab you took. We tracked down the driver and he pointed out where he had let you off."

Holmes chuckled appreciatively. "My, my, Gregson, you have made great strides indeed."

"Mr. Holmes, I must impress upon you the seriousness of the situation," interjected the agitated Mr. Winthrop, wiping his forehead with his handkerchief. "If word gets out, it could cause a panic, even a run on the Bank."[54]

"Is it that serious, Governor Winthrop?" I asked.

"Indeed it is, Doctor. You are Dr. Watson, are you not?" he guessed, despite the hurried lack of formal introductions. "Every note of paper currency in circulation is backed with the full guarantee that you could walk into the Bank of England and exchange it for its value in gold.[55] If the public knew of the theft, we would not be able to meet our obligations. The resulting panic could bring down the government."

"How much did they take?" I inquired.

"Over a million pounds, most of it in gold bullion."[56]

The mention of such a vast sum made even Holmes' eyebrows rise in surprise. "A goodly sum, to be certain." He then shook his head. "I am very sorry, Gregson, Mr. Winthrop, but I am presently engaged in other matters. I am certain you will find your gold soon enough. It is no simple matter to transport such weight, and the thieves can hardly unload it quickly, for such a flood of wealth into the seedy underbelly of London would surely be noted upon and whispered around the bars and dives of the East End. I am certain the clues are plenty, the trail is still warm, and that time is on your side."

---

[54] Runs on Central Banks were greatly feared events. It is not hyperbole to suggest that the runs on the central banks of Austria and Germany in 1931, and their subsequent failures, precipitated the climate that led to the rise of National Socialism.

[55] This was established by the Bank Charter Act of 1844, which made the Bank of England the nation's central bank. The UK was on the gold standard until the outbreak of World War I. It was resumed in 1925, but finally abandoned permanently in 1931 during the Great Depression.

[56] By comparison, the Agra Treasure dumped in the Thames by Jonathan Small was estimated at half a million, which would have made Mary Morstan 'one of the richest women in England' (Chapter XI, *The Sign of Four*). Similarly, when the West County Bankers failed for a million, it ruined half the county families of Cornwall (*The Adventure of Black Peter*). The will of Sir Henry Baskerville settled upon his heir 740,000 pounds, which is approximately 85 million in today's money (Chapter V, *The Hound of the Baskervilles*).

"Mr. Holmes, on behalf of the Bank's directors, I am prepared to offer you a very generous reward. Shall we say twenty thousand pounds?"[57]

I was astonished by this astronomical sum, but my friend merely smiled and shook his head again. "No, no, Watson may be able to list my sins, but avarice will not be found amongst them."

"I thought you might say that, Mr. Holmes," said Gregson, in a very amiable tone. "Fortunately, the Yard is not without resources of our own. We have already investigated the matter quite thoroughly and made a very interesting discovery."

"Oh, yes, what is that?" asked Holmes, languidly.

"You see, the Bank of England does not let just any Tom, Dick, or Harry waltz into their main vault.[58] Even an employee is not allowed within until he has been employed at the Bank for at least ten years. We are questioning everyone on the staff with access, but Mr. Winthrop feels that their honesty is not in doubt. And, as you likely are already aware, there is a separate public vault for the general populace to utilize for their sundry deposits. In point of fact, only a few very select private clients are ever allowed into the main vault. These individuals, who number amongst them royalty and mighty industrialists, typically feel as if the main vault is more secure than the one used by the general public when they wish to move their plate to the bank."

"Not in this case, so it would seem," said Holmes, leaning back in his chair with an air of resignation, for it was plain that Gregson would not depart without being heard.

"Indeed, Mr. Holmes. But, you see, in this situation, the limited number of visitors to the main vault works in our favor. We were able to obtain from Mr. Winthrop's manager a list of every private individual who has accessed the main vault within the last two years. We could go back further, of course, but we doubt even the most patient of criminals would have waited so long."

"A reasonable starting deduction, I suppose, as long as you are willing to abandon it should it fail to raise any subject of interest."

---

[57] This was an enormous amount of money for a detective's fee. Compare this to the £1000 offered in 1886 by Alexander Holder to recover the missing fragment of the Beryl Coronet, or the £6000 offered in 1901 by the Duke of Holdernesse to recover his son Arthur and name the man who had taken him (*The Adventure of the Priory School*).

[58] The origin of this strange phrase is unknown. The earliest known citation is from the 17th-century English theologian John Owen who used the words in 1657 when he told a governing body at Oxford University that: 'our critical situation and our common interests were discussed out of journals and newspapers by every Tom, Dick and Harry.'

"Ah, but it has, Mr. Holmes," said Gregson. "You see, there have only been ten private clients of the Bank who have entered the main vault in the last two years." He consulted his official notebook. "These men include the Duke of Balmoral, the Duke of Holdernesse, The Duke of Belminster, Lord Holdhurst, Lord Bellinger, Lord Backwater, Lord Singleford, Lord Southerton, and Mr. J. Neil Gibson."

"Mighty names," murmured Holmes.

"Exactly, Mr. Holmes. And all but one of them has been a client for more years than I care to count. But the last person only began to make deposits within the last two months. The sums were not large, but his fame was such that the staff at the Bank made an exception for this particular gentleman."

"And his name?" Holmes asked, lazily.

"His name was Sherlock Holmes."

§

Holmes had so often flabbergasted Gregson and I in the course of his adventures that I presume it was with some sense of triumph that Gregson spoke those words and witnessed how completely he had astonished Holmes. Holmes bolted upright and stared intently at Gregson for a moment. After a long pause, he began to laugh heartily. "That is rich, Inspector, most rich. Very well, the gauntlet has been thrown. The only honorable action is to stoop and take it up." He stood up and glanced over at me. "Come, Watson, our trail starts in the City."

A fine carriage was awaiting us at the curb, and once the four of us had settled in, Holmes began to question the Bank's governor. "First of all, Mr. Winthrop, pray tell me exactly what has gone missing?" asked Holmes, cocking his eye at the man.

"It is all gold bullion, Mr. Holmes, packed in crates between layers of lead foil."

"The four hundred troy-ounce bars?"

"Exactly."

"Stamped?"

"Of course. Our private mark."

"So they will have to melt them down to be usable. That is something, Gregson. How many places in London are capable of reaching the temperature necessary to melt gold?"

"I don't know, Mr. Holmes, but will put a man on it immediately," replied the inspector.

Holmes nodded. "In any case, it's a heavy burden, indeed, to vanish from your vault in the course of a single night. That much gold must weigh some eighteen thousand pounds."[59]

"That is correct, Mr. Holmes," said the governor, a trace of suspicion in his voice.

Holmes waved his hand dismissively. "The calculation is a simple one. And was the main vault only used for storing gold? What about bank notes or Stock Exchange securities?"

"The only securities would be in the private deposit boxes. But yes, some of the higher denomination notes, the £500 and £1000 ones,[60] are stored in the main vault."

"And were the deposit boxes raided?"

"No, they were untouched."

"And the bank notes?"

"Also untouched."

"You amaze me, Mr. Winthrop! It is most unusual for burglars to be content with a limited plunder when there was so much more within their reach. What sort of criminal carries off only the gold, the heaviest, most difficult-to-utilize commodity, and leaves behind a vast fortune in legal tender and lucrative bearer securities?"

"Perhaps they did not wish to spend the time opening the individual boxes?" hypothesized the inspector.

"Pshaw, Gregson! Banker's safes have been forced before now. It is a simple matter for any competent cracksman, so why was it not effected in this case? It is most peculiar." Holmes turned back to the banker. "I suppose there is no hope for insurance?"

"What insurance could possibly cover this, Mr. Holmes? There is not enough money in the nation to replace what has been taken."

"And how is it that the theft was allowed to proceed uninterrupted? Is there not a permanent guard?"

"Of course, Mr. Holmes," answered Winthrop. "On account of the value of the wealth that we hold there are four armed watchman, all of

---

[59] In 1909, a 400 troy-ounce bar was worth approximately £1557 pounds. Each bar weighed 12.4 kg. Therefore, half-a-million pounds of gold would roughly equal 321 bars, which would be about 3980 kg or 8756 pounds, almost 4.5 tons! In the early 1900's there was a great debate regarding whether to switch the United Kingdom to the metric system advocated by Lord Kelvin. By calculating the weight of the gold in pounds, Holmes is clearly betraying his bias towards the so-called 'imperial system.' There were many of a similar mind, and the UK did not completely switch over to the metric system until approximately 1978.

[60] The £500 and £1000 notes were first issued c.1725 and continued until 1943, when they were removed from circulation in an attempt to combat forgery, such as was carried out by the press of Rodger Prescott (*The Adventure of the Three Garridebs*). The highest denomination note used today is the £50.

excellent character, who patrol day and night within the building itself."

"So how did the villains open the vault door?"

"That's just it, Mr. Holmes," said Gregson, a note of pleading in his voice. "We don't rightly know. The gold was there when Mr. Winthrop closed the vault door yesterday evening. The door could not have possibly been opened during the night, for it was constantly in full view of the guards. But when it was re-opened this morning, the gold was gone. We have inspected the walls, the floor, even the ceiling, but all are intact. It is as if the gold has vanished away by the sorcery of some genii from the Arabian Nights."

§

Holmes had listened to this narrative with an intentness which showed me that he was keenly aroused. His face was as impassive as ever, but his lids drooped heavily and I could tell that he was in deep thought. After a moment he opened his eyes wide and glanced out of the window. "I see that we are drawing close, gentlemen. Do you remark, Watson, on the left-hand side, the small angle in the wall where our friend Mr. Hugh Boone once plied his trade? And there is the famous banking firm of Holder & Stevenson, now, I think, run by the younger Mr. Arthur Holder. Ah, we are here. The Old Lady of Threadneedle Street, at last."

Our hansom deposited us outside the sturdy neo-classical façade of that august establishment. We quickly moved through the marble-lined main foyer of the Bank, which was conducting business as if nothing was amiss in the vault below. The employees were plainly putting on a brave show for the sake of the public confidence. Mr. Winthrop led us through a locked and guarded door, and down a set of stairs. These stopped at a long hallway, the end of which terminated at the main door of the private vault. This was secured with both an iron gate and a formidable steel monstrosity. The latter was festooned with thick bars which could sink into the surrounding frame when the door was closed and the great wheel spun. But both the gate and door currently sat ajar, revealing the forlorn vault behind it.

Several uniformed policemen milled about, but they all appeared to defer to a man in private clothes. He was about sixty years in age, tall and thin, but with broad shoulders. He had thick black hair and a smooth moustache, with peering leaden eyes deeply sunken into his head. His black suit was cut by the finest Savile Row tailors, and he wore it with the confidence of a man used to command.

"That is Mr. Philip Maurice," said Gregson softly, in answer to our unasked question. "He is the assistant to the Commissioner of Police. As you may know, Mr. Holmes, Sir Edward Henry is a fine policeman and an excellent choice for commissioner, but he lacks certain of the political wiles necessary to administer a force of some fifteen thousand men. Mr. Maurice aides him in this task. He is an excellent person, indeed I may tell you that it was through his good offices that I was made Chief Inspector. He has the interest of Scotland Yard very much at heart and he came to the conclusion that the C.I.D. was in need of some fresh blood at the top."

"He is not a policeman himself?" asked Holmes.

"No, but he thinks like one."

"Ah, I see." Any further comment of Holmes was cut short as we approached the man, who turned and studied Holmes with a most curious expression, which certainly seemed to be more threatening than benevolent.

Mr. Maurice continued to look my friend up and down with no very pleased countenance upon his dour features. "You are Mr. Sherlock Holmes?" said he, finally.

"At your service, sir."

"And, pray tell, Mr. Holmes, have you opened a deposit box in the vault of this bank at any point in the last year?"

"I have not, sir."

"Then why is your name associated with just such an account?"

"I do not yet know for certain."

"How about a theory, then?"

"It is a capital mistake to theorize before one has data. Insensibly one begins to twist facts to suit theories, instead of theories to suit facts."

"We are not here to debate philosophy, Mr. Holmes, but to solve a crime of the most terrible severity, as far as the security of our country is concerned. I know your antecedents. You must have a theory; what is it?"

The corners of Holmes' mouth turned downwards in something approaching a grimace. "Very well. Either this was an attempt to draw me from my retirement, to bring me into the case for some purpose which remains opaque at the present moment, or it was an attempt to discredit my name, to cast some doubt upon my honesty."

"If that was their intent, I should say that they have succeeded. At the moment, you remain the most likely suspect in the eyes of Sir Henry."

"Mr. Maurice, if I may?" interjected Mr. Winthrop. "I might be able to settle the matter, or this portion of it, in any case. According to the ledger, my day manager, Mr. Jasper Bennett, was the one who originally dealt with the man who gave his name as Sherlock Holmes. If we summon him, he could say whether or not it was the same man as the one who stands before you now."

The adjutant nodded tightly, and the manager was swiftly produced.

Mr. Bennett was a well-built, cleanly-shaven man of about five and thirty years, with a frank, honest face. He studied Holmes carefully for several moments, before he stepped back and shook his head. "It is not him. If this be the real Sherlock Holmes, then the other man was an imposter."

"I can assure you, Mr. Bennett, that this is the real Holmes, or my name is not Dr. John H. Watson."

"Aye, I can say the same," said Gregson. "I am hardly going to mistake the man with whom I tracked the Tiger of San Pedro."

Mr. Bennett shrugged. "I have seen your picture before, Mr. Holmes. In *The Strand Magazine*, it was.[61] The man looked just like you, close enough to be twins, I would say. Even the grey eyes were the same. I guess that is why I never questioned the matter."

"Very well," said Mr. Maurice with perceptible hesitation. "I shall inform Sir Henry that you are no longer to be considered a suspect, Mr. Holmes. However, I regret to inform you that your services are not, in fact, required in this matter. The official machinery is amply sufficient for the purposes of solving this threat to the nation. I am afraid that Inspector Gregson caught wind of the fact that you were in town, and sought you out on his own initiative, before I could arrive upon the scene. I fear that this is the sort of situation where it is essential that it be handled with the greatest of discretion. All possible gossip must be refrained from if we are to avoid a great public scandal."

"It may surprise you to know, Mr. Maurice, that I prefer to work anonymously and that it is the problem itself which interests me," said Holmes mildly.

"Is that so, Mr. Holmes? And tell me, would Inspector Lestrade agree with you? After your so-called biographer here," he motioned somewhat insolently in my direction, "published countless of his tawdry tales in which you are, in fact, given all of the credit, while the good men of Scotland Yard are made to look obtuse and imbecilic?"

"Sir," interjected Gregson, "I would like to point out that Mr. Holmes here was instrumental in solving the Whitehall Mystery, and Dr. Watson has never breathed a word about it."[62]

"Oh, yes?" Maurice paused at this bit of intelligence, and his manner thawed slightly. "I was unaware that you had a hand in that tragic and grotesque tale. Well, I suppose if you are already upon the scene, it cannot

---

[61] *The Strand Magazine* published fifty-eight Holmes stories between 1891 and 1927, with illustrations of the Great Detective by Sidney Paget.

[62] In 1888, during the construction of the new building, workers discovered the dismembered torso of a female. The case, known as the 'Whitehall Mystery', was never officially solved, though Watson here alludes to the fact that Holmes did so, but Watson was forbidden to set down the facts.

hurt to let you have a little look around. But be quick about it, and then please remove yourself, so that the professionals can do their job. Superintendent Gregson, I will be back at the Yard. Send word with any update, no matter how trivial."

With that dismissal, Mr. Maurice departed the corridor. Gregson and Mr. Winthrop moved towards the vault door, but Holmes held back for a moment, his hand upon my sleeve. "Mr. Maurice's attitude was a trifle cavalier, don't you think, Watson?" he murmured. "It is a mighty shame that he left, or I might be inclined to have a little amusement at his expense."

"So you think you can solve it?"

Holmes shrugged. "This is an outrageous crime, Watson. Those are the easiest to solve, for there is often only one possible explanation. The mundane offenses tend to be much more difficult. Now let us see what the vault holds for us."

This proved to be a classic strong-room, about thirty-feet square. The ceiling was rather low, no more than eight feet, and appeared to be a solid slab of concrete. The floor was made up of cemented flagstones. Although much disrupted by the recent passing of feet, dust outlines showed where the massive crates must have until recently sat. A few undisturbed boxes remained, which presumably contained the ignored banknotes. A step-ladder stood in the middle of the room, though its role was a mystery to me.

Holmes paused on the threshold of the room and surveyed the floor with some interest. "Gregson, I must protest. It looks like a herd of cattle has stampeded through here this morning. How many men exactly did you allow in here? Ten? A baker's dozen?"

Gregson had the good sense to look abashed. "Counting myself and Mr. Winthrop, it would make fourteen, Mr. Holmes."

"Well, had the object been to obscure every trace of the thieves' footprints, you hardly could have acted with greater rashness. Pray tell why precisely you pitched such caution to the winds?"

"It was on behalf of the note, Mr. Holmes."

"On behalf of the what?" asked Holmes, with a start.

"I am very sorry, Mr. Holmes, I should have mentioned earlier. But you hardly gave us time during the cab ride with all your questions."

"It was at six o'clock this morning, Mr. Holmes," interjected Mr. Winthrop, "that my butler brought into my chambers an urgent telegram. I tore it opened, and was not sure whether I should laugh or cry when I read the words."

"Which said?" asked Holmes, his brow bearing the telltale signs that he was growing ever more impatient.

"I can show you," said Gregson, holding out the telegram, which had clearly been impounded for evidence.

It was addressed to Mr. Winthrop, and ran thus:

> "Sir: I thank you for the withdrawal ongoing.
> JONATHON WILD."[63]

"As far as I can reckon, Mr. Holmes, Wild is a pseudonym," said the inspector.

"Yes, thank you, Gregson, I was aware of that," said Holmes, dryly. "Even if the real Mr. Wild had not been hanged from the Tyburn Tree almost two hundred years ago, it would be a rare criminal who would inform the bank governor of his true name. So what did you do when you received this unusual note, Mr. Winthrop?"

"I immediately telephoned Scotland Yard, where I was put in touch with Inspector Gregson."[64]

Gregson nodded. "And I gathered up a dozen of my best constables and rushed over here. Things were quiet as a church upstairs, and the two men down in the corridor here also reported nothing amiss. Governor Winthrop and Mr. Bennett swiftly opened the gate and the door and we all rushed into the room. But there was no one there. Just the empty spaces where the boxes once sat. You see, Mr. Holmes, the telegram used the word 'ongoing,' which made me think that we might still catch them in the act."

Holmes snorted derisively. "I admit that it is a strange turn of phrase, but how would the man possibly have sent a telegram if he and his companions were still in the vault?"

"So you think it was a gang?" I asked.

"Of course, Watson. One man does not move four and a half tons of gold by himself. I would estimate that it would take eight men at least six hours to perform such a herculean feat."

"Do you think it was a foreign agent? Someone trying to destabilize the nation?"

"Good, Watson, very good. Your theory holds together. This would explain both why they only took the gold, and the strange phrasing of the telegram. But on the other hand, this is not their normal *modus operandi*. I have crossed paths with many of these agents in my time, some of whom

---

[63] Jonathon Wild (c.1682-1725) was a great criminal mastermind during the Georgian era.

[64] Private telephones had become commonplace by 1909. Even Holmes had one installed at Baker Street by 1899 (*The Adventure of the Retired Colourman*).

are now out of commission, and while the remaining men would like nothing more than to see this plan carried out and the resulting political fallout, none of them has the intellectual audacity to plan such an attack. No, I fear we must consider other adversaries. Gregson, have you already obtained a warrant to see the counterfoil to the telegram?"

"Of course, Mr. Holmes, we should have it momentarily."

"Very good, then your morning has not been a complete catastrophe. Since the floor of the vault is a lost cause, let us enter."

Holmes spent the following twenty minutes engaged in a careful inspection of every nook and cranny of the vault. He even tapped his cane upon each of the flagstones to ensure that they were solidly mortared. He repeated the procedure along the four walls, which resounded with metallic thuds.

"Lead-lined, I assume?" asked Holmes of the governor, who responded affirmatively. "Excellent. Well," said he when his examination was complete, "I concur with your assessment, Inspector. The walls and floor seem solid. By the presence of the step ladder, I can deduce that your men have already checked the ceiling for any ingress, though even the bare eye at this distance makes it plain that they did not enter from that direction. In fact, I see no obvious method at all by which a gang of thieves could have made their way into this vault."

"Are you saying that it is impossible, Mr. Holmes?" cried the Bank Governor.

"Not at all. I am merely commending Inspector Gregson on his thorough inspection. But I have high hopes. Now, then, let us have a look at these deposit boxes."

Gregson and Mr. Winthrop stared at Mr. Holmes as if he had gone mad. "But, Mr. Holmes, the deposit boxes were not touched during the robbery!" protested the inspector.

"That is precisely why they are of such great interest. Why, pray tell, would my simulacrum so greatly desire to gain access to this vault that he would run the very grave risk of posing as me? I fear that I am no longer unknown, thanks in no small part to my Boswell here. Mr. Wild, as we shall call him, could easily have encountered someone who was acquainted with me during this visit."

"I admit that it is a mystery, Mr. Holmes. I suppose, if he were a cracksman, it might be so that he would have time to obtain some moldings of the locks."

"Now, now, Gregson," said Holmes admonishingly. "I highly doubt that Mr. Bennett here allows anyone, no matter how highly placed, to remain alone in this vault for long. There is not sufficient time to obtain an adequate molding. And we have already established that the deposit boxes were unmolested. No, I think the answer lies in the box belonging to myself. Let us have it opened, Mr. Winthrop."

"Mr. Holmes, we can hardly do so," he protested.

"And pray tell why not?" asked Holmes, acerbically. "In the absence of the owner's key, the Governor and the Manager may use their master keys to open any box. This is your failsafe in the event of a lost key, is it not?"

"But Mr. Holmes, in such a case, the box can only be opened in the presence of the owner. To do otherwise would be a major violation of British banking laws. In the event of an owner being deceased, we could obtain an order from a magistrate to open for his heir. Perhaps we should so inquire..."

"That will hardly be necessary, Mr. Winthrop. The owner is here."

"What!?" the man exclaimed.

"Did you not say that the box is registered to one Mr. Sherlock Holmes, Esq.? I am he. Or so, two trusted men, Dr. Watson and Inspector Gregson, can readily attest."

There was a calm assurance of power in Holmes' manner which could not be withstood. Gregson paused for a moment, and then chortled at this legalese twisting of words. "He's right, Governor Winthrop. Let's have it open."

"Very well," said Winthrop, with obvious misgivings. He motioned reluctantly to his manager to help. The pair inserted their keys into the Chubb's lock, swung open the door, and pulled out the box. We gathered round with considerable interest to see what was contained within. To our great surprise, it held only a stainless steel brandy flask, inscribed with the initials 'S.H.'

§

I glanced over at Holmes, whose face bore the expression of one who has seen his adversary make a dangerous move at chess. He carefully picked up the flask and examined it with interest. He unscrewed the cap and sniffed at the vapors that emanated from within. His eyes flashed, and I could see from Holmes' rigid appearance that he was vibrating with inward excitement.

He handed the flask first to me, where I noted no apparent scent at all. I passed it to Gregson who, by the puzzled look upon his face, plainly also failed to discern what had so animated Holmes. Meanwhile, Holmes had turned to once more scrutinize the room. He walked about for a moment, every aspect of the room minutely examined and duly pondered. Without warning he dropped to the floor with an alacrity lacking in most men of five and fifty years. He crawled about for a few minutes, and then rose with a hint of triumph in his eyes. "Here you are, Gregson, mark these. They are of great importance. I think this should be the final clue that you need," said Holmes, handing the inspector several grains of dust that had been carefully scooped onto one of his calling cards.

Gregson stared in baffled amazement at these specks. "Dust? I am afraid I miss the point, Mr. Holmes."

"Truly? I think it is quite evident now exactly what has transpired. These are deep waters, Mr. Winthrop, deep and rather dirty. I see that the vault is currently lit with the incandescent bulbs of Swan and Edison. Do you keep them turned on when the vault is closed for the night?"

"Certainly not, Mr. Holmes," he protested. "What would be the purpose? It would be a terrible expenditure for the sake of nothing, for not even a mouse can enter this vault at night."

"Ah, but someone did, Mr. Winthrop, someone did. I deduce from the Governor's testimony, Inspector Gregson, that it was dark when you and your men entered the vault?"

"Naturally, Holmes. We brought lanterns, of course."

"Of course, well, the whole thing hinges upon two points. I would invite your attention very particularly to them. One is that little mound of what you referred to as dust, Gregson. The second is the curious smell inside the flask."

"But the flask has no smell," protested the inspector.

"That was the curious smell," remarked Holmes in his typically inscrutable fashion.

"Mr. Holmes!" cried the agitated Mr. Winthrop. "I cannot bear the suspense! If you know how the thieves entered the room, please tell us!"

Holmes' eyes were bright and his cheeks tinged. "When I set foot in this vault, I put myself in the man's place and having first gauged his intelligence, I attempted to imagine how I should have proceeded under the same circumstances."

"How can you be certain of his intelligence, Holmes?" I inquired.

"Come now, Watson. In the supposed Mr. Wild, we have a man with the brains to rob the most secure room in all of England, and the audacity to impersonate me. Surely this is a remarkable individual. Dangerous, yes, but surely remarkable. His intelligence is clearly second to none. As I was saying, burglary has always been an alternative profession had I cared to adopt it, and I have little doubt that I should have risen to the top." He paused and turned to the bank manager. "Ah, Mr. Bennett, could I trouble you for a glass of water? I find that my throat gets a bit dusty down here." The manager looked startled at such a trivial request in the midst of an exposition that touched upon a theft of such gravity, but he scurried off to do as Holmes' commanded.

Holmes watched him go, and then returned to his explanation. "As I surveyed the room, I learned that there was no method by which the thieves could have entered either from above or from the sides. But the floor is another matter entirely. This would not be the first time I have seen a man tunnel into the floor of a bank vault."

"Mr. Holmes!" protested Gregson. "Have you gone mad? These flagstones are cemented in place!"

"Indeed they are, Inspector," said Holmes, with his enigmatical smile. "And I expect they have been so for many years. Ah, thank you, Mr. Bennett," said he to the swiftly returning manager, who handed Holmes his requested glass of water. My friend took the smallest sip, and then returned to his account. "Have you ever had any reason to replace one of the flagstones, Mr. Winthrop?"

"Not that I can recall," the man spluttered. "But, really, Mr. Holmes, how could a gang possibly pass through a base of cemented flagstones? They would have to be insubstantial!"

Holmes did not answer for a moment. He walked slowly and thoughtfully among the crates and around the room until he stopped. So absorbed was he in his thoughts, that the hand carrying the glass had carelessly spilled some of the water along behind him. "No, Mr. Winthrop, they would simply have to move one of the stones and replace it afterwards. Like this one, for example."

He pointed down at his feet. As we stared at the small puddle of water, we realized that most of the decades-old join-lines between the flagstones absorbed the water readily. But at the spot indicated, the water refused to be absorbed, which could only denote that the cement was freshly poured.

§

After some initial consternation, Gregson summoned several study constables armed with chisels, mallets, and pry-bars. They made short work of the cement indicated by Holmes' water-spilling expedient. Within moments, the large and heavy flagstone was lifted off to one side. A black hole yawned beneath, into which we all peered, while Holmes, kneeling at the side, leaned down into it with one of the constables' lanterns. A finely carved shaft, complete with steel ladder, lay open to us. At the moment, however, we had no thought for how the tunnel had been mined, for our eyes were riveted upon the bottom of the shaft, where we could see the unmistakable reflection of rippling water.

"Gentlemen," said Holmes. "I present to you the Walbrook River."

"But that's impossible," stammered Winthrop, his face turning a ghastly color of green.

"No, sir, merely improbable. Did you not know that the sewers of London ran directly under your bank?"

"The sewers?" said Winthrop, weakly.

"Indeed, sir. You see below you a glimpse into our distant past, like some parting of the veils of time. It was around this very stream that the Romans built this place. They built a temple or two in this garrison town on the far edge of their empire. But they also built a wall, and it was that which gave the brook below us its name. Many centuries later, foul and rank with the rubbish and waste of the City's teeming population, it was one of the first of London's rivers to be vaulted over and buried far beneath our streets. And now, like the Fleet, the Tyburn, and many others, it forms part of the sewer system created in response to the Great Stink of a half-century ago."[65]

"I cannot believe it," mumbled Winthrop. "All this time, a river under my bank!"

"But how could you have suspected the existence of such a tunnel, Holmes?" I inquired.

Holmes smiled broadly and his eyes shone from underneath his black brows. He was transformed when he was hot upon such a scent as this. Men who had only known the introspective logician of Baker Street or the quietly retired bee-keeper of the South Downs would have failed to recognize him. "I simply had to apply my maxim again, Watson. If they did not come through the door, the walls, or the ceiling, then they must have come through the floor."

"But how did you know it was this stone in particular, Holmes?"

"The scratches, of course, Watson."

I looked about in confusion. "But all of the flagstones are scratched, Holmes! It must be expected when moving around such heavy crates."

He shook his head. "But not like these specific abrasions, Watson," he pointed to the adjoining flagstone. "These are fresh, without time to fill in with the typical dust that permeates rooms such as this. The cuts on this particular stone must have been made very recently, when a particularly cumbersome item was moved on top of it. Such as the adjoining stone that we have just dislodged."

"You deduced all of this from a set of fresh scratches?" said I, wonderingly.

"Not at all, Watson. It was equally likely that the scratches had been

---

[65] The Great Stink, or the Big Stink, was a time in the summer of 1858 during which the smell of untreated human waste and effluent from other activities was very strong in central London. The stench was also (wrongly) associated with cholera outbreaks and prompted London authorities to accept a sewerage scheme proposed by engineer Joseph Bazalgette, implemented during the 1860s.

made while the crates were removed. But I knew that one of the stones must have been recently replaced, for that was the only possible explanation for the presence of what Inspector Gregson referred to as dust, but was actually a quick-drying Portland cement.[66] And the flask of water confirmed it."

"Water!"

"Oh yes, Watson. Why else would there be a spirit flask with no scent? The residuals of any other alcohol would have been evident. The water was used to cure the cement."

"But the cement!" protested Gregson. "How could it have been replaced from below?"

"It couldn't be. It was set from above," said Holmes simply.

"That's impossible!" spluttered Mr. Winthrop. "A man would have had to remain behind in the vault."

"That is exactly what I suspect happened. Why else do you think that you received that peculiar note from the so-called Mr. Wild?"

"What do you mean?" asked Gregson.

"It was intended to raise an alarm. Mr. Wild did not wish for you to calmly open the vault as your normal morning routine, for he would surely have been discovered standing within. Rather, he wished for a small regiment of constables to rush blindly into the darkened room, so that one additional man, also dressed in a false constable's uniform, could easily blend in and then safely sidle away."

Gregson shook his head violently. "Impossible. No man has such a cool hand, to lock themselves in the main vault of the Bank of England and wait for the arrival of the police. It would be foolhardy to the point of madness."

"And yet, Inspector, I believe that is exactly what happened. It is the only plausible theory that fits the facts."

"But Holmes, it would have taken a man of exceptional strength standing in that shaft to hold this heavy flagstone in place while the cement set," I noted.

"Yes, yes, but how does it advance us?" said he irritably, at the interruption to his narrative.

"Well, it may be of capital importance. Anything which will define the features of the gang will help us towards the criminal."

He considered this for a moment. "Capital, Watson! I concur completely with your observation. At least one member of the gang is

---

[66] The first quick-drying cement was developed by James Parker in the 1780s. The success of his so-called "Roman cement' led other manufacturers to develop rival products by burning artificial hydraulic lime cements of clay and chalk and it was largely replaced by Portland cement in the 1850s.

either a giant, or they have some deformity. For I have noted that weakness in one limb is often compensated for by remarkable strength in the others."

Meanwhile, Gregson shook off the torpor that had been induced by the stunning find of Holmes, and called out to his men. "Carson! Stevens! Get down in that shaft immediately. See if you can catch up to them."

The two constables looked somewhat reluctant to comply with these orders, and I could hardly blame them. It was not, I must confess, a very alluring prospect. They appeared much relieved when Holmes countermanded the order. "Hold a minute, Inspector. You and your men entered the vault at, say seven o'clock this morning. At that time, the shaft was already sealed. It is now almost ten o'clock. Mr. Wild and his men have at least a three or even four-hour head-start. Any man clever enough to pull off this escapade will have carefully considered his exit route and ensured that they had sufficient time to escape. They will not be caught by sheer swiftness of feet."

"What do you suggest instead, Mr. Holmes?" asked Gregson, somewhat peevishly.

"It is hardly an easy task to haul four tons of gold anywhere far. They must be using some sort of miniature barges to float that weight down the river. Such boats cannot pass the narrower aspects of the tunnels without leaving marks. If you leave the sewer to me, I will endeavor to trace them. But I prefer to have the watercourses un-trampled by your men in hopes of preserving whatever clues happen to exist."

From the fluctuating features scrawled upon his open face, Gregson appeared torn by this suggestion, as I suspected that his superior, Mr. Maurice, would little approve. But eventually his trust in Holmes, laid by long years of association, won out. "Have it your way, Mr. Holmes. Will you go down immediately?"

Holmes shook his head. "I think not. There is one thing that I must do first, and another hour will little alter things. Take heart, Mr. Winthrop, that it will be some time before they can melt down such a vast quantity of gold."

§

We had barely settled into a hailed hansom, when Holmes commanded the cabby to pull up outside one of the district messenger offices. He dashed inside, leaving me inside the cab, only to reappear a few moments later. The cab set off again and Holmes leaned back in his seat, gazing vacantly out of the window. We sat in silence for a few minutes, before I could stand it no longer.

"Would you care to tell me where we are going, Holmes?" I finally asked.

"A quick trip back to Mycroft's domicile is in order. Although I retain in my brain-attic a precise map of every tortuous byway in upper London, the world beneath our feet is a completely separate city with its own unique layout. It may surprise you, but in my prior career I had little reason to venture within its depths. I am therefore in need of some directions, not to mention a change of clothes." He motioned towards his well-cut suit and patent leather shoes. "It will not be pleasant down there, I am afraid."

"I was thinking, Holmes," said I, slowly. "Could they have simply sunk the gold and planned to return for it when the coast was clear? They surely would not have thought that their shaft would be discovered so rapidly. This might explain why they did not take the bank notes or bearer securities, for they would be ruined by the water."

"Excellent, Watson. I had considered that very possibility. If true, then we have nothing to fear. The thieves will not be able to accomplish anything with Gregson's constables standing guard at the top of the shaft. They would be heard. However, there is one very grave objection your theory."

"What is that?"

"Remember, Watson, that we are dealing with a man of vast cunning. He wanted that shaft to be found."

"Why do you say that?"

"Because he asked for me to be called in. Both the name used to access the vault, and the initials upon the flask, which easily could have been carried out in his pocket, were signals as clear as a Very flare.[67] And if he knew that I would be called in, then he expected to have his method of entry discovered."

"Then the sewer is a trap!"

"Perhaps, Watson, perhaps," said he, nodding his head slowly. "We certainly shall not enter unarmed. You have your service revolver, I trust?"

"Of course. I have learned from the long years of our association to keep it near me night and day whenever I am involved in one of your cases."

"Very good, Watson, then we are well prepared for whatever looms in that nether realm."

First, however, were the unusual items that awaited us at Mycroft's chambers. A package had been delivered for Holmes, who opened it and pulled out a thick blue overcoat, waterproofed and capable of being

---

[67] Edward Wilson Very (1847–1910), was an American naval officer who developed a single-shot breech-loading snub-nosed pistol that fired flares.

buttoned close over the chest. There were two versions of each uniform, the coats very long, descending almost to the knees, where they would be met by a matching pair of huge plain leather boots. These outfits were completed by a pair of fan-tailed hats.

"Pray tell, Holmes, what you have there?"

He chuckled. "Well, Mercer does not disappoint. His swiftness is to be commended. This, Watson, is the uniform of a flusherman."

"And what exactly is a flusherman?"

"The flushermen are the brave souls who are employed by the Court of Sewers to ensure that no stoppages build up. They can be considered the spiritual descendants of the nightsoil men. They are the formal denizens of that realm, as opposed to the toshers, who unofficially scavenge what little of value can be gleaned down below."

"And do you plan to wear that uniform?"

"No, Watson, I plan for us to wear it!" said he, laughing.

But Holmes' plan was not to come to pass. For just as he was about to hand me one of the overcoats, a telegram arrived for him. It ran:

> *Mr. Holmes –*
> *There was another recent crime which may have some bearing upon the matter of Threadneedle Street. Could you see Dean Percival at St. Paul's?*
>
> *GREGSON*

Holmes looked up from this note and studied me. "Would you go in, Watson? Your appearance would inspire confidence from a man of the cloth."

"And abandon you to face the sewers alone? I think not, Holmes."

"Do not fear, Watson, I will take Gregson's stoutest constable with me."

"Very well, if you think it wise," I reluctantly agreed.

The two of us made a strange pair as our hansom rattled its way along Fleet Street. At least the clothes that Holmes wore were clean enough for the time being, though I wondered if he would ever find a cabby willing to bring him back to Pall Mall after he spent several hours wading through those dank sewers. St. Paul's was perfectly situated on the way back to the Bank of England, as the Fleet turned into Ludgate Hill, therefore Holmes had the hansom drop me in the in the south churchyard.

"Remember, Watson," said he, before the cab started up again. "You are acting as my representative in this matter. As our association continued from one century to another, you have had hundreds of opportunities to witness me apply my techniques. In your stories, you have habitually underrated your own developing abilities, and I now have little doubt that your researches will soon clear up this new problem."

I must admit that his words gave me keen pleasure. "Thank you, Holmes. I will endeavor to do my best. Be careful down there."

He nodded grimly and I watched for a moment as the hansom set off. It was simplicity itself to locate Dean Percival, who proved to be an amiable man of advancing years. He had flaxen hair and mutton chop whiskers. His weak blue eyes were covered by pince-nez, and he was dressed in a black ecclesiastical suit.

If Dean Percival was upset that Holmes had sent a delegate and not appeared in person, he hid it well. "I can hardly understand it, Doctor Watson. It has been almost a hundred years since the cathedral was last plundered. Upon that horrible occasion, the thieves broke open nine doors to get to the treasury. But almost everything of value was taken then, and nothing was ever recovered.[68] So there is now little to steal, unless they try to strip the gilding from the ceilings."

"But something was taken?" I asked.

"Oh, yes, though it's a rather trivial matter," said he, as he led me through a door in the southwest bell-tower and up a perfectly geometrical staircase to a portion of the cathedral which I had never before ventured. "We only reported it to Scotland Yard because we felt it was our civic duty. The cost of replacing it is negligible, even on our limited budget. I really can't imagine why anyone would want to take it. I hope if you do catch the individuals responsible that they are not harshly punished. If only they had turned to us in their hour of need, perhaps we could have aided them and turned them towards the path of righteous light, rather than this road of illicit darkness."

"So what was it, Dean Percival?"

"It is easier to show rather than describe. Here we are," he swept his hand over a dusty room filled with the detritus of men who worked with their hands. "This gallery is used as a work-room for the artisans who maintain the glory of the cathedral. There are stonemasons, painters, metalworkers, and glass-polishers, of course, but the men who reported the missing items are to be found over here." He pointed to a series of heavy tables and large wooden chests. "They are the gilders."

"Gilders? Do you mean the men who work with gold-leaf?"

"Exactly, Doctor Watson. We have so much of it in the cathedral that some part or another is always in need of restoration."

I turned this new information over in my brain. On the heels of the

---

[68] December 22, 1810 saw the cathedral's only robbery where thieves broke open nine doors to get to the plate repository, valued at above £2,000. The items were never recovered, obviously because Holmes had yet to be born!

great plunder at the Bank of England, here was more vanished gold! What could the thieves possibly be planning to do with it all? "Exactly how much gold was taken, Dean Percival?"

"Oh, no, you misunderstand me, Doctor. They didn't take any gold at all. They took every square yard of our goldbeater's skin."

"Your what?" I exclaimed.

"Well, I hardly know much about the stuff myself. To be honest, I didn't even know we had it lying around until the gilders informed me that it was missing. They tell me that it is a type of parchment made from the outer membrane of a calf's intestine. It is used in the process of making exceptionally thin golf leaf by beating the gold between layers of the tear-resistant skin."

My mind was racing with this new information. How did this fit into the thieves' master plan? Were they planning on hammering out the bullion, rather than melting it down? And who were these thieves? Were they fellow countrymen, solely out for gain, no matter what the cost to the stability of England? Or were they foreign agents, out to destabilize our great nation? Was this how they planned to smuggle the gold from our shores? Surely the transport of ultra-thin layers of gold leaf would be far easier to conceal than the large bars of its current form.

I realized that the Dean was watching me expectantly as I thought through the implications of what I had just learned. "And how did the thieves abscond with it, Dean Percival?" I finally asked.

He shook his head sadly. "I am afraid that we have only ourselves to blame for it. The gold itself is locked up, of course, but we never shut our doors to the needy. I suspect that they simply walked in one night and hauled it away."

"Do you know when?"

"The gilders reported it missing three days ago. It must have been in the handful of nights prior to this, as they mentioned that they last utilized it during the week before Hallow's Eve. But I told this to the policeman already."

"Gregson?"

"No, a Mr. Lestrade, I think was his name."

"And did he search the area for clues to their identity?"

"Yes, I believe so, but he said that there was nothing unusual to be found."

I smiled, thinking of the myriad of times that Holmes was able to discover some seemingly trivial item overlooked by the police but which, in point of fact, threw open the entire case. "You don't mind if I also take a look around?"

"Not at all. Take your time, Doctor. But if you do find them, please recall that I have no desire to press charges. I would see the men rehabilitated."

"And if they are past the point of no return?"

"Is there such an inexorable evil, Doctor, that cannot be cast aside by the light of good?"

"You speak of higher matters, Dean Percival, than I am used to contemplating. With Holmes, I have combatted many a terrible man in my day. And I daresay that some of them met a fate that they justly deserved."

"It is a heavy burden to make such a judgment, Doctor. Are you capable of shouldering it? Is anyone?"

With those profound words, the Dean left me. I spent the next thirty minutes examining every aspect of the room, focusing most of my attention on the area around the chests that once contained the goldbeater's skin. There were no obvious leavings on the floor. I had hoped for some tobacco ash, which I might collect and bring back to Holmes for identification, but it appeared that the thieves neglected to smoke during their raid. As to be expected in an area near where stonework was being done, there was much dust on the floor, and several fine footprints. But at least three days had passed. I realized that they could belong to anyone: the thieves, the gilders, Dean Percival, even Inspector Lestrade. How was I to tell which might provide a clue? I doubted if Holmes himself could decipher such an old trail. I wracked my brain to think of what strategy Holmes would employ in such a situation. And then I had it. For the goldbeater's skin was an animal product. And as such, it must possess a distinctive smell. And there was one being in London who had the power to track it.

My first task was to obtain a sample of the skin to use to set my chaser upon its track. Fortunately, the headquarters of the Goldsmith's Company was close by St. Paul's, at the corner of Foster Lane and Gresham Street. It took but a few minutes of explanation, and an invoking of the name Sherlock Holmes, in order to procure a small square of the special parchment. From there, I set out to No. 3 Pinchin Lane, near the water's edge at Lambeth. There I hoped to recruit a trusty companion to the adventure at hand.

The exterior of the shabby two-storied home of Mr. Sherman had not improved much in the one and twenty years since I first set foot upon its step. The stuffed weasel holding a hare, its remarkably-preserved shape a testament to the skill of the taxidermist, still served as a dubious decoration in the front window. I pounded upon the door for some time, before a candle glinted behind the blinds of the upper window and I heard the familiar gravelly voice yelling at me to 'be-gone.'

"Mr. Sherman," I called out. "I am here on behalf of Sherlock Holmes!"

Again, like the cave of Ali Baba, this magic phrase served to rapidly produce an unbarring of the door. I gazed upon Sherman, and was secretly glad that the old naturalist still drew breath, for his appearance had also deteriorated over time. His frame was still lanky and lean, with a stringy neck and stooping shoulders. His blue-tinted glasses appeared thicker than prior, and he was now nearer to ninety than eighty. But his memory remained, for he peered at me for a moment and then smiled. "Ah! It's Dr. Watson, is it not?"

"Indeed, Mr. Sherman, and a pleasure it is to see you looking well. I am in need of your dog."

"Toby?"

"That's the one."

"I am afraid that poor Toby is now sitting at the end of one of the feasting tables in Valhalla, Doctor, waiting for a tossed bone to fall."

"I am very sorry to hear that, Mr. Sherman."

"Of course, we've got Falstaff here, who is Toby's grandson." He indicated a handsome, lop-eared, thick-boned dog, its short coat a deep brown in color.

"He looks like a bloodhound."

"Yes, sir, of a sort. Toby was a right mongrel, of course, part spaniel and part lurcher. His mate was a beagle, and they produced Andrew, Falstaff's father. But Falstaff's mother was pure bloodhound. He's a fine tracker in his own right, to be certain."

"Excellent. Mr. Holmes and I are in need of him to track this calf's skin," said I, producing the sample from the Goldsmith's Hall. Falstaff wined eagerly at the smell of the parchment.

Sherman frowned. "Did it touch the ground with some regularity?"

"Not that I know."

"And how long ago was this?"

"At least three days."

Sherman shook his head. "What you ask is impossible, Doctor. Even Toby in his prime could not have done it. If the substance had been left in the roadway, like aniseed or creosote, that would be one thing. But to lay on a track from a substance in the air, after a span of three days... no, it cannot be done."

I turned away dejected at the thought that my plan had failed and I would have little to report back to Holmes.

"Where did you want to Falstaff to track the stuff, Doctor?"

"The theft occurred at St. Paul's."

"Ah, the City. Odd thing, that."

"What is odd, Mr. Sherman?"

"Well, of course, Falstaff and I go for walks round the local neighborhood. And he's smelt that same skin around here of late." He reached down and absently scratched the dog's head. "I can tell by the way he whined when you produced it."

"Are you certain?"

"Oh yes, it was at the Palace Gardens."

"Which Palace?"

"Lambeth, of course. The Archbishop's residence. There is a shed towards the back that recently caught Falstaff's attention."

I pondered this strange bit of intelligence. Mr. Sherman was pointing me towards the London abode of the Archbishop of Canterbury, the head of the entire Church of England. And yet, the goldbeater's skin had been stolen from St. Paul's Cathedral, the seat of the Bishop of London. Could this pair of great men be engaged in some secret struggle? It was too outlandish to consider. The most likely explanation was that the Palace had its own supply of the skin, to use for repairing the gold leaf within the ancient building. But would they really keep it in a shed in the gardens? I needed to follow up this lead before I returned to Mycroft's and related my findings to Holmes.

I thanked Mr. Sherman profusely, and a hastily-sketched map in hand, I set off on foot for the nearby gardens. There, I located, tucked up almost against the wall of the Palace itself, a ramshackle outbuilding roughly ten feet long and eight feet deep. As there was no other likely suspect in the gardens, it could only be the shed that Sherman had described.

Approaching it, I found that the door was solidly locked and the few windows blacked out. There was no obvious method by which I might see what exactly was held inside. I stood there for a moment, deliberating what scheme I might utilize in order to gain admission, when an angry voice called out.

"Go on, you vagrant. You'll find no shelter in here tonight," said the man. I turned to find a squat, dark, middle-aged man, with a deeply-lined face scowling at me. He wore the soiled uniform of a groundskeeper, and was shaking a large stick at me.

I attempted to disarm him with a note of gracious pleasantry. "Hello, my good man. My name is John Watson. I assure you that I am not thinking of trying to sleep in your fine shed. I was merely wondering what you might keep inside such a structure."

"You a copper?" said he, his voice surly.

"Not at all, Mr...."

But the name I hoped for was not proffered. "If you ain't a copper, I got no reason I need to talk to you. Go on, then!" He waved his stick again.

I held up my hand in a placating fashion. "Now, now, there is no reason to get rough. It's an innocent question. The only reason to refuse to answer it would be if you have something to hide."

"And if I do, what are you going to do about it?"

"I could very easily call in the aid of Scotland Yard and obtain a warrant. We'll have it open before nightfall."

He peered at me, his gaze malevolent. "You'd have to walk away from here first."

"Are you proposing to attack me with your stick here in this public garden? I assure you, my good man, that would be a poor choice."

"I will tell them I was beating off a robber." He raised the stick again.

"And I am no simple robber." I pulled my service revolver from my pocket and pointed it squarely at his chest.

In an instant, his manner changed. "There's no need for that, Mister. Just go on, and we'll forget all about this."

"Before I go, if you would be so kind as to tell me what you have in your shed."

"It's a garden shed, and I be the gardener. What do you expect? Garden tools."

"May I see them?"

"Get your warrant. Then I'll show you whatever you want, Mister," said he, his defiance returning.

I considered the possibility of threatening him further with my revolver, but ultimately decided that such a course was unwise, for my legal standing would have been tenuous at best. I instead beat a tactical retreat back to Pall Mall. For the time being, my clue had come to nothing, but once Holmes resurfaced from the depths of London I was certain that he would know what subsequent course to pursue.

§

I had little time to wait before a figure appeared in Mycroft's rooms, the likes of which had certainly never before passed his door. Holmes was covered head to toe with a substance that transformed his skin to black, and he reeked of a smell so foul that I can scarcely do it justice with mere words. Even knowing that he had intended to set out in the attire of a flusherman, I hardly recognized him. "A disguise, Holmes?"

"Hardly that, Watson," said he, laughing. He threw himself into one of Mycroft's upholstered armchairs, which I feared would never be the same and would perhaps require converting into firewood. "It is a tight fraternity under the streets and they know each other less by sight than by sound.

But the toshers do not mix with the official workers, so in order to draw out their confidences, I have made a series of minor adjustments to the standard garb of the sewer worker. I dare say that my modifications make it an eminently more practical outfit for exploring that nether domain."

"And what were the results of your investigations?"

His bushy eyebrows drew together in a scowl. "I found many miles of damp, green, fungi-lined tunnels. The water is dark and fetid, and there are places where the air is so thick with gas that an un-shuttered lantern could set off a giant eruption. The Walbrook may have once been a natural channel, but years of man's handiwork have linked it with a dizzying array of other streams, both true and artificial. Would you believe that there is even a bit of the River Westborne in the midst of the tube station in Sloane Square?[69] I followed a fresh series of almost indistinguishable marks in the direction of Hoxton, but they ultimately led to nothing.'" He shook his head. "It will take me days to explore every narrow tributary. Now, pray tell, Watson, what did you discover at St. Paul's?"

I related my findings at the cathedral, and how this had eventually led me to the gardens of Lambeth Palace. "I trust that there is nothing of consequence which I have overlooked?" I concluded with some degree of smugness that my afternoon had proved to be more profitable than his own.

Holmes had listened with careful attention to my long report, his finger-tips pressed together. "A singularly consistent investigation you have made, my dear Watson," said he. "I cannot at the moment recall any time when you have made more of a hash of things."[70]

"And what would you have done in my stead?" I cried, with some bitterness.

"I would have been more careful to not attract the attention of the Lambeth groundskeeper, and if I had engaged him, I certainly would not have told him my real name. Could you not have been Dr. Hill Barton one last time?"

"Why is my name of importance?"

He laughed merrily. "Come now, Doctor. Surely if my name is known far and wide, so then is the man whose words thrust that fame upon me.[71]

---

[69] This is quite true to this day, though it is now channeled through a relatively non-descript pipe.

[70] The expression was coined in the British Isles, probably not long before 1833, when Cardinal Newman wrote in a letter: 'Froude writes up to me we have made a hash of it.'

[71] Holmes is paraphrasing Malvolio here from Shakespeare' *Twelfth Night*: 'Some are born great, some achieve greatness, and some have greatness thrust

If the groundskeeper is crooked, he now knows the game is up."

"So you do believe that the groundskeeper is involved? Could the gold be kept in the shed?" I asked excitedly. "We should be off at once!"

Holmes shook his head. "There are serious objections to that theory, Watson. From your description it sounds far too small to serve such a purpose. And in any case, by the time we reached Lambeth, whatever was in that shed will have long been moved. Presuming, of course, that the groundskeeper is involved in the plot at all."

"But his attitude was so suspicious!" I protested.

"And that is why you should not have hesitated to force his hand. You should never have left without finding a way to see the inside of that shed, Watson. I can think of seven methods you might have employed. Only then could we know for certain whether or not he is one of the men that we seek. He may be involved in some completely unrelated, but equally nefarious activity, or simply be a deeply suspicious and violent individual."

"But you agree that there is a possibility that he is involved? Is this robbery some ecclesiastical spat between the bishops?"

"Hardly that, Watson. Even if we could admit the prospect of the Archbishop of Canterbury ordering a theft from his rival at St. Paul's, it is inconceivable that he would plunder the Bank of England. No, if your groundskeeper is involved, he is acting as an independent agent. He would not be the first servant, embittered after years of labor at a house where a single painting may be worth more than his life's savings, to jump at the first prospect of some easy coin. And what easier than to let some generous stranger store their items in the little-used garden shed for the span of a few days, no questions asked?"

"That is a plausible theory."

"It is more than plausible. I think that I shall have a few of my irregulars follow your groundskeeper for a few days, just to see if he can lead us to any other individuals of interest."

"Then my investigation was not in vain." I was proud to think that I had so far mastered his system as to apply it in a way which earned his approval.

He shook his head again. "I am afraid, Watson, that you benefitted from no small amount of Fortune. It was most propitious that Mr. Sherman happened to walk Falstaff in a northerly direction and not the opposite."

"And you have never profited from Luck, Holmes?"

"Never. I find the very concept abhorrent."

"What about the murder of Eduardo Lucas? Without his unhappy

upon them' (Act 2, Scene 5).

wife, where would those letters be? Would the Premier still be in your debt?"

"A touch, Watson – a veritable touch," said he, laughing.

"I say, Holmes, what if they floated the gold to the Thames, and then either up or down the river on a string of lighters? That would be simplicity itself, especially if they are using the grounds of the riverside Lambeth Palace as a sanctuary."

"Very good, Watson. It was in fact the very first possibility that I considered. It even occurred to Gregson, who has the men of the Thames Division combing its entire navigable length. Since the solitary river folk are notoriously averse to talking to the representatives of the government, I also have several less official forces in the field."

"Surely your irregulars must be grown men by now? Have you recruited other poor souls to take their place? What would the Children's Charter say?"[72]

Holmes shook his head. "While I much applaud the efforts of the Premier and his liberal government, the reforms do not go far enough. There are still plenty of urchins left on our streets and larks in our mud."

"If you are so concerned for their well-being, you could simply help them."

"Come now, Watson. Give a man a fish.[73] When I pay my irregulars a guinea, I do more than fill their bellies for a day, I instruct them that hard work will invariably lead to greater things. Look at me."

I frowned. "Were your parents not country squires?"

He snorted in derision. "A manorial lord can claim a fancy title, but also have not two farthings to rub together. My father may have given me two years at college, that is true, but it was only with many long years of hard training that I came by my especial techniques. Do you not recall the day we first met, when my purse was so under-full that I could not upon my own pay for a nice suite in Baker Street?"

"Of course, Holmes. It's not likely to slip my mind."

"Then you know of what I speak. I may have had a leg up on those poor lads, but my success I owe primarily to myself, with some assistance

---

[72] The Children's Charter of 1908 was a liberal reform legislation that established juvenile courts to prevent children from serving time in adult prisons. It regulated baby-farming and wet-nursing, and tried to stamp out infanticide. Local authorities were granted powers to keep poor children out of the workhouse, and children were prevented from working in dangerous trades, purchasing cigarettes, and entering pubs.

[73] This appears to be a shortening of the proverb, 'Give a man a fish, he easts for a day, teach a man to fish and you feed him for a lifetime.' The origin of this phrase is obscure, but it certainly originated before 1900.

from my Boswell, of course. And you may be surprised to see how some of the old gang has turned out, Wiggins, for example."

"So, what are we to do? Just wait?"

"Not exactly, Watson. You may sleep, if you wish. I, for one, plan to consume an unwholesome amount of shag. Perhaps by the first light of the rosy-fingered dawn, some new avenues may have occurred to me."

§

The rays of faint winter's sun were beginning to appear when I was awoken by sounds coming from the library of our host. A thick cloud of yellow smoke rolled down the hall, and made me think that either our rooms were on fire, or a window had been left open and allowed in the opalescent London reek. Instead, I found Holmes, sitting upon the floor like some strange Buddha, with crossed legs, and huge books all round him. One lay closed upon his knees, the slamming of which must have been the inciting noise. His face radiated unhappiness.

"Have you been up all night, Holmes?"

"I have."

"And are you any closer to a solution?"

He shook his head irritably. "Data, data, Watson! I cannot make fire without wood."

"So what are you doing?"

"I am taking advantage of Mycroft's excellent selection of classical works. I have often said that the bell chimes the same note. Everything has been done before. It seems that our friend Mortlock has either consciously or unconsciously taken inspiration from the ancient past, so I decided that the most practical thing I could do now is to study the same. I have just finished Herodotus, and found him to be quite instructive."

"So what do you plan to do now?"

"I have seven different lines of inquiry underway. It is to be hoped that one of them will draw blood."

But it was not to be. All that day and the next Holmes was in a mood which I would generously call reserved, and less generous people would call miserable. He ran out and ran in, smoked incessantly, and played snatches on his violin, which had been sent up from Fulworth by his old housekeeper. He sank into reveries, devoured sandwiches at irregular hours, and hardly answered the simple questions which I put to him. It was evident to me that things were not going well with his quest.

Inspector MacDonald stopped in to see if Holmes would assist him with a robbery at the Lane Gas Plant on Horseferry Road in Westminster, but Holmes dismissed him with an ungracious snarl. Inspector Gregson dropped by at one point with a theory that the gold was being stashed in a warehouse in Wapping.

Holmes, however, was derisive of this idea. "You are as likely to find your bars of gold in Wapping as you are to find an honest man in the Bar of Gold."

All day I turned over the case in my mind and found no explanation which appeared to me to be adequate. I finally ventured to inquire of Holmes what had come of the shed in the Lambeth Gardens.

Holmes had been scratching a tune on his Stradivarius, which I thought might be a variation of Dvorak's 'Indian Canzonetta,' but he set this down with some asperity and began to lecture me on my investigative shortcomings. "I must say that the faculty of deduction is apparently not contagious, Watson. How else can we explain your failure to seize upon the possibly vital clue you held so briefly in your hands? Your shed has been emptied and the groundskeeper has vanished. I went over the entire area myself, but there is not a single clue to be found that might point me in the direction where they moved whatever it once contained. For someone to cover their tracks with such care, both in the garden and in the sewers, well, it can only be an audacious message to me. I tell you, Watson, this time we have got a foeman who is worthy of our steel."

"But you can track him?"

He shook his head dejectedly. "On the contrary, Watson. Without further clues, I fear we shall never find him amid the millions in this great city. There are simply an almost infinite number of places where he could hide."

"So what shall you do?"

"I am doing it. I am waiting. Eventually he will make a move, even if it is but a feint, and then I will seize my opening and sink my blade home."

"And how can I be of any assistance?"

"I assure you, Watson, that if some occasion arises that falls within your purview, I shall not fail to utilize you."

Fortunately, we had not much longer to wait. A telegram arrived for Holmes. It ran:

Mr. Holmes –
Your suggestion has borne fruit. If convenient, could you meet me at Silvester's Bank?

GREGSON

"What suggestion was that, Holmes?"

"I asked Gregson to send a man around to each of the banks in the city in order to obtain lists of all of the recent accounts established at the respective institutions. It would then be a simple matter to see if all of these individuals had actually opened those accounts, or if our Mr. Wild had replicated his behavior. From Gregson's note, it sounds like my name may have again been taken in vain."

I frowned in confusion. "I have studied your maps, Holmes. There is no river under Silvester's bank."

"Yes, what of it?"

"Well, how will they get in? A simple tunnel from a neighboring building?"

Holmes shook his head. "No, Watson, he has tried that before. We are dealing with a terribly clever man, who changes his method to suit the locale. We will have to inspect the site to see if we can deduce what method he might employ."

When we arrived at Pudding Lane, Gregson was standing in the foyer of the bank. The inspector was deep in conversation with a familiar looking man, but when he noticed us, he beckoned us forward. Gregson shook his head ruefully. "I don't know how you thought to investigate this, Mr. Holmes, but you were spot on. I, for one, believed you were backing the wrong horse."

"Indeed, Gregson, sometimes the dark horse is the one to stake your winnings on. So, you've found a suspicious new account?"

"Yes, sir. It is rather cool of him to consider another job so soon and so near, but it must be him, beyond all doubt."

"How do you know for certain, Gregson? Did they use my name again?"

"Not at all, Mr. Holmes. They used Dr. Watson's."

Holmes burst into a hearty laugh. "A salute, Watson, an undeniable salute to your role in the firm!" said he. "I feel the presence of an enemy whose broadside is as quick and as devastating as my own. As a matter of fact, burglars who have done a good stroke of business are, as a rule, only too glad to enjoy the proceeds in peace and quiet without immediately embarking upon another perilous undertaking. We can therefore safely assume that this is in fact the work of our Mr. Wild. I had not put Silvester's high on my list, however. I thought he might target Lloyd's or the City and Midlands Bank."

"I too am most surprised that anyone would be so foolish to target my bank," groaned the man with whom Gregson had been talking. He was a well-built middle-aged fellow, with a frank honest face and a slight, crisp, yellow moustache. He wore a very shiny top-hat and a well-cut suit. His face was round and ruddy and his mouth pulled down in an expression of distress.

With some amazement, I realized that I knew the man, though I had not seen him in a very long time. "Mr. Hall Pycroft?" I stammered.

"The very same, Doctor, and it is a mighty fine thing to see you and Mr. Holmes again after all these years. It's been, what, a score of them?"

If Holmes was surprised by Mr. Pycroft's presence he hid it well. "So you are now the Manager of Silvester's are you, Mr. Pycroft? I suppose that makes great sense that you have risen from the ranks of the clerks. I always recognized that you had great pecuniary ability, with your amazing memory for financial minutia."

"And you had the good sense, of course, to once hire Sherlock Holmes," said I, laughing.

"Indeed," said Mr. Pycroft, chuckling ruefully. "I have Mr. Holmes to thank for repairing my reputation, so that I could even have had this opportunity."

"Think nothing of it," said Holmes. "But you expressed surprise that Silvester's would be targeted. Why is that?"

"Well, Mr. Holmes, I have made some modifications to our security protocols, with Mr. Silvester's approval, of course. I am confident that it would be most difficult for a thief to make his way into our vault. In fact, our reputation has spread. We are now known, in circles that matter, as the most secure bank in the City. The Old Lady may have her share of titled folk, but the smart set deposits their wealth here."

"Would you show us what you have done? Pray leave nothing out, no matter how trivial," asked Holmes.

"It would be my very great pleasure. Now, then, Mr. Holmes, first of all, you can see, as soon as you enter the bank, our vault upon display. It is not tucked away in some dank basement where no one can keep an eye on it." He waved to the great steel doors in front of us.

"And is it lined?" I asked.

"Of course, Doctor. We spared no expense during the remodel five years ago. All six sides are lined with twelve-inch reinforced steel. It would take the most modern diamond drill at least fifteen hours to penetrate it.[74] Needless to say, the vault is inspected more often than that, even upon weekends and Bank Holidays. Either Mr. Silvester or I look in upon it every single day of the year. Thus, anyone attempting to tunnel in would be deeply disappointed."

"But could they not tunnel underneath a crate held within the vault, such that you would never see anything?" I postulated.

"Excellent, Doctor!" exclaimed Mr. Pycroft. "The same concern had occurred to me. Hence, all crates are set atop carefully constructed

---

[74] The diamond core drill was invented and put to practical use during tunneling in 1863 by Rodolphe Leschot, a French engineer. Their use rapidly expanded into drilling oil wells, as well as more nefarious schemes.

wooden frames about six inches high, such that almost every square foot of the vault's floor is able to be inspected."

"But they could always go through the main door of the vault."

"That would be most difficult, Doctor. First of all, they would have to enter the main building, into which there are only two doors. The rear door can only be opened from the inside, and the front door is under constant surveillance."

"What about the roof?" inquired Holmes. "I note that you have a very fine glass dome, which would be child's play for a thief to penetrate."

"Ah, yes, but you also may have noted, Mr. Holmes, the unique situation of our building. We border essentially no one, with streets on every side save one. And the building closest to us is far shorter. How would a thief even get on the roof? Unless you expect them to climb up six sheer stories?"

Holmes waved his hand. "But let us say that someone did make their way into the bank, they could then disable the guards and allow a master cracksman sufficient time to open the door."

Mr. Pycroft shook his head again. "I am afraid that there are no guards to disable, Mr. Holmes. Instead, we use a little contraption that I like to call the 'watchtower.'" He pointed to an unusual feature of the bank. It was a projection from high up on the front of the Bank. It was large enough to hold a seated man, and reminded me of an Egyptian oriel window.[75] A set of stairs led up to a stoutly-built door, which could be barred from the inside. Apertures on both sides allowed a clear view both into the bank and out onto the street. "As you can see," Pycroft explained, "the guard in the watchtower has a full view of the vault door throughout the night. He would instantly spot any man approaching it and could call the police on the installed telephone."

"Wires can be cut."

"The guard also possesses a very loud bell which can be rung in order to summon one of the constables on the street."

"He could be drugged with opium or some other narcotic," opined Holmes.

Mr. Pycroft shook his head. "First of all, the guard brings his own food. That significantly limits the access anyone would need in order to introduce some substance. Secondly, the rounding City constables check upon him every twenty minutes. Even the best cracksman in Europe could not get through that door so quickly, much less make off with anything."

"They could neutralize the constables as well."

---

[75] Oriel windows are a form of corbel-supported bay window which projects from the main wall of a building but does not reach to the ground. They are commonly found in Arab architecture, where they are called *mashrabiyas*.

Pycroft smiled at Holmes' multitude of clever suggestions. "But the rounds of the constables take them through police headquarters at Bishopsgate as well. If one failed to turn up, half of London would be roused along his route in order to locate him."

"You really have thought of everything, Mr. Pycroft. I commend you. Ah, what have we here?" Holmes' attention had been distracted by a portrait of an elderly and rotund gentleman. This depiction had a high level of verisimilitude, and included the man's balding pate, which was ringed round with tufts of white hair, and the fact that the man's formal suit strained at the cummerbund. He had clearly posed in the foyer of the very bank in which we stood, the vault at his back, his hands spread slightly open as if to welcome customers inside. My own expertise on portraiture was limited, but even I could tell that the artist had a remarkably realistic style.

"That is Mr. Aldous Silvester, the owner of the bank," answered Hall Pycroft.

"It is recently painted, is it not?"

"Yes," said Mr. Pycroft, frowning. "How could you know that?"

Holmes smiled. "I have very astute senses, Mr. Pycroft, and can still smell some of the turpentine-thinned paint, which can take up to three weeks to dry. Furthermore, since I do not detect any scent of varnish, I can deduce that the painting is less than a year old, for surely the master that painted this would have returned to seal his work for all of eternity."

"Is that important? I cannot see how it could have any possible bearing upon the case?"

"Perhaps not," said Holmes, "but as Watson could tell you, I consider myself something of a connoisseur of paintings, and I imagine that I have seen the work of this artist before. Do you recall his name?"

"Let me think," said Mr. Pycroft slowly. "He was a Frenchman, or perhaps a Belgian. Achille Pendré was his name. Mr. Silvester seemed to think that he was rather well known, with works hanging in many of the Bond Street galleries."

"Yes, I think that is correct. Perhaps even in some of our finer museums. In any case, I have seen enough and bid you adieu."

"But Mr. Holmes," called out Hall Pycroft, "do you think we are at risk of an assault?"

"I very much fear so, but how and when are still matters that I have yet to determine. When I do so, Mr. Pycroft, I promise you will be the first to know. Until then, I urge you to remain vigilant."

Holmes was silent during much the cab ride back to Pall Mall. I could tell that he was deep in thought about what we had learned at Silvester's Bank. For my part, I was much perplexed. The precautions put into place by Mr. Pycroft seemed insurmountable. Only a great fool would attempt to penetrate them, and I had little hope that our enemy was so imprudent.

Finally Holmes sighed and glanced over at me. "What do you make of it, Watson?"

"I confess to being mystified, Holmes."

He smiled wanly. "Yes, we hold many of the threads, but enough have slipped through our fingers that the picture is not yet clear. However, our adversary is not infallible. He has constructed a plot of great intricacy, and like any complicated machine, it takes but the smallest snag to snarl it. He will make another mistake, and when he does, I will have him."

Little did Holmes know that his words were prophetic, for we were soon blessed by the appearance of Inspector Lestrade on the doorstep of Mycroft's Pall Mall chambers. His small, wiry, bulldoggish features were contrite as he gazed at my companion in a slightly reverential way.

Before the inspector could even state his case, Holmes cut him off. "Really, Lestrade, as you may have heard, I am somewhat busy today," said Holmes brusquely. "I will get to your missing museum items in good time. It is as if some gaping maw has opened and swallowed both your treasures and Gregson's gold."

"So you think the same man was involved in both crimes?" I asked.

He nodded. "Although it is unusual, Watson, for a criminal to carry on two such feats so temporally joined, and with vastly different *modus operandi*, I think it highly unlikely that two such masters are at play simultaneously."

"I've heard about the Old Lady, Mr. Holmes," interjected Lestrade, "and I know that Gregson has claimed your attentions, but something else has occurred with which I needed a bit of assistance. Even if you cannot come in person, perhaps you could suggest some starting point?"

Holmes sighed with impatience, but motioned for Lestrade to continue. "Pray tell, what great mystery has arisen this time?"

"Well, Mr. Holmes, it is something strange down at Runnymede."[76]

"Has the Magna Carta also vanished?" asked Holmes, with no small degree of sarcasm.

"No, Mr. Holmes, there is a dead man in the Long Mede pasture. We are uncertain of his name, for he was missing both his coat and his identity papers."

"I am afraid, Lestrade," interjected Holmes, "that the death of an

---

[76] Runnymede is a is a water-meadow alongside the River Thames in the English county of Surrey, approximately twenty miles west of central London. It is famous for being the location of the sealing of Magna Carta in 1215. Only four of the original charters still exist, none of them kept at Runnymede (two are in the British Library, one in Lincoln Cathedral, and one in Salisbury Cathedral).

unknown man can hardly take precedence over the matter at hand here in London. If you are in need of outside assistance, perhaps Barker..."

"But Mr. Holmes, you didn't let me finish. This is no ordinary murder. The examiner has completed his report and concluded that the man has been dead for no more than twelve to fourteen hours. However, the body was found on the pasture by Mr. John Black, one of the park wardens. Black is as old as the hills he patrols, and his honesty is above suspicion. If you will recall, Mr. Holmes, the weather was unseasonably cold last night, such that there was a dusting of snow in that part of Surrey which began around five o'clock. But Mr. Black is prepared to swear that there were no tracks in the snow anywhere near the body."

"You mean that he saw none."

"I assure you, Mr. Holmes, that I have examined the spot myself, and there were none."

Holmes chuckled appreciatively. "My good Lestrade, I have investigated many crimes, but I have never yet seen one which was committed by a flying creature. As long as the criminal remains upon two legs there must be some indentation, some abrasion, some trifling displacement which can be detected by the scientific searcher. I assure you that this meadow must contain some trace which could aid you."

Lestrade shook his head. "I know your methods, Mr. Holmes. You've used them to show me a thing or two in my day. There is something mighty peculiar about this Runnymede case."

Holmes sighed. "I suppose that we must follow-up on all crimes of a particular outré nature, Watson, no matter how unlikely they are to be connected to the cases of the Museum and the Bank."

"You will go down?" I asked.

"No, my dear fellow, you will go down. This may be some trivial problem, and I cannot excuse myself from the center of London for the sake of it. Your natural acumen should be more than a match for this snowy afternoon. Leave no stone unturned."

§

The pale sunlight of that late fall day was fading by the time Lestrade and I arrived at that site where the greatest of the English Charters had come into being, and where later Henry romanced Anne under a Yew Tree.[77] After the previous night's storm, the weather had turned somewhat

---

[77] The Ankerwyke Yew is a huge and ancient tree close to the ruins of St Mary's Priory, the site of a Benedictine nunnery built in the 12th century. The tree is at least 1,400 years old and is located on the opposite bank of the River Thames from the meadows of Runnymede. It is said to be the location where Henry VIII

for the calmer, though the temperature remained low with an exhilarating nip in the air, which set an edge to a man's energy. The dark blue sky was flecked with little fleecy white clouds drifting across from west to east. Lestrade led me to the play where the man's body still sprawled, a pair of constables stationed nearby to ward off any accidental intruders upon the scene.

I at once went very carefully round it to observe if there were any traces in the snow which might help me, as they had once helped Holmes prevent a great scandal. Fortunately the cold day had served to harden the crust of frost. Unlike the subtle impressions left on trampled grass or wet dirt, which often required careful examination with a lens, my reading of what had transpired on that sloping hillside was a simple one. There was a double line of tracks of a booted man, which could only belong to the groundskeeper Mr. Black. He had advanced towards the body at a run, but his return was more slow and careful. I noted that three additional prints approached the area, presumably belonging to the local constable, the medical examiner, and Lestrade himself. The local man had outdone himself, for he had carefully laid down a long piece of matting and stood upon it while looking at the body such that these new prints would not contaminate the scene.

Turning my attention to that of the body, this proved to belong to a middle-aged man, about forty by his looks. He was laying full length on top of the snow. The back of his head appeared to have been caved in by a ferocious blow. His shirt had a well-cut look to it, though the cuffs were heavily stained with some dark substance. Pushing them up, I noted that his hands were heavily calloused and his fleshy left forearm was dotted and scarred with innumerable puncture marks. There was no sign of any bullet holes. Utilizing my training in such matters, I independently verified from the extreme rigor of his muscles that the examiner's estimate of time of death was accurate. This confirmed that the man's demise must have transpired after the snow had begun falling.

A minute examination of the scene served only to make the case more complex. Immediately about him, the snow was somewhat tumbled, but everywhere else it was still smooth. I cast my eye about for any horse or vehicle which could have brought the body to that spot, but nothing of the kind was to be seen. I could confirm that Lestrade was not mistaken. There were no other prints in the snow. Either the man had died of natural causes, taken his own life, or Mr. Black himself had killed the man for reasons unknown. But the blow upon the back of his head ruled out the former two possibilities. And furthermore, how had the man come to

---

met Anne Boleyn in the 1530s.

the site of his death? There were no signs of wheels, or a horse, or of any other man, save the tracks that I had already mentioned. How did the stranger find himself there, more than a quarter of a mile from a road or a house or even a tall tree, without breaking the snow or leaving a track?

All these details I jotted down, and felt that Holmes himself could not have been more adroit in collecting his facts. I then put myself in Holmes' shoes. If he was on the scene, he would have considered how the murderer placed the body in this precise spot. I used my imagination, which Holmes' had often accused me of possessing to an overactive degree, to think about how I would undertake it. And from what I saw there were only two possibilities.

"Have you found anything of note, Doctor?" asked Lestrade when the silence had grown overlong.

"Beside the fact that he was a user of morphia and that he worked with tarred ropes, like a sailor, no there is nothing."

"Yes, we noted those signs on his hands and arms as well. Anything else?"

I am, in my advancing years, finally developing a subtle wisdom. I did not live for years with Sherlock Holmes for nothing and had learned to keep my own counsel. But I deigned to dole out a further pair of clues to Lestrade.

"I say, Inspector, what direction did the wind blow last night?"

"The wind?" he spluttered. "What does the wind have to do with anything?"

I shrugged. "I think the wind's direction may be as critical as the light of the moon."

"But it was a cloudy night with the snowstorm," protested Lestrade. "The moon would have been blotted out."

"That is what is so critical," I replied cryptically. Already in my mind the mystery was beginning to define itself, as figures grow clearer with the lifting of a fog. But what horrible purpose, what deep design, lay behind these events, and how did they relate to the plot that revolved around my friend?

Determining that there was nothing more to see at the location of the incident, Lestrade and I took the dog-cart back to Egham Station and there caught a train for the twenty miles back to Waterloo.

§

When I finished listing the details to Holmes, I then proceeded to expound upon my theory. "And so, as I see it Holmes, there are very few methods by which the body of this unfortunate man could have ended up on that snow-covered hill."

"Pray tell," said he, with hooded eyelids.

"One possibility is that his body was launched there, by something like a catapult or trebuchet."

Holmes broke into a whimsical laugh. "Oh, Watson, I fear you are reading far too many adventure tales. This is not the Middle Ages![78] Do you think one of Runnymede's neighbors is planning a siege? I ask you now, is such a theory tenable?"

It took all my self-control not to smile. "I said, Holmes, that this was only the first possibility. I did not say it was the most likely."

"And what is?"

"The key to this mystery is that the death of this man and the theft of the goldbeater's skin are linked. For I recalled that goldbeater's skin has another use beyond that of making gold leaf. It is also used to line and make airtight the reservoir bag used for the inhalation of the chloroform anesthetic.[79] If it could contain a small quantity of gas, surely it could also be employed to create something much larger, something large enough to lift a group of men into the sky?"

"An aeronautical balloon!" exclaimed Lestrade.

"Southwest of Runnymede, from which direction the wind is most often blowing,[80] there is, the town of Farnborough. I believe that is the location of the Army School of Ballooning,[81] having moved there from the enclosed Aldershot site, after first being established three decades ago at Woolwich Arsenal. I would inquire there, Inspector, whether they are missing an engineer," I concluded.

"Brilliant, Watson!" said Holmes. "A veritable triumph! You have demonstrated that you have finally mastered my methods. It proves that it can be done. The only problem is that you are of my same age. I should

---

[78] Examples of such adventure tales would necessarily include *The White Company* (1891) and *Sir Nigel* (1906), both penned by Sir Arthur Conan Doyle, Watson's first literary agent.

[79] This use was invented by Dr. Joseph Thomas Clover (1825-1882), one of the pioneers of anesthesia, in 1862.

[80] According to the Meteorological Office, the wind around London is most often out of the south west (20% of the time), the west (20% of the time), and occasionally the south (16% of the time) or the north (11% of the time). Despite Holmes' allusion to the contrary, an east wind is rare (*His Last Bow*).

[81] Large quantities of goldbeater's skin were used to make the gas bags of early balloons created by the Royal Engineers at Chatham, Kent starting in 1881–82. The method of preparing and making gas-tight joins in the skins was known only to a family from Alsatia called Weinling, who were thus employed by the Royal Engineers for many years. The British had a monopoly on the technique until around 1912.

have perhaps trained some younger person to do the same." He shook his head. "Now we must hope that my magnum opus, *The Whole Art of Detection*, will accomplish the same."

"Then you agree?" I said, somewhat surprised to find that for once in our long association Holmes actually concurred with my deductions.

"Oh, yes. Clearly this man was employed at the Ballooning School as you suggested. His salary however, could hardly match the cost of his opioid habit, so he was forced to supplement it by working for our Mr. Wild, or Mortlock, or whatever we shall call him. The villains were practicing a moon-less run last night, when the man must have heard too much, or became suspicious of their plans. He was therefore jettisoned over the fields of Runnymede."

"But, Mr. Holmes," cried Lestrade, "would not the Army know if one of their balloons suddenly went missing?"

"Not if they made their own," I pointed out.

Holmes looked thoughtful and remained in silence for some moments. "Well, Watson, there is this to be said for your theory. It does tie together many of our loose threads. It explains why the goldbeater's skin was stolen and what was hidden in that Lambeth Gardens shed. It even explains the theft of Mr. Mac's hydrogen gas. But it still does not tell us who is behind this masterful plot. I don't suppose, Lestrade, you have any more peculiar crimes that you have yet to share with us?"

"Well, now that you mention it, Mr. Holmes, there is one."

"Oh, yes?" said Holmes, with some interest.

"Something notable vanished from the Scotland Yard Museum a few nights ago."

I laughed. "You have a museum at Scotland Yard?"

"Indeed, Doctor. It is where we keep all of those objects that we confiscate from the scenes of notable crimes. And the particular object that was stolen could be considered the pièce de résistance of our little collection. It is the famous air-gun of Von Herder."

Holmes sprang upright, apparently thunderstruck by Lestrade's news. "Moran!" he exclaimed.

These words sent a chill to my heart. "Surely he is dead by now?"

"No, Watson, it would take a mighty force to bring down that old *shikari.*"

"But was he not given the death sentence for his murder of the Honorable Ronald Adair?"

Holmes shook his head. "There was a commutation of his sentence due to some political maneuvering on behalf of his father, the former Minister to Persia. I am afraid, Watson, that Moran is very much alive."

"But he must be in prison?"

"So I was led to believe, however, I think we must now verify whether or not this actually remains true." He refused to speak another word, but sat with his chin upon his breast, and his eyes closed, sunk in the deepest thought. I had the sensation of an unseen force, a fine net drawn round us with boundless skill and care, holding us so imperceptibly that it was only at the ultimate moment that one was indeed fully ensnared in its tangles. Perhaps Holmes felt it too, for even after Lestrade finally left us, he sat motionless for so long that it seemed to me that he had forgotten my very presence.

"Watson," said he, as he finally stood. "I am about to make several telephone calls from Mycroft's splendid system. You may take this time to avail yourself of a brief rest, for I fear tonight may be a long one." He glanced at his pocket watch. "In an hour we will head out. When we do so, kindly put your revolver in your pocket. We have an excursion to make this evening, and I think it best that you go armed. You would also oblige me by bringing with you your very excellent field glass."

"What about you, Holmes? This may not be the time for loaded hunting crops or canes."

"Indeed, Watson, you will be happy to learn that I had more than just my violin sent up from the Downs. I now have my old favorite Webley with me, and I fear that it may see some use tonight."

The appointed hour flew by, and soon I found myself bundled with Holmes in the back of a brougham, on our way to some critical dénouement. The thrill of adventure was again in my heart as we dashed away through the endless succession of somber and deserted streets, which widened gradually, until we were flying across a broad balustrade bridge, with the murky river flowing sluggishly beneath us. Beyond lay another broad wilderness of bricks and mortar, its silence broken only by the laughs of drunken revelers. A star or two twinkled dimly here and there through the rifts of the clouds. I suddenly recalled that tonight was Bonfire Night, the annual commemoration of the end of the Gunpowder Plot and the arrest of Guy Fawkes.[82] Soon, the sky would be filled with the lights of burning effigies and fireworks.

Holmes was monitoring our progress out of the window, his extraordinary knowledge of the by-ways of London allowing him to determine our location when all was twisted and confused to me. "We could, Watson, attempt to determine where exactly they plan to launch their airship," he explained. "Given the most common direction of the wind, it is probable that they would still choose to utilize a base to the southwest of the City, such as Spring Gardens or in the fields near

---

[82] Guy Fawkes (1570-1606) was an English Catholic who planned to assassinate King James I and blow up Parliament in the failed Gunpowder Plot.

Bedlam. But there are far too many spaces to search, and too little time, I fear. Instead, we must spring their trap. We shall be waiting for them at the locale upon which they plan to descend."

"And where is that?"

"Is that not obvious? We are here."

We had rattled through an endless labyrinth of gas-lit streets until we emerged into King William Street and the cab stopped in front of Silvester's Bank.

"But, Holmes," I protested, "I distinctly recall us crossing the Battersea Bridge. We had no reason to traverse back and forth over the Thames."

"On the contrary, Watson, we had every reason to cross the river. For our every movement is being watched. The coachman is an old associate who is aware of our quest, and who took every precaution to ensure that we threw all pursuers off of our tracks."

We were met at Silvester's by Mr. Pycroft, Inspectors Gregson and Lestrade, and six stout constables. Mr. Pycroft was shaking his head as we arrived. "I still don't understand how you propose that these thieves plan to rob us, Mr. Holmes?"

"I am afraid that you are vulnerable from above, Mr. Pycroft. I suspect that a dirigible will land a gang of men upon your roof this very night."

"Impossible. For a balloon to precisely target an area the size of our roof... it beggars the imagination."

"Not if it is powered by some engine that allows it to control its direction. Not if it is an airship."

"Do such things exist?" he asked.[83]

"They do indeed, Mr. Pycroft. It is a brave new world that hath such things in it. But what one devious mind can turn to ill-use, another equal mind can counter. And that is why I am here. Now, if you will lead us to the roof, I think the men of the Yard would like a word with the gang that plans to pay you a visit."

Hall Pycroft nodded his acquiescence to Holmes' plan, and the eleven of us climbed a series of stairs that led to the rooftop of the building. The front half of the roof was made up of the great glass vault, while the rear was flat, a perfect landing place for a balloon. From this perch we gazed out over the shadowy City, half-parchment-colored lamplight and half deep murk. Holmes attempted to utilize my field-glass, but I doubted that he could make out much. A half mile away, the dome of St. Paul's gleamed in the moonlight. Throughout the City, great roars erupted as the populace celebrated the burning of numerous effigies of poor Guy

---

[83] In fact, by 1909 airships had been in the development stage for several decades, with the first fully-controllable free flight conducted in 1884, and the first German Zeppelin in 1900. The British Army built their first dirigible in 1907.

Fawkes.

Holmes directed the constables to conceal themselves amongst the pipework, so that a descending airship would not know that they were being ambushed. He suggested that Mr. Pycroft repair below, as the gang might be armed and the initial scuffle could prove to be dangerous, but the brave man elected to remain at his post.

As Holmes and I settled into our positions, he spoke in a low whisper. "It is no coincidence that our gang has chosen this night, Watson. First of all, their propeller cannot possibly run silent; however, tonight it will be covered by the noise of the fireworks and celebrations. Secondly, the moon is full, which will aid their navigation, and if they are seen, they can hope that their device is thought to be part of the festivities. It is a brilliant plan, but they did not reckon that we would discover their target so rapidly. Now, let us see how long we have to wait. It may be several hours."

The night was bitterly cold, so that it promised to be a weary vigil. However, despite the bone-biting chill, I could not but stop and smile at the memories of similar vigils that I had staked at Holmes' side. The room at Stoke Moran, the rocks at Merripit House, the moat at Birlstone Manor, the window at Camden House, the outhouse of Woodman's Lee, the street lamp by Laburnum Villa, and so many others. No matter their length, they always had the sort of thrill about it that the sportsman feels when he lies beside the watercourse and waits for the big game to appear.

In absolute silence we crouched amongst the shadows of the rooftop, which had lengthened to the point where I could no longer even see Holmes at my side. An absolute stillness had descended upon the rooftop, save for the chimes of the surrounding churches as the hours ticked by, and the distant celebrations.

It proved, however, that our vigil was not to be so long as Holmes had led us to fear, and it ended in a very sudden and singular fashion. In an instant, without the least sound to warn us of its coming, a giant shape dropped out of the sky. Everything was painted black, but I could vaguely make out that from the gondola dropped several ropes, and down these slithered four men. Before they could move but a few steps, the Scotland Yard men jumped out of their nests and a great fracas erupted. The gang was putting up a stout resistance, and several of the constables were attempting to secure the ropes connected to the balloon, perhaps in hopes of capturing any additional members aboard. Mr. Pycroft lit a lantern near me, and with the addition of this light, I could tell that additional assistance was going to be required in order to subdue these criminals.

"Come on, Holmes!" I shouted and leapt into the fray.

As I did so, there was a strange, loud whizzing sound and the lantern exploded. I turned about in confusion, for I had heard no bullet. It was then that I realized that Holmes was missing. A cold hand seemed to close round my heart. Where had Holmes gone? He would have only deserted this critical post for an even more pressing duty.

Focusing my attention back upon the raging conflict, I realized that the Inspectors had ordered their men to abandon the airship and instead focus on capturing the four men that had comprised the villain's erstwhile 'boarding party.' This maneuver well underway, I could plainly see that the gang was soon to be fully subdued, even as the airship slowly drifted away back up into the sky. It was then that I heard a cry echo out from the top of the nearby Monument to the Great Fire.[84] Gazing towards that massive column, I realized that a struggle was taking place upon its viewing platform two hundred feet in the air. At least three men were involved, one of which could only be the wayward Holmes.

Abandoning the men of Scotland Yard and Mr. Pycroft, I dashed for the stairs back down to Pudding Lane. Injuries and advancing years may have stolen much of the former swiftness from my feet, but there were no signs of those ailments on that night. I flew downwards and out of the bank as if chased by the very hounds of Hades. Within moments I was at the entrance to the narrow spiral staircase within the great Doric column. I ran frantically up the stairs, scarcely realizing the magnitude of the feat, and little caring how winded I would be when I finally reached the top. Sheer terror pumped the blood through my veins, and within minutes I burst out onto the platform.

"It is most good of you to join us, my dear Watson," said that well-known voice. "I hope you do not feel the same as other biographers, and find this place monstrous, for I think the view above London and its spires to be quite refreshing.[85] Would you care for a pipe?"

There I was stunned to see Sherlock Holmes calmly standing and smoking his second-favorite pipe. With Holmes was a huge, coarse, red-faced, scorbutic man, whose pair of vivid black eyes were the only external sign of the very cunning mind within. I knew him at once as Shinwell Johnson, the dangerous villain later turned ally and agent of Holmes.

---

[84] The Monument to the Great Fire of London is a 202-foot tall Doric column which stands at the junction of Monument Street and Fish Street Hill, 202 feet from the spot in Pudding Lane where the Great Fire started on 2 September 1666. Completed in 1677, it is the tallest isolated stone column in the world.

[85] The Edinburgh-born writer James Boswell visited the Monument in 1763 to climb the 311 steps to what was then the highest viewpoint in London. Halfway up, he suffered a panic attack, but persevered and made it to the top, where he found it 'horrid to be so monstrous a way up in the air, so far above London and all its spires.'

Johnson appeared very interested in something occurring over the side of the railing, so I joined him there.

The shocks continued when I found myself staring into the malevolent glare of a pair of blazing deep blue eyes. These belonged to an elderly man who was hanging on to the edge of the rail with both hands, the knuckles white with tension. He possessed a fierce, aggressive nose, a high, bald forehead, and a huge grizzled moustache. His face was gaunt and swarthy, scored with deep, savage lines. I immediately recognized our old enemy, Colonel Sebastian Moran.

Moran's features worked convulsively as he stared at me. Then he burst into a bitter laugh that marked the cold composure of despair. "You fiend! You clever, cunning fiend! What now, Holmes? Do you plan to wait for my strength to fade and allow me to plunge to my death? That seems to be your *modus operandi* when dealing with foes that you cannot outwit."

Holmes snorted with amusement. "You are a fine one to talk, Colonel Moran. You who have had little qualms with shooting innocent men, either in order to ensure that your card cheating went unnoticed, or simply for financial gain. You have more blood on your hands than there is water in the Ganges with which to wash it off. The world would be a safer, better place with your crumpled corpse lying on the Eastcheap Road. But as for your fate, I think we should let Dr. Watson decide."

"Me?" I cried. "Why ever should it rest in my hands?"

"You were his original captor, Watson. If Moran had not of late been set loose to again terrorize London, he would still reside where you had safely locked him away. Do you wish to return him to that state, or should he pay the ultimate price for his murder of your poor balloonist? I care little, as long as he is declawed. However, I do think this beauty," said he, hefting the powerful air-gun with its curiously misshapen butt, "undoubtedly requires a more secure location that some dusty shelf in Scotland Yard."

I stared at the dangling man, who had carried out so much evil in his ill-spent life. Innumerable murders, and multiple attempts upon the life of my friend, suggested that Moran little deserved to live. And yet, such power over life and death should not rest in the hands of one man. I would have him face a jury, who could hardly fail to convict him for his great crimes. "Haul him up, Mr. Johnson, if you please."

The sizable man shook his head, but followed my orders after a quick confirmatory glance in the direction of Holmes. As soon as Moran was tossed upon the floor of the platform, Holmes sprang forward and with a sharp click and jangling of metal, Moran found himself locked in a pair of glittering steel handcuffs. "You will be interested to note, Colonel Moran, that a better man than you has also worn those cuffs. They are of my own design, and I recently liberated them from the same museum where you came by your old air-gun. I had donated them to the Yard after they were used to capture Mr. Jefferson Hope, in the first adventure in which I was joined by my Boswell. Since that man just saved your life, you may now show your gratitude to Dr. Watson, if you so wish."

Moran's response was an incoherent snarl of frustration and hatred.

Holmes shrugged. "Well, no matter. As to you, Watson, I owe you every atonement for having allowed your natural curiosity to remain so long unsatisfied. Should we now escort the good Colonel here back to our friends on the roof of Silvester's Bank? They must be wondering to where we have vanished."

As I followed him, Johnson, and their prisoner down the stairs I contemplated what had just transpired. "But, Holmes, why did you depart Silvester's, and furthermore, why not inform me of your plans?"

"My dear Watson, you were born to be a man of action. Your instinct is always to do something energetic. I was concerned you would not be able to stay your hand, when we needed Colonel Moran to declare his attentions to the world. We have little proof that he was involved in the matter at Runnymede, but we now have the word of two respected Chief Inspectors of Scotland Yard that Colonel Moran was taking shots at them."

"If I was trying to hit them, they would be dead already," snarled Moran.

"So you say, Colonel. Perhaps your aim is, in fact, still that steady after all these years. But you have learned little in the way of guile. I am surprised how easily I sprung your trap and ensnared you in one of mine own making." Holmes turned to me. "The wax model of Monsieur Meunier would hardly serve in this setting, of course, Watson, but the good colonel knew that where-ever strode Dr. John H. Watson, Sherlock Holmes would not be far behind. That is the other reason I had you remain on the rooftop, for your very presence distracted Moran from realizing that I was creeping up behind him. And of course, I have little forgotten that Moran here might have gotten the better of me at Camden House if you had not intervened. Therefore I brought Mr. Johnson here to ensure that we had the upper hand." The large former ruffian smiled severely at the mention of his name.

"And what now, Holmes?" I asked.

"Let us see precisely whom Lestrade and Gregson have caught in their nets."

Once we had made our way back to Silvester's Bank, we found the lobby swarming with constables. To one side lay several coils of rope and a pile of the muffled tools utilized by cracksmen, clearly how they planned to penetrate the vault door. Next to these was a stiff tube about eight feet in length, whose exact role in the planned robbery was to me not immediately apparent.

Four familiar-appearing men were fully bound and under heavy guard. The first was a middle-sized, dark-haired, dark-eyed, black-bearded man, with a large hooked nose, while the second was of such a similar look that I presumed them to be brothers. Their brows glistened with perspiration, their cheeks were of the dull, dead white of a fish's belly, and their eyes were wild and staring. The first man licked his dry lips before he addressed Holmes.

"We are innocent, I swear to you," he protested sharply. "These two men shanghaied us, and forced us to help with their plans." As he spoke, I saw a gleam of from the second tooth upon the left-hand side, which had been very badly stuffed with gold. At once I knew him to be the supposed Arthur Pinner, whose true name I had never learned. Therefore, the man beside him could only be his brother Beddington, the famous forger and cracksman.

Holmes only shook his head sadly. "I am afraid that the criminal records belonging to you and your brother are far too long for any jury to believe such a preposterous story."

Meanwhile, one of the men next to Pinner appeared outraged by this accusation. He was a lithe and small man, with a pale face and a shock of very red hair. His companion, however, took it with an indifferent attitude. Of the latter, it was challenging to say his age, though he was not short of forty. He too was fairly small, but stoutly-built, with quick mannerisms. His still-boyish face was lacking in hair, though he had a white splash of acid upon his forehead, and his ears were pierced for earrings. A wicked scar crossed his throat, a wound that must have been so severe it was a great wonder that the man survived the blow which had dealt it.

"Why, Watson, if it's not our old friend, John Clay and his pal Archie!" exclaimed Holmes. "I thought I recognized signs of your handiwork in that tunnel under the Old Lady. Your attention to bracing and shoring is really quite exact. I must commend you."

"I would prefer you address me as Your Grace, Mr. Holmes. The old gent died, you know."[86]

"Yes, well, I heard you had died as well."

"Reports of my demise are greatly exaggerated,"[87] the other answered,

---

[86] John Clay was the grandson of a Royal Duke with royal blood flowing in his veins (which king produced such a wicked descendent is never specified), and by this comment appears to be implying that he has inherited the title.

[87] Clay is paraphrasing quoting Mark Twain, who said something to this effect in

with the utmost coolness. "As I see were your own, Mr. Holmes. I myself wore a black armband when I heard you were lost over the falls."[88]

Holmes smiled. "You always had a rather daring attitude, Your Grace," said he, with hardly a trace of sarcasm in his voice. "It is a great shame that you turned your cunning brain to the role of murderer, smasher, thief, and forger."

"So you say, Mr. Holmes. Only the third was ever proven."

"You draw ever closer to the hangman's noose, Your Grace."

"For a simple robbery? I think not."

"And what about murder?"

"You will have a hard time sticking such a charge upon me, Mr. Holmes, especially since I am innocent."

"That is not what Colonel Moran here just told us. He claims you pitched a man from a balloon not two nights ago, a balloon mighty similar to the one that you just arrived on."

Clay's eyes widened slightly before he glanced over at the silent Colonel. "A good bluff, Mr. Holmes, but you will have to do better than that. The sun will set upon the British Empire before an Eton man peaches on one of their own."[89]

"This may be your last chance to tell all, John Clay, before the quality of my mercy is strained past the point of no return," said Holmes, severely.

"Ah, yes, well, it has been some time since England last shed a drop of royal blood. I fear not," said he with utter insouciance.

§

As that was the last word that John Clay or the others would utter, we soon left the five captured criminals in the capable hands of Scotland Yard and decamped back to Mycroft's rooms, though Holmes was careful to take the eight foot tube with him as we left.

I remained silent during the cab ride back, turning the events of the case over in my mind. However, once we had settled in to the study's armchairs, I turned to my friend. "There are a few things, Holmes, that I still do not fully understand."

1897, in response to a false newspaper account that he was gravely ill.

[88] When the British pubic read of Holmes' supposed death in *The Final Problem*, they reportedly reacted with great despair. It was not uncommon for people to wear a black armband in mourning.

[89] Eton is the famous boarding school, established 1440 near Windsor Castle, where generations of British aristocracy were educated. Only two men are recorded in the Canon as having attended it: John Clay & Sebastian Moran.

"Pray tell, Watson."

"I see that Clay, Archie, and the Beddingtons planned to land upon the roof, cut their way through the glass dome, and then rappel down into the lobby. But how did they plan to crack the vault door while under the constant view of the guardsman in Mr. Pycroft's watchtower? Was the guard eliminated in some fashion? Or did they bribe him?"

Holmes laughed. "Neither, Watson. Your methods would have been considered by the mastermind of this scheme, but both would have been rejected as excessively risky. Mr. Pycroft did far too good a job ensuring that the guard's position was both unassailable, but also well-recompensed. I learned that Mr. Pycroft had an ingenious method of dealing with bribed guards. They were expected to report any such approaches, and said report would immediately generate a payment to the guard from the bank in the same amount offered. Only once or twice has he actually been required to pay out, for most criminals have learned that Silvester's is far too tough a nut to crack. Instead, our friends employed a rather curious strategy, which can be found within this tube." He hefted the eight-foot long cylinder.

"What is it?"

"See for yourself, Watson." Holmes unscrewed the end and drew forth a rolled canvas. It proved to be a perfect reproduction of the lobby of the bank, but curiously devoid of any people. I immediately recognized it.

"The painting of Mr. Silvester!" I exclaimed.

"Very good, Watson. Yes, I recognized the hand of Victor Lynch, the forger, in the brush strokes of the supposed Achille Pendré. It was then I realized how they planned to fool the watchtower guard – by showing him the empty lobby that he expected to see each time he peered through the grill."

"And what were they trying to steal from Silvester's?"

"Ah, now you come to the heart of the problem, Watson. Given the involvement of Colonel Moran in this matter, one cannot but wonder if perhaps his old master had stashed some old deposit box within? One that escaped the attention of both myself and Inspector Patterson when we were cataloging the list of his assets. It would be curious to identify it and see what secret documents lie within."

"So you believe Moran to be the mastermind? Is he our Mortlock?"

"Honestly, Watson, I reject that possibility. Moran is a weapon. He can be pointed at something or someone, but he is no brilliant thinker. I fear that we may be putting out small fires when we enable the arrest of Windibank, Parker, Clay, Archie, the Beddingtons, and even Moran himself. But the bonfire still blazes. We have yet to identify the man himself, and I am certain that he still possesses forces that he has kept in reserve. The question is where shall he deploy them next?"

I had no answer for this question, but we had not long to wait before our secret adversary reared his head. The door to the study opened and Mycroft's ancient butler, Stanley, appeared with a note for Holmes. It had been folded over twice and sealed with a red wax pressed down with an 1889 Victoria Jubilee Crown coin. The note was superscribed to "Sherlock Holmes, Esq. To be left 'til called for." It was written upon ordinary cream-laid paper without an identifying watermark. My friend tore it open, and we read it together. It was not dated, and ran in this way:

> *atuaoltrnfntaxeenwieimeaefgieoihrfritnoetigohetiirsntraeya eehrmryulfrmsprmeyaanlytsdrauyaethkdmevhnsopiohdhe felaceaogtohlpeeothtiliegmneoaafhttodtsuyortte.*
> *- MORTLOCK*

Holmes studied this for some minutes, his face grave with unease. Finally, he set it down, and looked over at me. "As you are aware, Watson, I am familiar with virtually all forms of abstruse cryptograms, from the absurdly simple extra words of Mr. Beddoes, to the fiendishly clever little men of old Patrick. I believe, from the frequency distribution of the characters, that this is a rail-fence cipher. You can see that Mr. Mortlock has given us a fairly long strand to work with, and we can thus tell that the letter 'E' appears no less than twenty times. As 'E' is the most common letter in the English alphabet, one can hypothesize that this is not a complex polyalphabetic cryptogram, such as was devised by Mousier Vigenère,[90] where one letter is substituted for another using multiple shifting alphabets. Rather this is a transposition, where the plain-text is written downwards and upwards on successive rails of an imaginary fence, with the cipher-text then read off in horizontal rows. It is an ancient technique, dating back to the *scytale* rods of the Greeks, and has been widely used in recent wars as a battlefield code.[91] It is easy to decrypt if you know the number of rails used by the authors, and even without that key, it can be done by brute force and sufficient time."

"But we have the key," said I quietly.

"We do?" he exclaimed.

"Try 'Four.' As in 'The Sign of.'"

He stared at me for a moment, a curious expression upon his face. He then bent to work for some time at the table. Finally he looked up and

---

[90] Blaise de Vigenère (1523-1596) was a French diplomat who served under King Henri III and invented a new cipher in order to protect sensitive documents.
[91] Such as during the American Civil War, primarily by the Confederate side.

handed to me a piece of paper, covered with agitated scribblings that were far removed from Holmes' usual precise hand. I had to mentally insert spaces in order to form the string of letters into words, and when I had done so, the result turned my blood cold:

> *Again I tell you, it is harder for a guilty man to enter the kingdom of heaven than it is for a sphinx to thread the eye of a needle.*[92] *What crimes are you guilty of, Mr. Holmes? Prepare to meet thy fate.*
> *- MORTLOCK*

"What does it mean, Holmes?" I whispered.

He looked at me, his face a somber mask. "It is a threat, of course, but from whom exactly I still cannot be absolutely certain. Not yet. I now hold in my hands several of the scarlet threads that are running through the tangled skein of one of the strangest cases which ever perplexed a man's brain, and yet I lack the one or two which are needful to complete my theory. But I will have them, Watson, I'll have them!"

§

---

[92] A paraphrase of: 'Again I tell you, it is easier for a camel to go through the eye of a needle than for a rich man to enter the kingdom of God' (*Book of Matthew*, 19:23-26).

THE FALLING CURTAIN

A great man is dead. The embodiment of his age, with his passing marks a close to that era. And with this fallen curtain comes the realization that I too may have outgrown my usefulness on this earth. What little remains is for me to attempt to finish the documentation of as many of the adventures that Holmes and I shared together as I have breath to write and, of course, which are not of so sensitive a nature to reveal to the world.

I refer, of course, to King Edward VII, son of our beloved Queen Victoria, who had passed the throne to him a short nine years earlier. The date was 6 May 1910. The King had been ill for months, even collapsing while visiting Berlin and France weeks earlier, though certainly no mention of this was made in the press. He returned to Buckingham Palace, where he suffered several attacks of severe angina pectoris. But he refused to rest, saying: "No, I shall not give in; I shall go on; I shall work to the end." What glorious courage!

Two weeks later, Edward VII was buried under the intricate Perpendicular Gothic stone vaulting at St George's Chapel in Windsor Castle. His funeral marks the greatest assembly of rank and royalty ever gathered in one place and, as the sun sets upon the Isles of Scilly, it is well to ponder whether we should ever witness such a thing again.

I know all of this because I was there, accompanying my friend Sherlock Holmes. For he had finally accepted the knighthood that he so richly deserved, and yet had resisted for so long.[93] The incidents of those

---

[93] The precise services for which Holmes was offered and refused a knighthood are not yet known. However, Watson makes clear that they took place in 1902 (*The Adventure of the Three Garridebs*).

days which led to this honor are indelibly graven with fingers of fire upon my recollection, and I can tell them without any need for consulting my notes from the time. Although the events that I am about to set down occurred over five months prior, it was not until now that I felt capable of setting it down properly, so wracking was the experience to my mind. But when I went down to Fulworth last week to visit Holmes, he encouraged me to finally lay this adventure before the public. As such support from Holmes for my publications is quite rarely obtained; I will therefore endeavor to do so before his permission is revoked.

The events in question began on a wild, tempestuous night towards the close of November. Several weeks had passed since the capture of James Windibank at the British Museum, and subsequently the arrest of both John Clay and Colonel Sebastian Moran near the Great Fire Monument. But Holmes seemed no closer to discovering the identity of the mastermind who had set these men and their robberies in motion. Holmes' mood could, generously, be described as foul. I doubted that there were many others who would tolerate such a houseguest, though Mycroft's long absences at Whitehall and the Diogenes Club likely explained much of his forbearance. Even I, who was long familiar with Holmes' irascible temperament, found myself longing for a return to Southsea. After some particularly tuneless scratching upon his violin, which had been sent up from his villa by his housekeeper, I forcibly suggested that Holmes take a turn around St James's Park in order to help clear his mind. Holmes studied me for a moment, and then smiled. "I think I am not the only one who is brooding over the inaction of the last few days, am I, Watson? Every possible lead has dried up, and we seem to be at an impasse."

"Perhaps Mortlock has abandoned his schemes?" I ventured, referring to the mysterious individual whose coded messages portended grim threats against Holmes' life.

Holmes shook his head. "Even if that were true, Watson, there is still the small matter of recovering the artifacts removed from the Museum, and the gold liberated from the Bank of England. I cannot desert the field when such a crucial mystery remains unsolved."

I smiled at his not-insignificant conceit. "Then what is your plan of attack?"

"An excellent question, Watson, and one I have been pondering for some time now. But inspiration has not been summoned by the powers of the strings, so perhaps you are right. I shall attempt some other method of stimulating my mind, and if a walk does not serve, then I think a pile of pillows and two ounces of shag tobacco may perhaps do so. Would you care to join me?"

I waved him off, eager to have some uninterrupted time to myself, so that I might pen a letter. As I noted, we were, at the time, still residents in the Pall Mall rooms belonging to Holmes's brother, a domestic arrangement which was now marking its fourth week. My understanding wife had, of course, been apprised of the attempt upon Holmes's life, and while understandably nervous for my own safety, she comprehended that I could not possibly forsake Holmes in his hour of need. Nevertheless, to quell her fears, I sent daily reports of our progress, which was unfortunately, very scant of late.

After this task was complete, I attempted to emulate Holmes by reading the accounts of the daily newspapers in hopes of spotting some small anomaly or clue which might have escaped his attention but, if located, would give us one more datum for use in pinpointing the identity and location of our secret adversary. After the span of some fruitless forty minutes, I had just thrown the *Evening Standard* aside when the tall, spare figure of my friend stumbled into the room, his lip cut, an enormous discolored lump upon his forehead, and his left coat-sleeve drenched with blood.

I sprang up and caught Holmes just as he was about to collapse to the carpet. Calling out for Stanley, Mycroft's ancient butler, I guided Holmes to the settee. I rolled up his shirt-cuff, exposing his thin, sinewy arm, whose innumerable puncture-scars along its veins were now obscured by the presence of a terrible cut from a serrated knife. Once Stanley appeared, I ordered him to bring me all of the carbolized bandages and alcohol that he could procure. As soon as these were in hand, I proceeded to tend to Holmes' wound.

Holmes finally stirred and smiled. "Thank you, my dear Watson. I hope this is the last time that I have need of your astute judgment and medical talents."[94]

"What happened, Holmes?" I exclaimed.

"I was foolish, Watson. I thought I saw someone trailing us yesterday evening, when we left the performance of *Lucia* at Opera House.[95] But I paid him little mind, for we were only coming straight back here, and our base of activity is far from secret, what with the constant comings and goings of Gregson and Lestrade."

"But why did you not accost the man then, when I was there to assist?"

Holmes shook his head irritably. "No, no, Watson. That would have

---

[94] While Watson can be seen attending to the wounds of Victor Hatherley and others, he never records treating Holmes himself, so this may be an allusion to another unrecorded case.

[95] This is presumably a reference to Donizetti's *Lucia di Lammermoor*, the performance given at the Royal Opera House on Bow Street.

served little purpose. I knew that the man would be a little more than a flunky, no more entrusted with the true identity of his employer than a barnacle knows the name of the ship to which it is attached. However, this evening I made a critical error. I ignored the crying in my ear."

While it was not quite as troubling as 'oysters,' these nonsensical words were said in all seriousness. Given that Holmes presently had little reason to persuade me that he was dying, I was suddenly much concerned that Holmes had suffered a concussion in the attack.[96] I would need to employ every possible strategy to calm his nerves, in hopes of preventing this damage from escalating to a florid case of brain fever. Such a thing might knock him out of commission for weeks. "It is all right, Holmes. Let me see you to your bed. A tincture of laudanum will help you recover."[97]

Holmes chuckled softly, wincing at the pain that such laughter brought on. "Do not fear, Watson. I assure you that I am in full possession of my faculties. I suppose that I never told you of the technique that I learned while studying with the grand Llama in Tibet? It is a talent that they have developed, which warns them that an avalanche is about to crash down the mountain. When a skilled local hears a crying in his ear, he realizes that it is time to move away from the dangerous area. I in turn should have recognized that my old enemies are resurfacing and that one would soon make such a move. But I disregarded the warning and went for a walk in the very park where he might expect to find me. That is where I was set upon."

"Surely your knowledge of boxing and baritsu...."

"Unfortunately, Watson, baritsu is of only partial utility against the attacks of a ferocious hound."

I frowned in confusion. "This is hardly the mauling of a dog attack, Holmes. This is a cut from a knife."

"Ah, yes, it was while I was occupied with fending off said hound that his master crept in for the kill. First he landed the vicious backhander which I am afraid has not improved the symmetry of my face. He then flew at me with his knife, and I had to grass him twice, procuring this cut along my arm for my troubles. He had rather more viciousness than I gave him credit for."

"Who did?"

"Harry Peters, also known as the Rev. Dr. Shlessinger."

"Peters! I thought he and his hideous wife were in jail?"

"Unfortunately, it seems like that scheming pair must have slipped

---

[96] The term 'concussion' has been used by the medical community since the Sixteenth Century.
[97] Laudanum, a 10% tincture of opium, was much in vogue during Victorian times for treating virtually any ailment.

through the overly-slack net of Inspector Lestrade."

"So Peters is behind all of these crimes!" I exclaimed.

Holmes frowned. "Do not be absurd, Watson! Peters has a certain crude cunning, sufficient for beguiling foolish old women, but do you honestly think that his small mind could have planned the masterful thefts at the British Museum and at the Old Lady of Threadneedle Street? Do you think that Peters could convince Sebastian Moran to make another attempt upon my life? No, Peters is but another cog in this infernal machine. In order to stop its relentless motion, I need to find the central mover."

"And who is that?"

He shook his head. "That at present remains a mystery, Watson. But he knows me; that much is now certain. The warning is a useful one. Don't you see, Watson? I have been dreadfully careless. I am falling into my old patterns. Attending concerts, walking in parks – this is exactly what he expects from me. I have been playing into his hands. I have given him the weather gage.[98] But it is now time to change the battlefield to one more to our liking."

I gazed upon his aquiline face and saw an inexorable purpose in his grey eyes. I felt that an evil time might be coming upon those whom Holmes had set himself to hunt down. "As your physician, and your friend, Holmes, I must advise that you delay at least until dawn before you begin your assault. Judging by the quantity of blood upon your sleeve, you have just suffered a severe shock to your system."

He laughed. "Very well, Watson. But surely even a wounded general can dictate a few telegrams before retiring for the night?"

"I will allow that," said I, with some reluctance.

"Very good, Watson. If you would be so kind as to send round to the district messenger office for the services of their keenest lad, one that can faithfully take down some legible notes, I will relay to him the information that we require in order to plan our attack."

§

The greater part of the night's tempest had cleared by the morning, and the sun was shining with a subdued brightness through the dim veil. When I entered Mycroft's library, I knew from the pile of telegrams upon the breakfast table that Holmes had received answers to his messages of

---

[98] The weather gage is the advantageous position of a fighting sailing vessel relative to another, especially if it is in any position upwind of the other vessel. An upwind vessel is able to maneuver at will toward any downwind point. A vessel downwind of another, is much more limited in its ability to attack upwind.

the night before, though his mood had little improved. He showed few ill effects of his rough treatment the night prior beyond a healing lip, a fading bruise upon his forehead, and the bandages with which I had wrapped his left arm. As always, I was amazed by his constitutional powers, even as his age advanced in pace with my own.

"No luck, Holmes?"

He sighed. "As I have told you before, Watson, I abhor the concept of luck. A detective needs only knowledge, observation, and deduction to bring a successful conclusion to any case."

"And have you been successful?"

"Not yet, but I will. It is merely a matter of time. It is no small task, mind you. I have accumulated a vast number of enemies of the years, Watson, as anyone who knew me and my methods might expect. For every commonplace crime, such as the dilemma of Mr. Hilton Soames, there has been a more serious one. While some, such as Dr. Roylott, Captain Calhoun, Lattimer and Kemp, Jack Stapleton, and Mortimer Tregennis have shuffled off this mortal coil, there are still near a hundred men who have good reason for ending my life. Brooks and Woodhouse may take the lead in the quest for vengeance, but there are many others who stand directly behind them in the line."

"Pray tell, Holmes, what was the precise nature of your telegraphic inquires?"

"I adopted the obvious method of sending to the various prisons in which my enemies have been locked up, and thereby obtained a list of precisely who is still safely secured and who has been let slip."

"And the results?"

"Well, you will be happy to hear that Brooks and Woodhouse remain safely ensconced in **Pentonville Prison**, for starters."

I nodded my gratification at this news, and pondered who else might so desire Holmes' death. "What of Sir George Burnwell? He was a man without heart or a conscience."

"Yes, Watson, he was indeed one of the most dangerous men in England. Fortunately, he is no longer in England, for as you recall, he fled to the Continent with the poor Miss Mary Holder in tow." He waved his hand towards one of the scattered telegrams. "My sources tell me he has yet to return to our shores."

"How about Alec Cunningham and his father? They were quite the pair."

"I wholeheartedly agree, Watson. As I recall, if not for you and Inspector Forrester, my windpipe might be a tad narrower today. Fortunately, the old man is dead now, and Mr. Alec, who has all the tender qualities of a wild beast, is still a guest at Reading Gaol."

"Joseph Harrison?"

"Hah! Be glad, Watson, that you are not your friend Mr. Phelps, to have such a loving brother-in-law," said Holmes, with no small measure of irony in his voice. "That was a gentleman to whose mercy I should be extremely unwilling to trust. He was eventually picked up by Inspector Forbes and is a currently resident of Princetown."

"James Ryder?"

"Come now, Watson. Did I not tell you that Mr. Ryder was too terribly frightened to continue his life of crime? During one of those periods of inactivity which I so abhorred during my active practice, I looked in on him and ensured that he continued to walk a straight line."

"Culverton Smith?"

Holmes shook his head. "He put on a brave show through the trial, but once he was convicted and his sentence passed, the coward took a fatal dose of the *upas* poison of the Javanese mulberry tree."

"How about Jonas Oldcastle? If I recall correctly, he threatened to pay his debt to you one day."

"Unfortunately for him, Clotho cut his thread before his fully-allotted time at Parkhurst Prison expired. A far too common occurrence in those unhealthy locales, as Colonel Valentine Walter also discovered."

"But what of Hugo Oberstein, who only got fifteen years for the murder of Cadogan West?"

"Yes, which does not put him out from Portland Prison until next year. I inquired, and was assured that he has not been set loose early for good behavior."

"Williamson and Woodley?"

"The defrocked priest got only seven years for his presiding over a forced marriage, but upon release he resumed his evil ways and met his end at the hands of some, perhaps justly, outraged individual. Roaring Jack Woodley received ten years and was last seen departing for the South African mines, again striving to obtain a fortune, more honestly this time."

"Huret?"

Holmes' eyebrows rose. "The Boulevard Assassin? Guillotined by the French Republic."[99]

"Wilson?"

"The Canary Trainer? Drowned."

"Abe Slaney?"

"Deported to America. He still resides at Joliet Prison near Chicago."[100]

---

[99] Although commonly associated with the French Revolution, in fact, the guillotine remained the only legal method of execution in France until the death penalty was abolished in 1981, and it was last used in 1977.

[100] Joliet Prison was the main prison for Abe Slaney's hometown of Chicago. It

"Josiah Amberly?"

"Hung himself while awaiting trial. He beat Jack Ketch to the punch."[101]

"James Wilder?"

Holmes nodded. "A good thought, Watson, but he is still seeking his fortune in Australia. I confirmed with the Duke of Holdernesse that he has not returned to our shores."

"Reuben Hayes?"

"Hung for the murder of Heidegger."

"His wife?"

"Ah, an interesting suggestion, Watson! I confess that I do not see the hand of a woman in these matters. Save one, I have yet to encounter one that possesses the necessary degree of cunning required to set these traps."

"We could go on with this all day, Holmes," said I with some exasperation. "There must be a hundred more men whose desire for vengeance is great enough that they have sworn your death."

"Yes, Watson, so many have tried to break me for crossing them, and yet here I am. But most of them were small minds, with little ability to conceive of such grandiose and elaborate schemes."

A dreadful thought occurred to me. "I say, Holmes, could it be the Professor? Has James Moriarty returned?"

Holmes laughed sharply. "I think not, Watson. I am certain that he died in those falls, even if his body was never recovered. He lies at the bottom of Lake Brienz. Moriarty could not possibly have been silent for so many years. I would have caught a sense of his presence. When he first rose to power, I became conscious that there was a deep organizing force, from which a thousand threads led out to the individual criminal. There would be a vast web, with the Professor lurking at the center. And I do not detect the same force this time."

"But there are similarities...."

"Yes, Watson, but on a more limited scale. Here we have a person whose goal is not to set up a shadowy empire of crime, but solely to revenge themselves upon me."

"Surely, the robberies at the Bank of England and the British Museum suggest a motive to enrich themselves as well."

He shrugged. "Perhaps to a small extent. Though I suspect that these outré crimes were done more to ensure my continued presence upon the board."

I shook my head and wondered if Holmes' vanity was blinding him to the truth of the matter. To rank himself as more valuable than four and a

was built in 1858 and closed in 2002.

[101] Jack Ketch (d.1686) was an executioner for King Charles II. His name became synonymous with executioners in general.

half tons of gold bullion and the treasures of Ancient Britain was a great conceit.

"No, Watson," he continued. "I have heard these fevered dreams before. How many have tried to postulate over the years that the Napoleon of crime survived? He lurks in their brains like something vaguely horrible, all that is monstrous and inconceivably wicked in the universe. But he was human after all. He could not have survived that fall."

"So what is our next move, to continue your chess metaphor?"

"An excellent question, Watson. The stalemate has been broken. To date, we have been forced to play a defensive strategy, where we can only react to our opponent's moves. We have been unable to plan an attack, for the simple reason that we know not where his pieces are even located on the board. But it is possible that he has just made a critical error, which may shine some light upon the disposition of the battlefield."

"And what is that, Holmes?"

"By moving Peters against me, he made it very clear that this army has been purposefully assembled from my old enemies. Unhappily for him, he has also exposed his rook or perhaps even his queen, if such a term could be employed to describe the nasty piece of work that is Colonel Sebastian Moran. Windibank, Parker, Clay, Peters, they are all pawns. But Moran was once the lieutenant of Moriarty himself. If anyone knows the location or identity of the king, it will be him."

"But Holmes, you have already questioned him at length," I protested. "It has been three weeks since he was snared atop the Monument. I do not doubt that he could be concealing information from us, but how are we to extract it? Nothing has changed."

"On the contrary, Watson, much has changed. I am at death's door."

I frowned. "What are you talking about, Holmes? Even at your age, your iron constitution will have you back at peak power within a day or two."

"Ah, but whom precisely is aware of that? I was half-carried back here by a local constable, who came upon the end of the battle between Peters and I. Peters and his hound escaped, but he at least is certain that I was severely bloodied. The night was dark, so Peters has little idea of precisely how seriously he wounded me. It only remains for us to tell Moran the story we wish him to believe."

"You plan to use the press again?"

"I do indeed, Watson."

"But if you are dying, Holmes, then who will question Moran?"

He chuckled. "I must admit, Watson, that I was moved by the outpouring of emotion demonstrated by the British public when they first thought I had perished, but it is a long way from wearing an armband to confronting one of the most dangerous men in the world, even if he is safely behind bars. Mycroft would never exert himself to do it. And I have no real friends, save one. I can but think of a solitary man who would be the most distraught at my crucial wounding. You must question him yourself, Watson."

I was quite astonished at this request. "But Holmes, have you not before commented upon my lack of talent with dissimulation? Is that not why you kept me in the dark when I confronted Culverton Smith? Or when I accompanied Sir Henry to Baskerville Hall?"

He nodded. "There is no doubt, Watson, that your strengths lie in directions other than the stage. As Dr. Hill Barton, you fooled Baron Gruner for mere moments. But you have studied my methods for almost thirty years now, excepting some small hiatuses. I believe that you are ready for this role."

I was touched by this vote of confidence. "Then what must I do?"

"I have a few more telegrams to write, and we need entertain some visitors this afternoon. By the time the evening papers are printed, I think it will be time for your cue."

§

The afternoon visitors proved to be a veritable parade of the best physicians in London. Sir Leslie Oakshott, who once stitched up Holmes after the ambush at the Café Royal. Sir Jasper Meek and Penrose Fisher were finally allowed to call upon Holmes. Benjamin Lowe and Sir James Saunders, who both owed Holmes great debts. Percy Trevelyan, and even the renowned Leslie Armstrong, called out of retirement, all stopped in to see this most important of patients.

Holmes believed that our base at Mycroft's was being monitored by agents of our mysterious adversary Mortlock. Thus, if no physician other than me visited these chambers, it might give the lie to our deception. While invisible within Mycroft's curtain-drawn rooms, with only the loyal Stanley to witness what transpired, we conversed gaily with each of these eminent medicos about adventures long past. But as they departed one-by-one into their fine carriages, each man was carefully instructed to appear grave with concern. As one who had watched many lives slip through my fingers over the years, it was not a difficult emotion to conjure, simply by thinking of the still face of some once-beloved patient.

For his part, Holmes was in a merry mood as he read the agitated account in the *Evening News*, which ran as follows:

> *It is with great sadness that we report that Mr. Sherlock Holmes, the celebrated consulting detective, has been grievously wounded in an attack by persons unknown. Mr. Holmes, who retired six years past, was in London on private business. We have been informed by Inspector Lestrade of Scotland Yard that a constable on his rounds found Mr. Holmes being set upon by a ruffian and his hound while walking in St. James's Park. Given the terrible wounds sustained by Mr. Holmes, the constable rightly felt that his first priority was ensuring his safety, such that the unknown assailant has yet to be apprehended. Despite the attention of several of London's top physicians, Mr. Holmes has still to recover consciousness and his life is feared for. Scotland Yard assures the public that additional constables have been assigned to patrol St. James's Park until this villain has been caught and safely imprisoned. Inspector Lestrade states that there is absolutely no need for the public to avoid the park at this time.*

I need not say that, for my part, I read this paragraph with considerably more sang-froid than I did the last time Holmes utilized this particular strategy, when I was not forewarned about its hyperbole.

Holmes chuckled as he set the paper down. "Excellent, Watson. The stage has been set. I think it is finally time for your entrance. Gregson should be here at any moment to facilitate your appointment with the good Colonel."

As predicted, Gregson soon appeared, his face grinning with pleasure at being included in such a subterfuge. The two of us bundled into a hansom cab and, in swift progression, passed through royal London, affluent London, Bohemian London, over New Battersea Bridge, and finally through industrial London, till we came to our destination.[102]

As I entered the grey-bricked walls of Wandsworth Prison, I noted a comely-shaped woman departing from the building. She held a silken handkerchief over her face, hiding tears of shame from the world. I thought it must be a bitter blow indeed to have a loved-one locked behind those grim walls. Fortunately, my mission was not to visit a treasured

---

[102] From a glance at a map of London, it is clear that Watson is referring to Buckingham Palace, and then the boroughs of Belgravia, Chelsea, and Battersea. The New Battersea Bridge was built by Sir Joseph Bazalgette (engineer of London's sewers) in 1890, replacing the decaying but romantic old bridge which had been the inspiration of many famous painters.

relative, but rather to call upon a virulent enemy who richly deserved to be so incarcerated. At Holmes' request, Gregson had swiftly obtained for me the necessary orders and permits that allowed me access to Moran's cell.

I recalled Holmes' words as I departed Pall Mall. "Use every natural shred of cunning at your disposal, Watson," said he, sternly. "I tell you that it is his evidence which I depend upon to reveal the identity of our adversary."

Moran looked up as the door to his fetid cell opened. The glare from his blazing, deep-blue eyes was no less malevolent than every other occasion when I had the displeasure to encounter him. Although he was dressed in a shabby prison uniform, his fierce, aggressive nose, high, bald forehead, and huge grizzled moustache bestowed upon him a gravitas much out of place for his current squalid surroundings. His face was even gaunter than I recalled, and the deep, savage lines scored therein suggested that a great anger blazed within his breast. The décor of the cell was Spartan in the extreme, with nothing hung upon the dull grey walls. The table at which he sat held a pad of lined paper, a blunt-tipped fountain pen, a cigarette case, and a tray that held the remains of his evening meal. A discarded copy of the *Evening News* lay upon the floor.

He laughed cruelly when he saw me. "Ah, Dr. Watson, I expected you sooner."

"You villain!" I cried. "Are you responsible for this attack?"

"How can you blame me, Doctor?" said he, mildly. "Do you not see that my claws have been pulled?" We waved his hand around the stark cell.

"Then you know of what I speak!"

He gestured to the paper. "The amenities of His Majesties' prisons leave much to be desired, but one cannot accuse them of denying a gentleman his daily news."

"You are no gentleman!"

He laughed again. "My father, the late Sir Augustus, might argue with you on that point." He looked at me keenly. "You know, Doctor, we are not so very different, you and I. Did you yourself not formerly tread the hills of Afghanistan in the service of our beloved Queen, as I once did? Were not your friends and companions mercilessly shot down at your side for little reason? Do not a modest number of the King's shillings still ring in your pocket?"[103]

"Is that what turned you down this path of evil? Some friend of yours was killed by a Jezail bullet? Does that give you license to murder fellow

---

[103] Moran appears to be speaking metaphorically, as Watson's war pension of 'eleven shillings and six-pence a day' ran out after a span of nine months (Chapter I, *A Study in Scarlet*).

Englishmen?" I said, hotly.

His eyes blazed, but he merely smiled. "Ah, Doctor, did you come here to debate philosophy? Tell me, why is it considered honorable to shoot down savages at the orders of some distant, pampered monarch, but it is a terrible crime to use your inborn skills in order to enrich yourself at the expense of some weak fool?"

"Do you consider Holmes to be a fool?" I shouted at him.

"Any man who would challenge Professor James Moriarty could stake claim to such a title," said he, mildly.

"And yet it was Holmes that triumphed on top of those falls, not your beloved Professor."

"Did he, Doctor? Was Holmes truly the one who was triumphant? Holmes, the man forced into exile by his great fears? Holmes, the man who eventually returned to a quiet London little of his liking? Holmes, the man who even now lies at death's door as a belated retribution for his pride at challenging the Professor?"

"Are you saying that this latest attack was done by orders of Moriarty?"

He chuckled. "Oh, Doctor, don't you know that the Professor is dead? But ask yourself who stands to gain from the death of Sherlock Holmes? Not I. I am merely a tool."

"What are you talking about?"

"How do you think I came to be in possession of my favorite weapon?"

"The air-gun?"

"Very good, Doctor. A man such as me does not just stroll into Scotland Yard and retrieve it without anyone noticing."

"So who did?"

He laughed again. "If you want me to do all your work for you, Doctor, I expect to be recompensed."

"What do you want, Moran? Money? That will little help you in here."

"Want?" he suddenly yelled. "I want my life back, of course! Before Sherlock Holmes took down the Professor, I had everything I could desire in this world. I can assure you, Doctor, that fifteen years in prison made it very clear what I was missing."

"That is what I do not understand, Moran. Upon emerging from such a long spell of penal servitude, you immediately commit an act that lands you back in the same predicament?"

Moran resumed his calm attitude. "On the contrary, Doctor, I tell you that I committed no crime. Yes, I stand accused of an attempted assassination. However, I am afraid, from what you and the *Evening Standard* tells me, that my accuser may not be able to prosecute such a claim in court. I feel certain that I shall soon be once more set free.

Furthermore, with the impending change in government, I feel a shifting of the tide.[104] Perhaps an ambassadorship to some small potentate; one that will care little for the more illicit affairs of my past. I have always had a hankering for a small palace in Brunei, or perhaps the Straits Settlements."[105]

"You are bluffing!"

He snorted in derision. "Am I, Doctor? Only time will tell what cards I have in my hand, and which you have in yours. But I am afraid that your trump has already been played out, and the last trick will fall to me." He reached for a small silver case and pulled from it a cigarette. With a mocking smile, he offered one to me, but I only glared at him. He shrugged, as if little bothered by my slight and proceeded to strike a match. He puffed contentedly upon the Alexandrian cigarette for a moment, clearly waiting for me to make another move.

I stared at him in frustrated consternation. He had done nothing but taunt me, and I had learned little in return. What more could I ask that would induce him to reveal some clue to the identity of his employer? As I puzzled over this, hesitant to leave without some piece of useful information to report to Holmes, Moran began to cough.

He looked at me, his eyes wide with fear, though I could hardly understand the source of this emotion. "What have you done to me?" he exclaimed, dropping the cigarette.

"What are you talking about, Moran?"

"My lips, my tongue," he stammered, his voice starting to slur. He held up his hands in front of his face, and rubbed the tips of his fingers together. He suddenly began to retch, and then toppled out of his chair onto the floor. I sat frozen for a moment, suspicious that he might be malingering in order to induce me to lower my guard and attempt to take me hostage, but the sudden convulsion was too convincing to be fictitious. Even Henry Irving, or Holmes himself, could not have feigned such a fit. When Moran's lips began to turn blue, I knew that this attack was most serious.

Calling out for assistance, I sprang into action and attempted to support the man's airway. But the spasms in his lungs were too great for air to be forced down his bronchi. Try as I might, I could not make the man's chest rise, and within minutes I knew my effort to be futile. As two constables

---

[104] On 30 November, 1909, the House of Lords rejected the Budget, forcing a general election to be held six weeks later. This resulted only in a reduced Liberal Party majority, rather than an outright victory by some other party which Moran believed to be more sympathetic to him.

[105] Brunei was a British Protectorate from 1888 until its independence in 1984. The Straits Settlements were a group of British territories formed in 1826 and which dissolved in 1946 into Malaysia and Singapore.

watched in dismay, I reached over and felt the artery at the side of his sinewy neck. To my extreme mortification, no vital force moved through it any longer. Under my very eye, Colonel Sebastian Moran, the best heavy game shot of the Eastern Empire and the second most dangerous man in London, had been struck dead.

§

A subdued Inspector Gregson accompanied me back to Pall Mall in order to report this singular event to Holmes. We found him in Mycroft's library hunched over a map of London. His amber-stemmed pipe was reeking of a particularly poisonous shag, and he had clearly been studying it for some time.

He looked up at our entrance. "Ah, Watson, you will see that I have not been idle in your absence. I have been tracking various crimes described in the papers of the past months, the unique nature of which might suggest... I say, Watson, whatever is the matter?"

"Colonel Moran is dead," I said quietly, still shaken by what had transpired within the walls of Wandsworth Prison.

The look upon his face and his clenched hands betrayed Holmes' acute displeasure. "What!" he exclaimed. "How?"

I shook my head. "I can only assume that he was poisoned."

"Poisoned?" cried Holmes. "That should have been impossible, Gregson," said he, accusingly. "Were you not testing his food?"

"Of course we were, Mr. Holmes!"

"Then how was it introduced?"

Gregson shook his head dejectedly. "We don't rightly know."

Holmes stared at him. "I will need access to his corpse. Samples must be taken. If we can learn the identity of the poison, it will be a major clue. Poisoners are like homing pigeons, they find their favorite and stick with it. Morgan always used *aqua tofana*. Hughes, from Farnham, was a Prussic acid man. Mrs. Peterson was loyal to belladonna, *etcetera, etcetera.*"[106]

"Very good, Mr. Holmes," said Gregson. "I will speak to the examiner immediately."

Once Gregson had departed, Holmes turned to me. "Tell me everything, Watson," he commanded. "Leave out no detail, no matter how minor it might appear."

I carefully recounted everything that had transpired from the moment I entered Moran's cell. When I was finished, Holmes shook his head irritably. "It really will not do, Watson. You learned almost nothing of

---

[106] The story of Mrs. Peterson has yet to be unearthed, but we assume that she is no relation to Commissionaire Peterson (*The Adventure of the Blue Carbuncle*).

interest, and watched as our prime witness was murdered in front of your very eyes."

I was stung by this criticism, as I felt that I had done my best. "But what of Moran's claim that he was being aided by someone within the government? That they procured the air-gun for him and promised to ensure his luxurious retirement?"

Holmes scowled. "Lies and deceptions, Watson. Do you honestly believe that our own government is conspiring against me?"

I shrugged. "You have knowledge of many secrets, Holmes. Secrets pertaining to the defense of the nation, as well as the private details of Royal Houses throughout Europe. Is it not possible that someone decided that you knew too much and that the best method to guarantee your silence would be to eliminate you entirely?"

"I think not, Watson. Have I not once said that Mycroft is at times the government itself? He would know if such a wide-ranging conspiracy existed."

"But perhaps not one originating from a small handful of men?"

He sat silently for a moment, puffing on his pipe. "Perhaps not," he finally admitted.

"Then what should we do about it?"

"We should play our cards close to our vest, Watson. If we do not know who to trust within Scotland Yard, then we shall trust no one. In any case, we have nothing in which Gregson or Lestrade could possibly act upon."

The hour had grown late, and as I saw no further avenue of investigation that evening, I retired to my room, leaving Holmes gloomily hunched over his map of London.

§

In the morning, I was little surprised to find my friend seated at the dining table, plainly enjoying a hearty repast of rashers and eggs, all washed down with a prodigious amount of black coffee.

"You look cheerful this morning, Holmes. Have you come across some new piece of evidence?"

"No, but I plan to make use of the current impression that I am out of commission to conduct some clandestine inquiries in certain of the less salubrious corners of London."

"I have never known you to make such a late start when going about in disguise."

He chuckled. "An excellent observation, Watson. However, need I remind you that we are not at 221B any longer? I have no ready stock of appropriate attire and greasepaint with which to effect my transformation. I have sent out for something suitable and am awaiting its delivery."

At that moment, Stanley entered with an urgent telegram. I assumed it would be for Holmes, and was therefore startled when he handed it to me. I opened it eagerly, hoping to hear news from my wife, and was astounded to find that it was from someone else altogether. I read as follows:

8, CATHEDRAL GREEN, Wells, Nov. 29th.
Re Hags
SIR, –
As a means of personal introduction, may I recall to you that we were once classmates in the fifth form at Winchester School. From a reading of the daily papers, we have been made aware that you and your friend Mr. Holmes have returned to London, in what we can only hope is a permanent capacity. We have a terrible mystery on our hands here in Wells, with the reappearance of an ancient legend and the subsequent disappearance of a gentleman of our acquaintance. We therefore wish to call upon you at your earliest convenience and lay the matter before you.
We are, Sir,
Faithfully yours,
Dr. Basil Gennery
Curator, The Wells Natural History Society, Mendip Hills[107]

I looked up at my friend. "What do you make of it, Holmes?"

He made a noise which I interpreted to be a snort of derision. "Really, Watson, how many supposedly supernatural sightings do I need to expose via the harsh light of reason before people will stop bringing them to my doorstep? Were the events of the supposed Pharaoh's curse not less than a month ago?"

I shrugged. "There is something intrinsic to human nature, Holmes, which is attracted by the notion that there may be something mystical lurking just beyond the limits of our senses. You cannot stop it any more than you can stop the sun from rising."

"You have succinctly summarized precisely why I have retired to the South Downs. My bees comprise an eminently practical society, with none

---

[107] There is a Wells and Mendip Museum, founded 1893, located at 8 Cathedral Green in Wells. The Mendip Hills are famous for their particular geology which resulted in the highest concentration of caves in all of England.

of these absurd human failings."

But any further philosophical discussions were halted by the appearance of Stanley, who announced a visitor for me and Holmes. A glance at the man's calling card showed him to be the forewarned Dr. Gennery.

"Send him away, Stanley," ordered Holmes, irritably.

"We shall do nothing of the kind, Stanley," I countermanded. "You need not listen to the man, Holmes, but I will not turn away an acquaintance, no matter how tentative."

A resigned wave of Holmes' hand was sufficient to signal Stanley that he might see in our guest. Dr. Gennery proved to be an elderly gentleman, whose bald pate was fringed with tufts of white hair. His pale blue eyes were magnified by a pair of thick spectacles. His manner was agitated, and he seemed unsure of precisely what to say beyond the initial introductions.

Clearly Holmes did not intend to be helpful, so I took the lead. "Perhaps if you would start at the beginning, Dr. Gennery?" I said.

"Yes, of course, Doctor, you are correct." He paused for a moment, and seemed to gather his thoughts. "As you may be aware, gentlemen, the caves of the Mendip Hills are famous throughout Britain for being sites of great natural wonder and beauty, but also for their immense historical interest."

"How so?" I inquired.

"First of all, certain of these caves, such as Banwell, contain animal bones of an immense age. From them we have learned a great deal about the days when the creatures who would eventually become modern man still dragged their knuckles upon the ground. Furthermore, these caves have been occupied since the first era of prehistoric man. In Aveline's Hole, for instance, a cemetery of over two-score individuals has been unearthed from the days when the pyramids had yet to be built."

I nodded encouragingly. "I see, please proceed."

"Our troubles began roughly three weeks ago. It began with reports from the local farmers that they were witnessing strange lights at night in the area near Haybridge. Mr. Howard Kidd, my assistant, became convinced that the appearance of these lights was evidence that the fabled Haybridge Cave had been re-discovered.[108] You see, Doctor, over the years, many of these caves have attracted a series of legends. This particular cave was, as the stories go, the home of a foul spirit that haunted the countryside for miles around. This spirit formed from the mist of a

---

[108] I have been unable to verify the existence of a cave named Haybridge, but the village of Haybridge is very near Wookey Hole, which was haunted by the Witch of Wookey Hole, a sort of 'Hag of the Mist,' a Welsh spirit comparable to the Irish banshee.

pool deep within the cave, and could materialize as an old and hideous woman, whose cry would bring down terrible misfortune upon any who heard it. After many years of suffering at the hands of the Hag of Haybridge Cave, the locals finally gathered together enough gold to attract the attention of a famous monk from Glastonbury Abbey. He came and called down a powerful counter-curse upon the Hag, which sealed the entrance to her cave, so that she could go forth in the night no more."

I listened with some thrill at this tale, for it vaguely recalled the legend once laid out to us by Dr. Mortimer. "And why did Mr. Kidd think that the cave had been re-opened? Would not such a find be reported at once?"

Dr. Gennery shook his head ruefully. "People are stumbling across new caves all the time, Dr. Watson, and you are correct that most folks immediately notify the authorities. But there are some less scrupulous folk who keep the find to themselves, in hopes that their discovery may contain a treasure hoard."

"Is such a thing possible?"

He shrugged. "Not to our knowledge, Doctor. But the British countryside is replete with hoards from all manners of invaders: Romans, Saxons, Norsemen, even Royalists. It is always possible that some poor soul might have buried a hoard in one of the caves in advance of some approaching army, and was sadly never able to return and reclaim it."

I glanced over at Holmes, who appeared to be following Dr. Gennery's tale with ill-concealed scorn. "Do you think, Holmes, that this could be connected with the early British objects stolen from the Museum? Some unscrupulous collector of such treasures?"

Holmes shook his head. "It is a capital mistake to theorize in the absence of facts, Watson. For all we know, like those Neolithic animals before him, Mr. Kidd could have simply fallen down a hole from which he was unable to climb back out."

"I assure you, Mr. Holmes, that Mr. Kidd was an experienced spelunker," protested our guest.

"Even the world's greatest climber would be hard pressed to do so if his leg was broken, for example. In any case, I fail to see how we can be of assistance?" said Holmes, tersely.

Dr. Gennery licked his lips. "Well, Mr. Holmes, it is the impression of the board of directors that something foul is afoot. I am not saying that there is any truth to the legend of the Hag, mind you. As a man of science, my first inclination is to discount such notions in favor of a more rational explanation. But Mr. Kidd vanished for a reason, and we mean to see that he is found. And there is no doubt that you are the best man in England when it comes to getting to the bottom of a mystery."

I have mentioned previously that Holmes was on occasion susceptible to such flattery, but in this case, he resisted it. "You are correct, of course, Dr. Gennery. However, if your tale is accurate, then your case is a timely one if you wish to find Mr. Kidd alive. I am afraid that I am unable to offer assistance at the present instant, for my attention must remain fixed in London."

"Perhaps I could go, Holmes?" I volunteered.

Holmes peered at me for a moment. "You feel strongly about this, Watson?"

"I do," I replied, nodding vigorously.

"Very well," Holmes slowly agreed. "But I cannot spare you either. For there is no one else I trust fully in the present matter."

"But we cannot fail to assist Dr. Gennery and Mr. Kidd," I protested, waving my hand at the anxious curator sitting before us.

"No, you are correct, Watson. Fortunately, I have someone who owes me a very great favor, and I am willing to call it in now."

"Who is that?"

"Barker."

"Your rival from the Surrey shore?"

"Exactly. He is not in my league, of course, but he is also not without some small merits of his own. I will wire to him and ask him to join you, Dr. Gennery, at Haybridge immediately. I am confident that he can rapidly solve your little mystery."

Dr. Gennery looked somewhat disappointed by this decision from Holmes, but as I saw him to the door, I assured him that Holmes was understating Barker's talents. For no detective could be seriously considered a rival of Holmes without also possessing a very great deal of both acumen and skill.

§

Holmes had no sooner dispensed with dictating his promised wire to Barker when Mycroft and Inspector Lestrade appeared. Considering how we were staying in Mycroft's rooms, it was no small irony to see him approaching his brother like any other client in need.

"Mr. Holmes, Mr. Mycroft and I are in need of your assistance with a small matter," said Lestrade.

Holmes sighed and glanced at his brother. "Really, Mycroft. I am engaged at the moment. Can you not figure it out yourself?"

The elder Holmes shrugged. "Perhaps I have spent too long pondering the intricate dance of nations, Sherlock, but I fail to see how precisely it was done. I think this is more along your line of expertise."

"Very well. Pray tell what great catastrophe has occurred."

"A train has gone missing," said Lestrade, with some hesitancy.

Holmes laughed. "Trains do not go missing, Inspector. People go missing. But the British railway companies take great pains to ensure that their trains fail to vanish from sight."

"Yes, well, technically it was only the brake van[109] and rear-most carriage."

"A prank?" I interjected. "Some bored aristocrats, perhaps?"

Lestrade shook his head. "The train was moving at the time."

Holmes' eyebrows rose, a sure indication that his interest had been piqued. "Do you mean to say, Lestrade, that a moving train lost its final two cars and no one knows what happened to them?"

"That is exactly correct, Mr. Holmes. At first it was thought that they must have become uncoupled by some freak accident. But in that case, the next train along would have happened upon them."

"And that did not occur?"

"Not at all. The line superintendent then feared that the cars somehow ran off the tracks, but a close inspection of the entire length revealed that no such thing occurred."

"How many people are missing?"

"Only one. The guard."

"So it was a freight train? It must have been carrying something quite valuable for my brother to become involved." He glanced over at Mycroft.

The man chuckled, his corpulent belly shaking with rueful mirth at Holmes' perception. "That is correct, Sherlock. This train had originated at Waltham Abbey."

"Is that not where King Harold Godwinson was buried after the Battle of Hastings?" I asked.[110]

Holmes looked at me queerly. "I never get your limits, Watson. Why exactly you chose to clutter your brain with such unimportant trivia is beyond me. I presume that Mycroft is more concerned with a certain factory that sprung up at Waltham after the monks were dissolved from their lands by good King Henry?"

Mycroft nodded his agreement, while Holmes proceeded to explain. "You see, Watson, there are only three Royal Gunpowder Mills on our shores. Faversham in Kent, Ballincollig in Ireland, and Waltham Abbey. For reasons of security, their identities remain largely unknown to the general public, though of course, those with an especial interest in methods of violence are aware of their existence. It was from the

---

[109] The brake-van is the equivalent of an American 'caboose.'

[110] The last Anglo-Saxon King of England, Harold Godwinson was killed on 14 October 1066 by the Norman invaders under William the Conqueror.

idyllically-named Waltham Abbey that poured the agent which stoked the engine of the three wars: against Napoleon, in Crimea, and against the Boers. So I assume that a load of gunpowder was seized from the missing van?"

"It was guncotton, actually" replied Mycroft. "Bound for Canary Wharf, where a ship would take it to Gibraltar."

Holmes frowned. "An odd thing to steal, don't you think, brother? Useful for the Royal Navy, of course, but hardly to the common criminal. Especially as dynamite is much more stable, and therefore far safer if you plan to blow up a bank door."

"We are not here to debate why they stole it, Sherlock," said Mycroft testily. "We are here to determine how it was done."

"Then tell me the precise details, if you will."

"The train set out as usual at five minutes past three o'clock," began Lestrade.

"Do you mean to say that they have regularly transported this highly dangerous substance at a predictable time? That was most careless of them."

"Yes, I have already brought this to the attention of the Comptroller of the Mills," interjected Mycroft. "The man pleaded difficulties of avoiding conflicts with passenger trains coming from the north, but that is simply no excuse. This practice has been discontinued effective immediately."

Holmes nodded. "Pray continue."

Lestrade continued his narration. "The train passed through Enfield Lock on schedule and without incident. The station master confirms that the brake van was still attached. Same with Brimsdown and Ponders End. The master at Angel's Road admitted, under some pressure, to being asleep at the time, while the man at Park was occupied by a call of nature. So it was the master at Tottenham Hale who was the one that finally noticed the missing van. He telegraphed ahead to Stratford station, which signaled for the advancing train to stop.[111] An inspection quickly confirmed that the last two vans had been uncoupled. But the van and carriage could not have travelled far under their own power."

"Was the guard a loyal man?"

Mycroft nodded. "In point of fact, he was a relatively new hand."

Holmes sat for a moment with his fingers pressed together and then leapt from his seat, his injuries of two nights prior apparently forgotten. He pulled out a few of the drawers built into the bookcases, obviously searching for something.

Mycroft watched him with some consternation. "I say, Sherlock, you

---

[111] Clearly not the far-more-famous Stratford-upon-Avon, but rather the similarly-named London suburb of Stratford.

do realize that you are ransacking my own library? If you are looking for something in particular, you need only ask."

"Never mind, Mycroft. I have it here." Holmes had pulled out a rolled sheet of paper which, when opened, proved to be a map of greater London. He looked at it for a moment and then laughed. "Really, Lestrade, it is one of the elementary principles of practical reasoning that when the impossible has been eliminated, the residuum, however improbable, must contain the truth. It is certain that the train left Ponders End intact, is it not?" He pointed to a spot on the map. "It is certain that the final cars did not reach Tottenham Hale, here," said he, pointing again. "It is the highest degree unlikely, but still possible, that it may have taken one of the available side rails, though an external source of power must have been supplied. It is obviously impossible for a train to run where there are no rails, and therefore, we may reduce our improbables to any open lines that cross it."

Mycroft was shaking his head. "We don't need you to tell us that, Sherlock. There are no open lines. They have all been closed since the printing of that particular map."

Holmes looked taken aback at this piece of information. He spent a few minutes filling his pipe with shag tobacco and puffed at it silently while contemplating the paper before him. Finally he pulled the pipe out from between his lips and smiled. "But there are closed lines, are there not?" he asked calmly.

"What good are closed lines?" spluttered Lestrade. "Their rails have been pulled up. The train did not fly over them!"

But Mycroft seemed to follow his brother's train of reasoning. "Are you suggesting that some gang of criminals employed platelayers to replace the rails that previously connected a side-line, making it once more temporarily operational?"

Holmes nodded. "I confess that I am unable to suggest any other solution. I should certainly advise you to direct all your energies towards looking for such a closed line. The criminals would have removed the new rails afterwards, of course, in order to cover their tracks. But that particular stratagem would have afforded them the time required to set a pump-trolley upon the tracks.[112] They could then use it to push the cars onto the side rail, unload the carriage of its contents, and then dispose of the cars themselves. A dredging of the Tottenham Marshes might possibly bring some suggestive facts to light."

§

---

[112] In America, more popularly known as a handcar.

Once Lestrade and Mycroft had departed Holmes appeared to be in a better mood, despite these interruptions which had no relevance to the primary matter at hand. Perhaps the intellectual besting of his brother, often acknowledged to be his superior in intellect, sufficed to restore some of his confidence. He rose, and taking up his Stradivarius from the corner, he began to play a Dvořák Humoresque. I have always enjoyed Holmes' performances when they resulted in an actual tune, and was mildly dismayed when yet another visitor appeared and interrupted him.

This proved to be Inspector Alec MacDonald, who was one of Holmes' favorites upon the force. In the years since we first met, his deep set, lustrous eyes still conveyed a keen intelligence from beneath the bushy eyebrows of his great cranium. Only his brown hair, now dusty with grey, and his tall, bony figure had changed, the latter now conveying a sad sense of declining physical strength.

"Mr. Mac!" cried Holmes, as he steered the man to one of the armchairs. "What can a poor retired consulting detective do for you?" he asked as he sank into the settee opposite.

The silent, precise man hesitated a moment before speaking with his hard Aberdonian accent. "Well, it seems to be but a trifle, Mr. Holmes, but there was something about it that suggested I should notify you, given that you are back in town."

"Very good, pray proceed."

"This morning, Scotland Yard was called by the hospital at Blackheath to come take a look at a man who had been burned in a house fire down near Charlton. When we arrived, we found a horrific scene. The poor chap was more mummy than man, with nary an inch of his skin that had not been torched and subsequently wrapped by the doctors. The only parts of him that were unharmed were his hands."

"Both of them?" asked Holmes.

"Yes."

"That is most remarkable," said Holmes, eagerly leaning forward in his seat.

"Was it?" remarked the inspector. "I thought it an interesting coincidence, nothing more."

"I assure you, Mr. Mac, that it is not an easy task to burn every part of your body while sparing your hands," said Holmes, gravely.

I shook my head sadly. "Burns of that size are likely to prove fatal."

The inspector nodded. "Yes, that is just what they told me, Doctor. The man had, of course, been given strong doses of morphine in an attempt to make him comfortable, but he refused to rest. Instead, he continued to murmur one word over and over again. His lips were burned to such a degree that the word was hardly intelligible, but at last they realized what exactly he was saying. That's when they called the C.I.D."

"And what was the word?" asked Holmes, eagerly leaning forward in his seat.

Inspector MacDonald looked peculiarly at him for a moment, and his voice dropped to almost a murmur as he answered. "It was 'Holmes!'"

"Ah," said Holmes, settling back, his brows furled as he considered this new piece of information. He finally smiled at the inspector. "So, Mr. Mac, are you here to ask me my whereabouts during the time of the crime? For I presume that the house fire was not natural?"

"Yes, I was just getting to that, Mr. Holmes. But I can assure you that you are not considered a suspect. There is not a man of the Yard who would suppose you to be responsible."

Holmes smiled innocently. "So what was unusual about the fire?"

"The speed."

I frowned. "What do you mean?"

Before the inspector could answer, Holmes provided the explanation. "The brave men of the city fire brigades are no fools, Watson. They do not rush blindly into burning buildings without a reasonable expectation that they will be able to make their way out again. In order to make such a calculation, they have turned to science. There are formulas, not precise ones, mind you, but fair estimates of how long a certain type of building is expected to burn, based on various factors, such as the number of floors, approximate age, predominant materials, *etcetera*." He turned back to the inspector. "So how discrepant was the estimate?"

Inspector MacDonald shook his head. "Very much so, Mr. Holmes. The fire superintendent tells me that a fire at Hornfair House ought to have lasted at least an hour, and given the amount of brick, a sizable proportion should have still been left standing when all was said and done. He cannot explain why the entire house burned to minuscule ashes within fifteen minutes of the first sounds and notice of smoke."

"Fascinating," said Holmes. "So who is the burned man?"

"That's an excellent question, Mr. Holmes, and one we hoped you would be able to answer, since it appears that he may be an acquaintance of yours."

"But surely you can tell me the name of the owner of the house?" asked Holmes crossly.

Inspector MacDonald shrugged. "The owner is Sir Wilson Maryon, but he hasn't been near it in years. His estate agents lease it, and about two months ago it was taken by a Mr. John David Moore. However, by all accounts, Mr. Moore was a man of at least seventy years, stooped and hard-of-hearing. He claimed to be a retired botanist. The estate is quite private, and the neighbors are uncertain if he was home at the time of the fire. And even if he was, as I said, the fire burned so hot that we may not even be able to find any remains."

"But how do you know that the scorched man is not Mr. Moore?" I asked.

"By his hands, Watson," said Holmes.

"Exactly, Mr. Holmes," said Inspector MacDonald, smiling. "The burned man has no liver spots or other signs that they belong to a man of more than forty years of age. Though there are some unusual features that might help you identify him, Mr. Holmes."

"Such as?"

"There are innumerable old scars on them, though I am unable to precisely determine what profession would have caused them."

"Excellent, Mr. Mac," cried Holmes. "I have often said that the hands are the key to a man.[113] It is most fortunate that they were preserved in this situation. It is of no matter that you could not identify them, Mr. Mac. I would be happy to go down to Charlton and investigate."

"You mean 'we,' Holmes," said I.

"No, Watson, I am afraid that would be impossible. For now, we must hope that our adversary believes that I am still incapacitated. I will utilize one of the disguises that you did not record in your adventures, perhaps that of a Southwark costermonger looking for new wares.[114] Mortlock will not be expecting that."

"Do you think this course of action wise in your current condition? You only recently received several serious blows to the head. What if you are set upon again?"

"I think it a reasonable risk, Watson. Mr. Mortlock has proved to be a man of many resources, but he cannot be everywhere and see everything. I still have a few tricks up my sleeve that will permit me to avoid being followed."

"Very well," I acquiesced.

Holmes bade farewell to Inspector MacDonald, promising to wire if he learned anything of note and vanished to his room. When he returned, he was wearing the apron, cap, silk neckerchief, and bright yellow, pointed

---

[113] Actually, Holmes never said that, though he did mention the writing of a monograph on 'the influence of a trade upon the form of the hand, with lithotypes of the hands of slaters, sailors, cork-cutters, compositors, weavers, and diamond-polishers' (Chapter I, *The Sign of Four*).

[114] A costermonger was a street seller of fruit and vegetables, ubiquitous in mid-Victorian England. They would use a loud sing-song cry or chant to attract attention. The term is derived from the words 'costard' (a now-extinct medieval variety of large, ribbed apple) and 'monger'; a seller of goods.

boots that typified the guise of a costermonger. I shook my head in mild disapproval of his premature stirrings before his body was fully healed. "Take care, Holmes. If the police see a man dressed in an outfit like that poking around a burned house they will assume you are a looter. Inspector MacDonald may not have considered you a suspect, but you might still see the inside of a Bow Street cell before the day is done."

Holmes laughed sharply. "I will take care to avoid notice both official and unofficial, such as those posted by our friend Mortlock." He paused and grinned at me. "Mr. Mac is as fine a detective as can be found in the C.I.D., but he is far too trusting. For I have upon occasion been forced to veer outside the narrow scope of the law in order to right a greater injustice. Do you not recall, Watson, the odious tale of Charles Augustus Milverton, or the repulsive story of the Red Leech?"

"I prefer not to think of them, Holmes. For the one almost landed me in the clink, while the other..." I could not find the words.

"Yes, of course, say no more of it, Watson." He clasped my hand and vanished out of the door.

§

Despite the fact that Holmes did not see the hand of Professor Moriarty in this elaborate plot against him, I was less certain. This suspicion led my feet in the direction of the close-by Trafalgar Square. I knew that within the hallowed walls of the National Gallery lay an item once inexorably linked to the evil Professor.

The neo-classical building appeared like a Greek temple that had developed massive arms projecting off to the sides, and it dominated the northern elevation of the square. I climbed the grey steps up to its porticoed entrance and once inside, I obtained a map from the information stand. I studied it for the most probable location of works by late 18th Century French artists. Making my spot, I ascended to the upper level and made my way to a room in the far eastern corner of the building. There on the south wall, past several fine works by Corot and Bouguereau, I found the painting that I sought.[115] It depicted a young woman, with her head on her hands, peering sideways out at me. She wore a translucent shawl, part of which formed a halo over her dark curls, while

---

[115] Jean-Baptiste-Camille Corot (1796-1875) was a French Romantic landscape and portrait painter, while William-Adolphe Bouguereau (1825-1905) was a French Realist painter. Over time the paintings have been moved about, and currently, the Gallery's paintings by Greuze are located on Level 0 in Room E, along with two paintings by Claude-Joseph Vernet (1714-1789), a relative of one Mr. Sherlock Holmes.

a cloudy sky sweltered in the background. It was a most lovely composition by an obvious master.

"'*La Jeune Fille*,' by Jean Baptiste Greuze," said a voice near my right shoulder.[116]

I turned and found a man gazing expectantly at me. He was a small, balding man of about fifty years. His face was pleasant, though his eyes were much wrinkled, as if permanently affected by great periods of time spent squinting closely at objects. He wore a modest brown suit with a neat bow tie.

The man smiled benignly and spoke again. "I am most sorry to bother you, sir, but I thought I recognized you from your likenesses in *The Strand*. You are Dr. Watson, are you not? I am Joshua Goldfield, the Assistant Curator of the Gallery."

"I am sir," I replied, somewhat flattered that a portion of Holmes' deserved fame had brushed off onto me.

"If I may ask, Dr. Watson, are you particularly attracted to that painting?"

"How did you know that?"

"I saw you pass straight through the prior gallery. One can be forgiven perhaps for skipping the Kneller or the Reynolds,[117] but it is a rare individual who can walk through past Turner's *Temeraire* or *Odysseus* without pausing."[118]

"You are, in fact, correct. This painting interests me greatly. You are most observant, Mr. Goldfield."

"Yes, well, it comes from years of studying the minutiae of my paintings," he shrugged modestly. "A connoisseur must train himself to patiently observe the entire work in order to determine precisely what secret meaning the artist had intended for us to comprehend."

I smiled wanly. "You sound much like a certain friend of mine. Do all works of art contain hidden meanings?"

---

[116] Jean Baptiste Greuze (1725-1805) was a French artist whose working career flourished between the years 1750 and 1800. This particular painting fetched not less than four thousand pounds at the 1865 Portalis sale, despite the fact that Professor Moriarty's official university salary could be ascertained at seven hundred a year (Chapter II, *The Valley of Fear*).

[117] Sir Godfrey Kneller (1646-1723) and Sir Joshua Reynolds (1723-1792) were famous English portrait-painters.

[118] J.M.W. Turner (1775-1851) was the greatest of the British Romantic painters. Two of his most famous painting are *'The Fighting Temeraire'* (1839) and *'Ulysses Deriding Polyphemus from Homer's Odyssey'* (1829), the former especially a meditation upon obsolescence and the demise of heroic strength, the work of an artist confronting his own mortality.

"No, of course not. But the works of the great masters? Definitely. They all, even the simplest portrait or still-life, tell some story that may not be apparent to the untrained eye. Take this painting for example. Most visitors simply glance at it briefly, see a pleasant depiction of a young girl, and move on to the next work. It is one of the great disadvantages to having such a rich collection – people feel they have to see everything, and in consequence they observe nothing. In this case, Monsieur Greuze is contrasting the vitality of childhood with the stormy gale that is developing behind her. It is a metaphor for the ephemeral nature of youth, soon to be embroiled in the tempests of adulthood."

"That is most interesting, Mr. Goldfield. But I thought that perhaps you meant that your eye for detail was to be used to search out possible counterfeits?"

"Of course, Dr. Watson, that is a secondary object of any scrutiny. The smallest brush-stroke out of place, or a crack in the varnish where none should be, can serve to indicate that a painting is a fake. Of course, that is rarely an issue here at the Gallery. The provenances of our various works are impeccable, and our security is exceptional."

"And this painting here, are you aware of its provenance?"

"Of course, Doctor. It was purchased during an auction at Sotheby's. It had previously been owned by a man whose estate was confiscated, as everything had been purchased with money obtained illegally. I think you know of whom I speak, since it was Mr. Holmes who brought about the end of his empire of crime. I wonder if it is on Mr. Holmes' behalf that you have come, Doctor? I hope this is a sign that he is recovering from his wounds?"

"I am afraid that I cannot comment on Mr. Holmes' ongoing investigations."

The man nodded. "Of course, I completely understand. But was there some particular purpose to your visit? Some way that I may be of assistance?"

What was my motive for this visit? It had been a mere hunch that led my steps to Trafalgar Square. A desire to seek out some connection to the one man who seemed capable of coordinating such a series of brilliant thefts and attacks, even if he had in truth passed beyond the veil. And then a thought occurred to me. "Yes, now that you mention it, Mr. Goldfield, there is one thing you could do. The Gallery inspected this painting to certify its authenticity before it was purchased, did it not?"

"Certainly."

"I was wondering if you have had any reason to re-inspect the painting since then?"

He shook his head. "None."

"And is there a procedure by which the paintings are routinely examined, to ensure that no substitution has been made?"

The curator laughed softly. "First of all, Doctor, as I mentioned before, our security has detected no breaches, so it would be impossible for such an exchange to occur. Secondly, look about you," he waved his hand around the crowded gallery. "We have thousands and thousands of paintings in our collections. There are far too many to routinely inspect."

"But there is a method to do so in case of concern?"

Mr. Goldfield shrugged. "Of course. The painting is taken down from view, for reasons ascribed to 'conservation.' After a visual inspection of the strokes and the craquelure, we then analyze the age of both the paint used, but also the canvas itself.[119] Finally it is transported to University College, where it is placed under one of the Röntgen machines.[120] That tells us whether the surface painting has been painted over a prior work."

"A palimpsest?"[121]

"Very nearly. Some exceptionally skilled forgers are aware of the techniques for dating a canvas, so they paint over some minor work from the same era. While that first work is, of course, destroyed in the process, because of the lead in the paint, its soul is never truly lost, and the miraculous rays of Mr. Röntgen can bring it back to life, or at least a pale shadow of it."

"And do you have any trepidation about this particular painting?"

Mr. Goldfield paused and removed a pair of pince-nez from his waistcoat pocket. Settling them upon his nose, he studied *La Jeune Fille* for a span of nearly five minutes. He finally turned back to me. "No, I have no fears about its authenticity. Do you?"

"What if I was to tell you, Mr. Goldfield, that my friend has discovered that a particularly skilled forger is currently active in London? And that we have concerns that this painting may have been an especial target?" I blushed at this slight falsehood, suggesting that Holmes shared my concerns, since he had no notion of my impromptu visit to the Gallery.

"In that case, I shall ensure that it is tested forthwith. Where should I send word in the unlikelihood that an irregularity is found?"

I gave Mycroft's address to the curator, thanked him, and then made

---

[119] Craquelure is the fine pattern of cracks formed on the surface of an oil painting, usually due to the process of aging.
[120] Wilhelm Röntgen (1845-1923) is considered the discoverer of X-rays in 1895. The first documented use of X-rays to authenticate art occurred by a year later in Frankfurt, Germany, so it's dissemination to London by 1909 is entirely likely.
[121] Holmes was much interested in palimpsests, manuscript pages which have been scraped or washed and then reused, during the time preceding *The Adventure of the Golden Pince-Nez.*

my way back out to Trafalgar Square. Once there, I hesitated, unsure of my next move. I cudgeled my brains to find some possible explanation that covered all of the strange happenings that revolved around Holmes. The riddle of the sphinx and the problem at Threadneedle Street were certainly connected to the greater scheme, but what of the Hag of Haybridge Cave, the vanishing brake-van, and the burned man? Were they somehow linked to this monstrous conspiracy? Holmes would not likely return for several more hours. Where else could I go to find some vital clue that might unlock this vast puzzle? Who else could I turn to? Excepting Holmes and his brother, of course, the next smartest individual whom I knew was my old friend Walter Lomax, now head librarian at the London Library. His assistance had been invaluable in several prior cases, and perhaps he could once again see some light in the darkness.

I therefore turned my steps towards St James Square, which was a short walk away. But I was not to reach Lomax. As I was passing along Charles II Street, an enormous man, nineteen stone of solid bone and muscle, suddenly appeared out of an alleyway to my right and blocked my further progress.[122] My feet halted, and I gazed up at the crooked nose upon his craggy face, which was easily six inches above my own. The look that I found in his eyes was as cold as ice, and it dawned upon me that this was just the sort of man whose rock-like biceps could hold a flagstone above his head for the time required to allow mortar to dry. Had I just blundered into one of Mortlock's assistants at the Bank of England? If so, it was surely no accident.

I quickly spun on my heels hoping to put as much distance between this brute and myself, but when I did so, I found myself staring into the eyes of an even more fearsome individual, who had closed in on me from behind. This adversary was a short, powerful man with a round, fresh, clean-shaven face. His cheeks tended to roundness, such that I once considered him to have a childlike appearance despite his more than fifty years. However, one glance into the dead black color of his pupils made abundantly clear the fact that this was a man devoid of any sense of human decency. His name was 'Killer' Evans, and I thought him to be safely ensconced in one of His Majesty's most secure correctional facilities for his crime of once attempting to kill me. At the sight of my dawning recognition, his face split into a cruel grin. His right hand repetitively twirled a heavy sand-bag, which I feared was about to be utilized to smash my head into a pulp.

---

[122] A stone is an English unit of weight equal to 14 pounds or 6.35 kg, thus this man clocked in at about 266 pounds. Compare this to the enormous Godfrey Staunton, who was only 'sixteen stone' (*The Adventure of the Missing Three-Quarter*).

Over the years of my association with Sherlock Holmes, I have held my own in many a struggle. However, even if my advancing years and increasingly sedentary life were not an unfortunate fact, I little cared for my odds between this veritable Scylla and Charybdis. Before I could even begin to formulate a plan, the giant behind me reached out his massive hands and pinned my upper arms against my side in an iron vise. Despite this predicament, I was glad that he had not thought to go for my throat, or my senses would have swiftly departed. Instead, the nameless giant appeared to be content with merely restraining me, perhaps so that his partner Evans could finish me off. Nonetheless, I had little intention of complying with their nefarious plan and instead managed to reach my hand into my coat pocket, where my fingers clenched around my Eley's no. 2. Pulling it out as best I could, given the constraints upon my upper arms, I aimed it at Evans and did not hesitate. Although I had carried it upon innumerable dangerous missions with Holmes, there have been only a few instances where I was actually required to fire my trusty service revolver: the islander Tonga, the ferocious mastiff Carlo, the terrible hound of Stapleton, and of course the Gila monster of Eastland, marked the limits of the adversaries so dangerous that they required the persuasion only provided by a bullet. And yet, I felt the same of Evans. He had already shot me once before, five years earlier. I had no intention of allowing him to repeat his attempt upon my life.

My aim proved to be true, and a blossom of red erupted upon his chest. Evans stared dumbly down at the wound, lifted one hand to it, perhaps in a vain attempt at staunching his life's blood, and then collapsed upon the street. Although I could not see my other opponent's face, this turn of events clearly enraged the giant who held me from behind. He threw me against the side of the closest building with such great force that I felt a wave of pain burst from my right shoulder. As I slumped to the ground, I lost my grip upon the revolver, which rattled out of my reach. I wearily looked up and saw the giant advancing upon me. Attempting to ignore the agony lancing from my shoulder, I scrambled towards my weapon, certain that I would not make it in time, but that the effort nevertheless needed to be attempted.

My salvation came in the form of a passing blue-uniformed constable, his attention likely attracted by my gunshot. His brass police whistle blew excitedly as the man ran in our direction, though for a moment, I feared that the constable might prove to be an insufficient relief force. However stalwart the man and his gutta-percha truncheon, I was concerned that they were no match for the mighty fury of the giant's arms.[123] But my opponent

---

[123] The truncheon or baton was typically made from the extremely hard wood of the gutta-percha tree, native to the Malaysian peninsula. To this day, the typical

hesitated and, for reasons only known to him, decided to disengage. Leaving me slumped against the wall, the giant took to his heels and fled in the direction away from the advancing constable. Although my rescuer continued to blow his whistle, I little doubted that my assailant would make good on his escape.

§

A span of two hours later found me in the accident ward of St. Thomas' Hospital, having renewed my acquaintance with Dr. Penrose Fisher. He ensured that the head of my humeral bone was properly relocated in the shoulder joint. That procedure was not without some degree of discomfort, but now that my arm was immobilized in a sling, it had settled down to a dull ache.

Constable Jenkins had, at my request, passed word along to Inspector Lestrade, who in turn agreed to notify Holmes. As soon as my friend returned from Charlton, he immediately diverted his steps to the infirmary, where his concern for my well-being was most gratifying.

He had sat quietly as the final adjustments were made to the sling, but as soon as the nurse had departed, Holmes sprang from his chair and paced about the room in uncontrollable agitation. A flush rose upon his sallow cheeks and his long thin hands clasped and unclasped spasmodically. "I will not stand for it, Watson!" he exclaimed. "To think that Killer Evans would have the gall to attack you again, after I warned him! It is a good thing for him that your shot proved fatal, or he would need answer to me." His face set like granite as he contemplated our deceased adversary.

"At least it's over, Holmes, and no permanent harm done. I will be right as rain in two weeks,[124] if not sooner."[125]

He frowned at me. "Whatever are you talking about, Watson? What is over?"

"Evans was also known as 'James Winter,'" I explained. "But was his other alias not 'Morecroft?'"

"Yes, what of it?"

"Surely he was the sender of the notes? Morecroft? Mortlock? The similarities..."

"A coincidence, Watson," interjected Holmes.

London constable does not go armed with a gun.

[124] This slang phrase first appeared in the Oxford English Dictionary in 1891.

[125] Watson is perhaps being overly optimistic. While it is possible to stop wearing a sling after a few weeks, it can take three to four months to completely recover from a dislocated shoulder.

"I did not think you believed in such things, Holmes."

"Normally I would concur with that assessment. But these are not normal times. Much like Holy Peters, Killer Evans was a man not without a certain measure of low cunning. But how long did it take me to expose his ridiculous Garrideb identity? Five minutes? No, this conspiracy is far too vast for the mind of Killer Evans, may he rest in peace," he said with no small degree of acerbity.

"And his partner – the giant – what of him?"

"I believe that I recognize him from your description, Watson. His name is Mathews, and I believe I once mentioned to you that he knocked out my left canine in the waiting room at Charing Cross. What I failed to report, in an attempt at modesty that some might claim I do not possess, is that I not only permanently rearranged his nose, but that my right hook left him in a stupor for three weeks. After he recovered, Mathews spent a considerable stint in gaol for the assault upon Major Broughton, and I sincerely doubt that he has forgiven me.[126] We will ask Lestrade to send over a picture from the Rouges' Portrait Gallery for you to confirm it, but I think it is a safe supposition that very few malignant giants are roaming the streets of St James's Square."

"So we now need to track down Mathews?"

"No, Watson. We must, of course, first send an urgent telegram to your wife informing her of your safety. A man was shot and killed on the Haymarket. That will have attracted the attention of the evening papers, and your name is certain in some way to be attached to the incident. If they report that you were injured, she will have a chill pass through her heart when she opens the morning edition and lays eyes upon that particular heading."

"That is an excellent point, Holmes."

"And it is far too late for you to catch a train to Southsea tonight, but we will tell her to expect you tomorrow."

I did not understand his logic. "Is there some clue that points us to Southsea?"

He laughed sharply. "No, Watson. No clue, but I am afraid that it is past time for you to retire from the field. This is not your fight. Mortlock, whoever he may be, is determined to revenge himself upon me. He knew that an attack upon you would be a simple way to wound me. He is trying to weaken me, like a picador injures a bull before the matador delivers the fatal blow."

I shook my head. "I will not hear of it, Holmes. You and Mortlock may consider me to be but a piece upon your metaphorical chessboard,

---

[126] Another unchronicled case, why Mathews assaulted Major Broughton is not known.

but this chessman has yet to be captured. And I too am more than ready to extract some measure of revenge for the harm dealt to me by Mortlock."

"Watson, with your shoulder in a sling, you cannot even properly aim a gun," Holmes pointed out.

"I would prefer to think, Holmes, that my contributions to the firm over the years have not solely been on the physical side of things. Have I not provided an idea or two in my time?"

Holmes smiled. "My dear Watson, you really are a wonder. So you propose to continue the fight, despite your wounds?"

"Did Nelson hide at Merton after he lost both an eye and an arm?[127] This is but a mere strain. I can do no less."

Holmes raised an eyebrow. "You have on occasion, Watson, remarked that my self-esteem was not small. But I do believe that you just compared yourself to one of the greatest heroes of our nation."[128]

§

The telegraph to my wife duly dispatched, Holmes and I sat in the hansom cab back to Pall Mall, when he began to chuckle appreciatively. "It is very good of you, Watson, to refuse to depart. It makes a considerable difference to me, having someone with me on whom I can thoroughly rely."

"You did not honestly think I would slink off to Southsea, did you?"

"No, but I had to try. I cannot overstate, Watson, precisely how dangerous this particular adventure is proving to be. Inspector Patterson and Captain Powell are dead, and on our enemies' side, both Killer Evans and Colonel Moran have shuffled off this mortal coil. I am unable to foresee how many more may fall before this matter has been resolved."

I shrugged. "Once more unto the breach, Holmes, once more..."

He smiled. "Follow your spirit and upon this charge, eh? In any case, I blame myself. I should have deduced from the attack of Peters that Mortlock is aware of our haunts and that he would consider you a fair

---

[127] Merton Place was the country estate purchased by Admiral Horatio Nelson during the temporary Peace of Amiens. Despite having previously lost the sight in his right eye on Corsica and his right arm at Santa Cruz in the Canary Islands, Nelson stood fast upon the deck of his flagship, the HMS *Victory*, as it crashed the French lines at Trafalgar. There he was struck down by the fatal bullet.

[128] After his death in 1805, Nelson was considered for many years the pinnacle of British courage, on par with Lord Wellington, and surpassing John Churchill, 1st Duke of Marlborough (1650-1722). Nelson was finally surpassed by Marlborough's descendent Winston, c.1945.

mark. If he has targeted you, then logically his next move would be to..." his voice trailed off, and an alarmed expression seized his face. He suddenly leaned out of the enclosure to shout at the driver. "Cabby! All haste, my man, and three sovereigns for you!" he commanded.

"What is wrong, Holmes?" I asked anxiously, as I felt the man whip the horse into a burst of speed.

"I hope I am wrong, Watson, but Mortlock is seeking to keep me off balance. He has eliminated our most promising source of information in Moran. He has attempted to eliminate my most trusted ally. The next thing for him to do is pull the literal rug from underneath me."

"The rug?" I asked, confused.

"Our base of operations, Watson." He leaned forward abruptly and gazed directly forward out from the window. "By Jove! I was right. Do you see, Watson?"

For a moment I did not, but then I realized that a small panic was brewing in the street ahead of us. All traffic had halted, and alarms were beginning to ring. I could see a plume of smoke rising in the distance, and realized where it must originate. "Mycroft's chambers!" I exclaimed as the driver was forced to pull the hansom to a halt.

Holmes nodded grimly. "Come, Watson, we must hurry." He dashed out of the cab and began to sprint in the direction of his brother's rooms. I supposed that at this time of night, Mycroft himself was almost certainly at the Diogenes Club and thus out of danger's path. But the same did not hold true for his butler, Stanley. I knew that Holmes would not forgive himself if any harm came to the old man. Unfortunately, as I attempted to run after Holmes the pain in my shoulder quickly proved to be nigh unbearable, and my friend soon outpaced me.

By the time I arrived, I found Holmes hovering anxiously over the supine form of Stanley, who appeared much shaken and sooty, but otherwise intact. The Fire Brigade was already upon the scene and doing its heroic best to both evacuate the nearby buildings while simultaneously fighting the flames that were roaring from every window.[129] I took a moment to examine Stanley, and recommended that the man be observed in a hospital overnight for signs of smoke inhalation. Holmes used his influence with one of the nearby constables to ensure that this was promptly carried out, and then he turned and stared morosely at the burning building. I tried to imagine what was going through his mind. Inside were all of the notes gathered upon this investigation, but Holmes'

---

[129] This was formed in 1865, first as the Metropolitan Fire Brigade and then in 1904, as the London Fire Brigade, following two centuries where various insurance companies established units to combat fires that occurred only in buildings that their respective companies insured.

memory attic was of a prodigious size and I doubted that he would fail to reconstruct those in a matter of hours. And then I realized that his beloved Stradivarius had been sent up from South Downs by his housekeeper. It was not just that a financially-valuable instrument had been destroyed, for Holmes had picked it up for a mere fifty-five shillings on the Tottenham Court Road, and with the money he had earned over the years, he could easily afford to replace it. I think it was the realization that a great masterpiece, something unique and truly irreplaceable, had just been lost to the realm of man. It was, perhaps, a metaphor for death itself. What would happen to the world when Holmes himself breathed his last breath? Truly, something far too dreadful to bear considering.

§

I shook off these morbid thoughts and placed my hand upon his shoulder. "Where to now, Holmes?"

He shrugged and scowled. "I don't know, Watson." He sighed heavily.

"What about one of those small refuges that you maintain throughout London?"

"They are hardly fit for prolonged habitation. And are they secure? Mortlock has clearly been watching me. Does he know of them? Will he just send men to slit our throats as we sleep?" said he, bleakly.

"Then we take shifts!"

He smiled wearily. "Good old, Watson. No, if your shoulder is to heal, you will need more than a hard pallet above a warehouse in Wapping. We might as well do as you suggested some time ago."

And that is how we found ourselves taking a suite of rooms at the grand Langham Hotel. Unfortunately, I was far too exhausted to take more than a superficial notice of the rich golden glow that resonated from its stone facings or the opulence of its marbled lobby. Shortly thereafter, as I lay back in my bed, my last thought before I rapidly passed into unconsciousness, was that it truly was a room fit for a king.

The following morn, I discovered that the adrenaline of the prior evening had worn off, and the pain in my shoulder was rather substantial. When I was a man of eight and twenty, I could stand a bit of Jezail lead being introduced into my body at high speeds, but as a man of seven and fifty, a dislocated shoulder proved to be a more significant matter. Nevertheless, I slowly arose and made my way out into the common room of our suite. The door to Holmes' room was ajar, but before I could look in to see if he had gone out, there was a knock upon the set of double doors that led to the hotel's hallway. Before opening it, I carefully inspected the eyehole to ensure that there was not a murderous band of thugs waiting on the other side. I could only see a young boy dressed as a hotel porter, and decided he appeared to be an honest lad. After I threw back the locks, the boy held out an envelope and departed as soon as I deposited a shilling into his outstretched palm.

I gazed at it with some confusion, wondering if Holmes had informed Mycroft the location of our temporary abode of the prior night. However, as the envelope was addressed to me, I shrugged and started to tear it open. Just then, Holmes erupted from his room, like tiger springing upon its prey.

"Drop it, Watson!" This instant, I say!" he cried with such vehemence that I dropped the envelope upon the floor.

"What is it, Holmes?" I protested.

"If you value your life, do not open it, Watson!" he commanded.

"Whatever is the matter, Holmes?"

"My correspondence is, as you know, a varied one. I have lost count how many packages sent to me contain some subtle poison. Knowing that I am upon my guard for such a stratagem, our adversary is therefore forced to seek some other method that may introduce a contagion into the room. You are the logical choice for an addressee of such a parcel."

I studied my friend, and excepting only the time that he feigned being struck down by his mythical Tapanuli fever, I could not recall seeing him in a worse state. His hair and attire were disheveled and his long white fingers trembled slightly. His face had taken on a terrible gauntness, as if food had not passed his lips for many days, which might well be the truth. But the sign that sent a chill to my heart were his eyes. His pupils were mere pinpricks, and it was with considerable horror and dismay that I realized what this signified. Long ago I had weaned him from a terrible practice, but it was now clear that the fiend had only been hibernating for all these years. Despite many trials and tribulations following his return from Tibet, his iron will had prevented any waking of the beast. But the calm had now vanished, as this terrible storm threatened to reduce Holmes to a drug-addled creature. "Holmes! Tell me that you are not using the seven-percent solution again!"

He shrugged as if it was of no concern. "It is clarifying for the mind, Watson."

I shook my head. "I thought you had rejected that fallacy?"

"Yes, but perhaps I was wrong to do so. Some of my greatest triumphs occurred during those numinous days."

"Correlation does not imply causation," I replied, appealing to the eminent logician that I knew lurked in the brain behind the dulled windows of his eyes.

He did not reply, but instead sank into one of the plush armchairs and leaned back, lost in gloomy speculation. As I watched him, I knew that his inner being had been terribly shaken. Inspector Patterson, a good man, had been killed for little reason other than to serve as the lure that would draw Holmes out of retirement. Did the man not have some wife and children who would never again see him walk through the door and hold them tightly to his breast? Stanley, a man whom Holmes had known for close to half-a-century, had escaped a terrible death by the smallest of fractions. Even my own wounding, slight as it may be, would pile up in his mental inventory as another innocent person who was harmed solely because of Holmes.

Despite our long and close association, due to his natural reticence, some small part of Holmes remained a mystery to me. But I suspected that the logical machine, the brain without a heart, was but a façade, and like any man, Holmes surely must have terrors that come to him in the small hours of this night. Had he always secretly dreaded that his actions might lead to the harm of those rare individuals he considered to be friends? Had this sudden realization of his worst fears bring on this black melancholy? Never had I seen him so utterly despondent, even after when we had witnessed some horror enacted by one man upon another, or after those rare times when Holmes failed one of the clients who had entrusted their lives to him.

He finally sighed and looked up at me. "Well, Watson, I do not jest when I say that we seem to have fallen upon evil days."

"It is during such moments when the great man rises to the occasion," I said, quietly. "There is nothing more stimulating than a case where everything goes against you!"

He snorted. "Who said such nonsense?"

"You did, Holmes."[130]

He chuckled sadly, and then shook his head. "We are in the grips of some inexorable evil, a relentless persecution, not by one man, but an entire society of those who wish me harm. But I can find no thread that leads me towards the foul mind that is the prime mover."

"We can but try! Compound of the Busy Bee and Excelsior!"

He finally smiled. "I don't know quite what to do, Watson, and I should value your advice."

"You must act, Holmes!" said I, a heat rising into my voice. "It is not like you to be so defensive. I had thought you would go on the attack."

"Attack against whom?"

"I don't know, Holmes." I looked around the room, searching for an inspiration, when my eyes landed upon the envelope that Holmes had

---

[130] In Chapter V of *The Hound of the Baskervilles.*

previously dashed from my hand. "Perhaps this contains some critical clue," said I, stooping to pick it up.

He glanced at it with some interest. "Let me see it first, Watson."

I handed it over and he inspected it closely, even going so far as to sniff it multiple times. "I can see no signs that it has been tampered with. If they introduced a poison, then they must have infiltrated the messenger offices. I think, on the whole, the odds suggest that you can safely open it, though it is likely just a message from your concerned wife."

I was barely listening to him, however, for the enclosed message was unusual in the extreme. I little knew what it meant, but I thought that perhaps Holmes might see some hopeful sign therein. Before I could speak, Holmes snapped. "Out with it, Watson! What is so interesting? Your face is an open book!"

> *TRAFALGAR SQUARE, Westminster, Nov. 30th.*
> *Re Forgery*
> *Dr. Watson –*
> *I write to inform you that I promptly followed your advice and took* Le Jeune Fille *to the University for a painstakingly complete analysis. I am most dismayed that your suspicions were correct and the painting that we have proudly displayed for some measure of the last eighteen years is indeed fraudulent. Although the paint and canvas are of an appropriate age, Jean-Baptiste Greuze was not in the habit of painting over landscapes of prior German Romantics, no matter how minor, as we discovered when the painting was subjected to the rays of Mr. Röntgen. I pray that this information is of some minor assistance in any investigations conducted by yourself and Mr. Holmes.*
> *Yours sincerely,*
> *Joshua Goldfield*

Holmes read this with growing excitement, and suddenly sprang out of his chair. His inexorable eyes gleamed out of his haggard face. I could now read in them a set purpose to devote his life to the quest, until the men who had already been harmed should be avenged, and until no further danger awaited any of us at the hands of Mortlock. "You are absolutely right, Watson. We have been passive for far too long. Now that we know the name of our enemy, it is time to take the fight to him."

"We know the name of our enemy?" I asked with some confusion.

"Oh, yes."

§

However, Holmes would say no more at the moment. He informed me that he would need to go out for a short while in order to perform the few tasks that would be required to prepare for the coming battle. Upon his return we would be decamping from the luxury of the Langham. He instructed me to rest my shoulder as much as possible while we still maintained our comfortable quarters, and to not let anyone through the door until Shinwell Johnson arrived.

He smiled at my question regarding the necessity of this action. "Shinwell is a blunt instrument, of course, Watson. But he is as loyal as he is intimidating. He will ensure your safety while I am occupied. It is a temporary measure only until you have regained some use of your arm and are able to defend yourself. Do not take it as any denigration of your use, Watson. In fact, without your little visit to the National Gallery, we might still be in the dark."

The rest of the day was quiet, with only the arrival of Mr. Johnson, some packages, and a light supper to break the monotony. Nevertheless, the rest did wonders for my shoulder, which admittedly had hardly felt up to the task of waging war against the forces of Mortlock. By the time Holmes returned, however, a series of hot packs applied by the surprisingly solicitous Mr. Johnson had me feeling, if not normal, at least upon my way towards being whole again.

Holmes did not identify our group's destination, but before he led our way out of the hotel, he gave Johnson and I a series of instructions. "We can be certain, gentlemen, that our adversary has already deduced our current location. As we are retreating to a new base of operations – whose location I would for the time being prefer remains a secret – we must ensure that they do not follow us there."

"Should we split up?" I suggested. "It will be harder to follow three men travelling alone rather than a group."

Holmes shook his head. "But even if one man is followed, it will give away the game. Nevertheless, your suggestion is a good one, Watson, and we shall indeed split up. Once we reach the lobby, Watson will engage the fifth hansom cab that appears, while Johnson and I will make our way upon foot. We will meet at St Pancras Station and will then proceed together to our final destination. Any questions? No? I see that you both changed into the suits I provided, yes? And you have the hats? Excellent, let us be off."

Earlier in the afternoon, Holmes had sent up to the suite a new suit for both Johnson and I, his brown and mine grey. These were accompanied by hats, an ascot for Johnson and a bowler for me. At the time, I thought that Holmes had simply believed that our previous attire might attract too much attention, as I noted that Holmes had also acquired a new suit and hat. But once we reached the hotel's lobby, I realized that he had a far deeper strategy in play. For in that magnificent space there was a congregation of men unlike anything I think the Langham had previously witnessed. As I gazed about in confused awe, I counted no less than twenty men dressed exactly like my friend, with an equal number of men who resembled either me or Mr. Johnson in both stature and attire. I could not help but laugh at the brilliance and wonder of it all, and I was certain that the poor employees and guests of the hotel would remain mystified about that bizarre gathering for many long years to come.

Before I could even note it, Holmes and Johnson had melted into the crowd, such that even I could no longer spot the real man amongst his doppelgängers. At some unseen cue, the crowd sprang into action and began to vacate the hotel from all possible means of egress. A handful of 'Holmes' and 'Johnsons' and other 'Watsons' joined me in hailing hansoms, but I made certain that I was the occupier of the fifth one to arrive. As my cab pulled away, I was still laughing at Holmes' subterfuge, and wondered from precisely where Holmes had managed to find so many willing actors and identical suits?[131]

Although my driver had clearly been instructed to take a roundabout track to the neo-Gothic railway station at St Pancras, it was a span of less than fifteen minutes before I found myself deposited at what appeared to be my first destination. Disembarking, I looked about in vain for Holmes or Johnson, but could not spot them. I stood there for a moment, unsure of what I should do, when a ragged young news-vender approached. Although I had weightier subjects upon my mind than the events of the day, I purchased a copy so as to have something to do while awaiting the arrival of my friends. I thought it would appear more natural than standing there idle. Imagine my surprise when the lad did not immediately move off, but instead spoke to me in a low voice. "I recommend the story on page four, Doctor." Before I could look up and ask him what he meant, he had vanished into the crowd. I shrugged and followed his advice, where I found a message scrawled in Holmes' familiar hand instructing me to proceed to a black brougham on the nearby corner of York Way and Caledonia Street.

This proved to be a rather plain conveyance, though heavy velvet

---

[131] Although not conclusive, Watson said that: 'the stage lost a fine actor when he became a specialist in crime' (*A Scandal in Bohemia*), and it has been widely considered that Holmes was part of an acting troupe before he changed careers. If these suspicions are true, those old personal connections might explain how Holmes managed to engage so many actors in such a short period of time.

draperies blocked the windows such that its occupants could travel unseen. Before I could knock upon the door, it swung open to briefly reveal Mr. Johnson, before he reached out and hauled me rather roughly inside. "Sorry about that, Doctor. Instructions from the boss."

"Yes, well," said I, rubbing my injured shoulder suggestively. "Where is Mr. Holmes?"

"Right here, Watson," replied my friend as he slipped into the brougham after me, which immediately sprang into motion. "I was watching you to ensure that you were not followed, but I think we are in the clear."

"So where are we going, Holmes?" I asked, somewhat crossly that he had kept me in the dark about all of his preparations for so long.

He chuckled. "I apologize, Watson. We are headed to an inn situated upon Hampstead. From there we will wage our offensive against Mr. Mortlock."

"And who exactly is that?"

"All in good time, Watson. All in good time. Much will be revealed tonight."

Finally, after climbing for some time up the ridge where I knew Hampstead to lay, the brougham ground to a halt and the three of us bundled out. I looked about for a moment before recognizing Parliament Hill, the highest point on the Heath. I had been there many times on fine summer days, when the hill was teeming with laughing clerks, tittering seamstresses, courting couples, off-duty soldiers, and folks from every other walk of life. They came up here for the clear air and fine views, to look back over the often dismal yellow-laden, smoke-covered city from which they had temporarily made their escapes. But in the late hours of the night, those merry-makers had fled back down to the river-side city below, leaving only a deserted landscape of hills, fields, and woods. I knew that Holmes had chosen this locale primarily for its topography which would make it impossible for us to be tracked by an unseen foe.

After surveying the area, Holmes set off briskly across the heath, Johnson, and I trailing close behind. The last slivers of the setting sun were fading to black, and the long, sloping plain in front of us was still tinged with hints of bronze, deepening into rich, ruddy brown where the faded ferns and brambles caught the evening light. But the glories of the wonderful autumnal panorama were wasted upon my companion, who was sunk in the deepest thought.

A walk of a mile or so across the wind-swept heath, the air filled with the crisp snap of advancing winter and its trees alive with the evening calls of the birds, brought us to a rear-gate that opened into the grounds of the public house. A path led us through a small tea garden, and we circled the building where, from the front window upon the left of the door, there peeped a glimmer of a feeble light.

At the reception desk, we were met by a rosy-cheeked young lass, who welcomed us to Wat Tyler's House.[132] Speaking for all of us, Holmes engaged three rooms, giving Mr. Johnson's true name, but registering himself as Mr. Harris of Bermondsey and myself as Mr. Price of Birmingham. We had nothing in the way of baggage, so there was no need to immediately visit our rooms. Instead, Holmes motioned for us to follow him into a back room, which seemed to be a leasable space for a private party. However, to my great surprise, the room was already filled with six individuals.

Holmes smiled at the sight of them and waved his arm as if to include them in our group. "Dr. Watson, Mr. Johnson, may I introduce you to the New Irregulars."

As I studied them, I realized that several faces seemed familiar. The first was a slender young man in his mid-twenties, with a clean-shaven face and a wise look in his brown eyes. His coat-less attire and well-stained apron suggested that he was the keeper of this establishment.

"Is that little Billy?" I cried. "Not a boy in buttons any longer, I see." For there was little doubt that this was our former page at 221B Baker Street.

He smiled abashedly. "It is mighty fine to see you again, Dr. Watson. Even considering the circumstances."

"What has become of you, lad?"

With a nod of his head, he indicated the roof above our heads. "You are looking at it, Doctor. With the money I earned from you and Mr. Holmes, I had enough to settle down and purchase this little inn."

"Congratulations, Billy. It is very well deserved."

I glanced over at the second man, who also appeared to be an old acquaintance. Although no longer a youth of fourteen, he still had a bright, keen face. His blue eyes were active, and his entire body quivered with energy. He wore a modest suit and though his head was uncovered, I immediately pictured him wearing the blue flat-topped cap that was once an essential part of his uniform.

"Cartwright?"

"The same, Dr. Watson."

"Are you still working for Holmes, after all these years?"

"Only after a fashion, Doctor," he replied. "I took over the district messenger office from Mr. Wilson, when his gout proved to be too great

---

[132] Although not all of the details fit precisely, it is thought that this is a Watsonian name-change for the former public house on Hampstead known as Jack Straw's Castle.

to continue."

"And we are glad to have you back in the Firm, faithful Cartwright," interjected Holmes, clasping the man on the shoulder. "Your appreciation for detail is excellent, Watson, as always. Can you also recall the names of these two lads?"

I looked over the pair of thin, hard-faced men, both well into their thirties. One was slightly taller and older than the other, and he carried himself with an air of longing superiority. He had black hair and dark brown eyes that bespoke of hardness and want, though the fine cut of his suit suggested that those days were long past. The other had sandy-colored hair, and blue eyes, but seemed nonetheless to be a spiritual twin to the first man. I could not for the life of me place them.

"I do not believe that I have had the pleasure," I replied, holding out my hand to the elder of the pair.

Holmes chuckled. "All, well, it has been a few years, to be certain. And both Mr. Wiggins and Mr. Simpson have come a long way from their former insignificant and disreputable situations."

"By Jove!" I exclaimed. "You don't mean to say that these are your original Irregulars?"

"I do indeed, though they are street Arabs no longer." Gesturing to the taller man, Holmes said, "Wiggins here, who always had a fine eye for color, secured an apprenticeship under the artist Hughes.[133] He is now an illustrator at Newnes Publishing."[134] He then motioned to the second individual. "And you may recall that Simpson here was a sentinel extraordinaire, who would stick to a man like a burr. With a reference from me to Mr. Merryweather, the chairman of directors, Simpson obtained a position at the Coburg branch of the City and Suburban Bank, which certainly needed some additional protection. Due entirely to his own merits, he has subsequently risen to the post of chief guard."

The two men nodded to me silently, as I vainly tried to reconcile their adult appearances with the ragged waifs of my memory. Meanwhile, Holmes had moved on to a man whom I was certain I had never met. He was a hearty, full-blooded man of a similar age to Holmes and me. Despite his advancing years, he seemed full of spirits and energy. Under his Burberry overcoat he wore a suit cut in a fashion that I knew to be unique to tailors who resided only in the far eastern edges of our colonies. He had a shock of grizzled hair, a brown weather-beaten face, and eyes which were keen to the verge of fierceness. Yet, when he greeted Holmes, his tone carried a note of kindness.

"Holmes, I have long owed you a great debt. Now that I am returned

---

[133] Likely Arthur Hughes (1832–1915), a Pre-Raphaelite painter and illustrator.
[134] Newnes Publishing was best known for printing the *Strand Magazine*.

to Norfolk after many long years abroad, I am happy to have the opportunity to finally repay you."

Holmes shook his head. "Say no more of it, but I am glad to have you here, Trevor. Watson, let me introduce you to Victor, one of the oldest friends from my college days, albeit one I have not seen for three decades."

I shook his proffered hand with great delight at finally meeting this man, of whom I had once heard such an extraordinary story. Finally, Holmes turned to the last man, also about the same age of us, thin, high-nosed, and large-eyed, who stood up in the corner. His hunting outfit was covered by a dark Mackintosh. He carried with him a finely-made mousetrap fowling piece.[135]

"Ah, Cavalier," said Holmes, warmly. "I am glad that you brought something more practical than your old battle-axe."

"Yes, well, I could not be certain from your terse telegram, Holmes, however I expect we may be hunting larger game than pheasants," the man replied. "Since the principal is the same, I raided my gun-room, even bringing with me a few extra for the other lads here."

"Excellent! Watson, may I present to you my old acquaintance, Sir Reginald Musgrave, baronet of Hurlstone."

Just as Holmes had once described him to me, his manner was exceedingly aristocratic, languid, yet courtly. His pale, keen face and the poise of his head put me in the mind of a venerable feudal keep. With time, his natural diffidence seemed to have faded, only to be replaced with the assured self-confidence that comes with years of public speaking.

"So, Holmes, are you going to explain this rigmarole to us?" Musgrave asked.

"Indeed, but first, unlike Napoleon, who always feasted after a battle, and who was eventually brought low, we shall dine now in hopes that it begets us greater fortune."

Having lived with Holmes for upwards of seventeen years, I was well-aware that his periods of self-starvation while embroiled in an investigation alternated with rare but lavish feasts of epicurean delight. At this moment, Holmes had clearly arranged in advance for some of his favorites to be served. Amongst the choices were a couple of brace of cold woodcock, a pheasant and a partridge, and a *foie gras* pie. The repast was crowned with a fine Montrachet and a rare Beaune.

While we dined, Holmes would speak of nothing save shared past experiences. Even the less-than-literary Mr. Johnson had read my prior published stories and thus all were familiar with the terrible events of both

---

[135] The fowling piece, or shotgun, was enhanced in 1871 by British gun-maker T. Murcott's hammerless model, nicknamed the mousetrap.

the *'Gloria Scott'* and the Musgrave Ritual. The loyal service of Cartwright amongst the grim mires of Dartmoor was roundly toasted. They knew of the roles played by Wiggins and Simpson in such affairs as the vanished *Aurora* and the treacherous Colonel. However, Wiggins' timely locating of the messenger boy Ned, which saved an innocent man from being hanged, was a new tale to our companions, as I have neglected to organize my notes on that peculiar case. Finally, none were aware of Billy's heroism during the matter of the barren grave, for Holmes has yet to give me permission to publish the details of that horrifying mystery, though I have it ready in the vault of Cox & Co. for the day when I hope to persuade him otherwise.

Therefore, our meal proved to be a merry one. Not since the early days of our association have I known him to be so dazzling a conversationalist. This intense humor marked the pendulum swing from his dark despair of the prior night. By the time that the table was cleared, Holmes stood and, like a general, looked over the eight men that served as both his *de facto* chief of the staff and entire army. It was an interesting lot, three old men, perhaps limited in strength, but long in experience; two former lads of the street, whose endurance once allowed them to thrive in the harshest conditions; two former servants, with unwavering loyalty to Holmes; and one former convict, now walking the path of light. Could this ragged band be the ones to bring down the mysterious Mortlock and his terrible gang?

Holmes' demeanor was somber, as if he knew the stakes against which we struggled, however, when he spoke his voice retained its typical jaunty gallantry. "Gentlemen, I wish to thank you all for coming. Save only Watson here, who was savagely beaten by members of the gang, none of the rest of you has any qualms with them, other than your long acquaintance with their primary target.... me. Once you hear what is ranged against us, I will hold no ill will to any man who wishes to leave."

"Get on with it, Mr. Holmes," growled Simpson. "We ain't here for a holiday. We all know what's at stake, so let's not blather on."

Holmes smiled, though his eyes remained grim. "I appreciate your candor, Simpson. Very well, then. These are the facts as I know them. The key is to separate those facts which are crucial from the others which are merely incidental."

He proceeded to launch into a careful explanation of all that had transpired since Lestrade and I had first implored him to leave his villa on the South Downs. I was, of course, aware of all of the details of the Pharaoh's curse which had lured him to London, and the nature of the Sphinx's riddle which had kept him there. The same was true of the audacious robbery on Threadneedle Street, and the attempted assassination of Holmes by Colonel Moran atop the Monument. However, there was one piece of information that was unknown to me. "An item of note that I have been able to establish, gentlemen," said Holmes, "is that the dirigible's propulsion system was built by none other than Von Herder, the blind German mechanic who once worked for the dearly departed Professor Moriarty."

"But, Holmes," I exclaimed at this news, "does that not suggest that – "

"Hold, Watson," Holmes interrupted. "As I have said before, it is a mistake to theorize in advance of all of the facts. Let me finish outlining the events for the others."

He continued with the attack by Holy Peters and his hound, the slaying of Sebastian Moran, and even the bizarre train robbery that so troubled Mycroft. He concluded with a description of what he had found at Charlton, the full details of which I had yet to hear due to the rapid events of Murderous Mathews' attack and the fire at 22 Pall Mall.

"You see, gentlemen," said Holmes, "I was able to quickly determine the identity of the burned man. His hands were definitive, both for the manner of their preservation, but also from what was revealed by their lack of injuries. He had numerous small circular scars, all of which were over two years in age. The dating of scars is a tricky business, but I am confident in my conclusion. I knew their cause immediately, for they are the scars of a chemist who works with strong acids, and my own hands were once so covered." He held out those long thin white fingers for our examination. "However, it was clear that the man recently switched to using some sort of retardant glove, and those are what protected that lone portion of his body from the horrific fire.[136] It was then simplicity itself to determine, from a reading of the agony columns, that Mr. Horace Wall, a chemist of Newcastle, has been reported missing these last twenty-odd days."

"But, Mr. Holmes, what caused the house to burn so quickly?" asked Cartwright.

Holmes shrugged. "I have not identified the precise chemical, but it was certainly an accelerant of some sort. Questioning of some of the closer neighbors revealed that most described hearing a muffled boom before any signs of smoke or flame. I am certain that was an explosion being set off inside the house." Holmes paused and looked each of us in the eye. "So you see, gentlemen, all the cards are at present against us, and we must do everything that is possible if we are to win clear."

---

[136] Fire-retardant gloves in 1909 were likely made of asbestos, which became popular in the 1860's. The health risks of asbestos were only beginning to be understood at that time. The major report on the link of asbestos to pulmonary fibrosis was published in 1903.

"What do you propose, Holmes?" asked Victor Trevor.

"We must draw him out. He has attempted to ensnare us in his net, but we have our own web to weave! We shall muster all our resources and trick him into revealing himself."

Billy raised his hand, and once Holmes motioned to him, our former page-boy offered his ideas. "What about telling him where you are staying, and then setting up one of those wax busts and playing a phonograph recorded with your voice? When they come to kill you, we can spring our trap."

Holmes smiled and nodded as he considered this. "An excellent idea, Billy. However, we are dealing with a man far more cunning than Count Sylvius. Mr. Mortlock has clearly studied those cases that I was rash enough to allow Watson to publish. He will be expecting such a trick, and thus it will fail to snare him."

Holmes' continued disparagement of my stories failed to offend me, for I was occupied in thinking about the facts that he had just listed. "Holmes, do not forget the disappearance of Mr. Howard Kidd."

"I think, Watson, that we can leave out the illusory Hag and her supposed victim."

But my interjection had piqued the interest of Reginald Musgrave. "What is this, Doctor?"

I told the group the story of our visit by Dr. Basil Gennery and his supernatural tale of the Haybridge Cave, with my hypothesis that the some nefarious operation was being concealed therein. When I finished, an inpatient Holmes waved his hand dismissively. "Yes, very good, Watson. Now if we can return to the task at hand."

But Musgrave was not to be dissuaded. "That is interesting, Doctor, though it is hard to imagine that anyone is using one of those caves as a headquarters. You see, Doctor, since the events down at Hurlstone, I have developed an amateur interest in the history of the Cromwellian Terror.[137] Did you know that the Royalists took refuge in caves under the old college at Stourbridge in order to escape the passing notice of a superior force of Roundheads?[138] But they didn't use them for long, as they did not appreciate sharing the space with all of the bats."

Holmes stared at him intently. "By Jove, Musgrave! That is it!" he cried.

"What is it, Holmes?" I exclaimed.

---

[137] What less biased folks would call the English Civil War (1642-1651), fought between the Loyalists of King Charles I and the Parliamentarians of Oliver Cromwell.

[138] Stourbridge is a town in the West Midlands. Musgrave is most likely referring to King Edward VI College, founded 1552.

"I have been a fool, Watson. These are not three separate mysteries, but rather aspects of a greater whole. Ockham would be most pleased.[139] I should have known that Mycroft's guncotton was stolen for a specific purpose, and I should have recognized why the place at Charlton burned down so rapidly. Guncotton, as you know, gentlemen, is a type of nitrated cellulose. In small quantities, it can amaze as a magician's flash-paper, but in larger quantities it can be used for blasting. Meanwhile, the occupants of Hornfair House were clearly experimenting with nitroglycerine, which as you are all aware, is dangerously unstable. Whether the destruction of the house was an accident, or a purposeful attempt to cover their deeds once their plans were complete, may never be known. However, the stories of the Hag of Haybridge Cave are clearly a ruse utilized by this gang in order to scare away the locals from prying into their activities in the cave."

"Which is what?" asked Cartwright.

Holmes smiled. "Harvesting the guano of the native bats."[140]

"Guano?" exclaimed Trevor. "Whatever for?"

"To make saltpeter," explained Holmes. "Once you combine guncotton, nitroglycerine, and saltpeter, you produce a substance known as gelignite, or jelly.[141] Unlike dynamite, this is one of the most stable of the high explosives."

"But how is Mortlock going to use this jelly, Holmes? Is he planning another bank robbery?" I asked.

Holmes shook his head. "No, I think it probable that he is planning something far more dramatic."

"An attack? But what is his target?"

"Besides me?" said Holmes dryly. He shrugged. "He may have decided to strike a blow against Britain itself to avenge some as of yet unknown grievance. Both of his prior strikes were directed at significant foundations of our nation, both cultural and financial."

"But that leaves so many monuments – Parliament, St. Paul's, the Tower of London – the list could go on," I stammered.

Holmes was silent for a moment. "Yes, but he wants to tell us, Watson."

"He does?"

"Indeed, he needs me to be there to witness his strike. It is not

---

[139] William of Ockham (c.1287-1347) was an English philosopher, whose famous razor can be boiled down to: 'entities should not be multiplied unnecessarily.'
[140] In fact, the caves are home to the greater horseshoe bat, the largest in Europe.
[141] Gelignite, also known as blasting gelatin or simply 'jelly,' is an explosive material invented in 1875 by Swedish chemist Alfred Nobel, as an improvement over his earlier creation of dynamite (1867). Its composition makes it easily moldable and it cannot explode without a detonator, making it safer to store.

sufficient for him to destroy some pile of bricks and stone. He wants to destroy me as well, so I must be there. And he will lead me to it."

"How?"

"I will simply ask him," he answered enigmatically.

§

It was not until the following morn that I learned what he meant. During the wee hours of the night, Holmes had sent Billy and Cartwright back into the City with an important errand. When the assembled Irregulars gathered to read over the morning edition of the *Daily Chronicle*, we found within the agony column Holmes' message to Mortlock. Unlike that secret adversary, Holmes refused to hide behind codes and riddles, but rather addressed him directly, as he showed us:

> LONDON, Dec. 1st.
> Re Threats
> SIR/MADAM: –
> Referring to your telegrams of the 1st and 5th November, I beg to state that I have solved both the Riddle of the Sphinx and the Problem of the Riverbank. However, as the final matter has yet to be brought to a satisfactory conclusion, I await your command.
>   I am, Sir/Madam,
>   Faithfully yours,
>   SHERLOCK HOLMES, Esq.

Once we all had a chance to read it, Holmes leaned back in his chair and grinned. "Let us see if that draws him out, eh, gentlemen?"

The unfortunate inconvenience of this peculiar method of communicating via the newspapers, however, necessitated a significant delay in Mortlock's anticipated response. While the other members of the Irregulars were allowed to venture out of the inn for some fresh air upon the heath, Holmes forbid me from departing, claiming that I was too recognizable a figure, and that notice of my presence in Hampstead might divulge the still secret location of our current base. I therefore tried to interest myself in the most recent yellow-backed edition novel of Haggard.[142]

After what seemed an interminable amount of time, Wiggins and Simpson returned holding a copy of every evening edition paper printed

---

[142] This might be *The Lady of Blossholme*, an intriguingly-named 1909 novel by Sir H. Rider Haggard (1856-1925).

in London. Holmes reached for them, and rapidly skimmed to the end. "Mortlock is aware, gentlemen, that I am – or used to be, at any case – an avid reader of the papers' agony columns. Thus, that is where he will posit his response." Holmes turned his attention to the copy of the *Evening Standard* for a few moments, and then smiled. "Ah, yes, I see it now. Here is the first one, Watson," said he, pointing with his long, thin finger at an apparently innocent advertisement, which ran as follows:

> *Hoped to hear sooner. Terms agreed to. The Abbbot of Blackfriars is dissolved.*
> *- TOM LOCKR*

Holmes smiled broadly. "All is plain now, Watson!"

"Are you suggesting that Mortlock plans to destroy Blackfriars Station?" I asked with some confusion.

"Not at all, Watson, though Mortlock's play on the word 'dissolved' is most amusing."

"I see nothing else amiss, Holmes. What is it?"

"Come now, Watson, is not the word 'abbot' misspelled? Mortlock is not a careless man. I find the extra 'B" to be significant."

I shook my head. "How does a single letter further our case?"

"It is not a single letter, Watson, but rather eleven of them, scattered through a series of messages," he pronounced, waving his hand over the page.

"Mortlock put eleven advertisements into today's *Evening Standard*?" interjected Cartwright. "Perhaps I could go down to their offices on Fleet Street and inquire as to the identities of those responsible?"

Holmes nodded. "An excellent idea, Cartwright. It is most probable that Mr. Mortlock will have covered his tracks well, and there will be nothing to gain, but we should leave no stone unturned, in case he has finally slipped up."

"What do the eleven letters spell?" I asked.

"Reading them in order, we have 'B - O - W - R - E - D - T - I - G - E - R.'"

"Bow Red Tiger! What the devil does that mean?" exclaimed Musgrave.

Holmes smiled. "Mr. Mortlock, for 'Tom Lockr' can only be him, has time and time again shown a proclivity for the various forms of the cryptogram."

"It's an anagram," said I, suddenly realizing its meaning. "It spells out 'Tower Bridge!'"[143]

THE ASSASSINATION OF SHERLOCK HOLMES

"Capital, Watson! I had just worked that out myself. Clearly, Mr. Mortlock plans to make a rather spectacular attempt upon one of the prides of our nation. This fits well with the events at Hornfair House, for it is close to the Greenwich Line. From there it would be a straight shot on a special to the London Bridge Station, right around the corner from Tower Bridge."

"But when will he do it?" asked Trevor.

Holmes leaned back in his chair, and pulled out his cherrywood pipe. He proceeded to light it and after taking several puffs, he spoke. "It will be soon. We have baited the bear with our advertisement of yesterday, and now he is uncertain of precisely how much we know of his plans. He will not delay. It will almost certainly be tonight."

"At midnight," said I with some conviction.

Holmes glanced curiously at me. "Why do you say that?"

I shrugged. "He told us, Holmes. In his first Mortlock message: 'What walks on no legs at midnight?'"

Holmes smiled, though no touch of amusement rose to the level of his eyes. "Ah, yes, indeed he did. Very good, Watson. Midnight it is." He glanced at his watch. "We have just a few hours to plan our approach."

"But is this not a trap?" I protested.

"Of course it is, Watson. As was the little episode at the Monument. The trick is to trigger it in such a way that the spring does not catch our tail, while still absconding with the bait. Can I anticipate what Mr. Mortlock has planned, and prepare for each eventuality? I believe so. It is no different than playing chess against a grand master."

"Except in chess, no one dies." I pointed out.

He smiled wanly. "Indeed, Watson. It is a four-pipe problem, if I ever saw one."

§

Most of the evening had passed before Holmes summoned his new gang of Irregulars back to the private room that I had come to regard as our headquarters.

"Gentlemen, we are about to embark upon a most dangerous mission. There can be little doubt that Mr. Mortlock plans to catch me in his explosion, and any man who accompanies me is at risk of soon finding themselves participating in a closed-coffin funeral. So I reiterate that I will perfectly understand if there are any who wish to reconsider now that the stakes are perfectly clear." He paused and looked around the silent room.

[143] This neo-Gothic span was constructed from 1887-1894.

"No? Excellent. Then let us proceed. The problem before us is not an insignificant one. Mr. Mortlock has deigned to inform us that something of consequence will occur upon Tower Bridge at midnight. A small advantage working in our favor is that we know conclusively the nature of this threat, in no small part to the fortuitous visit of Dr. Gennery, the overly dramatic theft of the brake-van and freight carriage, and the fact that Mr. Wall heroically managed to remain alive for a sufficient time to make certain that I was made aware of the goings-on at Hornfair House. Mortlock cannot be certain that we have worked out all of these details, but he is a meticulous planner, so we must assume that he is prepared for this eventuality and has taken pains to prevent us from easily disposing of the device.

"Furthermore, we cannot be certain of the precise location of the explosive. It may be in either one of the towers or even situated in the high-level walkway overhead. Given the amount of gelignite that will be required to bring down one of those mighty structures, the most obvious method of setting it off would be to utilize a timed detonator. However, if Watson is correct about the time of the attack, it would be far too simple for us to arrive before the appointed hour and simply disable it. Of course, Mortlock would never allow his trap to be so simple, thus he must also have an alternate method of detonation. We can presume that he will be nearby, watching for my approach, and ready to prematurely throw the switch that would bring about my doom. There must be a copper cable that connects this location to the device itself. If we can find that cable, we can cut it, and by so doing, we can ensure that the approach to the explosive is safe.

"We come now, gentlemen, to our greatest advantage, which is in fact you. Save only Watson and Johnson, the odds are that Mortlock has absolutely no conception that the rest of you are aiding me in this endeavor. He will instead be expecting us to either utilize Scotland Yard, where he clearly has spies, or come alone. While they will be on the look-out for the approach of me or Watson, the others should be able to safely reconnoiter the surrounding buildings. Mortlock's men may have attempted to disguise the cable in some fashion to fool an innocent passerby, but it should be obvious now that you know what you are looking for. Musgrave, you will take Wiggins and Simpson and inspect the north bank of the river, while Trevor, Cartwright, and Billy will inspect the south."

"What about me and the Doctor?" asked Shinwell Johnson.

"Do not fear, Mr. Johnson, you both have an important part to play in this little drama. You see, while Mr. Mortlock does not know to be specifically watching for our friends, you can be certain that he will have men monitoring the cable itself. Any attempt to disable it will be met with resistance. I will therefore provide a distraction. If I can train their attention upon me, then this task will be made much easier. Your job, Mr. Johnson, and Dr. Watson too, will be to guard my back. I will be exposed during this time, and we don't want them deciding that it is easier to simply shoot me, and skip blowing up the bridge. Once someone has located and cut the cable, you will fire three rapid shots into the air. This will serve two purposes. First, it will inform me that it is safe to proceed to the location of the explosive and disarm the timed detonator that I assume Mortlock will have installed in the eventuality of a cut cable. Secondly, it should bring every constable within four blocks running. We can trust that Mortlock's men do not wish to engage in a full-scale battle upon the streets of London and will retreat before our reinforcements arrive. That will help clear my path to the explosive. Any other questions? No? Excellent. Of course, gentlemen, I need not warn you to take all the necessary precautions," concluded Holmes, as he meaningfully slipped his revolver into his pocket.

§

Holmes' gang of Irregulars split into the three assigned groups and we all climbed into dog-carts that were waiting outside the inn, plainly assembled at Holmes' request. Holmes himself drove the cart in which Mr. Johnson and I sat, his head covered by a close-fitting cap. It was a cold, dark evening, with a sharp wind and a fine rain beating upon our faces, a fit setting for the wild common over which our road passed and the tragic goal to which it led us. Eventually we returned to the familiar streets of Camden Town, and from there, Holmes wound his way down to the City. As we approached St Katherine's Way, Holmes paused.

As if sensing the question I was about to ask, he turned back to us and said in a low voice, "We want to give Trevor and Cartwright sufficient time to cross over to Southwark."

I pulled my father's gold watch from my waistcoat pocket and noted that it was twenty minutes to midnight. We did not have a surfeit of time, but I trusted Holmes' judgment. Finally, after a span of five minutes, he started the cart up again. I watched with some horror as he proceeded to drive the cart onto the bridge itself.

"Holmes!" I cried as softly as I could manage. "What are you doing?"

"This is my distraction, Watson," said he, calmly.

"This is madness!" I protested. "He will blow the bridge!"

Holmes shook his head, as he pulled up the horse in the very center of the span. "I think not, Watson. From here it would be a relatively simple matter for us to dive into the Thames, which is presently at high water, and drift to safety. He cannot be certain that bringing down either Tower would be sufficient to ensure my destruction, which you will recall is his primary purpose. No, he will wait until I am in the correct position. By the way, Watson, once we hear the pistol shots that signify the success of one of our colleagues, I will need you and Mr. Johnson to inspect the south tower, while I examine the north. If we do not find it in either locale, then it must be in the overhead walkway, and thus we will meet in the middle."

Without waiting for my response, he leapt from the driver's seat of the cart, and whipped the cap from his head. In the glare of the illuminated bridge, the distinctive clear-cut, hawk-like features of Sherlock Holmes were suddenly discernable to any who knew him. If Holmes was right and Mortlock was nearby, he would now know that we had arrived.

For several interminable minutes nothing happened. If Holmes was perturbed by this, he gave no notice of it. Instead, he calmly walked back and forth from edge to edge of the sparsely-travelled bridge. Meanwhile, Mr. Johnson indicated with a nudge that I should watch the northern approach for any signs of an assassin, while he monitored the south.

And then everything occurred at once. Three shots rang out on the northern bank, and Holmes' face lit up with triumph. But moments later, an identical trio of shots sounded from the southern bank. I could not comprehend what was transpiring, but Holmes knew at once the problem.

"They were decoys!" he exclaimed.

"What?" I cried.

"There is no need for two cables, one upon each bank. They were placed there for us to find and cut. The real cable must be..." his voice trailed off as he gazed about wildly, "there!" He pointed at a small boat that was moored close to the bridge on the eastern side. I had hardly noted it, but once Holmes drew my attention to it, I could see a thin black cable that ran from it to the upper walkways of the bridge. I then realized that the bomb was directly above our heads. The only way to reach it would be to climb one of the towers, but as soon as we did that, Mortlock would blow the explosive and bring the entire thing down upon our heads. He would then float cavalierly away down the river. We were trapped.

I think even Holmes was momentarily confounded as to the next course of action. Fortunately for us, the brave Shinwell Johnson had no such doubts. With a roar, the man ran as fast as he could in the direction of the anchored boat, whose cabin was plunged in darkness. A solitary man, his head covered by a dark hood, could be seen hunched behind the gunwale on the stern. It took mere seconds for Johnson to reach the edge of the bridge, and he then threw himself off into space. I watched with amazement as he sailed through the air with a grace I thought little possible given his massive frame. His momentum and leap were not quite sufficient to carry him as far as the boat itself, but that did not seem to be his goal. For he reached out and, with his large hands, grabbed the trailing cable itself. This had the effect of ripping a small box from the grasp of the man on the boat, while the cable, detonator, and Johnson himself proceeded to sink beneath the white swirls of the waters.

I moved to help him, but Holmes forestalled me. "No, Watson!" he cried. "Johnson can hang onto the cable until the others pull him out."

"What of Mortlock? He must be on the boat!" I exclaimed, watching as the hooded man cast off his mooring line. "We could stop him!"

Holmes shook his head. "There is no way, Watson. We have no police launch at our disposal. He will be out of our reach in moments. But the gelignite will have a back-up detonator, timed to go off in," he paused and consulted his watch, "ten minutes."

"Then there is no time to waste!" I rushed for the slightly closer south tower, where I knew a stairway led to the walkways above our heads. Holmes on my heels, I threw open the door and took the steps two at a time. Fortunately, the task was a lesser one than my frantic climb of the higher Monument, and it took us a matter of only three minutes.[144] As we burst onto the landing of the walkway, I pulled my watch from my pocket. "We have seven minutes, Holmes!" I cried. "We will be there in time!"

Holmes nodded grimly as he pushed past me and strode onto the walkway towards the north tower. "There it is, Watson," he pointed towards a wooden crate that was incongruously sitting midway along the span, a cable protruding from it and through one of the small windows. This opening allowed a rush of bitterly cold air to howl into the enclosed space, but I little felt the chill after my recent exertions.

Rushing towards it, Holmes tore off the lid and peered down into the crate. Joining him, I could see that it was filled with a row of about twenty brown paper tubes. Judging from the depth of the box, I estimated that it went roughly five tubes deep. These were all wired together with a copper filament and via this attached to an ornate silver pocket watch. I glanced at the clock, which was inexorably counting down towards detonation. To my dismay, I noted that there was less than a minute left. "But that is too short!" I protested.

Holmes shook his head ruefully, "It was a mistake, Watson, to think that Mortlock would ever play by the rules."

"But you can deactivate it?"

He pursed his lips and frowned. "In my little brain-attic I possess some

---

[144] The Monument is 202 feet tall, with 311 steps to its viewing platform, while the pedestrian walkways at Tower Bridge are only 143 feet (44 m) above the river at high tide.

knowledge pertinent to the neutralization of bombs, but I fear that there is not enough time to bring it to bear."

"Then what shall we do?" I cried.

Holmes looked about the walkway. He nodded towards a larger window nearby. "Throw that open, Watson!" he commanded. "Quickly!"

While I carried out this order, Holmes reached into the crate and pulled the bomb forth, its weight heavy even in his strong arms. He staggered to the window and with a great heave tossed it into the night. We both leaned against the window and watched it fall towards the river. If Holmes had flung it too late, it might explode in the air, and still destroy the roadway and anyone passing over the bridge. I could feel every beat of my heart as it sank towards the waves, and I cheered as the Thames covered it. Seconds later, an enormous burst of fire and steam were thrown into the air, with great sound and fury.

§

Fortuitously, as we soon discovered upon our descent, no serious harm had been done to either man or bridge. However, if I had thought that Holmes would be pleased to have narrowly avoided both his death and mine, not to mention the destruction of one of London's finest landmarks, I was much mistaken. Despite the fact that our Irregulars had fished Shinwell Johnson out of the frigid river before the bomb fell, and all were safe and sound, Holmes' mood could generously be described as taciturn. In short, he was cold and aloof for the entire drive back to our headquarters at Wat Tyler's House, and in turn, this gloom infected me and the rest of our companions. It was a grim lot that finally laid down our heads that night, each of us aware that although one plot had been hindered, Mortlock himself was still at large, and could strike against us at any moment.

In the morning, I found that Holmes had arisen before anyone else, and in a fit of uncommon courtesy, he had repaired outside to the rear garden of the inn. There he had paced back and forth long enough to wear a small furrow in the winter-browned grass, but when he joined us in the war-chamber, I noted that the bright shining of the sun seemed to have erased some of Holmes's black depression. The bright, eager spirit that greeted us in turn also served to revitalize the mood of the Irregulars.

After acknowledging each of our compatriots, Holmes sat down in the head chair and leaned back. He then proceeded to chuckle, as if he found something hilarious. "I have been terribly obtuse, Watson. I fear that I have not been operating at the heights of my powers, or I would have seen that springing Mortlock's trap was not in fact the most efficient method to go about our offensive. Instead, we should hunt him down in his bolt-hole."

"How do you propose to do that, Holmes?" I inquired.

"Tell me, Watson, what was the point of that little escapade outside of Silvester's Bank four weeks past?"

"Do you mean on top of the Monument? Why, Sebastian Moran was trying to assassinate you and Inspector Lestrade. It was intended to be Moran's revenge for Lestrade capturing him, with no small assistance from you, Holmes, fifteen years ago."

Holmes raised his bushy eyebrows. "Was it? I wonder." He tapped his pip against the arm of his chair.

"What else could it have been?" interjected Shinwell Johnson.

"A test. And perhaps a trap," said he, enigmatically. "Watson, I should have gone with you to interview Moran. This was a capital mistake. Perhaps I could have prevented his death, or at least delayed it until we obtained more useful information from him. And there is no substitute for direct observations made at the scene of the crime."

"I described everything to you, Holmes," I protested.

"You described everything you saw, Watson. That is not the same as everything I would have observed."

"Then go now," I replied, with some peevishness at his recitation of my apparent limitations.

He shook his head. "No, I am afraid it is far too late for that. You will just have to tell it again."

I sighed and proceeded to do so, as his eyelids drooped and he attempted to visualize the scene. When I was finished reciting Moran's last breaths, however, he simply sighed. "It will not do, Watson. How could you have let him die before your eyes?"

"How was I to know that the cigarettes were poisoned, Holmes! And the speed by which they acted...."

He suddenly sprang upright. "That is it, Watson! Unless there was only one poisoned cigarette, amongst a case of normal ones, then this must have been a new package. Something that was delivered shortly before you arrived!"

I thought back. "There was a woman..."

"What!" he exclaimed. "You only mention this now?"

I shrugged. "How could I have known that the trivial matter of a woman leaving the prison just as I arrived would be of any note?"

Holmes shook his head. "Watson, Watson. How many times must I tell you that there is nothing so important as trifles? We may take it as a working hypothesis that this woman was the vector of Moran's doom. The question is why?"

I frowned. "Is not the question the nature of her identity?"

"Not at all, Watson." He turned to the former district messenger boy. "Cartwright, this is exactly the sort of task that you excel at. We shall send you to Wandsworth Prison forthwith in order to determine who precisely had the necessary permit to visit Colonel Sebastian Moran."

"What if she used a false identity?" I protested.

"Possible, Watson, possible. But Moran was no simple smash-and-grabber. Not just any person could waltz into his cell. They would need a good reason. And from that we should be able to deduce her true self."

§

Several hours passed before Cartwright returned from this errand, and it proved that there was little deduction needed to be made. For the woman had brazenly signed both her name and provided the location of her London residence. The latter was at 98 Finchley Road, at a Camden inn called the Swiss Tavern, and the former was listed as 'Patience Moran.'

This was, of course, a name that I recognized, like a specter from the past. "Could it be the same girl, Holmes?" I asked, aghast.

He shrugged. "A girl no more, Watson, for the McCarthy case was twenty years ago. But there are stranger things in heaven and earth."

"Is she a relative?"

Holmes nodded slowly. "Perhaps a niece. Her father was the local lodge-keeper, was he not? Possibly a by-blow of the late Sir Augustus? At the time of the Boscombe Valley affair, I had yet to determine that Sebastian Moran was serving as the chief lieutenant for Professor Moriarty's empire of crime, and thus, I took little notice of the girl's name. In retrospect, that may have been a mistake."

However, it is difficult to say how Holmes could have possibly suspected the transformation of the girl we found waiting for us in a private room at the Swiss Tavern. She proved to be but a few years over thirty and her face was still unlined. Her piled up hair was golden blond, which contrasted vividly with her eyes, so dark brown to be almost black. She wore what was plainly an expensive grey muslin dress and her neck was adorned with a golden necklace studded by a dozen exquisite rubies. Sitting in a high-backed chair, her posture was ramrod straight, as if she was a sergeant-of-arms just off the parade ground. I thought her beautiful at first glance, but further inspection revealed the blazing eyes that I recognized from portraits of such zealots as Joan of Arc or Bloody Mary. As soon as she spoke, I realized that she was far gone from the paths of decency.

"Good morning, gentlemen," said she, in a voice like being entombed in a glacier. "I have been expecting you for several days now. I had been told to anticipate far more from you, Mr. Holmes, but it is now clear that you were put out to pasture for a reason."

If Holmes was upset by her slights, his face did not show it. "And your uncle? Were you also instructed to put him down, like a maimed thoroughbred?"

She chuckled, but there was a curiously-hollow tone in her laughter, as if she was merely aping the emotion rather than actually experiencing it. "Very good, Mr. Holmes. But are you simply guessing, I wonder?" When Holmes failed to respond, she continued. "He was never very kind to me, you know, or to my father, who was but his half-brother," she shrugged. "So once he had outlived his usefulness, it was time to make certain that he could betray no confidences."

"And who precisely trained you to be a lowly assassin?" asked Holmes, harshly.

But Holmes' blistering words made little impression upon her rosy cheeks. Only her cold dark eyes narrowed dangerously. "Those are dangerous words, Mr. Holmes. If you were to repeat them in public, you can be certain that you would be hearing from my solicitor. Do you truly want your last appearance in the papers to be the story of how you libeled a defenseless young woman?"

"It is not libel if it is true."

"If what is true, Mr. Holmes?" She opened her empty palms. "What proof do you have that I have ever committed a crime? Especially one so foul as the murder of my own uncle. Who could believe such a thing?"

Holmes shook his head. "I may not be able to directly link you to the Colonel's death, but once I imprison Mr. Mortlock, you can be certain that your source of income will be cut off. How long will you be able to eat after pawning that necklace on Tottenham Court Road? Three months? And then what? The workhouse? The back lanes of Whitechapel?"

She smiled cruelly. "You truly do not see, do you, Mr. Holmes? What do I care of fancy jewelry and fine dresses? These are merely props, stage settings for the great play in which we are all actors. Unfortunately for you, the playwright has deemed that this will be a tragedy. And like all great tragedies, it must end with the protagonist's death." She glanced over at me for the first time. "Only your Horatio here will be allowed to survive long enough in order to take up his pen and record the sequel to his prior false finale. What shall you call it, Doctor? *The Fall of Sherlock Holmes?* I think that has a nice ring."

"So you will not give him up?" Holmes demanded.

With a smile that dripped with false sweetness, she shrugged again. "Give who up, Mr. Holmes? Provide me with a name, not some *nom-de-*

plume, and perhaps I can help you." She stared at him for a moment. "No? Then be gone, I say!" she waved her hand, her tone no less commanding than a queen of old, though I knew her to be nothing but a country-bred lass.

Holmes stared at her for a moment, and then nodded coolly. "Very well, Miss Moran. If you will not listen to a voice of reason, then there is little I can do to save you when the sword falls. And fall it will. Even the great Professor Moriarty was no match for me. What hope does Mr. Mortlock have?"

He strode out imperiously, matching her manner with a similar aloofness. As I followed behind him, I glanced back to see if he had made any impression on the fanatical soul that resided in the bosom of what looked like nothing more than a modest young lady. But I feared that there was nothing hopeful in her lifeless gaze.

As we departed, I threw my hands into the air. "Why will she not give him up? Does she not realize that he is a monster?"

Holmes shook his head. "As you know, Watson, I am not a whole-hearted admirer of the so-called gentler sex. I find them to be capable of as many horrors as a man. And while their inner workings are more your area of expertise, I would suggest that she must be in the grips of a perverted love, much as were Maria Pinto Gibson or Violet de Merville. And a woman's love is not so easily set aside."

"But if she will not tell us anything, how are we to ever find Mortlock?"

"I can think of seven separate possibilities, Watson. For example, we could wait for either her to go to him or vice versa, but that could prove to be a long game. Who knows how long they are willing to go without seeing each other? And then we have given him sufficient time to devise some new scheme against us. No, we must maintain our momentum of last night, when we disrupted his carefully-planned attempt upon my life."

"So what do you propose?"

He stopped and looked at me. "Tell me, Watson, what poison was in that fatal cigarette?"

I frowned. "I do not know, Holmes."

"But surely you still retain the professional knowledge of all medical men on the pharmacopoeia of typical poisons, either deliberate or accidental, that you might encounter in your daily practice?"

"Of course, Holmes. But this was certainly no common poison," I protested. "Did you yourself not once write the definitive monograph on the various agents employed by the famous poisoners throughout the centuries?"

He smiled. "I did indeed, Watson. And that is what is so remarkable."

"So you do recognize it?"

"No, I do not."

"But you just said that it was remarkable!" I protested.

"Exactly, Watson. As I have said before, singularity is almost invariably a clue. The fact that Miss Moran employed a poison unknown to me suggests that it is singularly rare. If we can identify it, we should be able to determine from where it came. And there, unless I miss my mark, we shall find Mr. Mortlock."

"So it is to be a chemical experiment, then?"

Holmes nodded. "Of course. However, it is during moments like this that I regret my retirement, Watson. For while Mycroft's chamber served as a marginally adequate base, even if the repairs were complete, it cannot truly replace our flat at Baker Street. And of course, our Hampstead inn is remarkably lacking in chemical equipment."

I shrugged. "I have a suggestion, Holmes. Why not use the laboratory at St Bart's? I am certain they would let you borrow it one more time."

A smile lit up his normally grim face. "Ah, Watson, you are in a deplorably sentimental mood today. You wish to return to the scene where we were first introduced?"

I smiled in return. "Why not? While you are working, I may even pay a visit to the Criterion Bar."

Holmes shook his head and laughed. "I suppose if this is to be the end of us, there is something apropos of coming full circle. Very well, let us head to your old stomping grounds."

§

A hansom ride of some twenty minutes deposited us at the steps of St Bart's, though we stopped along the way so that Holmes could dash into a telegraph office and order Gregson to meet us there with a representative sample of the instrument of Moran's death. As I stepped from the cab, a profound sense of familiarity washed over me, and I knew I would need no guiding to our destination. Gregson, stalwart and true, was waiting for us with the requested package, which he handed carefully to Holmes. However, the Inspector seemed mildly dismayed that Holmes would not include him further in his confidence, and he departed morosely.

Once he was gone, Holmes and I turned down the narrow lane and through a small side-door into one wing of the great hospital. We climbed the stone staircase, even bleaker after an additional thirty years of wear, and made our way through the long corridors of whitewashed walls and dun-colored doors. Near the far end, a low arched passageway branched off to the old chemical laboratory. This lofty chamber had little changed since the last time I stepped through its doors. It was still lined and littered with countless bottles, while a plethora of students were absorbed in their work over the flickering blue flames of their Bunsen lamps.

Holmes spotted one unoccupied space and immediately set to work on the poisoned cigarettes with the pipettes, retorts, and test-tubes that he found there. I had accompanied Holmes up to the chemical laboratories in a nostalgic temperament, but the noxious fumes soon drove me from the place. I did not bother to inform the engrossed Holmes of my destination, for I knew that he would easily deduce it. I spent many fine minutes under the glistening ceiling of the Long Bar, whose gold mosaics were curled down into ornaments of blue and white tesserae. Over a glass or two of Château d'Yquem, I merrily conversed with a wide variety of acquaintances that I had not seen for many years. I had almost forgotten my *raison d'être* when Holmes finally appeared. His body looked haggard, which was hardly surprising given how hard he had been pushing himself over the last few weeks, and his hands were covered with small pieces of plaster where he had clearly had some recent mishap. But his manner was bright.

"He has finally made his mistake, Watson," said he, exultantly.

"You have identified the poison then?"

"I have indeed. And it can only have come from one place."

"Where?"

"All in good time, Watson." He leaned back and took a small phial from his pocket. "As I suspected, this has not yet found its way into either the pharmacopeia or into the general literature of toxicology. I shall have to revise Chapter Four of *The Whole Art of Detection*. But I have nonetheless found references to it in Eckermann. It is known as tetrodotoxin, and has some similar properties to curare, which you will recall is the favorite poison found on South American arrows. But unlike curare, which is a plant-based poison, tetrodotoxin derives from a certain species of *Pisces* known as the puffer."[145]

"Was there not a sea captain in English history whose crew and hogs fell sick from eating pufferfish?"[146]

"Excellent, Watson, you are scintillating this evening. And do you also know what nation is known for their consumption of pufferfish?"

---

[145] Tetrodotoxin is the neurotoxin found in improperly prepared pufferfish, or *fugu*, which only the most expert chefs are legally allowed to prepare. It can be fatal within thirty minutes of ingestion. It was first isolated in 1909 by the Japanese scientist Yoshizumi Tahara.

[146] In fact there was. Watson is thinking of James Cook (1728-1779), at the time captain of the HMS *Resolution*, whose log from 7 September 1774 records this incident. Cook and his men survived to go on to be the first Europeans to visit the Hawaiian Islands.

I shook my head. "Unfortunately I do not, Holmes."

He smiled. "Fortunately, I do. It is a practice common solely to the men of Nippon."

"How does that help us?"

"Because, Watson, the Empire of Nippon, or Japan as we call it in English, is a very isolated place. Unlike the denizens of Limehouse, who mainly hail from China and India, there are very few *nikkei* here in London. They live primarily in the area of Somers Town, where on Phoenix Street you can find the one eatery in London where pufferfish are sold."[147]

"You seem very well informed about them, Holmes."

"Remember, Watson, that I have some knowledge of baritsu, or the Japanese system of wrestling. Where do you think I learned it?"

"Holmes, I recall reading about the recent Anglo-Japanese Alliance.[148] Do you suspect that this is an effort to drive some wedge between our nations?"

"No, Watson. This is more personal. You may consider it a conceit, but everything to date has had a purpose directed towards Mortlock revenging himself upon me. The thefts and murder at the British Museum, the robbery at Threadneedle Street, the attempted destruction of Tower Bridge, none of them meant anything to Mortlock beyond being a tactic to be used against me."

"Who then is Mortlock?"

He smiled and nodded slowly. "You asked that once before, Watson. At the time, I had no answer, but I now have a theory. Let us gather our troops and see if I am correct."

§

Instead of returning to Hampstead, Holmes wired to Wat Tyler's House to inform his Irregulars that they should meet us at a ramshackle café on the Midland Road. There he left me for few minutes to reconnoiter the local area. By the time they had all assembled, Holmes had returned and dusk was falling.

"I don't understand why we are here, Holmes?"

"The clouds are finally lifting, Watson."

---

[147] The area of Somers Town was first populated by citizens of Japan c.1880, who had been sent to study at University College London. The *nikkei* are Japanese emigrants and their descendants that reside in a foreign country.

[148] The first Anglo-Japanese Alliance was signed on January 30, 1902, and the Japanese fought (albeit in limited fashion) on the side of Britain during World War I.

I glanced through the window at the sky, which still loomed an ominous grey. "I think not, Holmes. I see a storm approaching on the horizon."

"Good old, Watson!" he laughed. "I have every hope that the light of truth is breaking through. Gentlemen, I believe that I have identified the base of our elusive adversary. His lair is beneath an innocuous shop two blocks away."

"How can you be certain?" I asked.

He shook his head. "We will never be entirely certain until I have stared into the whites of his eyes, but I think it highly probable that we will find him within. For there are few other shops in this part of London whose back room is filled with crates that are being guarded by a man with a number twelve shoe." I think it highly probable that we will find Murderous Mathews within those walls."

"The giant?"

"Indeed, Watson. The very man who tried to remove your arm three days prior. Once Mortlock sacrificed Colonel Moran, it is simple to deduce that he would need another lieutenant to carry out his commands, so that he himself can remain in the shadows. Mathews may not have been blessed with a surfeit of brains, but his strength is second to none, and once bought, his loyalty is without question. Once we dispose of Mathews, our path to Mortlock should be clear." Holmes paused and glanced at me. "Have you a theory, Watson?"

"It can only be Professor Moriarty."

Holmes laughed grimly. "A fine guess, Watson, as you suggested once before. I admit that the similarities are most redolent of the dearly departed Professor's touch. One such example is what your friend Mr. Goldfield discovered under the counterfeit painting of *Le Jeane Fille*, which he told me in response to a follow-up telegram."

"I thought he said it was the work of a minor German painter?"

"Indeed, specifically a Romantic painter. From our days spent perusing the walls of the Bond Street Galleries, Watson, surely you recall that this group favored dramatic landscapes?"

"Of course," I shrugged. "What of it?"

"Well, this particular painting was of Reichenbach Falls."

I was stunned speechless by this news. "Then it is Moriarty!" I finally exclaimed.

"No, no, Watson. I previously assured you that Professor James Moriarty perished in that abyss, and I have seen nothing to make me alter my opinion."

"Who then?"

"Do you recall, Watson, when I said that the trial of the Professor's gang had left two of its most dangerous members free?"

"Of course. One was Colonel Sebastian Moran. And the other was...." I tailed off, thinking. "I don't know, Holmes. Was it Parker?"

Holmes shook his head. "Parker was never more than a lowly pawn in this game. He is not of sufficient importance to count in any tally. No, the other was Colonel Robert Moriarty."

"His brother!" I exclaimed.

"Indeed, Watson."

Cartwright frowned. "I thought there were two brothers?"

Holmes chuckled. "We shall forgive poor Watson here for not being overly precise in his descriptions of those days. He was much distraught in 1891, when he thought me to have passed on to the undiscovered country, and much excited in 1894, when my little deception was finally abandoned. He even called the man the same sobriquet as his elder brother, the professor. There was always but one brother, Robert by name. Like Sebastian Moran, Colonel Robert Moriarty was drummed out of the Indian Army for conduct unbecoming, though the precise details of the scandal are vague. He then seemingly settled into country life as a station master in the west of England. But where James was like a spider, Robert is a chameleon. He is completely unremarkable in appearance, and a natural actor to boot. He disappears into roles in a fashion that eclipses even my small talents in the way of disguise."

"He impersonated you at the Bank of England!" I exclaimed.

"Certainly, Watson. He also walked out of their empty vault in the guise of a policeman. I believe that he was also 'Andrew Morrison,' the missing guard from the British Museum, as well as the false guard on the munitions train. And I suspect that he may have played one other role in this drama, which I hope to confirm as soon as we confront him."

"So, we are going to crack the shop, Mr. Holmes?" asked Shinwell Johnson.

"Indeed we are," said Holmes, nodding grimly.

Johnson shrugged. "Maybe it's not my place to say so, sir, but why don't we bring in the official police force? Surely the Yarders are more equipped for this task than our little band?"

"An excellent question, Mr. Johnson. Do you recall the air-gun of Colonel Sebastian Moran? That gun was safely locked in the Scotland Yard Museum before it mysteriously made its way back into his hands. From this I can only deduce that someone within the ranks of the C.I.D. is aiding the efforts of Colonel Robert Moriarty. I have my suspicion as to this individuals' identity, of course, but no proof. Until that person is removed from their position of power, I fear that any attempt to enlist the aid of Lestrade, Gregson, and company would only serve to warn Moriarty of our impending assault."

"You can count on us, Mr. Holmes," said Billy eagerly. This affirmation was taken up by all present.

"Thank you, gentlemen. While Watson and I awaited your arrival, I carefully scouted the building of interest. Besides Mr. Mathews, there are at least ten other men inside, and we must assume that each of them is well armed. Any individual allowed this close to Robert Moriarty's base will be a violent and desperate soul, doubly-so if they are cornered. But we can allow none to escape, for Moriarty's skill with disguises is unparalleled, and he could easily slip through our fingers in the most innocuous of guises. Given the profound dangers, each of you will carry a weapon and no one will proceed unaccompanied in this task. There are four apparent exits from which Moriarty may attempt to escape. The two obvious ones are the front and rear doors. Cartwright and Billy, you will go in the front door. Mr. Johnson will enter though the back-door. As that is where I expect you will find Mr. Mathews, both Musgrave and Trevor will support you. The other two entrances are less obvious. There is a skylight opening onto the roof, from where it would be simplicity itself to cross to either of the neighboring buildings. Wiggins, you and Simpson, will enter from that direction. Finally, the villains have cut a hole into the basement of the eatery next door. This provides the ability to come and go unnoticed. Watson and I will enter via that aperture." He pulled his watch from his waistcoat pocket. "It will take some time for Wiggins and Simpson to get into position, so we will synchronize our watches and move on the strike of eight o'clock. Are there any questions?"

As there were none, our group disbanded towards our respective assignments. Holmes and I made for the eatery, where, our faces muffled by our scarves, we took seats in the darkest corner. Although the place was crowded with men who originally hailed from Japan, there were enough westerners that we did not immediately appear out of place. From the looks of these non-Japanese clients, it seemed that most were sailors who had made their way up from the docklands to sample the unique cuisine served in this establishment. Holmes and I were perhaps somewhat overdressed, but no one seemed to take especial notice of us.

A woman appeared to take our order and Holmes asked for several exotic-sounding items, the names meaning little to me. But I was never to learn what precisely the words signified, for before any food could arrive, Holmes pulled his out his pocket-watch and glanced at it. Holmes turned to me and smiled. "Now, Watson, we'll just take our luck together, as we have occasionally done in the past."

I nodded my agreement, and rose to follow Holmes. He pushed past a pair of startled waiters and made his way towards the back of the building, where we found a set of stairs heading downwards into the earth. Taking the steps two at a time, he bounded down them, and I endeavored to do the same, careful to ensure that my old-war wound did not flare at such an inopportune time. At the bottom, Holmes followed a brick-line passageway about fifteen feet, which ended at a door. This proved to be barred by a stout Chubb's lock, but that was little match for Holmes' quick pick-work. The door swung open, but Holmes caught it before it could make any sound. The corridor behind was lined with wooden panels, a change which made it clear that we had left one building and had proceeded into the cellar of the adjoining one, where Holmes believed our nemesis made his lair. Finally, the corridor ended at another door, this one unlocked. There was no way to see what might lay behind it. I tightly gripped my Webley Mark III .380 caliber pocket revolver, which more than once had been a good friend in need. Holmes nodded in approval and holding his own pistol, he pushed open the door.

We stepped into a large, vault-like room, with rough masonry walls and vaulted ceiling. Overhead, several electric bulbs flooded the chamber with a harsh light. It appeared to have been converted from the cellar of a warehouse into a fairly comfortable office, though the long-ago white-washed masonry was now old, stained, and grimy. There were no windows, of course, but rather the walls were covered by an admixture of Old Master paintings and maps of England, France, Germany, and Russia. Notably, there was also a heavily-marked map of London and many charts of buildings, with their floor plans, as well as diagrams of possible tunnels. Finally, the room contained many improvised shelves, which sagged under the weight of innumerable books. I noted, with a strange mix of pride and dismay, that my own modest works were prominently situated within arm's grasp of the owner of this illicit head-quarters.

Robert Moriarty himself was seated at a large circular desk facing us. He had been looking over a pile of letters, telegrams, and other assorted papers, but set them aside at the sound of our footsteps. Now that I had finally put a face to our mysterious adversary, I found him to be utterly unremarkable. He was a middle-aged man, but without any of the distinctive features that once marked his evil brother. There was no domed forehead, or deep-sunken eyes, or curious reptilian manner. It was in short, not a face full of character. Rather than the man of great intellectual force, the Professor's brother looked like little more than a mild grocery clerk.

With me in close pursuit, Holmes strode forward, his pistol trained upon the man. "Ah, there is your missing Greuze, Watson. And is that a Raphael I see?"

The man behind the desk looked up and smiled. To my consternation, his eyes betrayed no surprise. He appeared little upset by the sight of our guns. "Welcome, Sherlock, you don't mind if I call you that, do you?" he said. "And you too, John. There should be no formality between such old friends. As you may have deduced, I have been expecting you." His manner was as cool as ice, his voice silky and as soothing as a fashionable consultant, and as poisonous as a cobra. But the dead black of his eyes possessed all the cruelty of the grave.

Holmes seemed briefly startled at Moriarty's lack of alarm, but quickly recovered his composure. "It is a pleasure to see you again, Mr. Maurice."

It was with some surprise that I belatedly recognized the face of the man we had met in the Threadneedle Street vault in the form of the man before us. "The adjutant to the police commissioner!"

"Of course, Watson. How else do you think Colonel Moriarty acquired access to so many of my former enemies? The criminal fraternity that once belonged to his brother had been irretrievably fractured. However, using his official connections as the commissioner's assistant, he clandestinely recruited James Windibank, Parker, Beppo, John Clay and Archie, the Beddington brothers, Victor Lynch, Holy Peters, and Killer Evans. Promised a chance of revenge for their imprisonments, they all joined his scheme willingly, though I suspect that few of them knew exactly what Colonel Moriarty had planned for them. Certainly, Sebastian Moran was not expecting your master stroke."

Moriarty shrugged. "Moran was my brother's creature, not mine. He already failed my brother twice, first at the falls, and again at Camden House. I offered him one more chance to eliminate you himself. But after a third attempt faltered, there was little advantage to keeping him around. And Moran was a cunning soul, with a mercenary streak as wide as the Channel. He knew much about me and my plans. I did not wish to risk the possibility of him deciding that he would have more to gain by selling his knowledge to you or to Scotland Yard."

"So you used his niece to deliver the deadly package?" I exclaimed.

The man smiled cruelly. "Some women are overly impressionable, Dr. Watson. Do you not recall how readily Lady Frances Carfax fell under the spell of Dr. Shlessinger and his wife? Similarly, it took little effort to bend Patience Moran to my will, and I knew he would never suspect her to be the handmaiden of his doom."

"And your unnatural youth must have assisted you in that matter," said Holmes, dryly.

Moriarty chuckled. "Do you know that for a fact, Sherlock, or are you merely guessing?"

"I never guess. It is an appalling habit," replied Holmes. "I knew that Löwenstein had at least one other client in England, and I suggested to the

Doctor that he cut off future supplies of his extract."

"Which he eventually did," said Moriarty, shrugging. "But even that turned out to be a blessing in disguise, so I must thank you, Sherlock. You see, the youth and strength imbued from the Anthropoid extract have remained, while some of the more violent, animalistic tendencies have faded with time."

"Not from where I am sitting," I said, heatedly. I shook my head at the vast scope of his conspiracy against Holmes. "But such a scheme must have taken years to plan!" I exclaimed.

Moriarty smiled cruelly at me. "Oh, yes, John. When I first heard of my brother's murder at the hands of Sherlock here, my soul cried out for revenge. To think of it, my brilliant brother, slain by some inferior in mind, only because he possessed a slight advantage in physical strength! It was monstrous. What have you ever given the world, Sherlock? Where is your *Dynamics of an Asteroid?* No, you are merely the envious little assassin of a superior man. That is when I decided that revenge was a dish best served cold."[149]

"The old sweet song," said Holmes. "How often have I heard it in days gone by! It was a favorite ode of your late lamented brother and of Colonel Moran. Brooks and Woodhouse have also been known to hum it. And yet I live and keep bees upon the South Downs."

"So you did, Sherlock, so you did. But I do not think that you will be tending your apiary again after today."

"And the point of it all?" I interjected, exasperatedly. "The pharaoh's curse? The problem at Threadneedle Street?"

The man's eyebrows rose up on his forehead. "The point? Why, John, surely even you, the lesser partner of the Firm, has managed to deduce that by now! The point is Sherlock's death. Not some quiet death of old age, happily puttering with his beehives, but a death worthy of a celebrated man like Sherlock Holmes. He needed to be coaxed back to London with a case that was impossible to resist, then kept here by a series of ongoing mysteries, until I could set the stage for his funeral pyre."

I stared at him with some revulsion. He was like a madman – indeed I think he was a madman, subtly mad with the deep power of deception which insane people may have. He had so raging a hatred of Holmes in his heart that he could no longer be considered human.

Holmes merely yawned. "And yet, here you sit, alone and facing down the barrels of two guns. Your men have all been dispatched, your schemes foiled."

---

[149] The origin of this phrase is obscure. It has been attributed to the French diplomat Talleyrand (1754–1838) and has been in the English language at least since 1846.

"Have they?" said he, laughing enigmatically. "Did you not come to me, Sherlock? Is not the very first rule of war to choose the site of the battle? He who controls the ground typically wins." With the barest flick of his wrist, he pulled upon a lever and the room was suddenly plunged into darkness. I immediately fired my gun, as did Holmes at my side, the shots ringing out deafeningly in the enclosed space of the underground room. However, there was no cry of pain to signal that our shots had struck home. Instead, I thought I heard a noise like a heavy iron door creaking open, but I could not be certain of anything in the disorienting blackness of the room.

Moments later, the gloom was broken by the piercing glare shining from a tungsten torch, which Holmes must have had concealed in his pocket.[150]

"Where has he gone?" I cried.

But Holmes had already sprung to the spot behind the desk where Moriarty had been sitting. He was plainly inspecting the wall for the secret mechanism though which Moriarty must have fled.

"By Jove, Watson! He had one last escape route prepared."

"Can you open it?" I exclaimed. "What of the lever?"

Holmes shook his head, a motion I could barely make out in the dim wavering light. "That only appears to have dimmed the lights, Watson. I fear that the door is controlled by another mechanism."

"Could he have locked it from behind? Is he trying to trap us in this room?"

"To what end?"

"Poison gas, perhaps?"

Again Holmes shook his head. "No, Watson, Robert Moriarty is no Amberley. He wants to witness my demise, not see me slowly suffocate."

I threw the lever and brought the lights of the room to bear upon our problem. "Then he must want us to follow him wherever this door leads."

"Very good, Watson," said Holmes dryly, still examining the wall in hopes of finding some pressure point that might open the hidden door.

I looked about the room, focusing my attention upon the desk where Moriarty had been sitting. The various papers could wait, though I was certain that they contained a bounty of information on his criminal enterprises. There was a strange hollow tube leading up through the ceiling, which I finally decided that he used to communicate with his lackeys in the warehouse above. And then there was a foot and a half-high wooden frame, from which was suspended a bronze gong. "Holmes!" I

---

[150] Not an actual torch, but what Americans would call a flashlight. The flashlight was patented in 1899, and tungsten filaments invented in 1904, but Holmes is not recorded as having used one in any Canonical adventure.

exclaimed, pointing at it.

"What is it, Watson?"

"Is that not a Tibetan gong?"

Holmes stopped what he was doing and turned to look at it. "It is indeed," said he, quietly.

"Moriarty knew that you spent two years in Tibet after the events at Reichenbach Falls."

"Without a doubt, Watson!" Holmes became animated at this realization. "Everything he has done has been orchestrated to lead me back to that happy day, when a terrible blight upon society was finally brought low."

I picked up the wooden hammer, and tapped lightly upon the gong. The sound was quiet, so much so that our shots must have masked it previously. But immediately, the same creaking sound was heard as a crack appeared in the wall near where Holmes was standing. He reached out and pushed the iron door fully open.

Dropping the hammer, I joined him and gazed into the black maw that lay behind the secret door. At first I thought that within all was absolute silence and darkness. But then I made something out, sounding as if it was echoing from a great distance. "Is that water that I hear, Holmes?"

Holmes listened for a moment and then nodded grimly. "I fear that it is. This building must have been built over some covered tributary, perhaps even the Fleet itself. Now it has become part of the sewer system." He shook his head, plainly irritated. "I should have expected this, given his use of the sewers under Threadneedle Street."

"What are we to do?"

"There is only possible option for me at this time, Watson. I am going in."

"Then I am going with you, Holmes."

He shook his head. "Are you certain, Watson? You have almost died on multiple occasions. Your luck can only be pressed so far."

"The same can be said of you, Holmes, but you continue to do your duty."

He smiled. "Indeed. Well, we have not yet met our Waterloo, Watson, but this may be our Trafalgar."[151] He reached out his hand.

I clasped it in silence, and the die was cast.

---

[151] Here Holmes is mixing his metaphors. In *The Adventure of the Abbey Grange*, he compared himself to Napoleon, saying: 'We have not yet met our Waterloo, Watson, but this is our Marengo, for it begins in defeat and ends in victory.' But here Holmes appears to be comparing himself to Admiral Nelson, who won a great victory off the coast of Spain, but at the cost of his own life.

§

Before we entered the foreboding doorway, Holmes paused and reached into his pocket. He drew forth an envelope and handed it to me. "The endgame draws nigh, Watson. Should anything happen to me, should we become separated for some reason, I want you to open this immediately."

"I suggest that we avoid becoming separated down there, Holmes."

"I completely concur, Watson, but one must prepare for all eventualities. I need not remind you to keep your powder dry. You have already shown a steady hand when you were faced with the terrible threat of Killer Evans. But Robert Moriarty makes Evans look like a schoolboy by comparison."

"I understand, Holmes. I once swore an oath to preserve lives, but not all lives are worthy of that oath. Moriarty is something less than human."

Holmes nodded tightly and stepped through the doorway. Once inside, our path lit only by the frail rays sent off from his torch, I felt a crushing sense of claustrophobia unlike anything I had ever experienced before, as if the world above had ceased to exist. But this had the opposite effect upon Holmes, who was clearly invigorated by the challenge. All other extraneous players had exited the stage. Much like that terrible day above Meiringen, it was now just the two adversaries fated to meet in a struggle from which could emerge but one victor. However, Holmes had one advantage. Unlike that fateful day in 1891, this time I would not be lured from his side by some despicable ruse. I was in it until the end.

We found that the passage was entirely bricked; it's walls stained with damp and slime. It sloped downwards until we found ourselves in the curved tunnel of a sewer proper, a hazy, foul-smelling miasma lying over the water. In addition to the steady flow of the waste-laden water, I thought I could hear the skittering feet of the innumerable rats which I knew to haunt these warrens. After a moment's hesitation, as he determined the route taken by Robert Moriarty, Holmes followed the ankle-high current downstream, our feet soaked and slipping upon the wet stone. It was nigh impossible to gage distance in that malodorous underground hell, but I sensed that we had travelled at least half a mile, ignoring several side passages along the way. Holmes paused at each, but even I could easily determine that Moriarty had not passed through any of them, for the sludge piled at the junctions was thick and undisturbed. Finally, Holmes pointed towards a narrower tunnel that led off to the left. Stooping, so as to not brush our heads on the bilious green-stained bricks of the ceiling, he carefully entered it. The water was now rushing faster past our knees, and the sound level rising in the smaller space such that a herd of elephants could have been waiting for us at the end and we would have never known. Instead it would prove to be something far more terrible. Suddenly, Holmes stopped, as the tunnel opened into a far larger chamber.

"What is it, Holmes?" I whispered.

In response, Holmes shone his torch about. I could see that it was a fearful place, the subterranean equivalent to that torrential fall high in the Swiss Alps. I estimated from the sudden increase in whirling clamor that at least eight shafts identical to the one where we stood all came together here. Their combined burdens rushed down into a tremendous chasm. The glistening brick-lined shaft narrowed into a boiling pit of incalculable depth. I felt a terrible sense of déjà vu as I stood near the edge and peered down into the blackness below, the place from which Robert Moriarty surely intended that Holmes would never return.

A rusting metal bridge beckoned us forward over the abyss, but Holmes' torch could not throw its pale light over the entire length, such that the other side was lost in the gloom of the large chamber. If we crossed it, we would be fully exposed to anyone waiting upon the other side.

"We must turn back, Holmes," I protested, shouting above the din. "We must assume that Moriarty has a gun. This is the perfect place for him to ambush us."

Holmes did not answer at first. His pale, eager face had suddenly assumed that tense, far-way expression which I had learned to associate with the supreme manifestation of his genius. "Of course it is, Watson. That is why we must move forward. I will go first, and you will follow directly behind, your revolver trained over my right shoulder. If you see anything move on the other side, that is where you must train your aim."

"This is madness, Holmes!"

"Perhaps one must be a little mad to stop a madman. But the straight road of destiny leads onwards, Watson." And without another word, he strode forth onto the bridge. I had no choice but to follow him.

Holmes got about half-way across the slick metal slats of the bridge when he suddenly stopped and shouted in his loudest voice. "Ah, this is much like Reichenbach Falls, do you not think, Watson?"

The same terrible thought had of course occurred to me, but I had submerged it, rather than allow such a fear to consume me. Before I could even give voice to a response, a series of shots blazed out from the darkness. Without hesitation, I raised my pistol in the direction from which the muzzle flare had blazed and fired until all of my chambers were empty.

It was then that I stopped at looked at Holmes. Everything happened so fast, I could barely process it. Even as I had finished firing, I watched as Holmes, his shirt-front perforated by no less than four bullets, staggered backwards, tottering upon the brink. He looked at me and without a word, dropped over the edge of the bridge into the churning deep below. I gave a cry of surprise and dismay as I watched his body drop into that awful abyss. A sudden flood of horror utterly submerged my mind, and it was many minutes before I could feel function returning to my limbs.

A nobler man never walked the earth. And in a heartbeat, he was gone.

§

So, fortunately, was Colonel Robert Moriarty, but this time to his just reward. When I was finally able to walk, I found Moriarty's body, pierced with all six of my bullets, lying motionless on the far side of the bridge. I held my fingers against his throat for at least five minutes, far longer than required, so as to be certain beyond all possible doubt that his foul heart beat no longer.

As I knelt there, I realized that Holmes had determined that there was only one way out of the stalemate that Moriarty had devised. If Holmes had failed to press on, Moriarty would have escaped, and who knows how many more innocents would have been killed by that madman before we were once again able to track him down? But by moving towards Moriarty, Holmes had willingly sacrificed himself so that I could be in place to deliver the *coup de grâce*. He had made England safe once more, but at a price I found far too great to contemplate.

It was many hours before I was done speaking with Lestrade and Gregson. It seemed as if all of Scotland Yard had descended upon the warehouse at Midland Road, summoned there by Cartwright. Under the careful guard of an eccentric mix of amateurs and constables, a series of large crates were opened to reveal both the missing treasures of the British Museum, in addition to the half-million pounds sterling of gold bullion belonging to the Bank of England. Meanwhile, all of the men working for Moriarty had been rounded up by our Irregulars, save only Mathews, who had refused to surrender and was shot dead by both Musgrave and Trevor while trying to escape.

Despite my hesitancy in returning to that terrible abyss, I finally led Lestrade and a group of constables down to recover Robert Moriarty's body. I will admit to being relieved that his corpse was still where I had left it, for a part of me feared that, like some mystical bogeyman, Moriarty would have vanished and continue haunting my dreams. Lestrade made noises about sending men down the shaft in order to look for Holmes, but I knew this to be a futile task. Much like that of his first great nemesis,

Holmes' body would never be recovered.

Eventually, the corpses of Moriarty and Mathews, as well as all of the living prisoners were hauled away, and the various treasures were re-packed for careful shipping back to their respective homes. Once complete, I stood on the side of the Midland Road for a long time, uncertain of what precisely I should be doing. I knew that Musgrave, Trevor, Billy, Cartwright, Wiggins, Simpson, and Shinwell must have been nearly as distraught as I, but I could find no energy to provide them with any comfort. Billy finally asked if I wished to return to his Hampstead inn for the night, but I saw no point in such a journey. There was no reason to hide any longer. Our suite at Baker Street may have been gone, and Mycroft's rooms remained in a state of disrepair, but the Langham Hotel still stood. I would spend one final night there, before catching the first morning train back to Southsea and my wife.

Paying my distracted respects to the now disbanded Irregulars, and wondering if I would ever see them again, I hailed a cab. I directed the driver towards the hotel and leaned back to close my eyes. I reached into my coat pocket, hoping to find the comforts of my pipe. But instead my hand settled upon Holmes' envelope. I pulled it out, sat up, and stared at it for a moment. I then tore it open, only to find one of Holmes' laconic messages: "Watson – Come at once to Nevill's Baths if convenient – S.H."

§

Northumberland Avenue was some distance down Kingsway from Midland Road, and with several infuriating traffic delays, it was a span of some thirty minutes before I found myself in front of the old Turkish bath-house. When I entered, the attendant smiled and handed me a robe and towels. Without asking my name, he promptly directed me to drying-room number four. I paused before the door, anxious at what exactly I may find behind it. When I finally summoned the courage to swing it open, I found therein one Sherlock Holmes, enveloped in a swath of white sheets, smiling at me from one of the couches. I stared at him for some seconds in utter amazement, and felt a gray mist swirl before my eyes. I was nigh speechless.

"Holmes!" I cried, once I had recovered. "Is it really you? Can it indeed be that you are alive? Is it possible that you succeeded in climbing out of that awful abyss? I know you were in it. This time I saw you fall!"

He nodded. "Yes, this time I was actually in the abyss. It was a calculated risk."

"You knew!"

He shrugged. "I thought it highly probable. You see, Watson, the attack at the top of the Tower Bridge was the only true prior attempt upon my life. Moriarty, in his twisted vision of the endgame, wished for me to fall from some great height into a body of water, just as his brother once died." He paused for a moment, and appeared contemplative. "Human nature is a strange mixture, Watson. You will note that even a villainous murderer such as Professor James Moriarty can inspire such affection that his brother turns to crime to avenge him."

"But how did you survive?" I exclaimed.

"Ah, yes, well, it is thanks to this wonderful invention of Mr. Szczepanik. He has created a silken vest that is able to reliably stop bullets that are shot from a distance of eight paces.[152] Though, as I learned to my chagrin, the kinetic force is still sufficient to knock a man backwards and produce some impressive bruising. Fortunately, I had prepared for the latter eventuality, and made plans to recuperate here. Hence the envelope I handed you."

"Why did you not tell me? I thought you dead!"

He shook his head crossly. "I did tell you to open it immediately, Watson. You can hardly blame me for your oversight."

I sighed at Holmes' penchant for unnecessarily dramatic reappearances. It seemed that some things never changed. "I have only one word to say to you, Holmes."

His eyebrows rose with interest. "And what is that, Watson?"

"Norbury."[153]

"Hah!" he chuckled. "Perhaps I was overconfident that I would survive this encounter, Watson. The odds were high, but hardly one hundred percent. Still, I felt that it was a worthwhile gamble. Even if I died, if I could rid the world of the Moriarty-family plague once and for all, it would be one of the red-letter days of my career."[154]

I sighed and realized that Holmes would never change, nor would I want him to. He was a man unique amongst all others in the world. Thinking back over our many adventures together, I could want nothing to

---

[152] The invention of the folded silk ballistic, or bullet-proof, vest is attributed to Jan Szczepanik (1872-1926) of Poland, c.1901. In 1906, this material reputedly saved the life of the Spanish King Alfonso XIII, when a bomb concealed in a bouquet of flowers was hurled at him during his wedding.
[153] Holmes once requested of Watson: 'if it should ever strike you that I am getting a little over-confident in my powers, or giving less pains to a case than it deserves, kindly whisper "Norbury" in my ear, and I shall be infinitely obliged to you' (*The Adventure of the Yellow Face*).
[154] The term red-letter days dates from as far back at the Roman Republic (509-27 BCE), when important days were indicated in red on a calendar dating from the Roman Republic.

be different. "At least we no longer need to be concerned that our leisure time will again be disturbed by some mysterious cipher."

Holmes pondered this for a moment, and then shook his head. "Only the greatest cipher of them all, Watson."[155] Holmes laughed aloud. "You see, education never ends, Watson. Every day we still seek knowledge at the old university. Life is a series of lessons with the greatest for the last."

And with that maxim I can now set down my pen on this remarkable and sensational chapter of my association with Sir Sherlock Holmes, for as I previously noted, he received a knighthood for his preservation of the Tower Bridge. This final incident may now allow the curtain to fall[156] upon a career which has now outlived both its enemies and its shadows and promises to end in an honored old age.

§

---

[155] This appears to be a cryptic reference to the great question of philosophy and religion, i.e. the nature and meaning of the Universe itself. Holmes did dedicate at least a portion of his retirement time on the South Downs to the study of philosophy (Preface to *His Last Bow*).

[156] The curtain may have fallen, but that does not mean that Holmes would not return to take *His Last Bow*.

APPENDIX I:
THE EDGE OF THE UNKNOWN

That Sherlock Holmes is a committed skeptic of supernatural forces is a fact that cannot be refuted. As he says in *The Adventure of the Sussex Vampire*: "This Agency stands flat-footed upon the ground, and there it must remain. The world is big enough for us. No ghosts need apply." And yet, one wonders if something strange and remarkable lurks in the shadows of Victorian London, in a place that Holmes is unable, or perhaps unwilling, to see?

The Canonical adventures of Mr. Sherlock Holmes, in which he is typically accompanied by his friend and biographer, Dr. John H. Watson, contain multiple examples of seemingly-supernatural events. Most of these are ultimately proven by Holmes to be mere shams or products of overactive imaginations. The spectral hound of the Baskervilles was nothing but a phosphorescently-painted dog. The vampiric thirst of Mrs. Ferguson was but a valiant attempt to save her baby from poison. The horrific visions of a devilish world were simply the product of a hallucinogenic foot-shaped plant root. Even the simian transformation of the creeping Professor Presbury had a scientific explanation, despite the fact that the chemical formula utilized has yet to be successfully recreated. Similarly, in *The Adventure of the Pharaoh's Curse*, Holmes provides a plausible physical justification for the movement of the Pharaoh's effigy. However, this is not quite the same thing as actually proving his theory, and some readers might perhaps be left wondering whether or not a supernatural explanation may still be possible.

Are there other examples from the Canon where Holmes and/or Watson seemingly gloss over any cases that drift into the neighborhood of a realm beyond the veil? Incidents which are hard to reconcile with the settled order of nature? The cause of Colonel Warburton's madness, alluded to in *The Adventure of the Engineer's Thumb*, is never explained, nor the reason why Abrahams, mentioned in The *Disappearance of Lady Frances Carfax*, was in mortal terror for his life. What were the singular contents of that ancient British barrow (alluded to in *The Adventure of the Golden Pince-Nez)*? And why exactly was the world not yet prepared to hear the story of Matilda Briggs and the giant rat of Sumatra (mentioned in *The Adventure of the Sussex Vampire).*? These may be the realms in which even the most acute and most experienced detective is helpless.

Furthermore, are we seriously to believe that Sherlock Holmes, the finest mind of his generation (barring perhaps only his brother and the late, lamented Professor Moriarty), was unable to provide a final explanation on not one, but multiple occasions? In *The Problem of Thor Bridge*, Watson calls these cases "complete failures:"

> *"Among these unfinished tales is that of Mr. James Phillimore, who, stepping back into his own house to get his umbrella, was never more seen in this world. No less remarkable is that of the cutter* Alicia, *which sailed one spring morning into a small patch of mist from which she never again emerged, nor was anything further ever heard of herself and her crew. A third case worthy of note is that of Isadora Persano, the well-known journalist and duellist, who was found stark staring mad with a matchbox in front of him which contained a remarkable worm, said to be unknown to science."*

Watson refuses to provide further details, claiming that he did not wish to "annoy the casual reader." But was it, in fact, Holmes himself that was annoyed? In each unfathomed case, was there an explanation that Holmes refused to consider? As Watson's first literary agent, Sir Arthur Conan Doyle, once wrote in Chapter II of his 1930 book on spiritualism, *The Edge of the Unknown*:

> *"... However much our tiny brains may endeavor to comprehend and classify these extraordinary phenomena, there still remain so many unknown causes and unexplained conditions that for many a long year to come our best efforts can only be regarded as well-meant approximations to the truth."*

§

APPENDIX II:
THE BLACK MUSEUM OF SCOTLAND YARD

Other than the esteemed Dr. Watson and his assorted clients, the individuals that Sherlock Holmes interacts with most often during his almost twenty-year career as the world's first consulting detective are the various Inspectors of Scotland Yard, G. Lestrade and Tobias Gregson chief among them. It therefore stands to reason that Holmes might have spent considerable time at their headquarters, but a close examination of the Canon suggests that this is not the case.

In point of fact, the mighty Inspectors of the Criminal Investigation Unit (C.I.D. for short) of the Metropolitan Police Service almost always came, hat in hand, to the flat at 221B Baker Street whenever they encountered some remarkable case whose solution was beyond their limited means. Or at least this is the impression that Dr. Watson is careful to suggest in his accounts of Holmes' investigations. However, an intriguing undated scrap of paper, retrieved at the time that certain other completed manuscripts were unearthed, paints a slightly different picture, and also brings to light the vast esteem in which the members of the Yard held Mr. Sherlock Holmes. It ran as follows:

'It is still a peculiar sensation to climb the official staircase of the New Scotland Yard after many years of visiting the old building on Whitehall Place.[157] However, once I traveled down the second floor

---

[157] The Metropolitan Police was formed in 1829 by Robert Peel, who selected a private house at 4 Whitehall Place as their headquarters. This building backed onto a street called Great Scotland Yard, and from the public entrance that was located there developed a permanent nickname. The original building expanded

hall, immediately past the Rogue's Portrait Gallery, I found myself in a place that was intimately familiar. The prosaic inspectors of the C.I.D. might hesitate to call it by such an official-sounding sobriquet, but I prefer to think of it as the small, but exquisite, Scotland Yard Museum. This room, off-limits to the general public, was long and narrow. Dusty cupboards and cabinets stood all-round the walls. These were embellished and crowded with a great variety of curious specimens, the likes of which I little needed the nicely-typed name-cards in order to identify. In no particular sequence, amongst a myriad of other sundry items, I could plainly see:

1. *A pair of steel handcuffs, with a unique springing pattern: In which the hands of Mr. Jefferson Hope were caught by Inspector G. Lestrade.[158]*

2. *The coil of rope used to hang the bank-robber Sutton: Submitted by Inspector B. Lanner.[159]*

3. *A small tract containing a historical account of the Manor House at Birlstone: Submitted by Inspector A. MacDonald.[160]*

4. *A silk wedding dress, pair of white satin shoes, a wreath, and a veil, all somewhat discolored and water-stained: Dragged from the Serpentine by Inspector G. Lestrade.[161]*

5. *A small brass tripod for charcoal, whose poisonous fumes suffocated Mr. Paul Kratides: Confiscated from the scene of his murder by Inspector T. Gregson.[162]*

6. *A long, sharp, black thorn used to murder Mr. Bartholomew Sholto: Confiscated from the scene by Inspector A. Jones.[163]*

---

over the years to accommodate the growth of the Unit, but eventually a new headquarters needed to be built. In 1890, the C.I.D. moved into a new building located on the Victoria Embankment, very near Westminster Bridge and the statue of Queen Boudica. But the moniker followed them, and remains to this day, even as the 1890 'Norman Shaw' Buildings were vacated in 1967 for a modern structure on Broadway and Victoria Street.

[158] These handcuffs were actually invented by Sherlock Holmes (Chapter VII of *A Study in Scarlet*).

[159] As seen in *The Adventure of the Resident Patient.*

[160] As seen in Chapter VII of *The Valley of Fear.*

[161] Under questioning by Holmes, Lestrade denied dragging the Serpentine and claimed that a park-keeper found these items floating along its edge, but this description appears to contradict his statement (*The Adventure of the Noble Bachelor*).

[162] As seen in *The Adventure of the Greek Interpreter.*

[163] As seen in Chapter VI of *The Sign of Four.*

7. *A box of Benares metalwork, an image of a sitting Buddha upon its front hasp: Confiscated from Jonathan Small by Inspector A. Jones.[164]*

8. *The type-written statement of Mr. James Browner: As made before Inspector I. Montgomery.[165]*

9. *A wig of tangled red hair: Confiscated from the erstwhile beggar Hugh Boone by Inspector C. Bradstreet.[166]*

10. *The jagged unmarked stone used to murder Mr. Charles McCarthy: Submitted by Inspector G. Lestrade.[167]*

11. *The long-bladed knife of Mr. Joseph Harrison: Submitted by Inspector H. Forbes.[168]*

12. *A box of nickel and tin, for use in counterfeiting: Confiscated from the house of Dr. Becher by Inspector C. Bradstreet.[169]*

13. *A tin of luminous paste: Confiscated from an island in the Great Grimpen Mire by Inspector G. Lestrade.[170]*

14. *A small black and white ivory box with a sliding lid: Confiscated from Mr. Culverton Smith by Inspector L. Morton.[171]*

15. *A folded piece of old parchment written by M. Simon Renard: Submitted by Inspector A. MacDonald.[172]*

16. *A corner of woolen carpet, stained with the blood of Mr. Eduardo Lucas: Confiscated from his home by Inspector G. Lestrade.[173]*

17. *A pair of pince-nez mounted in solid gold with broken black silk cord: Submitted by Inspector S. Hopkins.[174]*

18. *A soft wax seal of a thumb-print: Confiscated from Mr. Jonas Oldacre by Inspector G. Lestrade.[175]*

19. *A vial of Fowler's solution: Confiscated from Dr. Benjamin Lowe by Inspector G. Lestrade.[176]*

---

[164] As seen in Chapter XI of *The Sign of Four*.
[165] As seen in *The Adventure of the Cardboard Box*.
[166] As seen in *The Man with the Twisted Lip*.
[167] As seen in *The Boscombe Valley Mystery*.
[168] As seen in *The Naval Treaty*.
[169] As seen in *The Adventure of the Engineer's Thumb*.
[170] As seen in Chapter XIV of *The Hound of the Baskervilles*.
[171] As seen in *The Adventure of the Dying Detective*.
[172] As seen in the non-Canonical *The Adventure of the Spanish Sovereign*.
[173] As seen in *The Adventure of the Second Stain*.
[174] As seen in *The Adventure of the Golden Pince-Nez*.
[175] As seen in *The Adventure of the Norwood Builder*.
[176] As seen in the non-Canonical *The Adventure of the Manufactured Miracle*.

20. *A mummified monkey strung with a double band of white shells: Submitted by Inspector T. Gregson (with assistance from Inspector Baynes of the Surry Constabulary).[177]*

21. *The steel harpoon used to murder Peter Carey: Confiscated from the scene by Inspector S. Hopkins.[178]*

22. *The advertisements of Pierrot in* The Daily Telegraph: *Submitted by Inspector G. Lestrade.[179]*

23. *The axe of Mr. George Blunt: Confiscated by Inspectors G. Lestrade and T. Gregson.[180]*

24. *The sideboard silver of Sir Eustace Brackenstall: Recovered from the Abbey Grange pond by Inspector S. Hopkins.[181]*

25. *The plaster footmarks of a middle-sized, strongly built man implicated in the murder of Mr. Charles Augustus Milverton: Prepared by Inspector G. Lestrade.[182]*

26. *A purple indelible pencil: Recovered from the body of Dr. Ray Ernest by Inspector T. MacKinnon.[183]*

27. *A fragment of a plaster bust of Napoleon Bonaparte: Submitted by Inspector G. Lestrade.[184]*

28. *A formidable horn-handled, two-edged dagger owned by Black Giorgiano of the Red Circle: Confiscated from his murder scene by Inspector T. Gregson.[185]*

29. *The counterfeit hundred-pound plates of Rodger Prescott: Turned in by Mr. S. Holmes.[186]*

30. *The air-gun of the blind German mechanic Von Herder used to assassinate the Honorable Ronald Adair: Confiscated from Colonel Sebastian Moran by Inspector G. Lestrade.[187]*

31. *The papers from Pigeonhole M used to convict the gang of Moriarty: Submitted by Mr. S. Holmes.[188]*

Standing amidst these relics of the past, I was moved to witness the

---

[177] As seen in *The Adventure of Wisteria Lodge.*

[178] As seen in *The Adventure of Black Peter.*

[179] As seen in *The Adventure of the Bruce-Partington Plans.*

[180] As seen in the non-Canonical *The Adventure of the First Star.*

[181] As seen in *The Adventure of the Abbey Grange.*

[182] Belonging to Dr. Watson! As seen in *The Adventure of Charles Augustus Milverton.*

[183] As seen in *The Adventure of The Retired Colourman.*

[184] As seen in *The Adventure of the Six Napoleons.*

[185] As seen in *The Adventure of the Red Circle.*

[186] As seen in *The Adventure of the Three Garridebs.*

[187] As seen in *The Adventure of the Empty House.*

[188] As seen in *The Final Problem.*

profound change in attitude assumed by the inspectors of Scotland Yard. Where once they regarded him with skeptical contempt and insolence, they had over the years, perhaps due to the fact that Holmes refused to take credit for the great deal of invaluable assistance that he provided them, clearly grown to regard him with a measure of respect, admiration, and even awe.'

As we mere mortals have never been granted access to this wondrous collection, we can only hope that Scotland Yard has perhaps since seen fit to add the sculpted head of a faux-Sphinx and the torn gold-beater's skin of an aeronautical balloon?

§

APPENDIX III:
THE WHOLE ART OF DETECTION

Over the last three thousand years that span the history of the written word, there have been many fabled lost books, ranging from a multitude of plays by Aeschylus to Shakespeare's *Cardenio*.[189] Each in its own was presumably a masterpiece, whose wit and wisdom have forever been lost from the world. But there is one book whose loss above all others is felt most keenly by Sherlockians worldwide: the fabled masterpiece of Sherlock Holmes entitled *The Whole Art of Detection*. This was, of course, besides *The Practical Handbook of Bee Culture, with Some Observations upon the Segregation of the Queen,* the other great magnum opus of his latter years, which distilled as much as his gathered wisdom into a tome that could forever be consulted by the would-be detectives of both the present and the future.

Until now, we only knew of this lost masterpiece from Watson's reference to it in *The Adventure of the Abbey Grange,* much like the tantalizingly brief mention of Homer's lost comedic poem the *Margites* in Aristotle's *Art of Poetry.*

But I have fortuitously unearthed a note containing Watson's expanded reminisces of its contents, some of which have been previously published, but only in monograph form. The contents read, as Holmes intended it, like a course of systematic and scientific lectures, and not a tawdry series of tales.[190] Like a pale specter, from this dim shadow, we can

---

[189] For an excellent discussion of lost works throughout history, albeit one that strangely omits the masterpiece discussed here, I highly recommend *The Book of Lost Books* by Stuart Kelly (Random House, 2005).

[190] Holmes to Watson: 'Crime is common. Logic is rare. Therefore it is upon the

perhaps better imagine how the whole work would have shone like the vivid sun. Perhaps it still may, if from some dusty vault an intact copy one day emerges.

§

Part I: The Book of Life.[191]
One: From a Drop of Water to Niagara Falls: The Great Chain of Life.
Two: The Building of a Memory-Attic.[192]
Three: A Sounding Board: The Role of a Partner.[193]

Part II: The Three Qualities of the Detective.[194]
One: Observation.
1. The Distinction between Sight and Observation.[195]
2. The Limitations of the Arm-Chair: Observations at the Scene of the Crime.[196]
3. Trifles: Little Things Matter.[197]

---

logic rather than upon the crime that you should dwell. You have degraded what should have been a course of lectures into a series of tales' (*The Adventure of the Copper Beeches*).

[191] Holmes appears to have expanded upon this treatise, partially quoted by Watson, for inclusion as the introduction to his magnum opus (Chapter II, *A Study in Scarlet*).

[192] It is with uncharacteristic modesty that Holmes refers to his brain as an attic (Chapter II, *A Study in Scarlet* & *The Five Orange Pips*) or box-room (*The Adventure of the Lion's Mane*), since the 'method of loci' is commonly referred to as the 'memory palace.' It is a mnemonic device that dates back as far as ancient Greek and Roman treatises. Holmes expands upon this in the non-Canonical tale *The Grand Gift of Sherlock*.

[193] Holmes: 'For nothing clears up a case so much as stating it to another person (*Silver Blaze*).

[194] Holmes on François le Villard: 'He possesses two out of the three qualities necessary for the ideal detective. He has the power of observation and that of deduction. He is only wanting in knowledge, and that may come in time' (Chapter I, *The Sign of Four*).

[195] Holmes to Watson: 'You see, but you do not observe. The distinction is clear' (*A Scandal in Bohemia*).

[196] Holmes on Mycroft: 'I said that he was my superior in observation and deduction. If the art of the detective began and ended in reasoning from an armchair, my brother would be the greatest criminal agent that ever lived. But he has no ambition and no energy' (*The Adventure of the Greek Interpreter*).

[197] Holmes: 'You know my method. It is founded upon the observance of trifles' (*The Boscombe Valley Mystery*), '...there is nothing so important as trifles' (*The Man with the Twisted Lip*), and 'It has long been an axiom of mine that the little

4. The Importance of Singularities.[198]
5. Bricks without Clay: The Requirement for Data.[199]

Two: Deduction.
1. The Profound Advantages of the *Tabula Rasa.*[200]
2. The Shocking Habit of Guesswork.[201]
3. Separating the Vital from the Incidental.[202]
4. The Greatest Deception: The Obvious Fact.[203]
5. The Trout in the Milk: The Utility of Circumstantial Evidence.[204]
6. The Shifting View: The Dangers of Circumstantial Evidence.[205]
7. The Capital Mistake: Theorizing Without Complete Evidence.[206]
8. The First Rule: Providing for Alternative Explanations.[207]
9. On the Provision of Theories and their Subsequent Explosion.[208]

---

things are infinitely the most important' (*A Case of Identity*).

[198] Holmes: 'It seems, from what I gather, to be one of those simple cases which are so extremely difficult.' Watson: 'That sounds a little paradoxical.' Holmes: 'But it is profoundly true. Singularity is almost invariably a clue' (*The Boscombe Valley Mystery*).

[199] Holmes: 'Data! data! data!' he cried impatiently. 'I can't make bricks without clay' (*The Adventure of the Copper Beeches*).

[200] *Tablula rasa* is a Latin phrase meaning 'blank slate' employed in the philosophy John Locke (1632-1704). Holmes: 'We approached the case, you remember, with an absolutely blank mind, which is always an advantage. We had formed no theories. We were simply there to observe and to draw inferences from our observations' (*The Cardboard Box*).

[201] Holmes: 'I never guess. It is a shocking habit - destructive to the logical faculty' (Chapter I, *The Sign of Four*).

[202] Holmes: 'It is of the highest importance in the art of detection to be able to recognize out of a number of facts which are incidental and which vital' (*The Reigate Squires*).

[203] Holmes: 'There is nothing more deceptive than an obvious fact' (*The Boscombe Valley Mystery*).

[204] Holmes: 'Circumstantial evidence is occasionally very convincing, as when you find a trout in the milk, to quote Thoreau's example' (*The Adventure of the Noble Bachelor*).

[205] Holmes: 'Circumstantial evidence is a very tricky thing,' answered Holmes, thoughtfully. 'It may seem to point very straight to one thing, but if you shift your own point of view a little, you may find it pointing in an equally uncompromising manner to something entirely different' (*The Boscombe Valley Mystery*).

[206] Holmes: 'It is a capital mistake to theorize before you have all the evidence. It biases the judgment' (Chapter III, *A Study in Scarlet*).

[207] Holmes: 'One should always look for a possible alternative and provide against it. It is the first rule of criminal investigation' (*The Adventure of Black Peter*).

[208] Holmes: 'One forms provisional theories and waits for time or fuller

10. From Effects to Causes: Reasoning Backwards and Forwards.[209]
11. Another Man's Place: The Value of Imagination.[210]
12: A Quiet Spot to Think: The Role of Seclusion & Solitude.[211]
13. Eliminating the Impossible: The Path to the Truth.[212]

Three: Knowledge.
1. The Annals of Crime and Past Horrors.[213]
2. On the Utility of Commonplace Books & Indexes.[214]
3. The Proper Study of Mankind is Man,[215] with the following sub-chapters:
   a. On the Uses and Limitations of the System of Bertillon.[216]

---

knowledge to explode them (*The Adventure of the Sussex Vampire*).

[209] Holmes: 'We have compelled to reason backwards from effects to causes (*The Cardboard Box*), and 'The ideal reasoner,' he remarked, 'would, when he has once been shown a single fact in all its bearings, deduce from it not only all the chain of events which led up to it, but also all the results which would follow from it' (*The Five Orange Pips*).

[210] Holmes: 'You know my methods in such cases, Watson: I put myself in the man's place, and having first gauged his intelligence, I try to imagine how I should myself have proceeded under the same circumstances' (*The Musgrave Ritual*), 'See the value of imagination' (*Silver Blaze*), and 'I have been sluggish in mind and wanting in that mixture of imagination and reality which is the basis of my art' (*The Problem of Thor Bridge*).

[211] Watson: 'I knew that seclusion and solitude were very necessary for my friend in those hours of intense mental concentration during which he weighed every particle of evidence, constructed alternative theories, balanced one against the other, and made up his mind as to which points were essential and which immaterial' (Chapter III, *The Hound of the Baskervilles*).

[212] Holmes' famous maxim: 'How often have I said to you that when you have eliminated the impossible, whatever remains, however improbable, must be the truth?' (Chapter II, *The Sign of Four*).

[213] Holmes: I am generally able, by the help of my knowledge of the history of crime, to set them straight. There is a strong family resemblance about misdeeds, and if you have all the details of a thousand at your finger ends, it is odd if you can't unravel the thousand and first (Chapter II, *A Study in Scarlet*).

[214] While in active practice, it was reported by Watson multiple times that Holmes kept a collection of book and files containing his accumulation of knowledge upon a wide variety of subjects. Some of the best examples are the extensive descriptions of volume 'V' (*The Adventure of the Sussex Vampire*) and 'C' (*The Adventure of the Pharaoh's Curse*).

[215] Actually said by Watson (Chapter I, *A Study in Scarlet*), suggesting that Holmes did more than just glance over his 'brochure' on the matter (Chapter I, *The Sign of Four*).

[216] The Bertillon system of measurements was much admired by both Dr. James

    b. The Influence of a Trade upon the Form of a Hand, with Lithotypes.[217]

    c. The Auricle: Natural Variations of the Helix, Tragus, Lobule, and Conchal Angle.[218]

    d. Accumulated Damage to the Ear: Accidental and Ornamental.[219]

    e. The Recognition of Tattoos and Skin Markings.[220]

    f. The Procurement & Dating of Bruises & Scars.[221]

    g. Graphology: Deductions from Handwriting.[222]

    h. A Study in Smells: The Distinction of 75 Perfumes.[223]

4. The Tools of the Detective, with the following sub-chapters:

    a. Small Becomes Large: Microscopes & Magnifying Lenses.[224]

    b. The Re-Agent Test for Hemoglobin: Superiority over Guaiacum & Corpuscles.[225]

    c. The Art of Tracing of Footsteps, with Some Remarks upon the Uses of Plaster of Paris.[226]

    d. The Earths and Soils of London and its Environs.[227]

    e. Upon the Distinction between the 140 Ashes of the Various Tobaccos, with Colored Plates.[228]

Mortimer (Chapter I, *The Hound of the Baskervilles*) and by Sherlock Holmes (*The Naval Treaty*).

[217] Shown to Watson in Chapter I of *The Sign of Four*.

[218] The auricle is the pinna, or outer part of the human ear. Natural variations are often inherited, such as the free or attached lobule, while the conchal angle describes how far the ear protrudes from the side of the head.

[219] Holmes felt that ears were of sufficient importance to devote two chapters to them, which were originally published in the 1887 edition of the 'Anthropological Journal' (*The Adventure of the Cardboard Box*).

[220] Mentioned in the non-Canonical story *The Adventure of the First Star*.

[221] Holmes attempted to verify how far bruises may be produced after death (Chapter I, *A Study in Scarlet*) and noted that: 'the dating of scars is a tricky business, but I am confident in my conclusion' (*The Falling Curtain*).

[222] Holmes was clearly a student of handwriting, as evidenced by multiple cases, perhaps most notably in *The Reigate Squires*.

[223] Never formally mentioned as being written up as a monograph, it is hardly surprising that Holmes would have done so, given the prominence it plays in Chapter XV of *The Hound of the Baskervilles*.

[224] Holmes used both a microscope and his famous magnifying lenses in a wide variety of cases throughout the Canon.

[225] Watson witnessed the final moments of the invention of this wondrous test, which was never again used in the Canon (Chapter I, *A Study in Scarlet*).

[226] Holmes showed this to Watson in Chapter II of *The Sign of Four*.

[227] Holmes was familiar with the various forms of dirt found throughout London, the tracking of which allowing him to deduce the movements of people whose shoes he examined (demonstrated in *The Five Orange-Pips*).

f. The Botany of Death: On Natural Poisons.[229]
g. On Secret Writings: Analyses of 160 Ciphers.[230]
h. On the Dating of Documents.[231]
i. The Elementary Distinction of Newspaper Types.[232]
j. The Typewriter & Its Relation to Crime.[233]
k. Human Conveyances and their Tracks: 42 Different Bicycle Tyres, with Lithotypes.[234]
l. The Multiple Uses of Malingering.[235]
m. On the Uses of Dogs in Detection.[236]

§

In *A Study in Scarlet* (Chapter II), Holmes himself states that 'no man lives or has ever lived who has brought the same amount of study and of natural talent to the detection of crime which I have done.' From a perusal of this list, I think it safe to say that he was not boasting. Who knows how many criminals have walked free, due to a lack of proper training of the world's official police forces? In conclusion, I can only mention that it is indisputable that the world lost a work of vital importance when Holmes neglected to ensure the preservation and dissemination of this masterpiece. Perhaps someday we will learn the reason for this dreadful lapse?

§

---

[228] Mentioned in Chapter IV of *A Study in Scarlet, The Sign of Four,* and *The Boscombe Valley Mystery.*
[229] Holmes alludes to writing in Chapter XXIII of *The Gate of Gold.*
[230] Mentioned in *The Adventure of the Dancing Men.*
[231] Mentioned in Chapter II of *The Hound of the Baskervilles.*
[232] Mentioned by Holmes in Chapter II of *The Hound of the Baskervilles* to be a "special hobby" since he was very young, this is the first proof that he finally formalized this knowledge into a monograph.
[233] Holmes mentions his plans to write in *A Case of Identity.*
[234] Holmes mentions this familiarity in *The Adventure of the Priory School.*
[235] Holmes mentions his intention to write in *The Adventure of the Dying Detective.*
[236] Holmes mentions his intention to write in *The Adventure of the Creeping Man.*

LITERARY AGENT'S FOREWORD
TO BONUS STORY

For several years I have been the recipient of as outlandish a deluge of letters as one could imagine. These deluded gentlefolk appear to imagine that I can simply summon additional works by Dr. John H. ₥n from thin air. Given the vast number of cases handled by his friend Mr. Sherlock Holmes while in active practice as the world's first consulting detective, it is a relative certainly that other tales by that esteemed author must exist hidden in some nooks and crannies of the dusty bank vaults and musty libraries of greater London. However, the intricacies of actually locating such manuscripts, ensuring their provenance[237] and completeness,[238] repairing the damage caused by the ravages of time, and wading through the convoluted complexities of the British Treasure Trove law[239] are such that it is not an everyday occurrence that such a tale

---

[237] As an interesting example, *The Case of the Man who was Wanted* (c.1914) was a type-written story found amongst the effects of Sir Arthur Conan Doyle, Watson's first literary agent. Believed for some time to be a genuine article, it was finally deduced that it had been written by a man named Arthur Whitaker and sent to Conan Doyle in hopes of a collaboration. It is also known as *The Adventure of the Sheffield Banker.*

[238] One such incomplete tale has come to light. Commonly known as *The Adventure of the Tall Man*, this outline was also located amongst the paper of Conan Doyle.

[239] Given that the concept of 'Treasure Trove' in English Law dates back to the time of Edward the Confessor (c.1003-1066), it is perhaps not surprising that this is quite complex. Boiled down, the object must have been hidden with an intention to recover later, and as such, belongs by prerogative right to The Crown. If simply lost or abandoned, it belongs to either the person who found it ('The

can be brought to light.

Although not directly related to the primary events detailed by Dr. John H. Watson in the three-part manuscript entitled *'The Assassination of Sherlock Holmes,'* this small narrative was unearthed in the same (presently–confidential) locale, of which the general details of its locating can be found in the Foreword to *'The Adventure of the Pharaoh's Curse.'* Given the mention of the 'Red Leech' therein, it seems appropriate to include this story in the special Collected Edition.

A careful reading of this early adventure will suggest why Watson may have written down the tale, perhaps for the sake of psychic restoration, but certainly never intended for publication during his lifetime.

§

Law of Finders') or to the landowner.

THE RED LEECH

I once reported that I was the means of introducing to the notice of my friend Mr. Sherlock Holmes solely the problems of Mr. Hatherley's thumb and Colonel Warburton's madness. However, this was a minor falsehood, for which I hope my readers will someday forgive me. At the time, I was not yet prepared to acknowledge the existence of a third case, which to this day fills me with unspeakable horror at the unfathomable evils that may inhabit the hearts of mankind.

At the time the circumstances of that particular adventure made such a profound impression upon me that it was exceptionally difficult for me to even cast my thoughts back upon those days. Not until six years later was I finally able to set down my notes into one of the massive manuscript volumes wherein lay those various cases of Sherlock Holmes in which I have been fortunate enough to assist.[240] I speak now of the repulsive story of the Red Leech.

It was in the spring of '88, not long after the publication of my first sketch, which I had entitled, somewhat whimsically, 'A Study in Scarlet,' that the blow fell upon my shoulders.[241] The day had started like any other, with me stretched out upon the sofa in the sitting room of our Baker Street flat, attempting to find something of interest in the morning

---

[240] This may explain why Watson claimed in *The Adventure of the Golden Pince-Nez* that the event in question took place in 1894, which is in direct conflict with the dates that he reports in the current manuscript.

[241] *A Study in Scarlet* was first published in *Beeton's Christmas Annual* 1887. Therefore, the events detailed in the current manuscript must have transpired in early 1888, after only a handful of early cases together, such as *The Speckled Band, The Beryl Coronet, The Resident Patient, The Reigate Squires*, and *The Five Orange Pips*, none of which had yet been published.

editions. Meanwhile, Holmes sat at his acid-charred work table where he was attempting to whittle a dagger out of a block of ice that he had obtained from the local fishmonger.[242] When I had questioned him about it, Holmes informed me that he was hopeful that the knife might prove sturdy enough to stab through a guinea fowl appropriated from Mrs. Hudson's larder. Holmes claimed this ice dagger was the most likely method by which Sir Lucian Sedgebrook of Rochford Hall, who had been found in his bed with a hole in his chest and the sheets damp around him, might have met his end. Personally, I thought it simply a sad end to what appeared to be a most appetizing bird.[243]

That morning I had considered a holiday from London, a notion encouraged by a glimpse of a brochure extolling the wonders of Gibraltar, which was currently pinned to the mantel by Holmes' jack-knife. Unfortunately, I knew that such lavish destinations were well beyond my limited means. I finally roused myself to pick through the day's letters when one in particular caught my eye. Tearing it open and skimming through it, I quickly fell into a black despair. I know not how long I sat, contemplating its contents, when out of the blue, my companion's voice suddenly interrupted my ruminations.

"On the whole, Watson," said he, "I must concur with you that, by-and-large, the legal profession is comprised of men to whom vampire-bats compare rather favorably."

"Blood-suckers!" I exclaimed, and then suddenly realizing that Holmes had recited the deepest reflections of my mind, I sat up in my chair and gaped at him in complete astonishment.

"Holmes!" I cried, upset at this invasion of privacy. "Have you been steaming open my letters? How else could you possibly know of my troubles?"

He laughed jovially at my amazement. "Surely, my dear Watson, you have seen a sufficient display of my methods that you can comprehend how such a thing is possible? In the same way that I am able to track a series of clues from the scene of a crime to the logical identification of the perpetrator, so I can follow your thoughts from the play upon your face of your emotions and expressions."

I shook my head. "That is impossible," I declared firmly.

He looked me over in his singular introspective fashion. "Not at all,

---

[242] Ice was imported to London from Norway beginning in the 1820's and stored in large ice wells, from which it was sold to restaurants and fishmongers in order to keep food children. This trades ended by 1921, when mechanical ice production became widespread.

[243] Unfortunately, Watson never provides any additional details of Sir Lucian's murder, including whether Holmes' solution was the correct one.

Watson. In this case, it was a mere trifle. I observed that you have been distraught ever since Billy brought up the day's correspondence. You sorted through the stack and opened only one envelope, ignoring all of the others. Although I did not observe the front of it, and therefore have no immediate knowledge of its sender, that particular envelope is unusual in its shape. It is clearly designed to hold a page of foolscap, rather than the imperial sized paper which is used for more common correspondence. I have made a careful study of various types of paper, which someday I may compile into a monograph. Since that particular quality of foolscap is primarily utilized for legal documents, I had now the first link in the chain. After reading it through no less than twice, you sighed heavily and sank back into your chair. You then gazed vacantly out of the window, your face bleak despite the beautiful day outside our walls, from which I can only deduce that you had fallen into a morbid gloom. Finally, you glanced over at the playbill for Anderson's performance of *2 Henry VI*, which we had attended last month at the Surrey. A grim smile came over your face, which showed me that you had recalled the most famous line from that play, the one in which Cade exclaims that: 'the first thing we do, let's kill all the lawyers.' At this point, the only thing left to do was to agree with your assessment that lawyers, at least those of a certain ilk, cause far more harm to society than good."

"Remarkable!" said I. "Even though you have explained it, I admit that I am still in awe that you could observe such small signs."

He shrugged. "It was a rather commonplace set of deductions, Watson, compared to some of the feats which I have performed in the past. Have I ever told you of the Arnsworth Castle business, which precipitated my departure from university?"[244]

While I have often attempted to draw from Holmes additional details of his early cases which occurred before I had made his acquaintance, I was, at the moment, not in a conducive humor for hearing his tale. Instead, an idea had germinated in my brain, which having sprouted, I was unable to abandon. "Holmes!" I exclaimed, leaning forward excitedly. "You have no work at the moment?"

"Only the trifling matter of the Bishopsgate jewel burglary," he replied, waving his hand at one of the letters he had left scattered about the room. "If my theory holds, this case should take no more than an hour or two in the Spitalfields Market to resolve. It will likely take me longer to explain the full matter to Inspector Lanner and his less-than-astute colleagues at

---

[244] Holmes again alludes to this case, which utilized the technique of compelling someone to reveal their most valued item, in *A Scandal in Bohemia*, but why exactly it precipitated his departure from university is sadly unknown, for he never related the full details to Watson.

the Yard."

"Then would you take on a case for me?" I inquired, my tone formal. "I am sorely in need of your advice, for this does not appear to be a matter for the police. I will pay your usual retainer, of course."

He snorted with amusement. "I am familiar with the depleted state of your pocket-book, Watson, which is rather threadbare at the moment, after the debacle at the Aintree National. No, if your case interests me, I will remit my fee altogether. Pray tell me about it." He leaned back into his chair and pressed his fingertips together.

"Very well," said I, my voice heavy at the thought of recounting the details of the Damoclean sword hanging over my head. I leaned back into the sofa and closed my eyes. "It all began two days ago with a letter from Ian M. Belmont, Esq. of Middle Temple. It took me a while to understand what he was going on about, as the letter was couched in a vast labyrinth of twisted legal parlance. Eventually, however, I realized that Mr. Belmont represents not one, but two, different parties that have objected to my recent publication of the Jefferson Hope case in *Beeton's Christmas Annual.* The first party is bringing suit against me for libel, while the other is claiming copyright infringement and plagiarism."

"Plagiarism!" exclaimed Holmes, shaking his head. "That is absurd. As you know, I glanced over your small brochure. It was filled with innumerable extraneous romantic notions, and was therefore a complete failure as a record of the exacting science of deduction which I brought to bear upon the case. However, I can see no grounds for plagiarism, given that you narrated the events as they took place, with only the most trifling degree of embellishment."

"Mr. Belmont stated that he was representing the estate of the American author Edgar Allen Poe. They assert that I have copied his stories of the Chevalier Auguste Dupin, whose methods you have, upon occasion, disparaged."[245]

"Fascinating," said Holmes mildly, apparently not much concerned about this attack upon my name. "Such a case may be difficult to prove, however. And the second party?"

I opened my eyes and sighed. "The leaders of the Church of the Latter-Day Saints. They claim that Part II of the story, *'The Country of the Saints,'* disparages their religion."

"Ah," said he, simply. Looking keenly at me from under his half-closed lids, Holmes nodded. "And what recourses have you adopted?"

---

[245] Edgar Allan Poe (1809-1849), although most well-known for his Gothic fictions and poems, is also generally considered the inventor of the genre of detective fiction, with the appearance of his detective Dupin in *The Murders of the Rue Morgue* (1841).

"I have inquired at both Grey's Inn and Lincoln's Inn, but even the services of a rising barrister are beyond my limited means. I did ask a friend of mine who works at the London Library what would happen if I was to lose such a case. He consulted the necessary legal tomes. It seems that the infringement charge would carry a penalty of a fine, which might be large enough to ruin me."

"And the libel case?" Holmes inquired. "What would transpire if you lost?"

"Imprisonment for up to two years!" I groaned.

"You did not appear excessively worried yesterday when we heard Adelina at Covent Garden,"[246] Holmes noted.

"Well, Holmes, for one, the debtor's prisons have been dissolved these twenty years, so I knew that I could not end up in the Clink like poor Dickens.[247] Furthermore, my friend, who is also familiar with the depleted state of my cheque book, felt it unlikely that Belmont would pursue his claim. The amount of money that Belmont could extract from me seemed hardly worth the effort required to bring this suit before Chancery. I therefore, at the time, resolved to completely ignore this foul correspondence."

"I see," said Holmes. "But now a new letter has arrived?"

"Yes," I replied with some bitterness. "And in it, he offers to abandon the two lawsuits if I agree to pay each claimant ten percent of all past and future earnings upon my writings."

Holmes pondered this for a moment. "You could accept his terms, Watson. Certainly your past earnings amount to very little, while the future is most uncertain. I cannot imagine that there are many people interested in reading romantic stories derived from our adventures together."[248]

I shook my head. "That is not the point, Holmes!" I exclaimed. "How can I set down any words knowing that a significant portion of it was being siphoned off to feed an unjust and ravenous maw?"

"Excellent!" laughed Holmes. "I never intended to truthfully suggest that you should take Belmont's offer. I simply wanted to test your mettle,

---

[246] Presumably a reference to Adelina Patti (1843-1919), a famous soprano of the day.

[247] The Clink was a prison in Southwark that shuttered in 1780 but was so notorious that its name has long been synonymous for prison in general. However, Watson is confusing the facts of the incident in question. In truth, it was Charles Dickens' father John who was forced by his creditors into the debtor's prison at Marshalsea (also in Southwark) when Charles was twelve years of age. Though John's wife and several of the younger children voluntarily joined him there, Charles actually resided with a family friend during that time.

[248] Perhaps the most striking example of Holmes being utterly mistaken!

in order to see how far you were willing to fight this claim."

"All the way, Holmes! All the way to the end, whatever the cost may be."

He smiled. "Hopefully, the cost shall prove to be very little. Will you give me *carte blanche* in this matter?"

"Absolutely," I replied with some warmth.

"Very good. As a start, I must reconnoiter the scene, and you are surely in no fit state to accompany me. If you would be so kind as to let me borrow that little letter of yours, I shall walk down to Doctor's Commons, or Somerset House, to be more precise, to examine some of Mr. Belmont's legal filings. I hope these may provide some clarity on the matter." He pulled out his pocket-watch and glanced at the time. "We shall meet at Wilton's at one o'clock for a full luncheon.[249] In the meantime, I suggest you attempt to improve your black mood with a vigorous stroll through Regent's Park."

Following Holmes' advice, I took up my hat and walking stick for a turn along the outer circle, past the boating lake and the Italian gardens. The park proven to be vibrant with the warp and weft of London's multitudes, strolling to and fro in a vast tapestry of life. Families were everywhere, the children laughing and shouting with youthful abandon while their exasperated parents vainly strived to rein in their youthful exuberance. Musicians were playing every type of instrument and tune imaginable, including some whose origin even I, who considered myself well-travelled, could not place. Food-sellers were hawking their aromatic wares, and merchants were selling virtually anything decorative a lady could desire. There were people sitting, standing, playing, sleeping, laughing, eating, drinking, smoking, and almost every other possible activity. It was like a microcosm of London as a whole, at least the slice of London known as the pride of the Empire. From this particular vantage point, none of its foul underbelly was visible, where harm was done for the sake of greed or sheer unbridled cruelty.

I eventually gave over my stroll in despair and, my nerves a quiver, I turned my steps to Wilton's where I discovered that Holmes had already begun his repast with a hearty helping of lobster pie. I had but little appetite and only listened morosely to his update.

"A more perfect compound of the tyrant, inquisitor, and malefactor than Mr. Ian Belmont, Esq. I have seldom encountered," remarked Holmes, as he pushed back his empty plate.

"You have met him, then?"

---

[249] Wilton's is a famous seafood restaurant in the St James area of London, which has been operating continuously (in various locales) since 1742 after getting its start as a simple oyster stall.

"Only in passing, as he was concluding his prosecution of an old lady who, I suspect, is half-demented, but as rich as Croesus. Nonetheless, I exchanged a few pleasantries with several of his colleagues, and learned that he is rather universally despised. They would not say it in so many words, but it was clear that the man has a reputation of being the intermediary for certain nameless individuals who broker in secrets."

"There is a trade in this?" I asked, aghast.

"Oh, yes, Watson. A most dirty trade. Compared to those of an opium trader or whoremonger their hands may be less physically blackened, but the stain is there all the same. Simply because many of the nation's most exalted families sprang from the loins of one or more kings does not make them any less susceptible to performing acts of complete and utter foolishness. Should such private secrets find their way into print, it would mean great consternation in many fashionable mansions. And so they pay."

"Then it's blackmail?"

"Oh, yes, Watson. That much is certain, and if one of the dog's hind legs is crooked, you can be certain the other is the same."[250]

"So you do not believe that the Poe Estate or the Mormon Elders are the ones litigating me?"

"I doubt it very much, Watson. First of all, Poe's wife died before him, and they had no children. So who precisely comprises his 'estate?' Some distant cousin? Pshaw. And, I fear that the Mormon settlers of Utah have bigger fish to fry than an invalided Army Surgeon with literary aspirations but an empty purse."

"Then is it Belmont himself?"

Holmes shook his head. "No, the man strikes me as being completely without either humor or imagination. He could no more conceive of such a scheme as he could stroll from London to Normandy without getting his feet wet. He is merely the tool of some greater evil."

"Then who is his master?"

"That is precisely what we need to determine. And that is why we shall be calling upon Mr. Belmont at three o'clock this afternoon."

"What?" I exclaimed.

Holmes chuckled. "Do not fear, Watson. In case Mr. Belmont is less dim-witted than he appears, I have not been so foolish so as to leave a card with my name upon it. Instead I used one of Lord Wentworth's."

I frowned in confusion. "Who then is Lord Wentworth?"

---

[250] The phrase 'crooked as a dog's hind leg,' which appears in the writings of Mark Twain, is likely of American origin, and Holmes must have picked it up while travelling around the United States before setting up as a consulting detective.

"Wentworth is a guise that I have assumed from time to time when I am required to be familiar with the young swells in the West End gaming clubs. Wentworth often appears to drink heavily before losing severely at whist, and he is thus beloved by all, who confide in him many interesting things. In this particular case, knowing his toady nature, I believe that Mr. Belmont will react most favorably to someone from the peerage."

"React in what way?"

"By taking on the case that we will bring before him. Mr. George Joyce Sliter, the famous explorer of the Zanzibar jungles, has been slandered and wishes for Belmont to prosecute."

I was thoroughly confused. "Who is George Joyce Sliter?"

Holmes frowned. "Why, you are, Watson. Pay attention."

Holmes spent the remainder of our hansom ride to the Temple explaining his scheme, the nature of which I was just beginning to grasp by the time we arrived at our destination. We disembarked near the Temple Bar and made our way through a series of arched grey stone passageways crowded with barristers in white wigs and black gowns.[251] As we strode through the brick-lined Pump Court, I glanced up at the 1686 blue and gold sundial set into the wall overhead. It read: 'Shadows we are and like shadows we depart.' I shook my head at this unhappy sentiment.

Holmes followed my gaze and nodded. "Ah, my thoughts exactly, Watson. Is not all life wretched and pointless? We reach. We grasp. And what is left in our hands at the end? A shadow. But we must go on, unless you plan to throw yourself from the Waterloo Bridge?"

I glanced over at my friend and shook my head. "Really, Holmes. It is a good thing you decided to become a detective, because you are a poor counselor."

He simply shrugged. "*Cura te ipsum*, Watson."[252] After another half-minutes' walk, he looked up and motioned to number five, pausing at the steps. "Here we are, Mr. Sliter," he said, meaningfully. "Recall your purpose." He knocked thrice upon the heavy black door adjacent to Belmont's brass sign.

We had a wait of some two minutes before the door swung open to reveal a scrawny young man whom I presumed to be Belmont's assistant. Upon the presentation of another of 'Lord Wentworth's' calling cards, we were rapidly shown by this lad into the solicitor's study. The room appeared to have not been altered since the days of Blackstone,[253] with

---

[251] Presumably Watson is actually referring to the dragon-topped Temple Bar memorial erected in 1880, since the original Temple Bar was dismantled in 1878.

[252] A Latin proverb meaning 'Physician, heal thyself.'

[253] Over a hundred years, if Watson is referring to Sir William Blackstone (1723-1780), a famous lawyer and legal commentator, whose works gave a complete

dark oak panels, faded carpet, musty wallpaper, massive tome-lined bookshelves, and a heavy desk littered with papers. Above the cold hearth was a framed picture of a man I supposed might be Fielding, which seemed an odd choice given the chosen livelihood of the current occupant of the room.[254]

Belmont himself proved to be a thin, anxious wisp of a man, with worried eyes and a twitching, hesitating manner – a man whom my own professional eye might assess to be on the verge of an absolute nervous collapse. He glanced briefly at Holmes' card, and looked me over as Holmes introduced me by my assumed name. Although it was several years since I clambered up and down the hills of Afghanistan, my frame still bore traces of the man that was once brown as a nut and as thin as a lathe. Therefore, the supposed identity of an African explorer was somewhat plausible.

After these introductions were made and he motioned us to chairs, Belmont leaned forward with his elbows upon his desk and licked his lips. "What precisely can I do for you today, Lord Wentworth?"

Holmes smiled and affected a languid manner. "Oh, it is not on my behalf that we came to see you, Mr. Belmont. The problem is Mr. Sliter's here. You see, the two of us were having a glass of Rémy Martin[255] at the Savage Club[256] and he was telling me about the terrible thing that has happened to him. I've heard around town that you have some experience in these matters and I got to thinking that we should come by and lay it before you."

Belmont blinked and nodded uncertainly. "Yes, of course," said he, non-committedly.

"Surely you have heard of Mr. Sliter?" asked Holmes.

Belmont shrugged weakly. "The name is familiar, of course, but the social pages are not something that I read regularly."

"Social pages!" exclaimed Holmes. "I did not expect you to have such a fine sense of humor, Mr. Belmont! Mr. Sliter here is one of England's

---

overview of English law, and were very influential in the early decisions of the US Supreme Court.

[254] Henry Fielding (1707-1754) was a dramatist and novelist (most famous for the novel *Tom Jones*. He was also a magistrate and helped found the Bow Street Runners, London's first police force. He had offices at Pump Court, perhaps explaining his place of honor in Belmont's office.

[255] Rémy Martin is a particularly expensive type of cognac that has been in operation since 1724. Holmes here was name-dropping in an attempt to convey the amount of wealth he and his 'client' Sliter hypothetically possess.

[256] The Savage Club is a gentleman's club in London, founded 1857 and catering to those connected to literature and the fine arts.

most famous explorers. Livingstone,[257] Burton,[258] Sterndale,[259] Selous,[260] Sliter! These men have no time for the social pages. Therefore, to see his fine name dragged through the mud, it is scandalous."

Belmont looked pained as he attempted to follow Holmes' rantings. "Do I understand that Mr. Sliter has been libeled by someone and you wish to bring a suit against said individual?"

"Exactly so! You have the facts spot on, Mr. Belmont!" beamed Holmes. "I am certain that you are aware of the romantic fictions of that scribbler H. Rider Haggard?[261] It is a well-known fact that his character Allan Quatermain was based upon my friend here. And now, in his most recent scrawls, Haggard has gone and killed him!"

"I strenuously object to being symbolically killed by Mr. Haggard. It is plainly libel," said I with some heat, as I warmed to my role.

"Now, now, Mr. Sliter," said Holmes, putting his hand on my shoulder. "Please calm down. You don't want to bring on an attack of malaria, do you?"

"I will not be calm!" I exclaimed, jumping to my feet. "The man has had the audacity to kill me! Me, who once wrestled a lion on the plains of Tsavo! Who once rode a rhino four miles across Ngorongoro! Who once swam the gorges beneath the great Falls of Victoria!" I began waiving my arms about like a madman.

Holmes leapt up and attempted to grab hold of my flailing limbs, but he instead clumsily knocked into Belmont's desk. This caused a great pile of papers to topple over onto the floor. Belmont uttered an angry curse as he gaped at the great jumble we had caused in his office.

"You've done it now, Mr. Sliter," said Holmes, coolly. "A pretty mess you've made..."

---

[257] David Livingstone (1813-1873) was a Scottish explorer best known for being the (European) discoverer of Victoria Falls.

[258] Sir Richard Francis Burton (1821-1890) was an English 'Renaissance man.' As an explorer he was known for his travels within Arabia, and as a writer for his translation of *One Thousand and One Nights*.

[259] Dr. Leon Sterndale was a noted African explorer whose exploits are best known to the world from *The Adventure of the Devils' Foot*.

[260] Frederick Courtney Selous (1851-1917) was a British explorer of Southeast Africa who was known as a big game hunter.

[261] Sir H. Rider Haggard (1856-1925) was one of the pioneers of adventure fiction. He is best known for *King's Solomon's Mines*, featuring the character Allan Quatermain. It has been widely supposed that Quatermain was in fact based primarily upon Selous, though strangely Haggard was once accused of plagiarizing the character and his exploits from a book by a Scottish explorer named Joseph Thomson. In 1887, Haggard killed off his famous character in the eponymous novel.

I immediately brought an end to my fictitious tirade and began to apologetically pick up the scattered papers, a task in which I was assisted by Holmes. After a span of some five minutes, order was restored to Belmont's desk, the papers neatly stacked, the pencils lined up in military order, and his great quill pen back in its well.

Holmes shook his head. "You must forgive my friend here, Mr. Belmont. He has been prone to these fits of violence ever since he was struck down by the Chikungunya bends while crossing Batavia."[262]

Although Belmont's anger had waned somewhat in the interval minutes, he did not appear much inclined to take the case of the supposed Mr. Sliter. Claiming an excess of work, Belmont instead directed us to a nearby colleague who might be able to assist. Holmes thanked him profusely, and we departed from the solicitor's office. Puzzled by what exactly we had learned by this charade, I followed Holmes as he made his way back to the Strand. He and I climbed into a passing hansom before he sat back and emitted a hearty chuckle.

"Capital, Watson! If you keep this up, we may make a fine actor of you someday. I especially enjoyed the mental image of you riding a rhinoceros."

"So was our expedition of some use?"

"I certainly hope so, Watson. Thanks in no small part to your excellent diversion, my pockets are now overflowing with various documents that appeared most promising, in addition to the most likely clue of all... his blotting paper."

"But how does that facilitate our investigation?"

"As you no doubt observed when you sat down to compose your little romance of our adventure together, your Gillott pen upon occasion requires blotting, the process of which produces a mirror image of said writing. Once we return to Baker Street and I examine my prizes, I will hopefully be in position to definitively identify your persecutor via the addresses of those to whom Belmont's regularly corresponds."

§

Back in our quarters, Holmes proceeded to light his cherry-wood pipe and set to work deciphering the pages purloined from Belmont's desk. Meanwhile, I paced anxiously about, and in so doing wore a small groove

---

[262] At first blush this appears to be an example of Holmes' inventing a fictitious disease, such as Tapanuli Fever or the black Formosa corruption (*The Adventure of the Dying Detective*). However, there is an actual disease caused by the Chikungunya virus, which is related to Dengue Fever. It has caused periodic outbreaks since at least 1779 and potentially originated in Batavia (now Jakarta).

in the back of our bear-skin rug. I would have sworn that at least four hours passed, though an inspection of my pocket-watch suggested it was a mere twenty minutes. Finally, Holmes smiled and pushed back his chair. Without speaking, he rose and strode over to the bookcase, where he reached out with one of his long, thin hands to pluck forth the index volume labelled 'S.' He proceeded to flip through it before pausing upon a page, which he read intently. He then slammed the book shut and looked up with a hint of triumph in his eyes.

"You have worked it out," I said.

"Oh, yes, Watson. I now know everything. The only thing that remains is to determine precisely how best to employ that knowledge."

"So you know who is behind Belmont?"

"I am familiar with her."

"A woman?" I asked, greatly surprised.

He shook his head. "She is no woman, Watson. She is a devil incarnate."

"In what way?"

"I have seen something of her work before. There were parallel cases, if you consult my index, with Robertson in '86,[263] and there was something of the sort with Peter Michael Picchetti in the early part of this decade.[264] I think her persecution may have even had a hand in his decline and death. You see, Watson, this harridan discovers some method to blackmail writers of all sorts, who then live in permanent fear of her. As in your case, to avoid being exposed to tribulations of prosecution they are forced to pay her a large portion of their income. In this way, one could argue that she is merely a more rarified version of those secret societies, such as the Camorra and the Black Hand, which plague the immigrants of Saffron Hill seeking so-called protection money."

"Then this is all rubbish and balderdash! There is nothing to these false claims of Poe and the Elders. We can fight it!"

Holmes puffed on his pipe for a moment. "Yes, well, it is not so simple, Watson. You are undoubtedly correct that her claims are meritless, but her resources are somewhat limitless, while your pocket-

---

[263] There was no widely-known author named Richardson who was publishing in 1886, however, that was the year that Robert Louis Stevenson's novel the *Strange Case of Dr. Jekyll and Mr. Hyde* was published. There is no record that Stevenson (1850-1894) was persecuted by a blackmailer, though this might possibly explain his flight to the South Seas and premature death.

[264] Similarly, there is no Peter Michael Picchetti, though earlier in the 1880's the famous poet Dante Gabriel Rossetti (1828-1182) was descending into a depression-induced spiral that eventually claimed his life. Was Rossetti secretly persecuted?

book is most certainly not."

"Whatever do you mean?"

"I denote that she can wage a protracted battle through the courts, Watson, while you cannot survive more than a round or two without utterly ruining yourself."

"But why would she do such a thing?" I asked, dumfounded. "Why spend such a sum with no hope of recompense?"

"Not from you, perhaps. But not all currency comes in pounds sterling, Watson. If she were to make an example of you, if she was to destroy you, then others will in the future fall in line that much more readily."

I shook my head at the injustice of it all. "So who is she?" I finally muttered.

"She has enjoyed many names in her long and dubious career. I understand that she was once a celebrated beauty, her hair that particular shade of Titian red that made her nigh irresistible to a certain order of men. But her external beauty has always masked a rotten core, with no concern for anyone other than herself. Her name, Watson, is Simone Elizabeth Kirby, née Delos. She was once the mistress of the Swedish diplomat Carl af Lindstrom, who you may recall attempted to murder his wife in order to marry the former Miss Delos."

"Of course!" I cried. "I remember that it was a terrible scandal when he was acquitted."[265]

"Yes, well, it helps when you pay off your witnesses. In any case, scandal has continued to follow this woman, like the stench of a tanner. After Lindstrom, she moved on to Bedloe Calvi, the Italian Ambassador, then Simon Chiffon-Roi, descended from French émigrés,[266] and then Norman Walters, the conductor at the Haymarket Theatre. Each of these men she married for a time, garnered their wealth, and then subtly destroyed. Who knows how long her current husband, Lord John Kirby, will survive her poisonous regard?"

"I don't understand, Holmes. How is she permitted to continue this reign of terror?"

"Ah, that is an excellent question, Watson. She is protected at the highest levels. Her current husband is a cousin to our illustrious Queen."

"So how are we to beat her?" I cried, despondently.

Holmes smiled ruthlessly. "Courage, Watson. A battle may look hopeless at first glance, but after surveying the field, a plan may arise that turns the table. Think of Crécy or Agincourt."[267]

---

[265] We are unable to find a record of this in contemporary newspapers, suggesting that Watson has altered some names, perhaps so as to avoid further prosecution.
[266] The émigrés were descendants of French nobility who fled to England in the early 1790's to avoid death at the hands of the French Revolution.

"But we prevailed on those fields due to a superior weapon. What, precisely, is our longbow?"

"Why, I am, of course," replied Holmes, without a trace of jest in his voice. "Mrs. Kirby has a modicum of low cunning, to be certain, but she is no match for my intellect. This is one of those cases in which the knowledge of pre-existing examples may serve us well. I will ponder the matter over another pipe or two, and by supper time, I expect to have an answer."

"And what should I do, Holmes?"

"Get some rest, Watson. There is a distinct possibility that this may be a very late night. And do not fear. I was beaten by a woman once, and I do not intend to repeat the experience."[268]

§

When I finally stirred in the shade-drawn room, I was startled to see Holmes sitting at my writing chair, smoking his pipe and gazing contentedly at the series of portraits upon my wall. I glanced at the clock upon the wall and was startled to note that it was but four hours to midnight.

"Ah, are you awake then, Watson? Excellent. I hope I did not disturb your repose. I have several items worthy of reporting and discussing. Perhaps I should ring Mrs. Hudson for a late pot of tea?"

I agreed with this suggestion, and after consuming several cups felt sufficiently restored to hear Holmes' plans.

"I have, Watson, devised seven separate schemes, each of which has certain merits, and also several surmountable problems. Clearly, at the most fundamental level, we are acting not only to extract you from her clutches, but we are hoping to prevent future victims of Mrs. Kirby. How would you go about doing such a thing?"

I shook my head. "I have no idea, Holmes. We are far out of my league at this point. I am but a simple Army surgeon...."

---

[267] Crécy (26 August 1346) was the decisive English victory of King Edward III over the French forces of Philip VI in the early part of the Hundred Year's War. Agincourt (25 October 1415) was another decisive English victory, this by King Henry V over the French army. Oddly, Watson does not mention the other great English victory at Poitiers (19 September 1356), which was dramatized in the novel *Sir Nigel* (1906), written by Sir Arthur Conan Doyle, Watson's first literary agent.

[268] Strangely, this does not appear to be a reference to Irene Adler, as *A Scandal in Bohemia* did not take place until 1889, after the events herein. Holmes also mentions this in *The Five Orange Pips*.

"No matter, Watson. For this is precisely my cup of tea. As I have noted, there are several avenues of approach open to us. For instance, it is plain that Mrs. Kirby does not soil her hands directly, but utilizes the iniquitous Mr. Belmont as her beard. We could perhaps fight fire with fire and bring a suit directly against her.[269] I suspect that she would strongly prefer to avoid any such scandal-inciting publicity."

I nodded slowly. "That seems promising."

"Unfortunately, it has drawbacks as well. It would be a slow matter, and at best would only induce her to abandon her persecution of you alone. She would still be free to turn her foul attentions onto other hapless souls. So astute a villain would see that our hands were tied in the matter, unless I was prepared to spend all of my time monitoring her moves via Belmont. And even then, she could simply hire some other dissipated solicitor to do her bidding. No, I think she must be more definitively neutralized."

"Perhaps she has records of her activities? If she has pressed numerous suits in the past, and has more planned for the future, she could not possibly be expected to keep track of them all in her head."

"Excellent, Watson! You have, I think, hit upon the heart of the affair. If we might obtain her note-book and papers, we could ensure, via various channels, that they found their way into the hands of a certain august lady, who might thereby be induced to withdraw her protection. If we are extremely fortunate, it is conceivable that Mrs. Kirby could even find herself banished from the realm."

"But how are we to acquire them, Holmes? She is hardly going to turn them over willingly."

"This is the precise problem that I have been pondering, Watson. It is most unlikely that she carries them about with her. As a whole, the records would likely be too bulky for concealment about a woman's dress. And while she has covered her tracks well, I am certain that I am not the only one who suspects her true nature. She knows that her enemies are capable of having her waylaid and searched. Though she does employ a rough-looking manservant of sorts, who I suspect acts as her de facto bodyguard."

"Perhaps she keeps them in her house?"

Holmes shook his head. "From a close tracking of newspaper reports that indicate police summonses to her Mayfair residence, I suspect that upon at least three occasions burglars have ransacked her house. You see, Watson, we are not the first to consider desperate means of opposing her foul influence."

"And how do you know that none of these attempts were successful?"

---

[269] The phrase to 'fight fire with fire' likely derived from Shakespeare's play *King John*.

"By the simple fact that she continues at large, her reign of terror unabated."

"Where, then?" I asked. "Perhaps her banker or her lawyer?"

"Very good, Watson. Though we can discount her lawyer. Belmont's offices are far too public and exposed. Any records kept there would at best be duplicates, in his hand, of what we require. They would not be sufficiently incriminatory. While you were resting, I have, however, sent telegrams with discrete inquiries at several of London's most prominent banking establishments. It is clear that she is the beneficiary of a veritable labyrinth of accounts, she retains no large security boxes. That is most singular, do you not think?"

I frowned in consternation. "I fail to see, Holmes, how the lack of security boxes helps our cause?"

"No? Well, you can perhaps be forgiven for not being at your best, given the personal circumstances of the matter. Come now, Watson, what fashionable lady of your acquaintance does not possess a set of expensive jewelry to be used for social occasions? And between soirees they keep their jewels in the bank, do they not? The notable lack of any security boxes informs us that Mrs. Kirby is not in the habit of keeping any incriminating papers at the banks, but also that she safeguards no other personal items there. However, as must have been made plain from the sheer number of prior assaults, she cannot possibly consider her Mayfair home to be a secure location for the keeping of valuable items. What can we deduce from this?"

I considered this for a moment. "Perhaps she has another house somewhere?"

Holmes smiled broadly. "Precisely, Watson! Like the lawyer Belmont, the Mayfair house is simply the public face for her operations, but her secret base is where the bodies are buried, metaphorically-speaking."

"But where is it?"

"This was the exact question that has been occupying my mind for the last several hours, Watson. She would want it somewhere nearby, where she would have relatively swift access to the records stored within. However, between the rails and the use of her coach, this could encompass a wide circumference about central London. Furthermore, the land records show no other properties registered to her name, nor that of any of her past husbands. She has been most clever in covering her tracks. However, she has made one mistake. Inquiries at the railway stations have failed to demonstrate that she often travels by train, unless she possesses a remarkable skill at disguising her distinctive red hair. Therefore, she must be using her coach to travel to her secret lair."

"So how are we to track her? Can we simply follow her the next time she leaves London?"

"Perhaps, though if her coach's path led into the countryside, it might prove difficult to continue our pursuit unobserved. Once her driver realized he was being followed, he would simply turn off on another path and lead us back to London."

I shrugged. "It would at least give us the direction that they were headed. That would narrow things down considerably."

"Good, Watson, but I think we can do a tad better. I had at first considered way-laying her bodyguard. I could hardly clap a pistol to his head unless I was prepared to fire it, but I might go a few rounds in the ring with the man and see if he was willing to talk afterwards."

"That hardly seems a subtle method, Holmes."

Holmes grinned whimsically. "I agree, Watson. Thus, I abandoned that strategy, and instead focused on learning more about the man himself. I first discovered that his name is Harry Jones, but other than his current occupation, no one I asked knew much more about the man. Fortunately, it appears that Mrs. Kirby is planning on spending tonight at Mayfair, which allowed me to loiter in the vicinity of her place in the guise of a lamp-lighter. Her bodyguard made only one appearance outside, but this was sufficient to tell me what I needed."

"Which was what?"

"Do you recall, Watson, the case of Mrs. Harrington's missing cymophane ring, where I noted that Woodard was a cork-cutter by the particular callus upon his thumb?"

"Yes, of course. I have noted on numerous occasions, Holmes, that your eye for trifles is astonishing. There was also the time that you concluded the identity of the retired sergeant of Marines by his tattoo, whiskers, and cane, or when you deduced that Mr. Kempson was actually a cobbler by the worn patch upon his trousers."[270]

"Indeed," smiled Holmes, with some measure of vanity at my recognition of his methods. "Though the former example is the most telling one. For the hands are the key to a man. And in this case, Mr. Jones has a very particular deformity of his thumb. It took me but a few moments to reason out what precisely it meant."

I frowned. "I cannot possibly guess what you inferred from a thumb malformation."

"Have you not observed, Watson, that game-keepers carry their brace of rabbits home in leather slings attached to their thumbs and draped over their shoulders? Over time, this leads to permanent damage to the ligament that attaches to the thumb."[271]

---

[270] Sadly, neither the case of Mrs. Harrington and her cat's-eye ring, nor of Mr. Kempson, were ever chronicled by Watson.

"So the man is a game-keeper? How does this advance us?"

"It tells us, Watson, that the secret base of Mrs. Kirby, née Delos, is likely to be found situated in a wooded area. And surely there are rather few of these within a short drive from metropolitan London. A quick perusal of land records at Lincoln's Inn Fields[272] told me that there is a secluded estate near Uxbridge, which is supposedly owned by a Mrs. Elizabeth Leto. If you recall your Hesiod, you will note that Leto was the mother of Apollo and Artemis, giving birth to them upon the Greek island of Delos."[273] He smiled like a cat that had caught a mouse. "I think the chain is complete. My suggestion is that you and I go out to Uxbridge tonight and see if we can strike at the very core of the matter."

"Are we to call upon her?" I asked, confused by Holmes' plan. "Did you not say that she was at Mayfair?"

Holmes smiled. "I cannot envision how a direct confrontation would further our object of permanently de-clawing the she-devil. No, I propose that we burgle her house, Watson. You don't mind breaking the law, do you?"

I hesitated. "Is it absolutely necessary?"

Holmes threw back his head and burst into a hearty fit of laughter. "Ah, Watson, I never get your limits. In every prior instance when I have asked you that question, you unhesitatingly replied in the affirmative.[274] But now, when your own hide is on the line, you pause."

"Well, in those other cases we were acting for the good of one who could not protect themselves. Mrs. Radford, for instance."[275]

"And so we are here, trust me. Your capacity for altruism is astonishing, Watson," said he, shaking his head. He turned and began to

---

[271] There is a diagnosis known as 'gamekeeper's thumb,' though the term did not make its way into the medical literature until 1955, when an orthopedic surgeon named CS Campbell noted this common condition amongst a cohort of Scottish gamekeepers. Their maneuver places a valgus force upon the abducted metacarpophalangeal joint, which over time, leads to insufficiency of the ulnar collateral ligament of the thumb.

[272] The Land Registry, formed in 1862, had its head office at 32 Lincoln's Inn Fields until 2011.

[273] Hesiod (c. 700 BCE), the Greek poet, tells of the myth of the island of Delos, a sacred spot off the coast of Mykonos. Leto had been cursed by Hera to be unable to give birth upon any lands, but since Delos was thought to float freely in the sea, it proved to be a sanctuary for her.

[274] Strangely, there are no recorded examples of this behavior which took place prior to the events chronicled herein. Later instances can be found in *A Scandal in Bohemia*, *The Adventure of Bruce-Partington Plans*, and *The Adventure of Charles Augustus Milverton*.

[275] Unfortunately, the affair of Mrs. Radford has been lost to posterity.

rummage through his desk. "Ah, here we have our tools for the evening. A nickel-plated jemmy, a steel chisel, some pass keys, and a dark lantern should suffice, I think." He looked me over. "I would wear your dark suit, Watson, and some quiet shoes."

I nodded in rueful agreement with his plan. "What about my service revolver?"

Holmes shook his head. "No, there is no room for violence tonight. We sneak in, we claim what we require in order to turn the tables upon Mrs. Kirby, and we exit unseen and unheard."

"How precisely do you propose to travel to Uxbridge, Holmes? I doubt that the typical cabby will be happy at the sight of your jemmy."

"Very good, Watson. No, it would not do for us to be reported as suspicious characters to the local constabulary. I have therefore taken the step of sending round to Forman, whose loyalty is unquestioned. He will drive us in his trap."

"You have thought of everything then."

Holmes nodded sagely. "This is my business, Watson."

§

Midnight found us sixteen miles east of London, our moonlit trip along the old Uxbridge stagecoach road and through Southall uneventful, for there was little traffic at this late hour. The silent Forman deposited us in front of two high park gates, each lichen-encrusted side-pillar surmounted by heraldic creatures, like sphinxes without the leonine body.[276] Beyond the gates, a long yew-lined avenue led back into the fine timber of the deep and ancient oaks. The two-story brown-brick house appeared to date back several centuries with its flattened pointed arches, square-headed windows, decoratively-shaped gables, and a large ornate chimney. As Forman could hardly wait on the side of the road for us without attracting the attention of any passersby, Holmes instructed him to drive on for the span of thirty minutes and then return in order to retrieve us.

Stepping from the trap, I buttoned my greatcoat, for the spring night retained a crispness in the air. "What is the plan, Holmes?" I asked as I surveyed the quiet and dark building nestled in the woods.

"Simple, Watson. We shall circle to the back, where there is less likelihood of our being spotted from the road. There, we will open one of the doors, by force if necessary, and make our way up to her study, which will typically be attached to her bedchamber. Even though her ownership of this estate has been well-concealed, it is probable that she will not keep

---

[276] Far be it for me to criticize Watson's descriptions, but a woman with bird wings but no leonine torso would properly be termed a 'harpy.'

anything compromising in plain sight. We will have to locate her safe, and open it."

"You can do this in the span of an hour?"

Holmes nodded with no false modesty. "I think it likely. To fully understand the capabilities of a criminal, Watson, one must study their methods. There are few locks that will delay me for so long. Barring some unforeseen catastrophe, I am hopeful that we will find what we need to definitively prove her misdeeds. Your troubles will soon be at an end, Watson."

Little did Holmes realize when he spoke those portentous words that a tragedy did await us inside, though one that strangely provided an even more definitive conclusion to my legal troubles.

§

Holmes had little difficulty scaling the wall around her estate, and with some assistance from him, I soon joined him in the enclosed woodlands. Holmes led me along a side deer-path rather than up the main avenue, and we slowly rounded the house. The back veranda was separated from the woods by a small clearing, which we sprinted quickly but silently across. The rear door proved to be amenable to one of Holmes' pass keys and, within five minutes of our arrival at the estate, we were already inside the silent building.

Holmes held aloft his dark lantern in order to illuminate our situation. "These old Tudor homes follow a standard pattern," whispered my friend. "We should find the room we seek on the first floor."

With me in close pursuit, Holmes crept quietly up the wide stone staircase and along a worn carpeted hall. He paused at each door before deciding, based on some small feature that was invisible to my eyes, that it was not the one he sought. He finally stopped in front of one that appeared much like all of the others and nodded slightly. Reaching out his hand, he swung the door open. The room behind was plainly utilized as Mrs. Kirby's study, as the center of the room was dominated by an elegant writing desk and comfortable chair, both resting upon a silken Persian carpet. The walls were marked by a gas-laid fireplace, currently cold, and several fine paintings, including one I thought I recognized as being a historical theme by Millais.[277] I was struck by the complete lack of books, which I thought rather ominous for someone whose ill-gotten wealth had been obtained by threatening humble authors.

After a moment's observation of the room, Holmes quickly made for

---

[277] Sir John Everett Millais (1829–1896) was an English painter and one of the founders of the Pre-Raphaelite movement.

one of the paintings situated to the right of her desk. He swung this back upon a set of cleverly hidden hinges in order to reveal a reinforced steel safe door secured by a six-lever Chubb detector lock.[278] I could see my friend smile with satisfaction at this challenge, and he proceeded to lay out his instruments around him.

However, he had just started to work upon the lock when the room was suddenly bathed in light. I turned and laid eyes upon a woman of some fifty-odd years, her hair marked by a singularly red shade that would have attracted the notice of any man with an eye for color. Her face was beginning to show lines unhidden by her carefully-applied make-up, and her figure was progressing past the point of voluptuousness, but I could still understand how she would have once been considered a great beauty. Her evening gown was of the finest scarlet silk, and a lustrous large white pearl shone at her neck.

"Good evening, Mr. Holmes," said the woman, who could only be Simone Kirby herself. "I am so happy you could join me this evening." She circled around us and serenely took a seat behind her desk. "Be so good to stoke the fire, would you, Mr. Holmes? I fear there is a chill in the air."

If Holmes was startled by her unexpected appearance, he hid it well. He moved to do her bidding, presumably to gain sufficient time to process the meaning of her words and determine our next course of action. Once this task was done and the fire began to crackle, he turned back to the woman who had calmly watched his every move. Holmes smiled. "Ah, Mrs. Kirby, we meet at last. I clearly erred in not coming up the main drive, or I would have seen the fresh tracks to inform that you had driven out to your country estate for the night. Nonetheless, I thank you for your hospitality. Pray tell, how precisely did you know that we were here?"

She laughed gaily. "I employ Mr. Jones not only for his strength, Mr. Holmes, but also because he possesses the keen senses of a huntsman. He noted that an unusual person was lighting the lamps outside of my Mayfair home, one that lingered far longer than should have been required. When you departed, he simply followed you home in order to learn your identity. Once I had that piece of information, I knew exactly what your next step would be, and we came out to Uxbridge in advance of your arrival. When you circled the house, Mr. Holmes, as I knew you would, you passed through that clearing that I had cut for just such a reason. Even with the dark suits that you and Dr. Watson are wearing, the moon illuminated you quite well from my particular vantage point."

---

[278] Chubb locks, famous for their impregnability, secured both the door at Briony Lodge (*A Scandal in Bohemia*) and the bureau at Yoxley Old Place *(The Adventure of the Golden Pince-Nez)*.

"Ah, I see," said Holmes, nodding his head. "And when the moon is down? What do you do then?"

She waved her hand. "Oh, the house is fully equipped with gas lights, Mr. Holmes. We keep those on whenever the moon is hidden. It would not do for us to receive unanticipated visitors."

"You infernal villain!" exclaimed Holmes.

She smiled. "The same criticism could be leveled at you, Mr. Holmes. Do you not also pry into the private secrets of England's elite?"

Holmes shook his head. "Only when called to do so by a client, whose cause is just."

"And who is the determiner of 'just,' Mr. Holmes? You? The doctor?" She laughed cruelly. "*Vae victus.*[279] I take what I desire, and that is precisely why you are here."

Holmes' eyes narrowed. "So you anticipated my involvement?"

She laughed gaily. "But of course, Mr. Holmes. Why else do you think I turned my attention on the good doctor here? Surely not for his small sum of money! No, once I read his little report of your abilities, I knew that you would be the perfect person to join the ranks of my employees. You, see Mr. Holmes, I am desirous of expanding the scope of my attentions beyond that of mere authors. I have a great number of people who provide me with information about potential candidates for my tender considerations, but none of them possess your particular skills."

"And why precisely do you think I would ever deign to cooperate with you?" asked Holmes calmly.

"If you do not, then you will have to familiarize yourself with the inside of a Princetown cell." She smiled cruelly.

"I fail to see your reasoning, madam," said Holmes, mildly.

"My man Jones is downstairs. He can easily summon the local constable, who of course, owes me a favor or two for overlooking some of his minor misdeeds. Once I point out to the constabulary precisely how you and the doctor illegally entered my house, I expect that you will find yourselves spending a year or two safely locked away. Possibly longer, if I can manage to convince the jury that you threatened me with bodily harm. By the time you are released, you will both be unemployable. No one desires to visit a physician or a detective who has spent time in gaol. How could such a man possibly be trusted?"

Holmes smiled. "Perhaps. But if not me, someone else will bring an end to your reign of terror."

She shook her head. "I think not. Do you see this, Mr. Holmes?" She motioned to a small package, wrapped in paraffin paper, which was sitting

---

[279] Literally, 'woe to the conquered,' meaning something akin to 'might makes right.'

on the side of her desk. "I have waited for your arrival in order to open it, as I wanted to demonstrate for you precisely the power of your new permanent employer. This little gift is from the Duke of Balmoral,[280] who sent it to me in exchange for my mercy and restraint on the matter of the bezique scandal.[281] I have always fancied the ring of William IV."[282]

She tore open the paper to reveal a small gilt-edge velvet box of the sort that normally holds fine jewels, such as a ring. Perhaps I had sensed something amiss, for I held my breath as she flung open the clasp with a leer of triumph upon her face. Suddenly, she cried out in horror and dismay. A metallic click sounded and appeared to engage some ingenious device. My brain could scarcely process what my eyes reported, but I thought I saw a slimy red horror flung from the box onto her face.[283] Her limbs flailing, she toppled backwards and her chair hit the floor with a loud thump. I moved to assist her, but Holmes threw up his arm and barred my path. We stared, aghast, as her screams slowly faded and her movements stopped. I watched as the beast rapidly engorged itself upon her blood.[284]

"I think she may be dead, Holmes." I finally whispered after a span of some minutes.

Holmes nodded and moved to the desk, where he pocketed the box and its wrappings. "Someone else clearly tired of being the subject of her malign attentions, but it will not do to have their name dragged into this

---

[280] There is no Duke of Balmoral, though Watson later claims that Lord St. Simon is his second son (*The Adventure of the Noble Bachelor*), that his horse Iris ran in the Wessex Cup (*Silver Blaze*), and that he lost money playing whist against Sebastian Moran (*The Adventure of the Empty House*). Who precisely Watson is concealing with this pseudonym has never been satisfactorily determined.

[281] Bezique is a card game for two players invented in France and imported to England during the Victorian era. Wilkie Collins and Christina Rossetti were enthusiasts, as was Winston Churchill later. It evolved into pinochle.

[282] Mrs. Kirby appears to be implying that she was promised the coronation ring made for William IV in 1831, and now part of the Crown Jewels. Few men in the nation could have made such a promise, even if they never intended to keep it.

[283] Although Watson never describes it fully, one must assume that the box's lid concealed a spring-loaded device that would fling out the occupant of the box when opened. This seems akin to the terrible device employed by Culverton Smith to murder Victor Savage (*The Adventure of the Dying Detective*).

[284] There is only one giant red leech that is known to science. It is endemic only to Mount Kinabalu in Borneo, where it can grow to a length of some 30 cm (12 inches). However, this particular leech is not hematophagic and instead feeds only on worms. Therefore, it cannot be the poisonous leech of this tale, which fortunately remains to this day unknown to science.

affair." He then seized a pair of fireplace tongs, pried the leech from her face, and, before I could stop him, threw it into the flames. There it writhed horribly before finally shriveling to a charred black husk.

"Surely that was a unique specimen, Holmes!" I protested, weakly. "A poisonous leech! Such a thing is unknown to science. It could have been studied by the Royal Society."

"Some things are perhaps better left unknown, Watson," said he finally. Holmes was silent for a moment longer as he stared into the fire. "In the end, Watson, which Red Leech was more repulsive, the worm[285] or the woman?"[286]

§

---

[285] Technically a leech is distinct from a worm, but we shall forgive Holmes' poetic license. He also calls mankind "poor, helpless worms" in *The Boscombe Valley Mystery*.

[286] One wonders if Holmes was ever successful in retrieving her papers, for within a decade another blackmailer, by the name of Charles Augustus Milverton, was plying the same trade in London.

ABOUT THE AUTHOR

In the year 1998 CRAIG JANACEK took his degree of Doctor of Medicine of Vanderbilt University, and proceeded to Stanford to go through the training prescribed for pediatricians in practice. Having completed his studies there, he was duly attached to the University of California, San Francisco as Associate Professor. The author of over eighty medical monographs upon a variety of obscure lesions, his travel-worn and battered tin dispatch-box is crammed with papers, nearly all of which are records of his fictional works. These include several collections of the further adventures of Sherlock Holmes (*Light in the Darkness, The Assassination of Sherlock Holmes,* and the forthcoming *Treasure Trove Indeed!*), two Dr. Watson novels (*The Isle of Devils,* and the forthcoming *The Gate of Gold*), and two non-Holmes novels (*The Oxford Deception* and *The Anger of Achilles Peterson*). His stories have been published in the *MX Book of New Sherlock Holmes Stories, Part I* (October 2015), the *MX Book of New Sherlock Holmes Stories, 2016 Annual* (May 2016), the *MX Book of New Sherlock Holmes Stories, 2017 Annual* (coming spring 2017), and *Holmes Away From Holmes: Tales of the Great Hiatus* (December 2016). He lives near San Francisco with his wife and two children, where he is at work on his next story. Craig Janacek is a *nom-de-plume.*

ABOUT THE TYPE

This book is set in Baskerville Old Face, a transitional serif typeface designed in 1757 by John Baskerville (1706–1775) in Birmingham, England. The typeface was designed to reflect Baskerville's ideals of perfection, for which he chose simplicity and quiet refinement.

It is unclear whether this John Baskerville is, in fact, one of the two sons of Hugo, who in 1742 set down the curious, old-world narrative of his eponym ancestor known as the Curse of the Baskervilles.

Made in the USA
Middletown, DE
12 August 2017